Hunger of the Heart

Wolves of Ravenwillow: Book 1

Magenta Phoenix

Big, Bold & Bearing

IMPRINT: Romance Paranormal Romance

Hunger of the Heart: Wolves of Ravenwillow: Book 1

Smashwords Edition

Copyright © 2016 by Magenta Phoenix

First E-Book Published August 2016

Cover Design by Melody Simmons

Magenta Phoenix

This book is dedicated to my friend, Meghann.
Thank you so much for finding my flash drive that held the finished
copy of this book. Without you I would have had to start again from
nothing.

o.x.o.x.

Special Thanks

I want to say thank you so much to my beta reader Heather. Thank you for all your hard work and encouragement.

You really helped me get this project off the ground!

o.x.o.x.

1

"Daddy,"

The small voice invaded Eric's sensitive ears as his crying daughter ran through the open door of his office at home. Her long, dark hair flew around her delicate face with every step she took. Blotches of red covered her button nose and trails of tears washing down her small cherub face. In her small arms was her favorite handmade doll, one of its arms completely torn off and missing.

Pushing away from his computer desk, he bent down, lifting her up to cradle his crying daughter against his strong chest. The scent of her sadness perfumed the air around them, pulling at his heart strings. Pulling her away from his chest, his eyes collided with her tear filled blue ones.

"What's wrong, Emma?" His thumb gently brushed a falling tear from her plump cheek. Biting her bottom lip, a small sob tore through Emma as she held up the torn doll.

"T-T-Travis tore it!" her tears came faster and her sobs more pitiful.

"It was an accident."

Raising his eyes from his daughter's distraught face, he spotted his son, Travis. Travis had the same dark brown hair as his twin sister. With his hands shoved in the pockets of his blue jeans, Travis looked away from the stern gaze of his father.

Travis's eyes hesitantly met his father's. "I didn't mean to. We were playing."

Eric sighed. He was so tired. Not that he disliked being home with his son and daughter, no, it wasn't that. He was just tired. Bone deep and he was ready to pull out his hair while pounding his face into his desk; that kind of tired.

It wasn't easy being a parent or hell even a single parent. Eric wasn't ready to admit it to any of his pack members that he ruled over; but he needed help. It was becoming impossible to juggle his architectural business, running his pack and caring for his children.

If only he had someone to help him…

Immediately he shut down the thought before he could begin it. A reminder of why he was alone wouldn't help his mood any. He'd put that can of worms in the past and that's where it would stay.

Emma buried her face against Eric's throat, drawing his attention as her breath continued catching with her small sobs. Before he could reprimand his son for his careless actions the sound of knocking at the front door intruded. Walking past his son, he gave him a stern look saying they were far from done with this discussion. His office opened out in to the living room. Eric wasn't all that surprised to see toys scattered across the hardwood floor.

Carefully he moved across the dining room and into the connected dining room and kitchen. Balancing Emma on his hip, Eric opened the front door and released a sigh at the sight before him. Not bothering to wait for an invitation, his mother; Sarah stepped across the threshold carrying a casserole dish in her small hands.

Just as he was about to shut the door a soft voice from his porch made him pause, "Excuse me,"

Turning to face the barely open doorway, Eric felt his breath sucked from his lungs. Opening the front door wider a small curvy woman stepped hesitantly into the kitchen, juggling two casserole dishes while trying to maintain hold of her tote bag that slid down her arm.

Walking toward the other woman, Sarah held out her hands. "Dear, let me take those."

"Thank you." Her voice was soft as a whispering wind.

While she handed the dishes over to his mother, Eric took the chance to take in her appearance fully. Her height appeared to only be 5'5 to his 6 foot tall frame. Her hair was the color of smooth milk chocolate, pulled away from her face by a simple green headband, allowing the silky strands to fall down her back. Her eyes resembled a doe's, bright brown and watchful. He couldn't help but allow his eyes to drift over the rest of her body. His eyes ranked over her full supple breasts and her smooth hips. Where most women were thin and lithe, this woman had curves and meat that would tempt a saint.

His nostrils flared at her scent; her luscious and unique feminine scent, her jasmine perfume. Everything about her threatened to draw him irrevocably closer to her; her scent and her laminating beauty caused his wolf deep inside him to leap towards the surface. Taking a step closer to her, Eric couldn't deny the intense urge to take her into his arms and mark her body with his scent. He imagined hearing her cries of pleasure and to feel her strong, meaty thighs cradle his body as he buried himself deeper within the depths of her heat. As he neared closer to her, another scent floated through the air. It was sweet, like melted sugar and left his mouth watering and his teeth clashing together with alarm.

Human.

Eric felt his heart stop dead in his chest. Why would his mother bring a human into his house, around his children? She appeared to be in her late twenties; too young to be a close friend of his mother's. Even with the feeling of foreboding in his chest, his wolf still continued to howl and lunge toward this unknown *human* female. Why would such a fragile and forbidden creature such as she, cause his wolf to fight him with such ferocity? Not ever had a female of his kind managed that.

"Really, Eric when is the last time you cleaned this kitchen?" The voice of his mother cut in.

"Last night." He growled out, his eyes never leaving the human in front of him.

Shoving his wolf back into seclusion, Eric pushed aside the erotic haze that clouded his mind and sought control over his body. No matter how much his wolf desired this woman, she was human and as such a threat to all like him if she ever was to learn the truth about him.

Sarah looked around the kitchen with mild distaste. Dishes sat piled in the double sinks, crumbs and trash was scattered across the counter tops. "Looks like I planned this out well."

Feeling uneasy, Eric gently put Emma down, his eyes quickly found his son's. "Travis; take your sister and go watch TV while Grandma and me talk."

The moment Travis and Emma were out of sight, he turned his hard expression to his mother. Folding his thickly muscled arms over his wide chest, his eyes flickered over the delicate looking human. Turning back to his mother, he gave her an inquiringly look.

"What's going on?"

Sarah turned her attention to her companion, "Rebecca, would you be a dear and put these away in the fridge. I need to talk to my son." Not waiting for a reply, Sarah; using her lupine strength, pulled Eric out of the kitchen, out the front door and onto the sun lit porch.

Pulling his arm away from the strong grasp of his mother's, Eric glared down at her. His heart pounded like a loud drum in his ears. Using his superior hearing, he could confirm that his children were in the living room watching TV. This gave him a small amount of comfort with the small distance between his children and the unknowing human woman in the kitchen.

"What is going on, Mother?"

She held her hands up in a placating manner. "Calm down, Eric." Her voice reasoned.

"*Calm down*? I will *not* calm down! You've brought a human in to my home, where my children are! How could you be so stupid?" He hissed out in anger as his blue eyes glowed gold with the presence of his inner beast. Curling his hands in two tight fists, he could feel his nails lengthening into razor claws, slicing into his skin.

"I've hired Rebecca as your nanny." Closing his eyes, Eric forced his beast back down before taking a calming breath.

"I don't need a nanny." He bit out slowly.

"A nanny for Travis and Emma, Silly." She scolded with a smile.

"Emma and Travis don't need a nanny." He bit out while pacing the length of the porch, his eyes flickering toward the kitchen window.

"Eric. Listen to me." She beseeched. Clasping his hand in both of hers, Sarah pulled him down onto the wooden porch swing. "There's been gossip that you no longer care about the survival of the pack. Your business is barely surviving, if it were not for your betas you wouldn't even have that. I'm concerned about you. Others believe you have become a weak Alpha, especially since your decision to form a peace treaty with the shifters of Darkwood Springs."

Eric couldn't help scoffing with disbelief. It wasn't until after he'd returned from his trip to Darkwood Springs that he could see the trouble mounting in his own pack. Doyle Mackenzie; a grizzly shifter and the Alpha over the many different shifters of the small town, Darkwood Springs, had opened his eyes after just a few days with him. It was strange. Wolves were pack hunters and born leaders among the many shifter casts. Where as, in most cases, bear shifters were more solitary. If it wasn't for the Mackenzie family, Eric suspected that all the shifters would be divided as most commonly were. But yet; Doyle's pack thrived.

Eric didn't fully understand what was going on with Doyle's strange mate, or the danger that he'd been pulled into while there, but he respected Doyle as a fellow Alpha. Why couldn't his pack do the same? The thought was laughable. Many thought his decision to form alliances with other packs was a sign of weakness. But he didn't care. He'd even secretly sent Mark; his close friend and a cougar shifter, to his own Alpha and secretive pack to inspire an alliance.

Many wolf packs were stuck in the dark ages. They kept to their own and weren't known for being capable of playing well with other shifters. Even members of his pack that he'd sent to watch Doyle years back still did what they could to get on the grizzly shifter's nerves.

With his peace treaties he was forcing his pack out of their archaic comfort zones and he knew none of them liked it. Quite frankly; he didn't give a shit. Times were changing and if the danger that Doyle's pack was battle was anything to go by, he knew that his pack needed to evolve. They needed to band together to become stronger.

There was only one law of his pack that he had no intention of changing and that was that all shifters avoided humans at all cost. The thought brought him back to his mother who was still speaking. No doubt she had been listing her reasoning for bringing a human into his home and endangering them all. He wouldn't stand for it. No matter her reasoning.

"I just worry about you, Eric." She continued on. "If you're not careful—"

"No one within our pack is stupid enough to challenge me." He said, slashing his hand through the air, dismissingly.

"Son, you've been ignoring pack business, it's time that you got back to it."

Eric rose with a huff. "I don't need some human hanging around and becoming suspicious. Did you even consider what would happen if she witnessed one of us shifting or if one of the pups did? I would be the one to end her life, is that what you want?" Sarah didn't shrink back from his narrowing eyes, but lifted her chin assertively.

"Of course it's not. It isn't as if I've brought some stranger to take care of my grandchildren. Rebecca came highly recommended from the very Alpha that you went to see a week ago."

"You're saying that Doyle Mackenzie recommended a human nanny to you?" he asked skeptically.

His mother winced before hesitantly answering. "Not exactly. One of the other grizzly shifters of his pack did. She told me that Rebecca had taken care of her children for a time and was the best. If she could take care of four bear-shifter children, two wolf-shifter children should be easy."

Planting his hands squarely on his hips, Eric shook his head. "No."

"Eric. Just hire her for a week, if it doesn't work out, you can fire her. Rebecca will just be here from morning till late afternoon when you come home. She'll clean and cook and take care of Travis and Emma, then leave. It's not as if she'll be living here. Please consider it."

Sighing, his hands dropped limply at his sides. "You are playing a dangerous game, Mother." He said in warning. "What do you think will happen if the elders find out about this? I doubt they will be as understanding as I am."

Waving her hand at him absently, Sarah rolled her eyes. "Don't worry so much. Our pack isn't really as old fashioned as the other wolf packs. I know you want to change things, Eric. So, start here. It would show the pack that it is possible for shifters and humans to mingle without the threat of Revealment hanging up in the air all the time."

Eric's lips pinched together at her words. As much as he hated to say it; let alone think it, she was right. He couldn't keep going on as he had been. Wolves worshiped strength and the only reason he was Alpha was because no one was strong or brave enough to take him down. If he continued on this way, that could change.

Gritting his teeth when he realized there was no way out of this, Eric turned and marched back into the house, striding straight into the kitchen. The human; Rebecca, his mother had called her, sat at the family dinner table, her eyes focused out the window on the clear summer sky. Striding closer, Eric glared down at her at ease expression.

"I didn't hire you, nor do I want you here." He growled out, pointing a threatening finger towards her. Rebecca turned to face him; her face didn't show with a hint of intimidation. When she didn't say anything, he continued. "Personally; I think hiring you to care for my children would be the biggest mistake of my life."

She merely shrugged her shoulders. "You're entitled to your own opinion." She commented, uncaringly.

Her words made his blood rush through his veins with anger. Who did this woman think she was? One thing was for sure, Rebecca wasn't a woman easily intimidated. Where most women, even shifter women would cringe from his angered expression and hard words, Rebecca didn't even flinch. Eric's wolf couldn't help but feel impressed at her bravery.

"Don't think to get too comfortable in your job here and don't think to run to my mother when I fire you. I will be the one paying your wages and I will decide the length of your employment. Furthermore, I don't give a damn about your references or how you acquire them."

Any other woman would have felt insulted, but not this woman. Rebecca simply shrugged her shoulders in acceptance. It was oblivious that she wasn't going to be an easy woman to control. But his mother was right; he couldn't go on stretching himself too far. He needed to focus on the pack and his business. If another pack or even a member of his own pack, felt his leadership was weak, challenges would be issued for his title.

"When did you usually show up for work in that past?"

"Six in the morning until three or four in the afternoon,"

"You'll start tomorrow. Be here at 4 A.M. Your shift will end at 6 P.M. We'll discuss conditions of your employment then. Don't be late. You can show yourself out."

Eric couldn't prevent the smile of satisfaction that came over his face as he strode from the kitchen and back into his office. He would be accepting her resignation by the end of the week. She wouldn't last three days after spending so much time in his domineering presence. He could guarantee it.

* * * *

Rebecca ignored the pain as her teeth sunk down into the soft flesh of her bottom lip. She prayed for patience, forcing her expression to remain blank as the man before her glared and growled. She'd seen his type before. How this man came from such a warm hearted person as Sarah Daniels was a mystery.
His looks favored his mother's but not his personality. He had the same blue eyes and hair with the same dark chocolate richness as her, with the exception of the silver streaks throughout Sarah's flawless locks. His skin held a dark, sun-kissed tan from the amount of time he must spend outdoors. His body was all hard muscle, unyielding and dominating.

Shaking her head, Rebecca forced her thoughts away from the image in her mind. She refused to be drawn in by his attractive good looks. She was here for a job, not to make friends. Eric would just one of the many jerks that she'd worked for in the past, and he wouldn't be the last. Rebecca needed this job. Not that it was her only option, but it was if she wanted to stay in Ravenwillow.

Ravenwillow had always been her home. Years ago, the death of her family had driven her away and forced her to make a change. She'd worked for a family in Darkwood Springs; a small town nestled in the woods of Canada. But it was time for her to come home and face her demons.

Ravenwillow a lot like Darkwood Springs, it was a small overlooked town in Virginia. It was seventy-five percent of forest land and not many jobs were available. Not that she was complaining. Rebecca loved children, despite their parentage. She'd finally gotten enough courage to come back to her hometown and she'd do just about anything to keep from resorting to relocating for work. She'd be damned if she let Mr. In-need-of-manners was going to change that.

When he strode from the room, Rebecca let out a sigh of relief. Uncurling her tightly clenched hands, she felt them slightly shake from fear. He had to know what she was, just as she knew what every person in this house was, Werewolves. He moved just like the men that guarded the compound where Doyle's pack resided.

Doyle's family or those that lived under his protection never knew her secret and she would make certain it stayed that way. Just by watching the way he moved and how his muscles shifted and danced under his dark skin, she could practically see the wolf that lurked beneath his skin.

Her small hand reached up to cover her racing heart. To any other person Eric Daniels would have seemed like an ordinary man, but beneath his rough skin, Rebecca saw a dangerous animal. Beneath her clothes she could still feel the scars, burning painfully against her skin as a silent reminder. Memories long buried, threatened to resurface against her will. Memories of the fateful night that she'd discovered the existence of shifters and the danger that came with them.

"Rebecca?" Jerked from her thoughts, she turned to see Sarah walking towards the table, a concerned expression on her face. "Are you alright? I know my son can be a brute sometimes." Sarah seemed to be at a loss to explain why Eric didn't want her here.

It's because I'm human, weak, worthless and unpredictable a threat in the eyes of all shifters

Rising from her chair, Rebecca plastered a false smile on her face.

"I'm fine."

"I hope he didn't make you reconsider taking the position. Travis and Emma are wonderful children, despite their father's personality."

"It would take more than some parent growling at me to do that." She teased lightly, hoping that her words didn't give away her secret. Smiling warmly at her, Sarah motioned toward the living room.

"Would you like to meet the little ones?"

"I'd love to."

Following Sarah into the living room, Rebecca silently prayed that Travis and Emma were as easily fooled as their father. All she had to do was keep her head down and survive long enough to do her job. And pray that her secret remained hidden. Because the moment they discovered what she knew, it would mean her life.

$\underline{2}$

Three Month Later…

"Damn you, Rebecca!" Eric cursed out from down the stairs; his voice flowed down the stairs into the kitchen. Emma and Travis looked up from their breakfast and then at Rebecca. Sitting next to two wide eyed children, Rebecca had found her morning beginning as normal.

For the last three months her routine had remained the same. Around 4 A.M. she showed up to cook breakfast for Travis and Emma then she would wake them up, get them ready for school. But every morning for a month she would sit at the table and share breakfast with the two wonderful twins while reading the news paper. It was usually then that Eric would come storming down stairs growling at her over some adjustment that she'd made in the household and how it infuriated him.

Setting her newspaper aside, she released a deep, tired sigh. Bringing her coffee mug to her lips, she was thankful for the rich caffeine that rushed through her. Something told her she'd need it today.

"Can I have some?" Emma's small voice asked.

Rebecca's heart nearly melted at the look of innocence in little Emma eyes. In such a short time she'd found herself growing impossibly more attached to Eric's children.

Laughing softly, Rebecca shook her head. "Coffee is for grownups. You wouldn't like it, drink your milk instead."

"Dad lets us have whatever we want after you go home." Travis remarked, while placing a fork full of pancakes and syrup in his mouth.

"Well, I'm not your dad and I say the last thing you two need is caffeine."

After both gave her a disappointed look, Emma and Travis turned their full attention back to their plates. The silence was short lived, just as Rebecca turned her attention back to an interesting news article, Eric's booming voice vibrated down the stairs.

"Rebecca! Get up here, now!" Rolling her eyes, Rebecca rose from her seat, tossing the newspaper down next to her steaming mug.

"Eat your breakfast. I'll be back."

Striding through the living room, she kept a relaxed pace as she climbed each step, leading to the second floor. Passing both Travis and Emma's bedroom, she stopped just outside of the master bedroom.

Inside the room, Eric was presently stalking back and forth across the length of his bedroom in a desperate search of something. His chocolate brown hair was slicked back, still wet from his shower as moister glistened off his square jaw. The strong columns of his legs were incased in gray cotton suit pants while his white button up shirt hung open, not a single button done. Against her will, she found her breath catching as a shiver of awareness that shot through her body at the sight of him.

Leaning against the door jam, she tried to look away from his glistening sculpted and defined chest. "You bellowed?"

Turning to glare at her, Eric approached the door, anger evident on his face. "Why do you do this to me? Of all days, why did it have to be on the day I have a meeting? Now I'm going to be late because you couldn't leave my things alone."

"Eric, if you want me to help you need to speak in plain English. What's the problem?"

"Where the hell are my ties?" he growled out.

Why don't you sniff them out? Biting down on her lip to keep her laughter from escaping, Rebecca folded her arms across her light blue t-shirt. "Did you try your sock drawer?" she smirked.

Narrowing his eyes at her, he stomped over to his dark five drawer dresser. After jerking the top drawer open, Eric rolled his eyes as he let out a sigh of relief. Jerking a silver silk tie out of the drawer, Eric quickly buttoned up his shirt while looking back at her.

"I don't care how you clean the rest of the house, but leave my room alone." He growled out, his hands busily tucking in his shirt.

Pressing a finger to her chin in an attempt to look pensive, she mumbled in a low voice. "I don't remember that clause in my contract."

Glaring at her, his fingers moved with efficient speed as he knotted the tie around his neck. "Enough of your sass, Rebecca, It's too early for it." Crossing over to the bed, Eric shrugged his arms into a dark gray suit jacket. Turning his attention back to Rebecca, his expression softened. "Listen. I'm probably going to be late getting home tonight, so if you could go ahead and put Emma and Travis to bed for me."

"No problem."

"Also, I may be bringing some of my workers back with me to go over this new house I've been commissioned to design."

"The work of an architect is never done?"

Chuckling, he shook his head, "Not for me. Any way; as soon as me and the guys get here, you're free to go home."

"Alright," She nodded in agreement. "Wait; your tie is crooked."
Approaching him, Rebecca leaned into Eric's warm frame.
With quick movements, she loosened his tie to straighten the knot around his neck. Unconsciously; Rebecca moved closer to Eric, examining her completed work with approval. Looking up at his face she was surprised to see that he was studying her. Not looking at her, but *studying* her. His eyes narrowed and Rebecca felt herself go still. Her heart pounded so loudly in her chest that she was for sure that he could hear it.

Out of nowhere, she felt a shift in the air around them. A heat swept through her body like a rush of liquid fire. The warmth of his body flowed over hers, bathing her in his masculinity. She longed to feel this hard arms wrap around her, caressing her, loving her. Her hand unwillingly slid from the smooth cloth of the tie to lie over the heavy muscles of his chest. At the soft touch of her hand, his muscles flexed and shifted beneath his sun kissed skin.

Struggling to fight off whatever had come over her, unwillingly, her eyes drifted from his tense expression to his firmly set lips. He possessed lips that made a woman just want to nibble on. The thought brought amusement to her and a strange need to attempt such an action herself.

* ~ *~ *

Her scent assaulted his nose, playing havoc on all his senses. Causing his wolf to awaken and fight for supremacy, fighting for the female he wanted. His wolf had never reacted to a female like this before and it concerned him. The worst part was; his wolf wasn't the only one to react to Rebecca's close proximity. Instantly he could feel his cock jump and pulse beneath the fabric of his clothes as her fingers brushed against his chest and her hand encircled his tie innocently.

Why was he reacting this way to *her?* She was human, after all. His interest should end right there because of that fact, but instead, he felt a strong force pulling him closer to her. The temptation was almost too strong to resist. In the last few months everything about her seemed…he didn't even know the right words to explain it to himself. All he knew was that she seemed…more, more than she had been since he'd first met her.

Her melted chocolate hair and eyes shined, nearly glowing with an ethereal beauty. Her smooth, porcelain skin nearly had him begging to place his mouth and tongue against it. His hands ached to glide over the soft curves of her flaring hips and round buttocks. And don't even get him started on her mouth.

Against his will, Eric watched as her eyes focused on his tie as her small pink tongue slipped out to wet her bottom lip. She may have meant the action to be innocent as she was lost in her concretion, but it stirred a need within Eric that he thought he'd long since buried. For a moment he simply watched her. There was something different about her.

Slowly he felt her hand drift down from his corrected tie to his covered chest. The brush of her small, soft fingers were like a drug and in the back of his mind it left him craving more. His eyes locked with hers before drifting down to her plump sinful lips once more. All he needed to do was to cut away the space between them and then he could taste the forbidden fruit standing tauntingly in front of him.

There's no harm in just one taste, is there? His inner wolf inquired.

Like fingers brushing at the inside of his mind, Eric jolted at the voice echoing inside his head. It was his wolf. Never had he heard his wolf's voice so clearly in all his life. His thoughts of surprise at his beast emerging were quickly pushed aside as a need beat through his being like a battle drum. His cock hardened and pulsed with a painful need that he couldn't name, it was a hunger for something— no, not something, it was for her.

No. He wouldn't.

Like a deer caught in headlights; he froze. He hadn't even realized that he'd been so enthralled with watching her that it was then he realized that his hands were reaching out to touch her face. What was he doing?! What was he thinking? Rebecca was not for him. Not even for this moment.

He had to put an end to this before it went any further and before he wolf gained power over his mind. With his wolf so close to the surface, he knew if he stayed in the same room with her a moment longer, he would do something that he would regret. He had to get away from her. Shoving his wolf back into its isolation, Eric forced his hands slowly back to his sides, praying that Rebecca had been so focused on her task that she'd not seen him move.

"Are you done yet?" He forced the harsh words from his lips.

Surprised, Rebecca stepped back, letting her hands fall away from him. Eric didn't miss the embarrassment that she quickly hid. More than anything he wanted to draw her close to him.

Hold her close? What was wrong with him? Why was he even thinking of doing something like that?

Shaking his head at the absurdity of the idea, he pushed it from his mind. Fearing that he may not be able to hold back from her any longer, Eric quickly grabbed his black leather jacket off his king size bed and left without a backward glance.

*~ *~ *

Left standing in Eric's room as he stormed past her, Rebecca found herself shaking her head with confusion. Closing her eyes, she covered her face with both of her hands before dropping them with a groan. What just happened? How did simply fixing his tie nearly turn into her nearly kissing him? What was wrong with her? Forget about how much she'd probably embarrassed herself in front of her employer.
Did she have so little regard for her life? The moment Eric or any other shifter discovered that she knew about them, her life would be forfeit. No amount of kisses or lust would change that.

Releasing a heavy sigh, Rebecca's hand stroked the scars that lied beneath her soft blue t-shirt. Reminding her that she could never trust Eric, no matter how much she wanted to. She needed to build some space between Eric, herself, and whatever this building infatuation was.

More likely his werewolf allure, simple chemicals in the brain, nothing more.

"Becca!" The high, sweet voice of Emma shot up the stairs, startling Rebecca out of her haze. Quickly leaving the alluring atmosphere of Eric's room, she made her way down the stairs with relative ease. Waiting at the bottom of the stairs, Emma was struggling to hold up her pink, Dora the Explorer book bag while she struggled to zip it up.

"Here let me." Gently taking the book bag from her and zipping it closed, Rebecca proceeded to help Emma slide her small arms through the short pink straps. "Ready to go?" she asked smiling down at Emma's calculating expression.

"Yep!" Emma beamed up at her, excitement lighting her eyes. Chuckling, Rebecca rose to her full height, "Let's get you and your brother to school before you're late." Enfolding Emma's small hand with her own, they made their way back into the kitchen. By the front door, Travis stood with his entire focus on the game boy in his hands.

"Travis, do you have everything you need?" She inquired while grabbing her purse and keys, with Emma still clinging to her other hand.

"Yeah," His mumbled out answer caused Rebecca to smirk. Shifter or just plain human children were all the same.

Her routine of getting Emma and Travis off to school began as normal. After a short drive up the road, she pulled up in front of their school, a familiar teacher waited by the curb to escort children from the vehicles and onto school property. The teacher smiled at Rebecca as he bent down to look inside her small gray Honda from the passenger side.

"Hey Becky, how's it going today?"

"Hello Rick, Just the same usual stuff." Rick Evert, Emma and Travis's teacher.

Rick was a thickly built man; he was tall, but not as tall as Eric. His hair was the color of dark wheat. Rebecca had met him the first time when Eric requested that she attended a parent-teacher conference with him, giving the teachers a chance to meet her.

Nodding with a smile, Rick moved away from the passenger door and opened Emma's door, helping Emma and Travis out of the car. As they disappeared inside the building, she couldn't prevent her eyes from roaming over to three small giggling children rolling around on the soft green grass. Often times she wondered how many teachers and students were shifters. She only prayed that Emma and Travis had a few fellow shifters that would understand them.

The blaring sound of a car horn from behind; startled Rebecca out of her previous thoughts. Putting the car into gear, Rebecca pulled out into traffic, fighting the feeling of fatigue that threatened to drown her. She still had too much to do before she could head to her small apartment, where she had a date with a scalding hot bubble bath and with her soft, warm bed. And it was that fantasy that would help her get through the rest of her day.

Hopefully, Eric would be too busy when he came home tonight to engage in another verbal battle with her and with any luck she could find a way to keep from throwing herself at him.

* ~ * ~ *

"You're late, Alpha." Looking up as he walked through the doors of Black Claw Hunting Lodge, the home base of his pack, Eric was greeted by his unhappy assistant and beta; Chris.

"I know. Has Damon arrived yet?" he asked while shrugging out of his black leather jacket.

"You're lucky today. He called a little while ago and reported that he'd be late. Just like you." Chris pointed out with an accusing look.

"You can drop the look anytime, Chris. I wouldn't have been late if Rebecca would learn to stay out of my room."

"I wouldn't be complaining if I were you. When do I get to meet her?"

"Later."

The subject of his children's nanny wasn't something that he was keen on talking about around pack members. He'd always been a private person and he intended to keep it that way. Looking around, he noticed that Chris and he were the only ones within the spacious walls of the pack's lodge.

"Where is everyone?"

"Jason called and said he was on his way, He's running late because Myra wanted a ride up here."

"Why the hell is Myra coming?"

Myra was one of the more attractive females of his pack and a pestering thorn in his side for the last five years. No matter what he did, she couldn't take a hint. She was too busy keeping her eye on his mating status to care about anything he said.

Chris didn't bother to hide annoyed but slightly amused smile. "She wants to show her respect and support to her Alpha by being by his side today." His first beta was enjoying his pain too much.

"Call Jason and tell him not to bring her." The last thing he needed was to have a lust crazed, she-wolf hanging around him all day long.

"Too late," Smirking, Chris nodded in the direction behind Eric. Knowing already who it was that had pulled up in front of the lodge, Eric couldn't suppress the groan of displeasure of what awaited him next.

Turning just as his other beta, Jason entered; he took in the unwelcoming sight of Myra. To others, Myra was considered an attractive woman; not that he could see why. Her long blonde hair fell around her high cheek bones and over her shoulders like a golden waterfall. Her thin and tanned body was overly exposed by the revealing red dress that she wore. With the low dipping neck line of her dress and how the thin material fell barely to her mid thigh, she was here for more reasons than to "Show respect and support" as Chris put it.

"Good morning, Alpha." Her voice coming out husky as she approached him, tilting her head to the side, exposing her neck to him; a sign of respect among shifters to their Alpha.

"Thank you for coming, Myra. But it really wasn't necessary." His hard voice growled out as he turned his eyes away from her.

Smiling coyly up at him, she sauntered closer to Eric. "Necessary or not, I'm here. I'm sure you'll find some way I can be of use to you."

Pressing her slender body against his, her small unrestrained breasts brushed enticingly against his chest. What should have made him harder than steel, Eric was surprised when his wolf growled and shrunk back from her touch. Myra's touch once brought him pleasure, now only felt like ice against him, having no pleasurable affect on him what so ever.

Clasping her upper arms, he pushed her away from his uninterested body. "I have stuff to do. If you insist on staying make yourself useful elsewhere." Striding past her, Eric headed for the quiet atmosphere of his office, slamming the door closed behind him. Hands braced on his hips, he began furiously pacing back and forth across the floor.

An unknown and undeniable rage flooded his mind and body. Myra's touch had enraged his wolf to the point of insanity. Even now his wolf clawed for freedom, a freedom he couldn't afford to give him now. His wolf was on edge.

Eric's hands tightened into fists as he fought dominance over his unruly wolf. He had never been out of control and neither had his animal half. Something was wrong, out of place; it was the only thing that could stir up his animal this much. What could it possibly be?

A loud knock on the office door interrupted his thoughts, pushing the door open his second beta, Jason stuck his dark head in between the door frame and the dark oak door.

"Chris and me thought we'd order some food before Damon gets here, if that's alright with you?"

Eric nodded, "Go ahead."

Once Jason closed the door, Eric found himself slouching down in his chair, looked over the tall piles of documents, floor plans, and sketches. Dragging a weary hand over his eyes, he wasn't looking forward to organize his messy desk before going home tonight.

Deciding not to wait, fifteen minutes later, he'd organized his neglected workspace and transformed it into a more manageable work area. Lain out across his newly cleaned desk was everything he need for the meeting today. Everything from the floor plans to the architecture design of the doorways and windows for a large three level house the Beta from a neighboring pack had hired him to design. All his attention focused on going over every detail lain out before him, in the back of his mind Eric recognized the sound of his office door opening.

At first he dismissed it as unimportant and assumed it was one of his Beta's bringing him some of their food. Until the strong smell of sweetened floral perfume filled his office and burned his sensitive nose. Looking up, he saw Myra leaning against the now closed door.

Her small manicured fingers swiftly flipped the lock into place, while flashing him a lusty smile. Slowly running a hand down the front of her dress, Myra's fingertips trailed down the low neckline of her dress and skimmed over her exposed flesh.

Rolling his eyes, he leaned back in his chair, his eyes moving back to the papers scattered across his desk. His wolf growled his warning as Myra approached from behind his chair. Her hands slid from his shoulder and over his hard chest. Once again her touch was cold, causing his wolf to want to snap his jaws at this unwanted female.

Ignoring the frightening glow of his eyes, Myra moved between the desk and his chair. Leaning back on the desk, kicking off her red stilettos, she planted one bare foot beside his thigh and the other on the opposite arm of his chair. Her position spread her thighs wide, flashing her black lace thong.

"Myra," His voice held an irritated tone. "I have work to do,"

Grasping a hold of his tie, she tugged him forward. "All work and no play make you a very dull wolf, Alpha." Leaning closer, a hairs length between their lips, Eric pulled away with a look of displeasure set on his face.

"You forget your place, Myra."

"Then show me my place, Alpha. I remember where yours was—"

Grasping his hand she pulled him forward, shoving his hand between her warm thighs. The thin thread of his wolf's control snapped and as his wolf leapt towards her in anger. Jerking his hand from between her thighs, his hand shot out, wrapping around the thin column of throat.

In his anger, he shoved her down on her back and pinned her against the wood of his desk. Leaning over her, his irises glowed brightly as his wolf rose to the surface. His jaw ached as it reshaped and his teeth lengthened. His killing gaze swept over her startled face as his face partially shifted. His facial bone reshaped with loud crunching sound until his face resembled a wolf's more than his human face. His wolf growled dangerously and snapped his jaws at the trembling female beneath him.

He growled in a deep rumbling voice, "Get out." Eric jerked away from her, his wolf slowly receding back within him. His partially shifted face slowly faded back to normal.

Glaring at him, Myra slowly slid off his desk and bent down collecting her heels. Intentionally lingering in her bent over position as her low neckline dipped lower, flashing her braless chest at his angry eyes.

"Get out before I throw you out." He growled out, as his eyes narrowed dangerously at her.

"She was never your mate, Eric. Open your eyes! She's never coming back! I'm the strongest female in the pack; I would make a proud mate for you." Her voice rose with each step she took toward him.

"Myra, you will address me as "Alpha" and nothing more if you value your place within *my* pack. Furthermore; were I ever to take another mate that wasn't my true one, it would never be you."

Instead of a look of hurt, he'd expected to cross Myra's features, her expression only shown with anger and the promise of revenge that she no doubt would collection on. Spinning away from him she marched towards the door with angry strides. Her delicate hand covering the door knob, Myra turned to look over her shoulder at him, angry flames filling her gaze. Jerking the door open she sent him a smothering glare before slamming the door shut behind her.

Breathing heavy, Eric slammed his hand down on his desk with a snarl. This wasn't like him, he knew that. Normally he could brush aside Myra's attempts to worm her way back into his bed very easily and without emotion on his part. But this time his wolf reacted so violently that he'd nearly ripped her throat out. He had to get a handle on whatever was happening to his beast before he lost control and harmed someone. He was Alpha; he was never out of control. It was unthinkable and unacceptable.

When the door opened again, Eric's anger filled eyes lifted. His lips peeling back in a snarl. "What?!" he shouted as Chris poked his head in between the door jam and the door. Seeing his fierce expression, Chris looked warily at Eric.

"Are you alright?" Chris asked. His wary expression gave away to a look of confusion.

Shoving a hand through his hair, Eric huffed out a heavy breath. "I will be once I get through today." He muttered. "What did you need?"

Slipping into the office, Chris closed the door behind him softly before turning back to look at Eric. His lips twisted into an uncertain expression. Hesitantly, he spoke. "The elders are here."

Scowling, Eric's lips pinched together while his hands moved to rest on his hips. "What?"

Why would the elders be here? In shifter packs; elders were the only individuals that held any semblance of power; other than the Alpha. They helped to maintain the laws and they irritated the shit out of Eric. If all four of the elders were here, it meant that something was up.

"They are waiting for you in the meeting room and have asked that you make yourself available now." Chris said with obvious distaste. His beta didn't like the elder's underhanded attitude any more than Eric did. Often times the elders abused their rights as councilors to the Alpha to push him around to their liking and he was getting tired of it.

Rubbing a tired hand against his forehead, Eric nodded. "Let's get this over with."

Striding around his desk, he followed Chris out into the wide lobby of the pack's lodge. Turning down a hallway to the left, Eric strode toward the meeting room with Chris following behind him. The long hallway was flooded with morning light from the countless chest high windows on the left of the long hall leading to their destination. Idly, Eric's gaze shifted out the windows as he walked. His gaze took in the sight of the lush forest that surrounded the pack's lodge. He'd rather be running in his wolf form out there than facing a group of sour faced elders.

His strides didn't slow when he entered the meeting room. The room was basically empty save for a long table that stretched the length of the room. Coming to a stop at the head of the table, Eric noted that the elders had already made themselves comfortable in the padded chairs at the middle the carved table.

Adopting a blank expression, Eric turned his attention on the scowling faces of the elders. The elders sat in a close unit with two sitting on either side of the table. He recognized the head elder; Peter Smyth, a willowy man that treasured tradition and hated anything that didn't glorify or strengthen the pack. He sat in his chair as straight and stiff as a board.

Pulling out his chair, Eric sat down in a relaxed manner; his eyes flickered over the room. Chris had pulled the door closed as they entered in an effort to keep this meeting private. For that, he was very thankful for. He highly doubted that the elders had ordered this meeting to talk about the weather with him.

"Good morning." He murmured. None of the occupants at the table returned his greeting.

This was going to be fun... he thought dryly.

"Alpha," Peter began, displeasure evident in his tone. "We have come to discuss several pack matters that concern us."

Ignoring the way the elder glanced at Eric like he was a child about to be reprimanded, he shrugged. "I wasn't aware of any issues among my pack."

"That is precisely why we are here." A second elder commented.

The second elder was a woman; not that he could care to recall her name, but he noted that her expression was aloof and stiff as she regarded him. "It has come to our attention that some of your decisions of late may not be in the best interest of our pack."

Before Eric could reply the Peter explained. "One of those being your decision to form an alliance with those filthy Mackenzie's," The elder's face held a look of distaste. "A *decision* that you neglected to share with this council before hand; I might add."

Eric had to fight the urge to smile. It had been months since he'd heard from Doyle and his pack, much to his relief. Doyle's pack may be an odd one among shifters, but Eric respected Doyle. As Alpha of his pack; Doyle welcomed many different shifters and offered protection where it was needed. He found it amusing that others of his pack viewed Doyle with such distaste.
The grizzly bear shifters may be a bit odd and extremely possessive of their mates, but they at least didn't fight amongst themselves like these people before him were doing. He didn't care about the challenges that Doyle was battling at the moment, it wasn't his business. He had enough to worry about with his own pack. What he cared about was their alliance, nothing more.

"The peace treaty with the pack of Darkwood Springs is what this pack needs." he stated firmly as he tapped his finger against the table.

"And who said that was what this pack needed?" Derik; the third elder stated with a scoff.

"What you should be doing is focusing on strengthening your pack; not making friends. There are several wolf shifters in Darkwood Springs, not to mention several rival packs nearby. Why haven't you made any attempt to expand this pack's reach?" He asked, giving Eric a rude, accusing look.

"Expanding the pack's reach" was just another way of saying to make war with other packs in effort to take control. In the past it's what was done amongst wolf packs. But the thought held no taste for Eric. He was by no means a peace loving man; he was a man that did what had to be done. Damn the consequences as long as the outcome was worth it in the end. He did want his pack to be strong. Constantly engaging in pack wars for more power was not what he wanted.

"The treaties with other shifter packs are important to the survival of this pack. One of these days, there will come a time that we will need the aid of the shifters of Darkwood Springs. For this pack to survive and thrive we need to have allies. *That* is what will increase our strength, not warring with other packs for more territory." His hard gaze fell on each of the elders as he spoke firmly.

Silence stretched through the room, as the elders must have seen that his mind wouldn't' be changed on the topic.
"Our pack will never be strong until we have an Alpha pair to protect and govern us." Jonathan; the fourth elder reasoned gently, earning several approving nods from the others.

And there it was, the true reason for the elder's ambush meeting today. Eric growled in the back of his throat. Why couldn't they just leave this matter alone? He was a strong and fair leader. What the hell would having a woman at his side matter?

"What does this have to do with the security of my pack?" his voice rumbled out with displeasure.

Peter folded his hands on top of the table before answering. "An Alpha female is required within any shifter pack. The reasons for this are unimportant, but it is something that needs to be addressed." At the end, his thin finger tapped against the table in emphasis. Peter's voice rang out with a tone of authority that he seemed to think he possessed in that moment.

"This is not the fifteenth century," Chris stated, moving from his guarding position by the door to come and stand beside Eric. Folding his arms over his chest, he frowned at the arrogant elders. "It's never been a requirement that our Alpha has to have a mate to control and run this pack."

Eric was grateful for his friend's support, but he was too furious to summon the effort to show it. None of the elders ever liked how he'd won the title of Alpha. Unlike most Alphas; who were born into the position and only had to challenge their parent for the title, Eric had been different. He'd been born of two low ranking parents that held no title within the pack. He'd always known that he wouldn't be content to follow the leadership of another. So, he'd fought and shed his own blood for his title and he'd be damned if some snooty elders were going to find ways to take that away from him.

"As of this moment, we've come to an agreement." The female elder said gently, responding to Chris's words as she waved her wrinkled hand toward the other expressionless faces around her. "We've agreed that it should be a requirement. Your recent interests have shown us that you are not concerned with what is best for all the members of this pack and its future and *that* puts the safety of this pack at risk of attack from another. By seeking out other; unnecessary alliances and your refusal to seek out a replacement for the position of Alpha female, you have made us appear to be a weak pack and we cannot tolerate that."

Eric's teeth gritted together, his eyes flashing with dangerous rage. How much more of this was he expected to sit back and listen to? If it were possible he would gut every elder before him and he'd do it with a smile. Releasing a slow breath, he leaned back in his chair.

"With all due respect—" he began; but was cut off as Peter shook his head and held up a staying hand.

Did he just shush me?! Eric raged silently. He didn't know how much more disrespect he could take before his beast exploded.

Rising from his chair, Peter smoothed a hand down the front of his silk tie with an unhurried motion. "With all due respect, *Alpha*." He practically sneered. "This isn't up for discussion. As elders of this pack we believe that you're no longer the best option for this pack."

"I don't like threats, Elder Peter." Eric growled out.

Peter simply smirked at him. Turning to nod at the other elders, he motioned for them to rise as though he'd just called the meeting to an end with the simple action. Without a word the other elders rose from their seats and left the room without a backward glance. Turning his attention back to Eric, Peter stepped as close to his Alpha as Chris's shielding body would allow.

"My suggestion to you, Alpha," Peter began. "Find yourself a replacement mate and show the pack that we have two strong leaders. A lone leader; no matter his strength is still an easy target. You have not met a challenge in some time and that can change very quickly with your recent disregards to the elder council."

"I rule this pack, not you or any of the other elders." Eric hissed out, rising from his chair to hover menacingly over the thin man.

Smirking, Peter shook his head; unafraid. "Regardless; give our words some thought. Otherwise, when you are challenged for your title, you will not have the support of the pack behind you." With those words uttered gently, Peter turned and left the room with slow strides.

The moment the door closed, Eric paced away from the table with a murderous expression falling over his face. His wolf rose to the surface. Fighting to break free and destroy any that opposed him. The elders had no right to tell him to get married or else loose the loyalty of his own pack. They were advisors for God's sake! They held no power over him!

"Eric?" Chris's voice cut through the murderous fog that shrouded his mind.

Drawing in a deep breath, Eric forced his wolf back into the cage of his mind before turning to face his beta. Releasing a deep sigh, he rubbing a tired hand over his stubble dusted jaw before returned to his chair.

As much as he hated agreeing with the elders, he knew they had a point. Without a mate, he was vulnerable. He'd been Alpha of the Ravenwillow wolf pack for twenty years, upon taking that title, he'd taken a mate. His wolf went still at the memory of Emma and Travis's mother. Rage boiled in his stomach like lava. Pursing his lips in anger, he pushed the memory of his mate-by-choice aside.

Pack law dictated that there must be an Alpha pair; if he waited much longer the elders would push the issue further. He needed the support of the elder council to have the loyalty of his pack. As much as the thought turned his stomach to think about it, he would have to consider finding a woman to fill the leader position beside him. He would either have to choose a mate from one of the available females of his pack or a neighboring one. Or he would face challenges daily for his position as Alpha and if defeated, his pups and he; if he wasn't killed, would be driven from the pack. But could he bear to enter into another loveless and despondent mating?

A light knocking at the door caused Eric to growl low in the back of his throat. "WHAT!" He snarled out.

 Slowly meeting room door opened, a tall muscle bound man stepped through. His body encased in a black and blue, pinstriped suit. The top three buttons of his silk, navy shirt undone. His short golden hair glowed against his rough olive skin.

"What type of greeting is that? Should I feel insulted?" A crooked smirk formed across his firm lips. "Jason told me I would find you here."

Pushing his present worries aside, Eric forced a friendly smile on his face. "Damon, I see you were able to pry yourself away from your current bedmate and your mirror for our meeting."

Chuckling Damon ran a hand through his hair with a mocking look. "Who am I to deny the desires of a beautiful woman when she looks my way?"

Rolling his eyes, Eric shook his head at his old friend's teasing. Damon was beta of one of the many packs of wolf shifters that Eric had formed treaties with. In all the years Eric had known Damon, he found him to be a playful lover of many and a strong wolf like no other.

"Whose bed did you slink from this time? You must have known her well if risk being late today."

Taking the seat near Eric's chair at the head of the table, Damon grinned with amusement. "I knew all I needed to know at the time. She has the largest—" He paused, holding his hands out in front of his chest as if he were cupping a bountiful pair of breasts. Damon shot a playful grin at Eric as he finished, "Heart."

"Right," Eric acknowledged disbelievingly. "Enough talk of women's *hearts*. Let's get Jason and get this meeting over with. I want to head over to the building site before it gets late."

"My friend you need to get out more and treat yourself." Damon stated with his usual teasing grin. Standing, he pushed away from the table. Walking around the opposite side of the long table, Damon's eyes flickered around the room. "I noticed the beautiful Myra has graced us with her presence today." His eyes searching Eric's for a reaction of some sort.

"Feel free to take her with you." Eric whispered with an unfeeling tone.

Shaking his head, Damon clicked his tongue mockingly at Eric. "Thank you for the offer, my friend. But *my* Alpha would have my head if I ever thought of taking another male's mate."

"*She's not my mate!*" he snarled, growling low beneath his words, causing him to sound more animal than man. His wolf snarled at the very idea. Myra…his mate; not a chance in hell!

"You say that as if you already know who it is." Damon stated, no doubt fishing for information in hopes that Eric would give him something to gossip about.

Rising to his feet as well, Eric's gaze shot to the watchful gaze of his first beta. Chris watched him with a cool silence that he was known for. Turning away from Chris's watchful eyes, Eric ignored the amusement that danced within Damon's expression. Pacing along the opposite side of the table, Eric shook his head in denial. "Don't be ridiculous."

Damon shrugged his shoulders carelessly. "Makes no difference to me, I was just hoping to hear that you had finally found your true mate. I've been dying to see the great Eric Daniels brought down a peg by a slip of a woman."

From behind him, Chris began to laugh only to cover it the sound with a round of fake coughing as Eric turned to look at him. His true mate? The fates weren't that kind to him. When he'd visited Darkwood Springs to meet Doyle face to face, he hadn't been able to push aside the feeling of jealously that surged through him at seeing Doyle with his own true mate. The bond between Doyle and his mate; Aria was evident to any that saw them together. It was as though they were linked together by thousands of ropes, with no way to separate one from the other.

He craved that; or at least he had at one point in his life. It was far past the time that he should have found his one true mate, if he was worthy enough to have one. After all this time, he seriously doubted that there was still any hope of finding her; the one meant for only him.

In his youth, he'd enjoyed many females of his pack and many not of his pack. When he'd searched for his true mate with no luck, he'd settled for a simple mating among his own pack and he'd chosen Beth.

He'd known that Beth; the mother of his children, wasn't his true mate. At the time; it hadn't seemed to matter much. As Alpha, it was expected that he would mate a strong she-wolf that would stand by his side and give him strong pups. Beth had been his best friend and it had made sense at the time. Even though she hadn't stirred his wolf, he'd hoped that they would have found some happiness in their mating. He'd been wrong.

Not soon after Emma and Travis's birth, it became obvious to him and others around him that Beth had found her happiness in someone else's arms. He hadn't expected love from her, but he had expected loyalty. Before he could confront her about it, she'd disappeared without a trace and her lover with her. For years he'd endured the sympathy filled looks from his family and pack.

He had long given up hope that Beth would return and be a mother to her children. He'd let go of the dream of waking up every morning with his unknown and unfound true mate, the dream of utter happiness and the feel of a true mates love. Hearing from many mated males, the overwhelming and powerful feeling of finding your one true mate, and the over rush of powerful emotions. No words could have been found described to him the intensity of emotions that he would never experience.

Shaking the thoughts away, Eric forced his mind to a more productive subject. There would be time to worry about his mating status; but now wasn't the time. Turning to look at Damon, Eric gestured toward the open doorway with his hand.

"Let's head to my office and I'll show you the blue prints that we've drawn up for your house before we head out."
Damon nodded. "I hope you made the bedroom extra large." He teased. "I need my space."

"For what? You're large ego and blow up dolls?" Chris commented from behind as they headed down the sunlight filled hall.

Scoffing, Damon turned to look at Chris as he continued walking.

"I'll have you know I graduated from blow up dolls a long time ago."

The combined teasing words and friendly laughter echoed behind Eric as he made his way to his office. He couldn't help the returning feel of a strange restlessness within his wolf all of a sudden. His beast was on edge. As one would feel as if they were being hunted or watched, neither of which Eric cared for.

Cautiously, Eric allowed his gaze to wonder around the wide open lobby area of the lodge as they moved toward his work office. Sitting with a lazy posture was his second beta; Jason. His eyes briefly lifted once Eric exited out of the long hallway, only to drift away and back at the motorcycle magazine he was glancing through. On the far side of the room was Myra; he dismissed her seeking gaze within the second he'd spotted her.

Something had put his wolf on edge and had left his skin crawling to the point of madness. But what was it?

3

"That's stupid." Travis grumbled, lifting his eyes from his game boy for the first time in the past hour.

Letting her head lull against the back of the soft chair she sat in, Rebecca closed the thick story book around her thumb, effectively holding her place within the many pages. For the past half an hour she'd done what she did every night, after getting the energetic twin in their separate beds one of the twins chose a book for their nightly bedtime story.

Emma shot a glare across from her side of the room to her disagreeable twin. "Shut up, Travis."

Turning her attention back to Rebecca, Emma clutched her stuffed orange and black striped tiger closer to the soft material of her purple Barbie nightgown. "What happened next, Becca?" her voice filled with innocent wonder.

"Maybe that's enough for tonight." Rebecca began to extract her thumb from the book, but was stopped by the sound of Emma's cry of denial.

"No! I wanna hear more! Come on, Becca; you promised." She cried out with a pout.

Rebecca winced when her gaze collided with Emma's beseeching dark brown eyes. The same big eyed, pleading look a small puppy gave. Emma always knew how to guilt her into anything. Glancing down at her wrist watch, she affirmed it was well past eight-thirty, within the time the twins should already be asleep.

"It's time for you to go to bed, Emma. We'll read some more on Tuesday."

Closing the book, Rebecca rose from her comfortable seat, replacing the book on the tall white bookshelf beside bedroom door. Tonight had been Emma's turn to choose which book would be read; unsurprisingly she'd chosen "Beauty and the Beast, The Madame Le Prince de Beaumont version". The very same book that Rebecca had given Emma as a gift, when she'd made the highest grade in her kindergarten class.

Turning around she made her way to Emma's bed, where she still sat up clutching at her stuffed tiger, idly rubbing one of the orange ears. Sitting down on the edge of Emma's flowered comforter, Rebecca reached for the small lamp that set in the large space between Emma and Travis's twin beds. Turning the small switch and with a small click the bedroom smothering the bedroom in moonlit darkness. Almost immediately a small crescent moon shaped nightlight on the bookshelf began to glow in the shadowy room.

"Why can't we read more tomorrow?" Emma asked grudgingly, when Rebecca stood, pulling aside the thick comforter, Emma obediently crawled under it.

"Because tomorrow you guys are going to your Grandma's and Monday night it's Travis's turn to pick the book we'll read."

Emma scrunched up her face in disagreement. "He only likes video games."

Smiling gently, Rebecca nodded her head in agreement. "That reminds me."

Walking across the room, Rebecca could clearly see Travis in the dimly lit room, the lit up screen of his game boy illuminated his small face. He still sat on top of his navy colored comforter; his blue eyes flickered back and forth across the screen of his black game boy. Coming to stop near his bed, her hands closed over the game boy, pulling it out of his two small clutching hands.

Travis made a hopeless grab for the game boy. "Hey! Give it back!" Turning the game boy off, she folded the screen down. "Go to sleep."

"I was almost to level twelve!"

"Well, Zeda can wait until tomorrow."

"It's Zelda." Travis grumbled with a pout.

Her unflinching gaze settled over his stubborn one. A look no doubt he inherited from his even more stubborn father. "Go to sleep Travis."

Giving her a pouting look, like his twin he crawled beneath his comforter and settled against the soft matching pillow. Laying the game boy down on top of the bookshelf, her eyes slowly swept over the twins bed one last time. Somehow both of Eric's children always seemed to fall asleep the second their heads hit the pillow. Travis had lain down with his back toward her, no doubt put out with the confiscation of his video game. Emma snuggled on her side; in her sleep she continually rubbed the side of her face against her pillow in effort to get comfortable. Her stuffed tiger still clutched to her small body.

Deep in her heart, she knew that she wouldn't always be needed for Emma and Travis. But in the past few months they both had found a way to weasel through her armor and into her heart. How would she walk away from them afterwards? No doubt Emma and Travis could tell she wasn't a shifter like them, but they had done nothing but treat her like a member of the family.

Quietly closing the door behind her as she left, Rebecca slowly made her way down the short hall way and down the maroon carpeted stairs. Her eyes drifted over the collection of framed baby photos and other pictures that documented Emma and Travis's memories. She spotted several photos of the twins with Sarah, their grandmother. But there was only one picture with Eric. It was her favorite picture out of them all, because it was the only photo of them that she'd taken.

Taken last month at the park, the photo showed Eric lounging on a blanket with Emma and Travis crawling over him in a mock of a wrestling match. Eric's handsome face glowed with happiness as his large arms wrapped around the two wiggling children. They really made a happy family. A family, Rebecca knew she'd never be a part of.

With her family gone, Rebecca found herself constantly marveling at the beauty of many family photos wherever she worked. But never had she stared at a picture of her employer the way she did now. She didn't understand the strange pull she felt towards him. It wasn't as if Eric even liked her. Several times she'd caught Eric looking at her, but it wasn't soon after meeting her gaze that he found an excuse to leave the room. No doubt; he found humans to be unattractive and beneath him.

Maybe if she'd been a shifter…

Rebecca immediately shook off the thought before her idle brain could complete it. Eric was her boss and he would remain so if she valued her job and life. He would never see past her weak human form and she couldn't look past the vicious beast that she knew lurked beneath the surface.

After straightening up the slightly cluttered living room, she found herself near the end of her nightly chore list. Standing in front of the double sink, her hands moved quickly across the soiled dishes. When one dish was spotless, she deposited it in the other sink, filled with clear, rinse water. From there she plucked it out and laid it gently on the wooden dish rack beside the sink.

Finally finished, she grabbed a dish towel and dried her hands. Turning to the dish rack, she began putting the newly cleaned dishes where they belonged. Setting the last of the dishes away, her ears picked up the sound of several male voices coming from the porch. Giving the clean kitchen one final look over, she headed to the laundry room located by the staircase.

Taking the last load out of the dryer, she focused on ignoring the conversation that became louder as Eric and his visitors entered through the kitchen. Not wanting to interrupt or be introduced to anyone in her rumpled appearance, Rebecca stayed in the laundry room as she sorted and folded the last load of the night.

The sound of heavy footsteps nearing the dimly lit room made her heart begin to race. She prayed they were just heading into the living room to watch some TV and had no intention of coming near her. When the footsteps seemed to draw closer, she felt her heart race more.

Looking down at the polished red washier, Rebecca winced at her blurry reflection. Her high ponytail was crooked and many strands of her hair fell tangled around her face and her blue t-shirt was dirty and damp from dish water. She didn't want to meet Eric's colleges like this! Her only hope was that she could finish folding the clothes and put them away quickly, then slip out before being seen.

"There you are." Gasping in surprise, Rebecca closed her eyes, holding a hand over her racing heart as Eric's tall frame suddenly filled the doorway. "Sorry I didn't mean to scare you."

"You didn't." Dropping her hand from her wet chest, she roughly shoved her tangled strands of hair behind her ears. "I'm just finishing up and then I'm out of here." Gently setting the three piles of folded clothes in the square basket, she tried to slip past him; but he refused to move from his position in the doorway.

"That can wait a second."

Reaching out he tried to gentlemanly extract the tan weaved basket from her delicate arms. Rebecca repositioned the basket on her opposite hip, away from him, her eyes flashing challengingly at him. Moving toward her, Eric tried once again to take the basket from her and once again she stepped aside, evading him.

Glaring down at her, he held out his hands. "Give me the damn basket."

"No. I want to put these where they need to go so I can go home. Now if you'll excuse me." Before Rebecca could walk around him, his hand shot around her, snagging the basket from her grip.

Ignoring her sound of frustration, he dropped the basket carelessly on top of the washier. Grasping a hold of her wrist, he tugged her out of the laundry room, causing her to stumble behind him. "Come, I want to meet some people."

Futilely, she tried to reclaim her hand. "Eric, you can't introduce me to your colleges with me looking like this."

"Why the hell not?" coming to an abrupt halt, he turned to face her, His hand still shackling her wrist.

"Look at me. My clothes are wet and dirty, my hair is messed up—"

Raising a skeptic brow, Eric scoffed. "So what? It's not as if they'd be interested in you anyway."

Finally fed up with being treated like a dog being led by a leach, Rebecca jerked her hand from his grasp. Shocked that she was able to pull from his hold, Eric turned to watch her quietly. Raising her chin, definitely at him, her hand reached up to shove her fall dark hair from her face.

"Fine, I'll meet your friends. But next time, I expect to be asked nicely and in advanced. Furthermore; you may be my boss, Eric; but that doesn't give you the right to drag me around like a dog." By the time she finished railing at him she was panting for breathe. Eric's surprised face turned to his normal stern one.

His forehead rippled with a deep frown and his full lips tensed in a hard line. Not bothering to answer her he continued the rest of the way across the living room and into the kitchen. Given no other choice, Rebecca followed him, all the while doing her best to straighten her appearance as the sound of male voices grew louder.

"Where'd you disappear to Alpha?" shooting a warning glance at Jason's question, Eric flicked his eyes toward Rebecca. Silently cautioning everyone to watch what they said around the human in the room.

Walking past the three watchful wolves in the room, Eric headed to the fridge, while calling over his shoulder. "Everyone this is Rebecca. She looks after the house and my children." Reaching into the fridge he withdrew a chilled bottle of water. Walking back to the group, he stood next to Rebecca and began introducing each male before her.

"This is Jason; he's my… assistant of sorts." He explained hesitantly.

Rebecca's gaze shifted to look up at Eric's as he quickly averted his gaze. Through his cool exterior she could see that Eric was on edge with his pack members; or at least that's what she assumed they were, around her. Perhaps he was concerned that one may say something to endanger their secret in front of her. Regardless what the reason for his strange demeanor, she had to play along.

As Jason stepped forward, offering his hand in greeting, Rebecca couldn't help but stare at his handsome face. His nearly black hair fell to his shoulders, pulled back tightly in a meager ponytail. She wasn't surprised to see his eyes mirroring the same richness of his hair color. With his dark olive skin color and his almond shaped eyes, she would guess that he had strong Native American Indian heritage in his family somewhere.

He smiled warmly down at her as his large hand cupped her smaller one. "So you're the elusive Rebecca? Eric talks about you all the time."

Rolling her eyes gently pulled her hand away from Jason's gentle grasp. "I'm sure it wasn't all good things. I have a habit of irritating people to the point of insanity."

Letting out a rumbling laugh, Jason's lips curved into a soft smile. "I doubt that."

* ~ * ~ *

Clearing his throat loudly, Eric's hard eyes bore into Jason's, giving a clear warning for him to back away from the small human. Nodding his head at Eric in acknowledgement, Jason turned and settled down one of the kitchen table chairs.

Only after making one introduction, Eric was seeing that introducing Rebecca to his Beta's and Damon was the worst mistake he'd ever made. His eye flashing over all their expressions made it clear. Every one of them watched Rebecca with a look of hunger and longing. How dare they look at her that way! He should kick them all out now, including Rebecca! How dare she look so tempting, so…something! Somehow he couldn't fight the growl that rumbled deep in his chest, the feeling of protectiveness that flooded all his senses.

Mine…Only mine… the thought came from deep down, from his wolf.

Shock rocked him, nearly causing him to crust the plastic water bottle in his hand. There it was again, the invasive sound of his wolf's thoughts. How was that possible? A shifter's inner beast only fully emerged like that when a true mate was near. This confused him, causing his gaze to focus on Rebecca's.

Growing impatient with the nonsense of his own thoughts he quickly finished introducing the last two, barely patiently waiting wolves before him. "And Damon and Chris, Damon is an old friend and Chris is another assistant." His hand gestured to each one as he rushed out their names past his snarling lips.

"It's great to finally meet you." Just as Chris stepped forward to shake her hand, he was shoved back by Damon as he moved in front of him. Smiling charmingly down at her surprised face, his large hand engulfed hers. Rebecca felt her breath catch in her chest.

"Rebecca…" he murmured her name softly as his head lowered to her hand. His firm lips brushed gently against her soft skin.

Pulling her hand away from sinful attentions of the handsome man in front of her, Rebecca couldn't miss the look of unrelenting anger that swam in the depths of Eric's blue eyes. What was his problem?

"There." Eric snapped, his eyes flashing dangerously at each of the moonstruck idiots in the room. "You've met her. Now let's get on with business." Looking down at Rebecca, he desperately tried to reign in his wolf before it broke free and he did something he'd regret. "You can go finish your duties now. Once you're done, you can leave for the night, no need to inform me when you leave."

Ignoring the way her eyes narrowed at him in outrage, Eric motioned for the others to follow him as he made his way to his office. But no one moved an inch. All their attention was on Rebecca as she smiled friendly at each of them.

"It was nice to meet all of you. Good evening." With a friendly wave goodbye she quickly left the drooling werewolves staring after her retreating form. Not that she was aware of her alluring effect on the three seasoned wolf shifters.

Chris let out a heavy, longing breath as he continued to stare in the direction vanished mortal. "I now see why you didn't want any of us coming over unannounced."

"God, I have never seen such a more tempting sight." Damon smiled dreamily as he took a deep inhale, drawing her lingering scent inside his body.

"She's not off limits, is she?" Jason asked with curiosity, leaning his face against his braced hand. Out of all three of them Jason seemed to be the only one retaining some of his sense.

Crumbling the plastic water bottle in his hand in restrained anger, Eric's sharp eyes flashed dangerously. "Yes, she is."

Tossing the demolished bottle in the small trash can, he couldn't help but allow his gaze to follow the same direction as the others. When had she begun to smell so good? Her scent made his wolf want to rub against every part of her body, marking her skin with not only *his* scent, but to brand hers into his also. Maybe she was wearing a new perfume?

Turning back the waiting trio, Eric let out a heavy breath. He couldn't wait for tonight to end. His body felt too strung while his mind was full of anxiety. Something in his life was unbalanced, the question was; what was it?

"Let's get this finished." Eric growled out.

Without another word he strode from the kitchen, not caring whether or not the others were following. One thing was for certain, he would never be introducing Rebecca to anyone ever again. Moments ago she had seemed to turn the most vicious werewolves he'd ever met, into obedient puppies. He just prayed that he continued remained immune.

* ~ * ~ *

This had to be the third time in a half an hour that Eric's eyes had shot to the small clock that sat on the edge of his desk. Chris and Jason's voices seemed to drone on in the background of his mind. Gathered around his desk, they had been reviewing changes in the blue prints for the past half hour, but Eric couldn't seem to get his mind to focus. For reasons he couldn't fandom, his thoughts kept drifting to Rebecca. What was she doing right now? His keen sense of smell and hearing told him she was upstairs, moving quietly from room to room putting clothes away.

"Alpha," Jerking his eyes up to Jason's studying eyes, Eric mentally shook himself. He needed to focus on the matter at hand and not on the forbidden mortal woman in his house.

"Maybe we could just meet up later and finish these last details at a later date?" Damon suggested from his leaning position against the far wall beside the door. Stuffing his hands in his jean pockets, Damon's hopeful eyes trailed out into the living room, no doubt hoping to catch gimps of Rebecca leaving.

"What's wrong, Damon? Are we making you late for a date? Don't you ever think of anything productive?" Chris mumbled as he wrote a measurement note on the blue print before him.

Damon smirked, "I'll have you know my thoughts *and* my actions are very *productive.*"

"Spare us the details, Damon. You've put off his project long enough and I do have more important things to do with my time than run after you to get your final approval on these." Eric indicated to the blue prints in front of him. "If we want to start building before fall comes we have to do it soon, so get over here and look at these damn papers."

"I must say, Eric; you seem a bit testy tonight. Nothing a night in the naked arms of a beautiful woman wouldn't cure." Damon suggested teasingly.

Rolling his eyes, Eric let out a tire groan, "If I recall correctly, there are a few females within my pack that have been *dying* to get their hands on your address and cell number. I recall them not sounding like they were fans of yours."

Holding up his hands in surrender, Damon crossed the distance between himself and the others. "Alright, Alright, Threats do not become you, my friend."

Smiling softly Damon looked over the spread out blue prints of his future house, while Chris described the measurements and structural design of each area and Jason suggested the best materials to choose from. Eric wasn't all that surprised when Damon asked as few as questions as he could. He knew the only reason Damon wanted this house built was so he had a place to live as far from his own pack as possible, not that he'd shared any further information beyond that.

"Do you have sample photos of what the living room windows could look like?" Damon asked curiously.

Eric as well as his Beta's narrowed his eyes in suspicion. "Why do you want to see photographs of window designs, when Chris as several sketches of them in front of you?"

"I just can't seem to picture it right in my head. Photos may help give me a better perspective."

Rubbing his tired eyes, Eric nodded toward waiting Chris. Not wasting a moment Chris and Jason walked over to Eric's tall black filing cabinet and began withdrawing several folders. As they flipped through each folder, Eric leaned his head against the headrest of his chair, none of them aware that Damon was quietly slipped from the room.

Opening his eyes, Eric rose to his feet to stretch. His irritated gaze falling on his Beta's as they flipped through the photos in their hands. "Did you find it?"

"Yes, Alpha," Jason mumbled straightening his collection of pictures.

"Alright, Damon, No more stall—" turning Eric was greeted by an empty space that Damon had previously occupied. Looking around the room, Eric let out a low growl. Where was that idiot now?

* ~ * ~ *

My feet hate me. Rebecca thought to herself as she quietly walked out of Eric's room.

After today's long day, she was looking forward to a long hot bubble bath and crawling into her warm bed. The aching of her feet made her so happy that she was off for the next two days. Emma and Travis were spending the weekend with their grandmother so obviously Eric would have no need of her until Monday.

Softly closing the door behind her, Rebecca was surprised when she bounced back against the door after running into a hard, warm wall in front of her, a warm wall, which came with a pair of large hands that wrapped around her arms to steady her. Looking up she was surprised to see the golden eye candy; Damon blocking her path.

He smiled warmly down at her. "Sorry. I thought you heard me call out to you."

"It's okay." She murmured, pulling her arms from his strong hands.

"I'm glad I caught you before you left."

"Why? Does Eric need something?"

Stepping closer, Damon reached out, stroking the arch of her cheek. "Don't worry about Eric. It's me you should worry about." He whispered, his face moving closer and closer toward hers.

"Excuse me?" bewildered, Rebecca tried to put space between their bodies.

"You're in danger of me kissing you right now. What do you think about that?" His lips hovered a mere few inches from hers. Slapping her hand over his hovering mouth, Rebecca slowly pushed Damon out of her personal space. Laughing softly at his flirtatious words, she shook her head. "I think your barking up the wrong tree."

In more ways than one, wolf-boy,

Turning his face, Damon rubbed his cheek against the palm of her extended hand, causing Rebecca to jerk it back. Planting a hand on the wall beside her head, Damon leaned dangerously close to her.

"Why do you say that? Am I not your type?"

"I don't have a type and I don't want to be used so you can gloat to Eric."

"Trust me it's you that I am interested in, not pissing off Eric. Are you free tomorrow night?"

Stepping around him, Rebecca turned to face him with her back to the stairs. "I'm not in a habit of dating men I just met."

Stepping closer to her, he reached down and took possession of one of her hands, enfolding his hands around hers. His blue eyes bore into hers, beseechingly. "Then get to know me. I know a great Italian place."

She shook her head, befuddled. What was it going to take for this guy to take a hint? "Damon—"

"What's going on here?" a rumbling voice boomed from the stairs.

Startled; Rebecca jerked her hand from Damon's loose grip and spun around, coming face to face with seething Eric standing on the top step.

"Eric. Damon and I were just—" Before Rebecca could begin explaining the awkward situation she'd found herself in, Eric's sharp gaze shot above her head to Damon.

"Jason has the pictures you need. Go take a look."

Shrugging, Damon smiled teasingly. "I don't need to see them. Everything looks great from what I see." His eyes trailed over Rebecca suggestively.

Narrowing his eyes, a low growl unwillingly tore through Eric's throat. "Wait downstairs, Damon. Now,"

Giving Eric a smug look, Damon made his way, slowly down the stairs. Eric's now glowing, predatory eyes following Damon's every step until he disappeared from sight. Moving with soft, graceful movements, Rebecca neared the steps and had almost slipped past Eric before his hand shot out toward the wall, blocking her path. His eyes flashed dangerous over her startled face. She was forced to step back as Eric advanced towards her, until she was trapped between the cool wall and Eric's hot body.

His chest fell and rose with his rapid breaths, his hard features seemed to be carved out of granite. "What the hell was that?"

She shrugged her shoulders, unconcerned. "Nothing, we were just talking."

"*Talking*? Talking about what?" he asked, his voice turning stone cold serious.

Cool and calm, Rebecca crossed her arms over the swell of her breasts, "None of your business." She instantly felt on edge by his questioning. Why should she tell him anything? She hadn't done anything wrong. "You're the one that introduced me to him; it stands to reason that we would talk to one another."

"Listen and listen carefully, Rebecca. I don't care what you do in your personal time, but when you are in *my* house you will behave as though you actually possess some doctrine. I can't have you distracting my workers with your provocative appearance."

Letting out a gasp of outrage, Rebecca shoved past him. "Provocative! There is nothing provocative about my appearance. Damon came on to me not the other way around."

"He came on to you? *How*?" Eric's wolf leapt toward the surface at her words, giving Eric barely enough time to face away from her to hide his partial shifting features and glowing eyes. His wolf was enraged that another male had dared approach her and for some reason, Eric didn't like the idea much either.

"Just tell me something, Eric." She continued, her voice was soft; but strung tightly. "What is so provocative about my appearance?"

Taking a calming breathe he was able to shove his resistant wolf back down within his soul. Turning to face her, he pointed at the rumpled and dirty blue t-shirt and jeans, thankful that his hand was normal and not covered in fur and claws. "This outfit is…inappropriate."

Planting her hands on her hips, Rebecca looked down at her food smeared and wrinkle ridden clothes. "How so?"

Her question caught Eric off guard. He hadn't expected her to inquire beyond his response. Her clothes weren't really inappropriate. They were sinful. Her t-shirt, though it was just a plain, high collar t-shirt, it cupped and molded against her full breasts and the soft curve of her stomach. His eyes traveled down to her faded blue jeans. They were made for her, hugging and cupping the meaty curve of her buttocks and strong thighs.

More than anything he wanted to peal her figure hugging pants down and sink his teeth into her meaty flesh. She was becoming too much of a temptation for him. But still he fought against his baser instincts. Unsure how to deal with his willful human, he lied, "You look like a street walker, if you weren't dressed like this; you wouldn't have to worry about Damon coming on to you. Remember to dress more appropriately from now on and we won't have to worry about you attracting unwanted attention from my workers."

His wolf practically wagged his tail at the sight of fire leaping into her eyes; he had become very fond of her temper. It had become his greatest ally in fighting this new born attraction to her that he couldn't fandom, and was the only thing that kept him from reaching out and taking her as he wished to.

"A street walker?" advancing on him, Rebecca now had Eric backing up, startled. " Let me tell you something, Eric; I will not apologize for how I look and if it bothers you so much I'd be happy to scratch your eyes out!" she raged, her finger jabbing into his chest warningly.

During watching her rage at him, something shifted inside him. Some strange invisible force seemed to make being this close to her unbearable. As if he'd go mad if he didn't touch her. The scent of her anger rose from her pores mixed with her personal alluring scent. Eric suddenly couldn't get enough.

Before either of them knew what was happening, Eric's hands gripped around her upper armed, jerking her stiff form against his. Bending down his lips covered hers in breathless urgency. Shocked; Rebecca froze under his assault. His tongue swept past her lips and into her gasping mouth.

His hands moved from her arms up to grip her unraveling ponytail and holding the back of her head still for his exploration. Leaving the haven of her mouth, his teeth nipped and pulled at her bottom lip before his tongue swept teasing over the plump flesh.

Rebecca felt herself being pulled inevitably closer to Eric through his kiss. How long had she wanted this? How long had she dreaded this? Her body softened against his hard frame, warm sensations from his gripping hands in her hair and the soft scratching of his nails against the back of her skull began to pour over her, causing goose bumps to rise on her arms.

As he broke away from her swollen lips, the temptation to pull him closer almost was her undoing, until Eric's husky voice broke through the heavy fog that covered her brain.

"Rebecca." Her name whispered from his parted lips, as his chest rose and fell with exhilaration.

His eyes burned over her flushed features and panting lips, his green irises illuminated in the darkness of the hallway. Instead of being fearful of the unnatural glow, Rebecca felt herself being drawn closer by the beautiful glowing orbs that gazed gently down at her.

Forcing his glowing eyes to darken to normal, Eric strived to put some distance between their desire ridden bodies. "You invite too much unwanted attention, causing males do things they would never do otherwise."

Jerking away from his warm hand that still held the back of her head, Rebecca rubbed furiously at her lips as she tried to rid herself of the delicious taste of him. The overwhelming desire for his strong body quickly turned to self loathing.

Did he mean that he wouldn't have kissed her if she hadn't enticed him in some unknowing way? How dare him! He was the one to kiss *her!*

Ignoring his still glowing eyes, Rebecca swung her hand at his face before giving it a second thought. Her hand stung as it met Eric across his face. Not waiting around to see his reaction, Rebecca raced down the stairs. Stopping in the kitchen to grab her purse she was surprised to see Damon leaning against the bar pulling a water bottle from his firm lips, a questioning look on his face.

Setting the bottle on the bar, he slowly began to approach her. "Are you okay?" His eyes filled with curious concern.

Glaring up at him as she snatched her purse off the bar, releasing a huff of breath. "You can pick me up at eight." Without another word she opened the front door, slamming is behind her for good measure. Storming over to her car, she jerked the door open in anger.

Inviting unwanted attention? I'll show him unwanted attention!

4

Rolling over, Rebecca gave up on her futile attempts to sleep in. All night her dreams had been plagued with visions of Eric kissing her, loving her, his warms rough hands roaming over her flushed skin.

With a cry of disgust, she tossed her pillow across the room, wishing she could have hit *him* with it instead of the wall. Swinging her legs out of bed, she climbed out of her small bed, padding bare foot into the connecting bathroom, her long t-shirt falling barely past her flexing buttocks.

Bending over the small tub, turning on the water she adjusted the water temperature to her liking. Leaving the water running she returned to her bedroom in search of a change of clothes. Just as she'd reached her small dresser the shrill sound of her phone on her bedside table grabbed her attention. Crossing to examine the caller I.D. she let out a grunt of disgust as the name: *Daniels, Eric,* flashed on the small lit up screen.

What does he want now?

She was tempted to let the phone continue to ring. It would serve him right to have to talk to her answering machine. After all; her answering machine would show him the same range of consideration that he deserved; none. Inhaling a steady breath her thin fingers curled around the black cordless phone and held it up to her ear.

"What?" her voice was less than friendly.

"Rebecca? What's wrong? You sound upset."

Rebecca was forced to bite down on her lip to keep from yelling into the phone, *Upset? Try pissed off, wolf man!* "I'm fine. Why are you calling me?"

"You left rather abrupt last night. I wanted to make sure you were alright."

"You're the reason I left *abrupt* last night, Eric."

"That's why I called. I wanted to apologize for the kiss. I can't think why I would behave like that much less with you. So I'm sorry."

Much less with you... What was that suppose to mean? Was he ashamed that he'd lowered his lupine self to kiss a mere human, as though she were beneath him? Seething with rage, Rebecca felt her volcano of anger over flow and explode.

"You know what, Eric? I'll see you on Monday, but until then why don't you go jump off a cliff!" stabbing one of the top buttons she disconnected the call. After slamming the phone back on its stand, she walked not two feet away before it rang again.

Storming back, she jerked the phone to her ear. "What?!" her chest rose and fell as her anger slowly drained with her outburst. Silence for the other end met her rage filled words. "Well? Did you call to talk to the street walker?"

"Actually, I called to talk to my extremely attractive date for tonight." The teasing voice of Damon floated through the earpiece, causing her to wince.

"Oh, Damon it's you..."

He chuckled softly. "At your service, so what was that about a street walker?"

Laughing nervously, she began pacing the length of her small bedroom. "I thought you were someone else. Wait, how did you get my number?" She asked freezing in midstride.

"After Eric ordered me downstairs last night, I went through his cell phone for your number. By the way do you know what you're listed under in his contacts? *"MY CURSE","*

"Why did you call?" she asked, choosing to ignore his comment about Eric's cell phone.

"Just to make sure you weren't planning on backing out on our date."

She had almost forgotten how she had agreed—well more like decreed that he could pick her up. When Eric had kissed her, she remembered feeling startled, confused and then desired; up until he had told her that she was inviting unwanted attention. Why shouldn't she go out with Damon? She deserved happiness, even if for just for a while.

"Of course not, I'll see you at eight." Without any hindrance she agreed to meet him at the restaurant. Murmuring a quick goodbye, she hung up the phone, surprised that she was actually looking forward to tonight.

The excitement over her impending date quickly faded and was replaced with the icy feeling of fear, fear that had her heart squeezing tightly in her chest. How could she have forgotten? Damon was a close friend of Eric's, did that mean he was a shifter too? In her mind she could see Damon teasing face turning cold as the form of a terrifying wolf over took his handsome features as he lunged for her exposed throat, her hand flew to her neck as her eyes widened in terror.

Shaking her head, she pushed the gore filled thoughts from her head. Chances were that she'd never see Damon again after tonight anyway, she wasn't all that convinced that he wasn't interested in her beyond pissing off Eric. The idea of Eric's reaction to finding out that she and Damon would be together tonight was almost too much for her smiling face to take.

After witnessing the way he'd reacted when seeing Damon standing close to her, holding her hand tenderly, she knew Eric was attracted to her on some level. This is why she was not missing her date for nothing. Nothing would please her more than watching him twist with envy, once he found out.

* ~ * ~ *

Pacing back and forth across his office, Eric was unable to take his eyes off the phone that sat untouched on the cluttered desk. There was no lie he could tell himself for the reason why he'd dialed Rebecca's number. After their encounter last night, his wolf was unreasonable, causing him to crave her even more than usual. He was beyond restless, feeling as though he'd destroy anything he'd touch if he couldn't have her in his presence.

Hours earlier; in a moment of desperation, he'd called her. The sound of her irritated voice had startled him, but just hearing her still felt like a soothing balm for the worst of his tight, burning skin. She may just be a mortal, but she had the temper of a she-wolf, with jaws snapping at him for insulting her and God help him it made him want her more.

Never before had he been so connected to his wolf aside from shifting when their souls joined as one. Now he could hear his wolf's thoughts, his feelings and desires as his own, a torn part of him had begun to mend back together. What had caused this change in him, in his wolf?

Mate...the familiar deep rumbling voice echoed in the walls of Eric's mind.

He knew now that it was his inner wolf and the realization terrified him. The only reason a shifter's inner beast fully emerged was when their beast sensed their true mate near. She was the one person in the world that completed both man and beast, his true mate. A mate beyond worth or description.
Could this explain his unexplainable mood swings? Was this what the mated wolves had meant? Had the feeling of completeness and other stronger, indescribable emotions mean not just the finding of his destined female, but becoming whole with the wolf inside him?

Mate. The voice now growled through his mind once more.

What mate? Eric finally asked. Every second the thoughts of his wolf sounded—*felt* more as his own.

Our mate; Find her and claim her now. I do not want to be apart from our mate. His wolf whispered with a beseeching tone before a growl rumbled out. *Find her.*

Eric found himself scoffing, his head shaking with disbelief. This was ridiculous. He didn't have a mate and it certainly wasn't Rebecca, the forbidden mortal. Why would the fates be so cruel to him? Forcing him to wait for his true mate and then to present a fragile mortal to him, a woman that he would forever long for but would never possess.

She is ours...

She is not ours. Eric responded adamantly to his inner beast.

Communicating with his beast felt strange, but a freeing rush coursed through him at the same time. *It is forbidden to claim a human as a mate and even if it weren't you know the pack laws as much as I do.*

Others have taken a human mate before, it is only impossible because you allow your stubbornness to cloud your mind. His wolf argued.

We are not bears! Eric yelled through his thoughts.

He refused to believe it. He would prove to his stubborn wolf that she wasn't his mate that was causing his basic instincts to go haywire, but the lustful idea of tasting the forbidden fruit that he was denied.

Snatching up the phone, he quickly redialed her number; after he saw her in person he'd be able to put all this disputable nonsense to rest.

* ~ * ~ *

Where the hell is it?

In a panicked rush, Rebecca dumped the contents of her makeup bag into the porcelain sink, each item making a loud crashing sound on impact. Sifting through the pile, she searched desperately for her lipstick. Go three years without a date and no use for makeup, much less lipstick and when you really need it, it's gone.

After Eric and Damon's calls, she had enjoyed her day off thoroughly, first with a long hot bubble bath and then by curling up on her couch with a romance novel and her favorite soap opera playing in the background, Then spending two precious hours making herself presentable for her date tonight, saving makeup for last.

Releasing a sigh of relief, her fingers closed around the thin cylinder shaped tube of scarlet red lip stick. Bending closer to the mirror, she very carefully brought the exposed tip of her lipstick to her upper lip. Her hand jerked off course when the startling sound of her phone erupted through the silence of her bathroom/bedroom.

Grabbing a tissue, she wiped away the spear of red across her cheek as she walked to the phone. Not bothering to look at the caller I.D. this time, she plucked up the phone, cradling it against the side of her face and her shoulder as she returned in front of her bathroom mirror.

"Hello?" she answered while concentrating once more on applying lipstick to her parted lips. Instead of hearing a return response, only silence greeted her. "Hello?" she repeated, seconds away from just hanging up.

"You sound like you're in a better mood."

The sound of Eric's smooth voice had chills racing up her spine, at least before her hard resolve fell into place. "What do you want, Eric?"

"I thought I'd treat you to dinner to apologize for my behavior last night. Interested?" he asked in a way that told Rebecca that he'd expected her to agree. His arrogance was so heavy that it seemed to float from the phone.

"No, thank you." As soon as the words left her mouth she could have sworn she heard a barely audible growl floating from the background.

Let him growl, he's not getting his way this time. She thought smugly

"Why not?" His voice rumbled out.

"I'm busy tonight, doing *street walker* things if you must know." She snapped, turning to her right, tugging open the third drawer of the mounted linen cabinet.

Reaching beneath a neatly folded stack of towels, she withdrew a small, hidden box. Inside was a collection of her most valued jewelry; all that she had left of her mother. Selecting a simple necklace she turned back to the mirror, still holding the phone to her ear.

"Is that why you're upset with me?" when she didn't answer, feeling his wolf becoming more anxious, causing him to pace around his desk before he continued, "I didn't mean it, Rebecca." She still didn't answer. What should he say?

"Eric, why did you *really* call? Are you bored and just wanted to torment me on my day off?"

Rubbing a hand against the back of his neck, he slowly settled in the chair behind his desk. "Possibly,"

"Well it will have to wait until after my date tonight. Speaking of; I need to finish getting—"

Outraged; Eric leapt from his chair, nearly crushing the phone with his lupine strength. "Date? What date? You have a date?"

"Aren't those all roughly the same question?"

A growl rumbled deep in his chest, while his wolf snarled at the idea of an unseen male courting *his* Rebecca. "Who is he?"

"Why do you care?" she asked uncaringly, while adjusting the simple oval, moonstone pendant necklace over the slope of her throat.

While gritting his teeth, his fist clenched tightly around the plastic phone as he fought his rising temper. "At least tell me his name." *So*

I know who to kill…

"Eric, I really don't have time for this."

"You'll make time!" he bit out, sounding as though his words came out through clenched teeth. "Where did you meet this guy anyway? How do you know he's not some psycho?"

Shrugging out of her terry bathrobe, standing in nothing but her red lacy bra and panties, she reached out for her folded purple blouse and black slacks on the edge of the sink. After pulling up her thin slacks, her eyes were drawn back to her reflection and her scars that seemed to illuminate against her pale colored skin.

Her hand hesitantly reached up to trace the white, raised scars that marred her soft skin, Scars from angry claws and lethal teeth, which had torn her skin like a knife slicing through butter. One scar was a short four claw slash from the center of her collar bone, across the swell of her right breast. Turning slightly to the left, in the mirror she surveyed the second scar leading from the back of her right shoulder and sloped diagonally down to her right hip.

She could hear Eric's voice droning on about the dangers of being alone with strange men. Looking at the eternal brand on her skin, she knew she would never make the same mistake she did years before.

"I'm a big girl, Eric. I can take care of myself."

"I need to see you tonight."

"Not happening, Eric." Shaking her head at his persistence, she shoved her arms into her sleek blouse, buttoning it up as high as needed to conceal her wide scars. Pulling her hair out of the collar, allowing the chocolate strands to fall over her shoulders.

"Where is he taking you? Is it public? Just don't get in the car with him. I'm sure women like you prefer driving yourself, so he doesn't know where you live. Right?" his questions sot reassurance; whether for Rebecca or him was undecided.

Unwilling to answer any of his questions about her date with Damon, she mischievously replied, "Oh look at the time…got to go!" without another word she quickly hung up and tossed it on her bed, Smiling impishly at how she'd hung up on him and envisioning him snarling in rage at being ignored.

Take that, wolf man! Looking at the time; she raced from her room, slipping her black heels on as she went. This was one date she refused to be late to, especially when it would annoy Eric endlessly.

* ~ * ~ *

Eric's elongated claws bit deep in the armrests of his brown leather recliner. Staring at the far empty wall, his sport's program playing on the widescreen in the corner was all but forgotten. At this very moment; Rebecca was on her date with some unknown man. He didn't want to think about it. He didn't understand why he felt such rage at the thought of Rebecca with another man. He supposed somewhere he'd become possessive of his human. He was more than willing to deny that she was anything to him.

She wasn't his mate. He couldn't explain why she had his wolf all riled up. However that didn't mean that he would willingly step aside and let another have her. He couldn't stand the thought of her sharing her warming smile and laughter with another male. With every image of her with someone else that floated in his mind, he could feel his beast rising higher and higher to the surface. If he didn't get more control over his emotions, Rebecca would find an unrestrained werewolf crashing her beloved date.

Rebecca may just work for him, but somehow he'd imagined her as a permanent fixture of his home. His children loved her and though he wouldn't admit it; he loved the fire that would flair in her eyes when her temper rose. She had somehow wormed her way into his mind and he wasn't beginning to see her as a simple human nuance any more, she was simply…his.

What did that even mean?

Just as he was seconds from leaping to his feet and searching out his wayward human, the phone hanging on the kitchen wall began its high-pitched ringing. Striding quickly from the living room, he nearly jerked the entire stand off the wall with his urgency. Jerking the phone to his ear, he answered with bated breath. "Rebecca?"

"'Rebecca'? Have you been holding out on us, Alpha?" Jason's voice floated out with mischievous waves.

Sighing heavily, he pinched the bridge of his nose. "This better be good."

"Actually; I just wanted to tell you about an interesting development that I just discovered as we speak."

"Is it about work?"

"No…" Jason said hesitantly.

His breath huffed out with irritation. "Is it about Pack business?"

"No."

"Good night, Jason." Pulling the phone away from his face, Jason's rushing voice assailed his lupine ears.

"Wait! Wait! Wait! You'll *want* to hear what I have to say!" rolling his eyes, Eric pulled the phone back to his ear, waiting patiently for his Beta to continue speaking. "Anyway; I stopped in Divinity, the old Italian restaurant in town and I saw Damon all fluffed up for a date."

"Damon has dates all the time; it's really not that special." He mumbled undaunted.

"*And* when I casually chatted him up about who he was meeting he—very smugly might I say—told me he had a date with—and I quote, 'Eric's human'."

All at once, Eric felt everything inside him go still. Deep inside his wolf rose up, growling dangerously at this new information of his rival. Damon? Of all the shifters and humans, she'd chosen Damon, the Casanova of all the wolf packs? Or should he say; former Casanova, because after tonight there would be nothing left of him to attract the most desperate of women.

"I guess she's not as off limits as you said."

Snarling loudly into the phone, he felt the plastic crack under his harsh hold. "Call the Alpha of the Black Cliffs pack."

"May I ask why do you want me to call Damon's Alpha?"

"Because he's going to need a new second Beta after I tear him limb from limb."

Completely shattering the cordless phone beneath his hands, Eric ignored the sound of plastic crunching under his bare feet as he walked across the tiled floor and out onto the porch. Gazing out over the spacious yard that led into the luscious forest that surrounded the back of his property, the scents of forest delimited the air around him, the chirping of the insects and the rustling of meager wildlife called his inner beast to the surface. It was then that he freed the untamable wolf inside him.

Big, Bold & Bearing

Eyes glowing in the darkness, flames licked under his tight skin as
he allowed the change to overtake him. Mist shrouded his body as
his human form blurred. His body shrank, melting his human form
away as bones broke and reshaped. His nose and lips morphed and
extended into a black, fur covered muzzle. As the searing heat faded
from his changed form, his powerful legs propelled him forward. In
the form of the wolf, he navigated quickly over the earthy forest
floor.

Darting over fallen logs and around heavy underbrush, the primal
nature of his wolf became unbearable and undeniable. The instinct to
reach his mate and destroy all that kept her from him was in the
forefront of his mind.

Each stride took him deeper into the woods and nearer to town,
nearer to *her.* The moonlight filtered through the towering trees, the
light sung through the darkness against the softness of his pelt. The
exhilaration that came from running free in his true form couldn't
compare to happiness that filled his heart at knowing Rebecca would
be his tonight.

Too long had he been alone. Simply existing in hopes that he would
find the female meant to complete him and it had turned out that she
found him instead. Pack law be damned! He didn't care if she was
human or that she was forbidden to him. No one had the right to hold
his mate from him, not even himself.

* ~ * ~ *

Walking through the propped open doors of the local Italian restaurant; Divinity, the entrance opened up into a wide and welcoming environment with vaulted ceilings and polished columns. Circular tables covered in white tablecloths, accompanied with large tea candles and small vases filled with flowers were spaced across the white marble floor. At the end of the entrance archway was a long red oak bar. Soft classical music played in the background as mouth watering scents floated in the air around her.

Rebecca found her hands going to her waist, making sure her blouse wasn't wrinkled and displayed as less skin as possible. Who was she kidding? She wasn't built for this "dating" thing. Her idea of a good time was cuddling up on the couch watching a movie with her nose tucked in a perfectly steamy romance novel. Why had she ever agreed to this in the first place?

"Rebecca!"

Hearing her name called from across the spacious lobby, turning her head her eyes fell on Damon as he stood from his seat, one arm raised in the air, waving her towards him. Navigating around nearby tables and moving patrons, she made her way to him with a nervous smile on her face.

Walking around the table, without a word; Damon lifted one of her hands to his lips. After brushing a soft kiss over the top of her hand he still retained possession of her hand even after raising his head. Damon was obliviously taking this date more seriously than she was. Dressed in a royal blue silk shirt; the first two buttons undone, displaying his muscular chest to her eyes. His dark blue dress slacks had to have made specifically for him only.

"I can tell that this was a bad idea." Her eyes jumped to his in surprise.

"What do you mean?" her hand shot her the gaping collar of her blouse, fearful.

"Look at you." he indicated with an open hand, a soft smile on his face. "You're breathtaking. How am I supposed to eat anything tonight with a sight like you before me?"

Laughing softly, she shook her head in disbelieve. This man was unbelievable. "Isn't it a little early in the evening for you to be throwing lines like that out?"

"You misunderstand me. I only speak the truth where you are concerned." Turning he pulled out a padded chair for her, waiting for her to be seated comfortably before he returned to his seat. Almost immediately a waitress came and took their orders and left them alone once again. The look in Damon's eye's as he ordered their wine and his food as well as his teasing words were not missed by Rebecca. He may be attracted to her as a woman, but he clearly had his sights set other where.

"So why did you ask me out?" she asked folding her arms over her cool plastic menu.

"Do I really need a reason? You're a beautiful woman. Why wouldn't I want to ask you out?"

Rolling her eyes, Rebecca leaned back against the soft cushion of her seat. "Oh come on. You really expect me to believe that? I saw the looks you were giving that waitress. You look like you could have tackled her to the floor and licked her skin off."

A chuckle rolled through his chest, "Nothing that drastic, I promise you."

"So, Why then?"

"Why not let us enjoy the evening and if you still want to know when I take you home I'll tell you."

Leaning closer, her eyes narrowed suspiciously at his smiling face. "Are you hoping to distract me?"

Also leaning closer, his firm lips curved teasingly. "Only if you want me to,"

Smiling at him, she couldn't fight the soft laughter that escaped her red colored lips. As his hand reached toward her face, she froze. Only did she relax when he was simply tucking a long strand of hair behind her ear. His hand lingered a few seconds more to caress the side of her face.

"So; tell me about yourself." his eyes flashed questioning at her as he settled comfortably against the back of his chair.

She shrugged her shoulders, indifferently. "There's nothing interesting to tell."

"I should warn you, I can always sniff the truth out." He flashed his white teeth at her in a teasing grin.

"You're welcome to try. But I think you'll find I'm more stubborn than even Eric."

A look of confidence flooded his features as his lips curved into a wolfish grin. "We'll see about that."

5

Leaping down from a low hanging rocky ledge, Eric's strong body flew over the soft earth and vegetation. The moonlight flashed and danced over his jet black fur with every flex of his muscles, each that burned with every movement that his lupine body took. Every ache and resistant movement only served to push him forward endlessly.

Nearing the end of the dark, dense forest, smells and sounds assaulted his senses; declaring that he was coming closer and closer to having Rebecca in his grasp.

Stepping out from the cover of the heavy laden maple trees, his eyes feasted on the sight of the small collection of buildings of Main Street. He found himself stepping out into someone spacious back yard; the back of a small house hindered his view of the rest of the main square. Taking in his surroundings he spied a filled clothes line tethered between two trees, he quickly returned to his human form.

The darkness of the night cloaked his bare form as he stalked across the cool grass covering the ground beneath his feet. Taking a pair of large black drawstring sweats from the white corded line, he quickly covered his nakedness. He highly did not doubt that Rebecca would appreciate him standing before her in nothing but his skin, nor would the town folk.

Moving around the side the simple one level home, he moved cautiously, making sure he was seen by no one. How would anyone go about explaining sneaking around in the dark with no clothing to speak of? Though most of the population of Ravenwillow was shifters, it was essential that human's remained ignorant to the existence of his kind.

Moving like a shadow in the night, Eric remained unseen until he stepped out beneath an illuminating street lamp. The main square was filled with people, families, friends and couples leaving the old fashion movie cinema, restaurants and local shops. Moving along the sidewalk, his nose fought to find Rebecca's scent trail as his eyes also searched for this all important restaurant that she was likely to be at. An unending variety of sounds and scents bombarded his senses making it impossible to locate his human's whereabouts.

How in the world was he to find her in a place like this? His wolf was becoming agitated and at any moment wouldn't be as compliant. But then, teasing scent from a distance, he caught it. The sweet, rich smell of his human that lingered beneath the lavender perfume she always wore. Uncaring about how many passing people he nearly plowed over, Eric took off. His wolf urged him forward, moving fast with hard desperation to reach her. With every stride he took, her scent intensified. Sliding to an abrupt halt he found himself looking up at the florescent lit word; *"Divinity"*.

Satisfaction filled his chest, tonight he would lay down the rules to his wary doe. His wolf was more than ready to battle Damon for the right of her. Her resistance mattered little. For some inexplicable reason, his wolf recognized her as his one and only true mate and for the time being he was more than happy to treat her as such, at least until they both came to their senses. But he refused to tolerate her gentle eyes looking to another for comfort. He couldn't deny that his wolf as well as himself was hoping she would put up a fight against his claim on her. The chase was always just as sweet as the victory.

Fighting the heat behind his glowing eyes that signaled his form shifting, he shoved his wolf deep, preventing him from fully emerging as he longed to do. Striding through the bolstered doors, he walked around the wooden podium and past a panic stricken waitress that tried to prevent him with a stalling hand from entering the exquisite dining area.

Searching through a sea of faces his sharp eyes finally fell on Rebecca. She looked stunning—No, not stunning; beautiful, hauntingly so. Why had she never dressed like *this* for him?

Being around more brazen females, Eric couldn't help but notice how modest she dressing for her alleged "Date". Her blouse was far from enticing, the cloth was too loose against her torso with buttons done up to the slope of her swan-like neck, but the illuminating color made her pastel skin glow against the candle light. The dark slacks she wore fitted loosely to her shapely legs.

The musical note of her laughter filled his ears as she laughed at something her traitorous companion said. Just as he began to move toward their table to render Damon into little confetti pieces, Eric found himself halted by a tap on his bare shoulder. Turning his head, he glared down at a very nervous looking waitress as her shaking hand pushed her loose red curls behind her ear.

"Excuse me, sir; you can't be in here without a shirt or shoes." She softly remarked, her blue eyes hesitantly flickering at his nearly bare form.

"Mind your own business." He growled out, before he could take a step a body stepped in his path. Eric's anger filled eyes fell on the owner Paul Delagari. Paul narrowed his dark eyes at Eric like he was bug at a picnic.

"Is there a problem?" his voice growled out, his bear-shifter temper shifting just below the surface.

"Stay out of this, Paul. I came to retrieve something of mine and won't be leaving without it." As Eric moved to step around Paul, he moved as the last instant blocking his path. Both males glared at each other in an unspoken battle of dominance.

"I will not have you causing problems in my place, Daniels. Look at yourself; you're on the verge of shifting in front of over thirty humans. Whatever has you riled up, go shake it off before you retrieve what you're after."

Narrowing his eyes, Eric refused to be shoved aside like some submissive pup. "Get out of my way, Paul. Before I make you wish you had." He growled, no longer fighting to restrain his inner beast.

"If that's the way you feel, we could always include the elder council. I doubt they'd take kindly to you risking exposure of our kind. I believe a few of them are here tonight."

Eric's wolf snapped and growled at the challenging Alpha before him, but Eric knew Paul would follow through on his threat if Eric continued to be an issue. Growling threateningly in the back of his throat, Eric fixed Paul with a killing glare.

"One of these days you won't be able to hide behind the elders, Paul. And when that day comes I'll make you sorry for tonight."

Spinning around, he held his shoulders tight as he exited the way he came. But; not before his eyes found Rebecca again. He nearly went feral at the sight of her red lips curving around a spoon that Damon held out to her, her eyes closing with delight at whatever she'd tasted.

Snarling; Eric strode from the restaurant. This wasn't over; tonight he'd make that sneaky traitor eat his own heart for even glancing at Rebecca. With that thought in mind, Eric began pacing the parking lot, laying in wait for his unsuspecting prey.

* ~ * ~ *

"Wow." Rebecca gasped as she licked her lips after Damon had withdrawn his offered spoon from her mouth. "That's incredible."

"Told you this place was the best." Damon grinned as he returned his attention to his plate. "So, tell me about yourself." he inquired, seeking to spark a conversation with is quite date.

"Trust me there's nothing remotely interesting about me you'd want to know about."

"Are you purposely trying to prevent me from getting to know you, Rebecca?" he teased. Rebecca just smiled teasingly as she returned to her dinner. "You don't want to tell me about yourself? Alright, why don't we just skip that and cut right to you telling me about how you came to know about my kind?"

Rebecca's heart stopped dead in her chest as heavy fear settled in her stomach. Forcing her bite of food down her constricting throat, she tried to slow her racing pulse. Looking fearfully at Damon's smiling face she hesitantly looked around.

"Your kind?" her voice shuddered with apprehension.
His eyes locked, unrelentingly with hers. "You know that I'm a shifter; a werewolf."

"W-What do you mean? I'm not sure I know what you're—"

"Come now, Rebecca. Did you really think that such a secret like this would stay secret forever?"

Suddenly feeling like a deer in headlight, her destruction nearing closer and closer. Feeling anxious, she shot him a pleading look. "Are you going to hurt me? Is that why you asked me out? So you could expose what I know?"

Bracing his elbows on the table top, Damon clasped his hands together. "You misunderstand, Rebecca. If I wanted to hurt you, I wouldn't have chosen to take you to a public place."

Her heart began to race impossibly faster with fear. "I beg you, at least give me some time to get out of town, I swear I haven't told a soul—nor will I ever. Please don't kill me, I haven't done anything wrong." her words rushed from her lips coated with icy terror as tears filled her eyes.

Sympathy filling his eyes, Damon reached across the table clasping her hand, though she flinched at his touch. Tears streamed down her cheeks as Damon made soft cooing sounds of comfort while he brushed her fallen tears away.

"Shh. Calm down. No one is going to hurt you, I swear this to you."

Her breath hitched with emotion. "Then; why did you…?"

"It wasn't hard to see how you purposely ignored things that others would have questioned. I had to discover how you came by this information, before the others discover what I have. Because trust me, they would kill you without hesitation. If you confide in me, Rebecca, I swear to you, I will do whatever I can to protect you from others that would seek to harm you."

"Why?" her red, swollen eyes flashed suspiciously at him. "Why would you care what happens to me?"

Leaning back in his chair, Damon's face turned very serious for the first time all evening. "I have known Eric all my life, Rebecca. Not once has he shown such protective and possessive emotions toward anyone, until you. Deep down I believe that you are Eric's true one, he's just too thick headed to admit it."

"'*True One*'?"

"I'll explain later, first I need you to tell me everything you know, so I can figure out how to protect you. I'm not sure if you're aware but half of the people in this place are shifters and many are ruling council members that would end your life with a snap of their fingers."

"Is it safe to talk here?" her eyes widening with fear.

Nodding slowly, Damon folded his arms over the table. "Tell me." He pled.

Taking an unsteady breath, closing her eyes, Rebecca took a moment to calm her rattled nerves. Slowly opening her eyes, Rebecca flicked her tongue over her suddenly dry lips. For years she'd dreaded this moment. The moment when a shifter discovered her story and made her paid for it.

"About five years ago, I was home from college on break the night it happened."

"What happened?" His voice whispered as her eye began to glaze over in memory.

"When I met a monster…"

* ~ * ~ *

Five years earlier

"Mom, you really don't have to go to all this trouble." Rebecca insisted franticly as she watched her mom working on; what seemed to be, a five course meal. "I'm only here for a few days. I would be happy with just a simple pizza."

"Oh, hush." Mary St. James scolded her daughter with a wave of her elegant hand, "I want to. Besides your father won't complain about having a full stomach tonight."

Shaking her head, Rebecca slid from her position on the kitchen bar stool at the kitchen counter. Coming up behind her; Rebecca watched as her mother vigorously stirred the contents of her mixing bowl.

Leaning her hip against the pale green kitchen counter, Rebecca found her eyes shifting out the pitch-black kitchen window. A heavy weight of weariness weighted heavy on her shoulders.

"Anything I can do?"

After the countless hours spend driving from her dorm in New York to her parents home in Ravenwillow, Virginia, more than anything; sleep was taking precedence over food. Not that it would stop her mother from her dominating plans of a large welcome home dinner for her only daughter.

Shaking her head, Mary concentrated on pouring her chocolate cake batter into her prized baking pan. "No. Go visit with your father until I'm done."

Not bothering to argue, she grabbed her open soda can, left the kitchen, following down the short hallway leading into the family room. There her father sat in his regular seat in the dark leather recliner. His worn eyes rose from his spread out news paper, flickering gently over her face as his thin lips curled into a slight smile.

"Hey baby-girl, what's your mother up to?"

"Cooking the Christmas feast for the White House." She mumbled, taking a slip from her cola.

Her father's hearty chuckled filled the air around them. "Never take a dog's favorite bone. First rule of women that I learned my first year of marriage, baby-girl, your mother is going to do whatever she plans regardless of what you or I think. Best to just let her be."

Letting out a deep sigh, she slunk down onto the couch. Tiredly rubbing her eyes, her body relaxed into the plush cushions. As her father went back to his evening ritual of reading his newspaper, they sat in silence, for how long; she didn't know.

Releasing a tired sigh, Rebecca allowed her head to fall back against the back of the couch. Just as Rebecca had begun to drift off, a loud sound of banging on the front door; startled her awake. Seeing her father struggling to remove himself from under his spread out newspaper, Rebecca quickly rose from her relaxed position.

"I'll see who it is."

Walking up to the door, she rose up on her toes and gazed through the peep hole. On the other side of the door stood a tall man that she didn't recognize. His features hidden and shaded in the confines of his dark blue hoodie, his hand were shoved in his jean pockets as he waited. Keeping the chain lock, she leaned against the edge of the door as it opened.

"Can I help you?" his hidden face remained lowered as he remained silent. After receiving no answer, exasperated; she added, "What do you want?"

Slowly the dark hooded face rose. Upon seeing his eyes, her heart froze in fear as lifeless eyes that stared through her glowed with a devilish crimson hue. His lips slowly curled up into a spine-chilling smile, revealing sharp canines. "Just a taste."

Before Rebecca slam the door closed, his powerful arm shot out, strong clawed fingers wrapped around the edge of the door. Hearing her father approach from behind she struggled to force the door closed. Tightening his grip around the door, Rebecca watched as he used the door as a battering ram into her face. As she was thrown backwards, her body crashing into a near end table and the large ceramic vase that sat on top. Pain exploded throughout her body as the sound of the metal linked chain snapping and hitting the hard wood floor. Screaming voices echoed around her. Struggling to move, the pain slowly made her world turn to darkness.

* ~ * ~ *

The coppery smell of blood slowly drew Rebecca back into consciousness; she coughed as blood from her nose flowed down the back of her throat from her reclined position. Too afraid of what she would find if she opened her eyes. The house was quiet, too quiet. No sound of her mother's soft humming or the sound of her father moving his newspaper around.

Steeling herself, Rebecca hesitantly opened her eyes. The front door was wide open, confirming that whoever or whatever had come to the door was now inside the house with her. Her heart began to pound faster than the hooves of a race horse. Pulling herself up into a sitting position, her ribs protested painfully at the movement.

With much difficulty, using the fallen end table as leverage, she stumbled to her feet. Gasping in pain with her first step as broken pieces of the flowered vase crunched under her bare feet. Cutting and tearing at her tender skin as she carefully felt her way along a near wall in the pitch black room.

With her next step, her foot slid along the cold and damp floor of the hallway. Gripping the side of the entrance way, Rebecca caught herself before she could tumble to the floor again. Moonlight from the kitchen window flowed over the hardwood floor, not a foot away was a sight that caused Rebecca to shove her fist into her mouth to prevent her scream from escaping.

Just beyond the entrance way was long, dark puddle of blood leading from her mother's slashed arm. Her lifeless finger's hung open with her blood splattered palm facing up, the rest of her body hidden down the dark hallway. Before she even realized her tears coursed down her cheeks, the sound of heavy footsteps near her mother's lifeless body had her freezing in terror.

Slowly she edged around the book shelf at her back, hiding her body from view of the entrance way. The small sound of a foot hitting the pool of blood on the floor revealed the killer now stood in the entrance way, just a few feet from her. Slowly looking around for an escape route, she eyes collided with the dark, empty eyes of her father. Sprawled on his back, his blood soaked the floor beneath him leading from the deep clawed slashes along his throat.

This time; she didn't have time to cover her gasp of alarm. Following her cry was the sound of a low rumbling growl and the continuing sound of slow, but steady footsteps, coming closer and closer to her.

Covering her mouth to prevent the rising nausea from the stomach turning smell of blood and death, her eyes quickly swept toward the open door. Could she make it before her parent's killer figured out where she was? Before she could move a muscle, a deep and emotionless voice cut through the dark room, darkly caressing the walls around her.

"Don't run. I would catch you before you could take a single step. I want to take my time with you."

Moving around opposite end of the couch, Rebecca leaned her back against the cream colored fabric, hiding herself from the dark stranger's view as he slowly entered the living room. Several times she heard him sharply inhale, as a predator would while gaining the scent of its prey.

"Come out. I won't hurt you." His voice then turned somewhat gentle as if consoling a frightened animal.

Trembling, Rebecca remained hidden trying to assure herself that she was well hidden as he tried to coax her out into the open. "It doesn't matter, I will find you."

Looking at his reflection in the dark TV screen, she watched as he slowly circled toward the opposite side of the living room, his face turning every which way as his nostrils twitched erratically. Her eyes widened as they dropped to his hands. He held his hand loose at his side; fingers splayed in preparation. His fingers were longer than the average person, baring long and sharp claws. As he moved dark trails of blood dripped onto the floor from the frightening points of his claws.

Her heart pounded with a heavy beat in her chest. She wasn't brave by any means, but even she knew that she couldn't just hide until he found her. She had to run and get help before she ended up like her parents. Sensing her opportunity, her legs glided through the air as she rushed towards the door.

Just a few more steps… Rebecca assured herself.

Her hope was short lived as a large hand tangled in her long hair, jerking her flight to a stop. Sharp claws dug into her scalp as he jerked away from the door, throwing her a short distance away. Landing on her injured side, she cried out. Her hand cover the painful area as she found a large piece of wood from the end table she had crashed into earlier, lodged between her ribs.

As her attacker slowly approached her, rolling onto all fours, she quickly tried to crawl away. She screamed in pain as five sharp claws thrusted through the fabric of her shirt and deep into the soft muscle of her shoulder. As he tugged her back, his claws ripped down her back, leaving behind five deep slashes as her blood quickly began soaking her shirt. Grabbing her by her neck, her attacker lifted her entire body off the floor before pinning her to against a nearby book shelf.

"Shh. It's alright." He murmured when she cried in pain and terror as he ran the back of his free bloody hand along her cheek. "This is how it's supposed to be." His lips curled into an almost frightening smile.

"What?" she gasped in fear. Pulling his hand away, he shoved the dark hood away, revealing his dark face to her. Her eyes fell on his with dread. His eyes glowed with a yellow hue as something moved beneath his skin. Suddenly his face seemed more animal, more monster than human. His teeth grew to sharp points as he grinned down at her maliciously.

His lips curled in amusement as he gazed down at the cold body of her father. "You're prey, every single one of you. It's time you vermin accept that."

Beyond terrified, Rebecca struggled against his hand that currently was wrapped around her throat. A loud growl erupted from between his parted lips, making her eyes go wide in fear at the frightening sound. "Your parents died too quickly. I never got the chance to enjoy their screams. But I am going to take my time with you." His voice hissed out, his hand tightened around the fragile column of her neck. "I'm going to slice you up into ribbons as you cry for death. But I won't give it to you too quickly. I want to watch you beg, beg for your miserable life."

While his dark words dripped from his lips, Rebecca reached behind her, her slender, shaking fingers slid around her father's silver letter opener. Before she could draw her tightly clenched hand back, he struck. Had it not been for his other hand around her throat she would have fell to her knees. His sharp talons had slashed diagonally across her chest from the left side of her collar bone to the underside of her right breast. His lips curved in satisfaction as he watched her life's blood began soaking through her the tears of her top.

Flexing his blood coated hand, he prepared to strike again. Not wasting anytime; she lifted her fisted hand, thrusting the letter opener deep into his chest as she could. The feel of the slightly sharp object in her hand embed in his chest made Rebecca sick with revulsion.

Jerking away from her, he released a howl of pain before he turned his anger eyes on her. Wrapping his lethal hand around the handle, he jerked the meager blade from his chest with slight annoyance.

"You'll pay for that." He growled low in his throat.

Before he could move, the sound of loud sirens outside the door exploded around them. Sliding to the floor, the pain and the intensity of her injuries suddenly drained all the strength from her. From outside she could hear car doors slamming as someone approached the porch.

"Police! Your neighbors reported sounds of screaming and a struggle, Is anyone hurt?"

Smirking at her, his eyes glowing once more. "This isn't over." He promise viscous snarl.

"Last warning! We're coming in!"

Glaring coldly at him she remained silent, if she was to die it would be on her own terms; not his. "I look forward to your execution. None of my kind will let you live now. Others will come for you and you will never know mercy from my kind." his dark laughter echoed around her.

Slowly his body began changing. The sounds of his bones snapping and reshaping startled her as his face also began reshaping. Until the man no longer stood before her but a large, snarling brown wolf.

As two officers rushed through the open door, their guns and flashlights drawn and pointed. "Shit…" one officer murmured his eyes darting over the bloody carnage in the living room.

"Look out!" the other shouted as the wolf charged past them.

Holstering his gun, he knelt beside Rebecca. "Call 911! Now!" he shouted to his partner. As his partner rushed out, the remaining officer tried to give what comfort he could.

"Hang on, we'll get you help. Hang on…" This time she welcomed the dark unknown that followed part of her prayed never to awaken again.

<u>6</u>

Rebecca's body shuttered as her words came to an end. Damon walked silently beside her down the sidewalk towards her apartment. Not once did he interrupt her or urge her on, he simply waited; allowing her to finish in her own time. Shoving his hands in his pockets, Damon tried his best to appear nonthreatening as possible.

"Did you ever figure out who he was or is?" he asked carefully as they passed under a street lamp. His eyes shifting over her averted face and her nervously, wringing hands.

"No. After lying in a hospital bed for days on end, I feared I had imagined everything. When the police came to question me, I didn't know what to tell them. I told them what I could, anything that sounded plausible."

"You didn't tell them the truth?"

Turning to face him, her arms folded across her chest defensively. "You mean; did I tell anyone that I saw werewolf viciously murder my parents and try to rip me into pieces of human confetti?" she sighed, wearily. "No, I did not. Even I knew that all that would earn me is a one way ticket to nearest insane asylum. There were times that I thought that it had all been a dream... or nightmare. There were times I feared if I closed my eyes he would be in the room with me, waiting to finish what he had started."

Damon's gaze softened, "It must have been hard, finding that such frightening creatures existed."

Rebecca solemnly shrugged her shoulders, "At times, but then I saw that your kind; aside from a few incredible gifts, aren't all that different from mine."

"And how did you become so enlightened?" he asked with a teasing smile.

"After I took a job as a nanny for the Morvelt family. They belonged to a pack in Canada." She explained, as she began walking again, Damon mirroring her steps right next to her.

"*Morvelt*? You worked for the most formidable bear-shifters within Doyle Mackenzie?"

Nodding with a slight smile, she continued. "I came to live with them not long after the attack. At first, there was no great connection between the three children I helped care for and myself. But one night, in the midst of a strong thunderstorm, I was awoken by the sound of the frightened moaning of a bear cub."

"One of the Morvelt's?" he asked curiously.

"Yes. At first I was too surprised to move and then this small black bear cub leapt into bed with me and straight into my lap. As it curled against my stomach, I could feel it trembling; it was then I realized this small child was just as afraid of the unknown as I was. I wrapped my arms around that small fuzzy creature, the fur and everything else melted away until I held little Anna, the youngest."

"Did her parents; your employers ever find out that you knew?"

Letting out a held breathe, she shook her head, "No, at the time; Anna was only four years old. I doubt she even remembers. My guess is; during the worst of the storm, when she couldn't find her mother; her terror caused her to seek me out." Turning to face him, her arms fell to her sides, "Now, your turn."

Damon's blonde eyebrows rose. "My turn?"

"I've told you everything you wanted to know. It's your turn to explain, why are you offering to keep my secret?"

"I'm offering to do a lot more than that, Rebecca." Looking up at her red brick apartment building, Damon released a light hearted sigh. "I'm offering to not only be your friend, but your protector. That is; until my friend Eric, comes to his senses."

"First off; if you wanted to be my friend, what was that display at Eric's house the other night then?"

"Eric is stubborn and too set in his own ways, but; of course you knew that didn't you?"

Chuckling softly, she nodded. Absently, Damon's eyes swept over top of her head to stare across the dark, empty street and into a dark alley. His sharp gaze collided with a pair of trained, green glowing eyes from a lurking figure in the dark. It was the same dark figure that had been following a small distance behind them ever since they left the restaurant.

Flicking his tongue over his bottom lip, he smirked down at her. "So I intend to playfully nudge Eric's head out of his own ass. Help him see the light, in more ways than one."

Raising a skeptic eyebrow, Rebecca looked up at him; not fully understanding where his meaning was. Get Eric to see what? "And how do you intend to do that?"

Sweeping his eyes over her head one last time, before his eyes returned to hers, he shrugged casually. "Easy and simply like so,"

Without a second thought or an ounce of hesitation, both of Damon's hands gripped the sides of her face, jerking her face to his. His lips settled over hers in a stilling kiss, cutting off her squeal of surprise. Too surprised to move, Rebecca held her body stiffly away from Damon's; her hands held up in defense.

A loud beastly snarl erupted behind them, with an unseen force; Damon and more importantly his lips were suddenly thrown away from Rebecca. The sound of Damon's surprised grunt as the air was shoved out of his lungs was quickly followed by the sound of an enraged fist hitting flesh. A short distance away, a dark figure was crouched over Damon, their fist tightly fisted at the front of his shirt.

"You conceited, bombastic son of a bitch!" a deep, yet familiar voice snarled out, before drawing back his fist again and smashing it into Damon's face as he did nothing to prevent it. "Touch her again and I'll wear your intestines as a necktie!"

Sprinting forward as fast as her high heels would allow, burning her hands in the soft dark locks she gave Eric's hair a sharp jerk. Caught off guard, Eric lost his balance and falling off of Damon and tumbling back on top Rebecca.

"Ow!" she cried out, as all of Eric's weight abruptly fell on top of her, sending the both of them roughly into the sidewalk. "Get off me!" she yelled in frustration as the sidewalk bit into her ankle. With a combination of shoving roughly at his back and Eric's effort to roll off her, she was able to crawl out from underneath him.

Glaring murderously at Eric's anger filled face, Rebecca walked over to Damon as he quickly stumbled to his feet. His left cheek, already swelled as both his nose and lip bled.

Running his arm against his bleeding nose, Damon absently waved at the fuming Alpha, "Good evening to you too, Eric."

"You will address me by my rank, beta" Eric's lips lifting in a snarl.

"Oh, now that was just hurtful, my friend."

Eric took a threatening step toward him, only to be stopped as Rebecca stepped between them, both of her hands pushing against the solid muscles of his chest. "You dare call me your friend, after what you did?" his voice whispered dangerously.

"I'm confused. Did or did you not say that you had no attachment toward her?" Damon asked coyly, flinching as his lips curled into a smile. "I was under the impression that Rebecca's heart was free game and free to claim."

"It is not! Make that mistake a second time; I will make you wish you'd never laid eyes upon her." His words hissed out as he tried; unsuccessfully, to side step Rebecca's blocking form.

"Stop it both of you!" Rebecca yelled over top of their arguing voices. Hitting Eric square against his bare chest, she turned her venomous gaze fully on him. "How dare you go around attacking people? If I don't want Damon kissing me, I will handle it myself. You're my boss, Eric and I don't answer to you outside of work."

Walking over to Damon, grabbing a hold of his hand she firmly tugged him up the cement steps to her apartment. Eric quickly followed, with his shoulders and hands tightening in aggression. "What do you think you're doing?" Eric demanded as she led Damon through the main entrance and up another flight of stairs.

"Not that it's any of your business, but I'm going to patch up the mess that you made of his face. Now, go home."

"I will not go home. You're insane if you think I'm going to leave you alone with that backstabbing traitor."

"Do whatever you want." Her words tossed callously down the stairwell as Damon and she reached their destination.

Pulling her keys out of her purse, she quickly let Damon inside just as Eric reached the top of the landing. Before he could step through the open door, using her high heeled foot, Rebecca shut the door in his face so hard that it actually wacked him on his nose. Biting back a growl, Eric was forced to open the door himself.

The door opened into a small, simply decorated living room. A small beat up green sofa sat near the door, a black coffee table in front and small TV sitting on top of a worn desk against the opposite wall. Leading out of the living room to the left was a small doorway into the kitchen and a short hall beyond that, more than likely leading to her bedroom.

In the kitchen, Damon sat too comfortable at a small table as sounds of Rebecca moving down the dark hallway. Damon looked up and smiled as Eric entered the kitchen.

"I'd like to thank you, Eric. If you had not nearly beaten my face into the pavement, I likely wouldn't have gotten invited into Rebecca's home," If possible his smug smile grew wider, despite his split lip. "And who knows, maybe even her bed."

Taking an aggressive step forward, Eric found his hands clenching so tightly that his bones popped. "You *even* fantasize about her bed and I promise you, I will—"

"You'll what?" Rebecca's soft, but sharp voice cut in from across the room.

Walking back into the kitchen, her arms filled with bandages and a tall bottle of peroxide. Dropping everything on the small kitchen table, her eyes raised to Eric's. There was nothing neither soft nor gentle about her gaze. Averting her eyes, she pulled the spare chair in front of slightly amused Damon, trying to ignore the small thrill that raced through her being at the knowledge that Eric stood, hovering behind her. His very presence made heated chills race over her skin. Ripping open a gauze pad and dousing it with peroxide, she tried to focus on cleaning up Damon's cut up face. An uneasy task, if not an impossible one.

Pausing; she focused on Damon's amused face, "This may hurt."

Damon smirked and then winced at the pain from his spilt lip, "Love hurts, baby. I'll take anything you can give me." The sound of Eric's pacing and aggression seems to grow tenfold.

Glaring at his flirtatious filled words, she went to cleaning his spilt bottom lip and a small cut over his left eyebrow, with more force than necessary for good measure.

"Ouch! Easy!" Damon gasped out in defense against her rough handling. "Aren't you women supposed to be gentle and tender at moment like this?"

Reaching for a dry bandage, Rebecca shrugged her shoulders, indifferently. "I warned you." Reaching out for his bloody nose she began to stop the slow bleeding, after wiping away the majority of the blood, she tossed the damp gauze on the table.

Gently; she reached toward his swollen nose, smirking slightly when he flinched away from her hands. Slowly her fingers brushed the sides of his nose with calculation. "Does that hurt?" at his slow head shake, her fingers trailed to the tip of his nose and gave a sharp squeeze.

"OW! Damn it, woman!" jerking away from her hands, Damon glared at her while cupping his pulsing injury.

Turning away, Rebecca went to the task of ripping open a wide butterfly bandage and leaning closer to the flinching and skeptic patient. She wasted no time pressing the wide edges of the bandage over his split eyebrow. Rising and disposing of the bloody gauze, she went to her freezer. Wrapping a small dish towel around a cluster of ice cubes, she returned to Damon's side, not missing the angry looks that Eric was shooting both of them as he leaned against her counter with crossed arms.

Pressing the ice pack to his nose, she waited until Damon replaced her hand with his. "You got lucky; it's not broken, just a bit swollen. The ice should help with that and with your lip."

Flashing his heart stopping smile, he pulled the ice pack away from his face. "I can think about something else I'd like to feel against my lips…"

Before she could tell him where he could put his good for nothing lips, Eric lunged forward. Jerking Damon out of his chair by the labels of his dress shirt, Eric jerked him roughly through the kitchen door way. Forcibly pulling Damon across the small living room, Eric violently wrenched the front door open and shoved Damon out into the dimly lit hallway. As Damon smirked and began to retort to Eric's rough handling, the door was slammed coldly in his face.

With a satisfied smile on his face, Eric turned the dead bolt into place. Turning; he faced Rebecca with a look of shock and irritation, her jaw hanging open. Eric and his wolf couldn't help but feel pleased. No man or wolf's scent would ever caress the air around his mate again; he'd make sure of it. Doing his best to ignore Damon's lingering scent, he looked around the meager room his eyes scanned the famed photos on the book shelf and on the walls.

"I've always wondered what your apartment looked like,"

Finally finding her words, she exploded. "What the hell was that about?!" turning to face her, he lazily crossed his arms over his bare chest.

"Do I really need to explain it to you? Don't you feel even a tiny bit ashamed of yourself?"

"Ashamed? Ashamed of what?" she scoffed, "How I conduct my personal life is my business, Eric. I don't need your permission to go out on dates. Damon asked me out and I accepted, what's there to be ashamed of?"

"That you lead one man along, while courting the attention of another." He stated simply as his hands closed over a porcelain frame that had been shoved between a few hardcover novels. Flipping the fame over, he paused as he recognized the picture before him. "Where'd you get this?"

Stomping up to him; Rebecca jerked the frame from his hands, hugging it protectively to her chest. She had no need to see which photograph it was; she knew it was her most treasured one.

"It's my copy. I didn't steal it from your house, if that's what you think."

"Then; why hide it? I remember the day you took that picture, the picnic at the park. Do you remember?" He smiled fondly, remembering how Travis and Emma had playfully attacked him in a tag team mock-wrestling match.

Walking past him, she replaced it between her small collections of novels. "I remember you threatening to fire me if I didn't delete this picture from Sarah's camera."

His eyes sweeping tenderly over her, a soft smile curled his lips as he moved closer, crowding her against the bookshelf. "I'm glad that you didn't listen to me. That silly photo means more to me than you know." Reaching forward his rough fingers; gently, brushed her fallen hair behind her ear.

"Sometimes; Eric I think you're like a rubiks cube, just when I think I've figured you out, you surprises me." Inhaling sharply; she focused back to their pervious argument, a much safer topic than their present. "What did you mean by leading on?"

He shrugged casually, "I must admit it was an ingenious plan. Accepting a date with Damon to get at me, especially after the kiss we shared."

"What?" she responded bewildered, "You mean the kiss you had no idea why it happened, much less with *me*. Come on, Eric; there is no way you would be jealous. It's not as if we're lovers or whatever. You're my boss, plain and simple."

Crowding closer to her, his hand cupped her chin carefully as if he were holding a precious piece of crystal. "Then maybe it's time I should do something to change that."

Bending down, his hard lips covered hers. This time the kiss was gentle, a slow dance between his urgent lips and her slightly resistant ones. As he felt the last of her body's resistance diminish, his animal nature rushed to the surface at her surrender. Wrapping his strong arms around her, he pulled her soft body against his hard one, rocking his hard, pulsing erection against the soft swell of her stomach.

Moaning against his lips with need, her hands fisted in his dark hair, holding his face to hers as she began to kiss him back.
Sliding one hand down her back, over her firm buttocks, his hand gripped the back of her thigh, forcing her to lift it around his hip and bringing her throbbing center in direct contact with his hard, jean covered bulge.

Moving his lips from hers, trailing down the column of her nearly exposed throat, a satisfied growl surfaced from within. For a second, Eric felt his wolf take over, allowing a partial shift of his face. Elongating his jaw, allowing him to give her a mating bite and to show all, including Damon; that she was his. As his sharpened teeth playfully nipped at her neck, he felt Rebecca stiffen in his arms.

It was easy to for her to ignore Eric's beastly growl of desire, she was used to hearing him growl. But she couldn't ignore the feel of his teeth, nor could she ignore the flashes of past images and fear that it induced. Did she want him so much that she'd endanger her life?

Fearful, her arms slid down to his naked chest, intent on pushing him away. "Eric. Please stop."

His lust filled eyes bore into her frightened ones. Taken aback, his hand released her anchored leg, allowing her to stand on both of her feet. He didn't like seeing the fear and uncertainty in her eyes. His beast was too close and whatever had been set in motion between them; he couldn't stop it. Deep down he wasn't certain he even wanted to.

His logical brain told him that he should back away from her and leave but his beast couldn't tolerate the idea of leaving her. He couldn't put the beast back; not now, not when his mate was finally in his arms. It somehow felt right.

Reaching out, his large hand cupped the side of her face as she attempted to avert her gaze. "Talk to me. Tell me what you want, what you need."

* ~ * ~ *

His gently spoken words had Rebecca's eyes jerking up to his face. Who the hell was this man that wore Eric's face? Because it certainly wasn't him, Eric never acted this way; at least not to her anyway. The Eric she knew was rude, abrupt, and didn't care about her.

Why should he? In his eyes she was a beneath him as he must view all humans. Regardless why he was acting the way he was she had to stop this. It was true that she felt a pull toward Eric and it had only gotten stronger over the past few months. But having him in her home, kissing her; was asking for trouble that she didn't need.

"Rebecca?" his voice was gentle, caring and it confused her. Slowly his thumb rubbed along her cheekbone, silently willing her to answer him.

"I want you to leave. It's not appropriate for you to be here."

His gaze hardened. "But it was for Damon?"

She didn't miss the flash of anger that swept across his face. She really poked the tiger; or in this case, wolf, when she'd accepted her date with Damon. It made no sense why he was acting like this. Why should she care what he thought anyway?

"Who I date and who I invite into my apartment is my business."
She stated stubbornly. Shoving past him, she walked to the front
door to open it, giving him an expecting look. "I think it would be
better if you would leave."

In that moment; Eric looked every bit the predator that she knew
lurked beneath the surface. His expression grew hard as he slowly
approached the open doorway. Rebecca held her breath as he drew
closer, her heart pounding. Without breaking a strike, Eric reached
out to gently, but firmly, pulled the door knob from her grasp to shut
it. Once the door was closed, he turned back and centered his
attention back on her. She stood frozen, not with fear but with
confusion.

"I don't want you bringing men here, Rebecca. I want you to
promise me that what happened tonight won't happen again." he said
with a hard tone as though he was reprimanding a child for breaking
a house rule. The thought made her blood boil. He couldn't tell her
what to do!

"As long as you don't come back here; I don't see this night
repeating." She said with a glaring look. "However I don't have to
promise you anything beyond that."

His eyes narrowed, causing a sense of foreboding to slip down her
spine like cold trails of ice. His lips pressed together firmly as his
bare muscular chest rose and fell with harsh breaths. He was angry.
Witnessing Eric's temper in the past; she knew that it was only a
matter of time before he started yelling at her.

"You damn well will promise it. I don't want anyone else here with
you."

She didn't know what she had expected him to say; but *that* certainly hadn't been it. "What's wrong with you?" she scowled pacing away from him. She didn't get very far as his hand reached out and clasped her wrist. Jerking her to a stop, she found herself staring up at his cool blue eyes as he stepped in front of her; still maintaining possession of her wrist.

"I don't want anyone else here with you." He repeated in a low voice. Each word was bit out between his teeth as the control of his temper seemed to be holding on by a thread. "I cannot explain it, but the thought of another man near you makes me…" he trailed off, shaking his head. "Do not test me on this, Rebecca. I don't share well and I have no intention of sharing you with another man. I am it."

Rebecca blinked up at him with utter confusion. "What are you talking about? You're not making any sense!" she said waving her hand at him. "I had a date. *One* date and now your acting like you own me? I am nothing to you but an employee and you have no say in what I do."

He watched her during her ranting, completely unaffected. She may as well have been conversing about the weather with the expression he held. Slowly he moved closer to her, his hand releasing her wrist as both hands slid up her arm to cup her shoulders.

"Tell me you don't feel it, Rebecca. This need I have for you. Tell me you don't feel it clawing at you in your dreams and every waking second."

"It's called lust, Eric. It's no different than walking down the street and noticing anyone else."

"It's different for me." He admitted softly his eyes boring into hers with a beseeching light. "If it were simple lust, that would be easy for me to ignore; but it's not."

"Then that is *your* problem." She bit out. With a glare she shoved out from beneath his hands before pacing away. "I want no part of you other than my paycheck. Now for the final time, I want you to leave. I think you've done enough damage for the night."

Crossing her arms, she glared at him as she pointed to the door like he was a dog. She almost laughed at the irony. Dropping her indicating finger, she waited. Eric stood still as a statue, his arms hanging limply at his sides as he studied her. His eyes narrowed slightly as though he was perplexed at her for some unknown reason. She attempted not to feel the edge of discomfort at his close scrutiny. Unwilling, her eyes fell from his scowling face to his bare chest. Eric didn't look like a model in the least. He possessed a strong physic; it was true. But he possessed a *man's* body. His shoulders where broad and his arms were comprised of roped muscles that flexed beneath his skin with each movement. His muscled chest was dusted with dark hair that led her gaze down over his hard abs and down further to the gray sweats that he wore.

Flush tore up her face as her eyes lingered on the tell tale bulge that pressed from beneath the sweats. Her womanly channel clenched in response to what her eyes had beheld. This was too much for her. Being this close to him, surrounded by his rough scent; it was maddening. A part of her wanted to tackle him and just forget every sensible thought in her head. She hungered to feel his strong, hot hands on her skin. More than anything she wanted to press herself against the hard plane of his body and drown in his embrace.

"Maybe I should make it your problem as well." Eric's sudden rough voice cut through her chaotic thoughts in an instant.

Raising her questioning gaze to his, she had no time to react as he ate up the distance between them in two quick strides. Startled, she jumped back, stumbling on her heels; she fell backward onto her couch. Eric had followed every terrified step of hers with confident movements.

Looming over her, he followed her down onto the worn cushions. Struggling to rise up, Rebecca pushed up with her arms, half dragging and crawling backward along the couch in an effort to escape his predatory gaze. With a slow movement, Eric's hand encircled her ankle with a gentle touch, slowly pulling her back to him.

Falling onto her back as he pulled her closer, Rebecca pushed up on her elbows, gazing up at him uncertain. "Eric, what are you doing?" she gasped out.

He didn't answer. His eyes flashed at her briefly until they lowered to her captured ankle. With a gentle and slow action, he slipped her heels from her feet to carefully set them in the floor beside the couch. Her womb tightened with awareness as his hand cupped her foot tenderly in his hands. His fingers dug into the bottom of her bare foot, slowly kneading the soft flesh. Almost as quick as he had begun, he lowered her foot to do the same to the other.

Rebecca's chest ached with how hard her heart was pounding. What was he doing? Somehow she knew this went far beyond him simply touching her. At the feel of his hands on her bare skin, a pulse of need grew between her legs. She had to push away this need if she had any hope of getting rid of him before she did something stupid.

"Eric—" she began, but ended with a gasp of surprise as he moved closer to her with a hard look.

Lifting her legs, Eric settled between them, his unrelenting hands smoothed up from her trembling knees and over her thighs until his strong fingers closed around the button of her dress slacks. Her stomach muscles bunched and tightened with desire and apprehension. Her hands quickly covered his and interrupting his task.

Seeing her nervous eyes flicker uncertainly over his face, Eric slowly crawled over her slivering body. Gently laying a kiss over her left eye and then the right, as her breath calmed; his lips covered hers in a soft kiss. His lips moved over hers seeking for the response that he wanted from her. Without realizing it, Rebecca found herself arching into his kiss, pleading for more.

Pulling back, he studied her flushed face. She lay under him; still as stone, staring at up at him with her frightened doe eyes. "Tell me you don't feel anything with me this close to you." He demanded in a harsh tone.

Panting, she shook her head mutely. Her lips felt bruised from his kiss and God help her; she wanted more of his rough kisses. Curling her fingers into the cushions beneath her, she forced her hands not to move and definitely not to reach for him and pull him to her as she ached to do.

Holding her gaze, his hands moved back to the clasp of her slacks with nimble fingers. At the brush of his fingers against her lower stomach, she was jerked out of her trance. Before she could react to what he was doing, Eric moved higher up her body, giving himself room.

Covering her lips with aggressive possession, planting one hand up near her head, Eric's other hand slid beneath the front of her open slacks. At the touch of his hand slipping beneath the armor of her clothing, Rebecca jumped, yelping fearfully against his pressing lips. Jerking his mouth from hers, he pressed his forehead against hers as his fingers slid between the folds of her sex.

Gasping, Rebecca eyes widened as her hands shot from their position to grip his wrist in a vain hope to restrain him. "W-What are you doing?" she nearly shrieked.

His fingers moved with confident strokes, first beginning at the bottom of her folds at her entrance, before sliding up to her clit to slide firmly around her swollen bud. Crying low against the sensations that had her belly growing hot with need, Rebecca fought for the strength to tug on his wrist that she held.

She would fight him. In...just..one…minute.

His fingers continued to slide her wet sex, coaxing a forbidden response from her as he bent to trail soft nips along her jaw to her ear. Licking at her lobe, he drew the soft flesh between his lips before biting it softly. Her gasp of pleasure was his reward.

"Tell me you don't want me now and I will leave without a backward glance." He breathed out against her ear.

Gooseflesh erupted down her neck and down her spine as his words flowed over her skin. She wanted to tell him to leave, to pull his hand from between her spread legs and cease his addictive touch, but she couldn't find the will to speak.

Alternating between licking and nipping at the skin of her neck below her ear, Eric's stroking hand began to become more demanding. His fingers moved quicker against her clit with devious strokes. The heat in her belly spread like raging flames, consuming everything it touched. Her inner muscles squeezed with need at each quickened stroke of his hand. God; she loved his hand. How had she not known that a single touch like this could inspire such a reaction within her?

In that moment; her body didn't belong to her, but to Eric. Drugged on the sensations that kept building stronger and stronger, she found she was more than willing to let him have whatever he wanted from her as long as his fingers kept moving against her.

"Let go. I'm right here. Let go." He whispered against the skin of her neck as his fingers pressed harder against her clit with quick movements.

Before she could fight it, the fire inside her exploded into an atomic bomb of sensations, obliterating every thought she possessed. Eyes wide, her back arched off the couch as she cried out. Over and over, her sex clenched so hard that her legs shook. Waves of pleasure shook her, flooding her veins with fire that she never knew existed.

Falling back onto the cushions, her hands falling away from his wrist, Rebecca's breath escaped in ragged pants. Dazed, she barely felt Eric pull his hand from her spasiming sex as he moved to caged her with both his arms. Smirking down at her, he smoothed her hair away from her face with his fingers.

"This is the part where I say *I told you so*."

Coming out from the drugging cloud that he'd created within her, Rebecca felt her horror at what had just happened flood her. Refusing to meet his eyes, Rebecca turned her face away, her teeth biting down into her bottom lip as she tried to block out the silent screams that echoed in her mind. What had she done? She couldn't do this with Eric. She couldn't allow herself to get involved him. The distance that had remained between them before tonight was necessary. It was her only protection.

"Please. Please let me up." A sigh of relief escaped her lips as Eric moved to sit next to her hip on the edge of the sofa. Not bothering to mess with her slacks, she pulled herself into sitting position, moving to the opposite side of the couch out of self-preservation. Her sex still hummed with the lingering tingles of desire. She had to get away from him and what he'd done to her.

"Rebecca." At the soft tone, she forced her eyes to remain adverted. She couldn't face this right now. She couldn't face *him*. When she didn't look his way, Eric's voice grew firmer. "What you're feeling will not go away. That hunger—is for me, for what only I can give you."

Shaking her head, her hands lifted to rub over her face. She couldn't deal with this. The feelings that he was bringing to the surface within her were too confusing to think about. "I want you to leave." She whispered, keeping her face turned away from him. She didn't trust herself to look at him. If she did…she didn't know what would happen.

The cushion beside her abruptly shifted as Eric rose to his feet. "Fine." he bit out.

She closed her eyes, praying that the next sound she would hear would be the slamming of her front door. She nearly jumped out of her skin as Eric's hand cupped her chin firmly, tilting her face to look up at him.

"Look at me." He ordered when she attempted to avert her gaze once more. Knowing there was no fighting him in that instant, she looked up at him. "Take tomorrow off and think about what happened here tonight. When you come back to work, we *will* talk about this; about *us*." His hand fell away from her. Stepping back, his gaze lingered on her face a moment longer before he turned and started for the door.

She frowned at his commanding tone. "There is no *us*, Eric." She called at his back firmly.

He didn't bother to turn to face her as he responded. "There is and you better get used to it. Don't be late."

Closing the door behind him, Eric felt his air explode out of his lungs. Forcing himself to step away from her closed door, it took every ouch of discipline he possessed to not storm back inside and finish what he'd started. He had been holding on by a thread as Rebecca had shattered against his hand. The scent of her orgasm filled his nostrils.

He very much doubted he would ever be able to forget that scent and he wasn't the only one. His wolf reacted to her scent and her presence with uncontrollable need. There would be no staying away from his little human now. He'd known that when she'd cried out her pleasure with his name on her lips.

Though she'd fallen to pieces in his arms, from the stubborn look in her eyes when he'd forced her to look at him, he could see that there was a fight looming ahead of him. Rebecca wouldn't be an easy woman to woo to his bed. Eric could help but smile as he sprinted down the steps. Rebecca would be his; he would just have to be sneaky about it.

<u>7</u>

Hands clasped firmly behind his back; Eric paced back and forth across the kitchen, all the while his wolf snarled within him with impatience. Where was she? For the third time, he glanced at the large clock that hung on the far wall of the kitchen. It was barely past two and Rebecca was due back from picking Emma and Travis up from school at any moment.

The seconds ticked by like hours. Several times he thought about turning around and heading to the seclusion of his home office instead of this senseless waiting. There still were piles of paper work that needed his attention, but every time he started to leave, he felt his wolf recoil and found himself turning back.

He shook his head with disgust. What the hell was he doing? His sudden—well; maybe not sudden—obsession with Rebecca was perplexing to say the least. He didn't know what hold she held over his body and his wolf; but he found that he wanted it. Craved it. He didn't know what had driven him to his actions the other night in Rebecca's apartment; but he didn't regret a single second of it. He smiled at the memory. The way her chocolate brown eyes watched him with uncertainty and then melted with need; a need only *he* could full fill.

He struggled not to dwell on what else had occurred that night, but it was impossible to push the images from his mind. Rebecca—*his Rebecca*—had actually gone on a *date* with Damon—that mongrel! He suspected that she'd only done so to prove a point to him, to prove that he held no control over her.
That's where she was wrong.

He didn't want to control her, but he'd be damned if he idly stood by as Damon put his roman hands on her or any other part of her body. Growling in the back of his throat, he fought against the memory of Damon pulling Rebecca into his arms as his lips crashed down over hers. His wolf became enraged at the image.

No matter how hard he thought about it, he couldn't figure out why he felt this way about her. He was unfamiliar with the feelings that roiled within his chest. It was a strange, belly clawing, heart wrenching feeling. It was obsession boarding on the need to possess her.

His pacing strides froze at the thought. Could that really be the reason? Did he simply just want her? Was it possible that he could simply claim her body and this unexplainable need would leave him? No. He shook his head in denial. What he was experiencing went far beyond a simple sexual attraction.

Before he could pondering on his thoughts any further, his head jerked toward the front door at the soft sound of a car coming up the gravel driveway. Inside his mind, Eric felt his wolf come to attention at the sound. She was here. His chest expanded with the knowledge as his lips curled into a smile.

Crossing his arms over his chest, he forced himself to remain still and wait. Just as he thought his impatience would be his undoing, the front door swung open; echoing with the excited voices of his children. The twin's eyes widened with happy surprise at seeing him home early. Both rushed at him with excitement as they both proceeded to tell him of their day simultaneously. Struggling to listen to both, he chuckled as his eyes lifted to see Rebecca cross the threshold.

Her eyes briefly lifted from the floor as she turned to close the door behind her. Moving further inside, the moment her eyes met his, she froze. Her face quickly paled at the sight of him. Eric had no doubt that she had hoped to avoid him after the other night, just as he had anticipated. All too quickly, Rebecca dropped her gaze from his and turned into the main section of the kitchen, pretending to do something in there. He smirked. Did she really think that she could hide from him?

We'll see about that...

* ~ * ~ *

Heart thundering in her ears, Rebecca felt her mouth go dry as she came into the house to find Eric waiting for her. What was he doing? Why was he home so early? Suddenly all her hopes of putting off facing him; especially after what had happened at her apartment, went up in flames. Needing to put some space between them for her peace of mind, Rebecca quickly ducked into the kitchen, keeping her back to Eric.

Emma rushed to her side as her twin's excited voice held Eric's attention. Curling her fingers around the bottom of Rebecca's t-shirt, Emma tugged insistently. Thankful for the distraction, Rebecca turned to smile down at Emma's soft face.

"Can I have a snack?" her voice was so soft, echoing with sweet innocents that Rebecca felt her heart squeeze.

Rebecca nodded. Turning away she moved past Emma to the opposite counter beside the sink, reaching for the white and blue ceramic cookie jar that sat against the wall. Lifting the lid, she pulled out two chocolate chip cookies that she'd made earlier in the week. Replacing the lid, she turned to hand them to Emma who eagerly held out her hands.

Holding the cookies out of reach for a moment, Rebecca paused handing them to her. "One is for your brother, Emma." She said with a firm look before lowering the cookies within reach.

"I will." Emma promising words were tossed over her shoulders as she ran from the kitchen and towards the living room. As she past her twin, Travis quickly followed her once his eyes fell upon the treat clutched in her hand. The excited voices of the twins were quickly droned out when the TV was turned on in the other room.

The soft smile on her face faded as a heavy stone settled in her stomach once she realized that she was now alone—with Eric. The sound of his footsteps drawing closer had her heart lurch. Frantic, she searched for any reason, any excuse to keep him at arm's length—or further from her. Turning to face the freezer, she began pulling out cuts of meat for dinner.

"I want to talk to you." Eric's voice slid out like a caress against the back of her neck, drawing a shiver from her in response.

Her stomach tightened. He felt so close. She drew in a shaky breath as her tongue darted out to lick at her bottom lip. What could he possibly want to talk about? Couldn't they just go back to him despising her? Things were much easier when he simply growled out his rude responses to her every time they'd talked in the past.

"I'm busy." She mumbled, keeping her back to him. Her shaking hands clutched the packs of frozen meat like a lifeline.

Moving to the side of her, Eric eyed her with a hard look. "No, you're avoiding me and I won't let you do that; not anymore." He argued calmly. Reaching out, he took the packs of meat from her hands.

"I'm not avoiding anything." She said with stubborn disagreement. "I just don't want to talk to you."

"Well, that's just too damn bad." Continuing to give her a hard look, he tossed the meat onto the counter to his left. The frozen meat landed with a loud bang, causing Rebecca to flinch at the sound.

"There's nothing to talk about." She bit out, lifting her chin stubbornly. Jerking her gaze from his, she attempted to step around him. Eric moved so quickly she barely saw his hand shoot out to snag her arm and spin her toward the counter until she was pinned, facing him.

"Let go of me." She hissed out, her eyes flashing up at him as he pressed her back into the edge of the counter.

She breathed out a gasp of surprise as she felt his hard bulge brush against her stomach. The touch sent electric sensations to her womb. Her cheeks flooded with heat when she recalled how he'd touched her and how he'd made her feel. She couldn't do this. She had to get away from him.

With him this close it was impossible for her to pretend. She couldn't pretend that the scent of him didn't fire her blood and she couldn't pretend that the other night hadn't happened. His hands slid slowly up her bare arms to massage her upper arms. His hands felt as though they were burning through her skin and stealing all the strength she possessed.

"Do you think about it?" his words softly whispered close to her face.

Startled, she pressed her hands to his chest in a vain attempt to prevent him from stealing more of her personal space. "Think of what?" she scowled.

"The other night." his lips curled into a teasing smile. One of his hands lifted to trail a finger teasingly across the high neckline of her t-shirt. "The way I touched you..." he slid his trailing fingers up the slope of her neck as she gulped nervously until he stopped at her mouth. "...and the way I kissed you." His thumb smoothing along her bottom lip as he moved closer to her.

Panicked, she shook her head and in doing so; dislodged his caressing fingertip. "No." she lied.

It was true that she had thought about what he'd done to her that night. She couldn't stop thinking about it, even when she was asleep. Sensual dreams of her and Eric; a tangle of limbs and silken sheets had invaded her night and left her needy. That night he'd awakened something in her that she wished would have been left buried. She couldn't trust what she was feeling.

Getting involved with Eric would put her in jeopardy. Her life was more important than submitting to the sexual need he'd awoken within her. Plus; if she had to, she was more than capable of taking care of the problem herself.

"I know you're lying." Eric whispered low, his tone dark. "Why are you fighting this?"

"Because it is wrong. You're my boss and I won't be one of your one-time flings and that's what I would be to you."

Much to Rebecca's relief, Eric sighed heavily before taking a step back from her. "I don't know what it is that I want from you, Rebecca. All I know is that you are *mine*." He practically growled out the word "*mine*".

Glaring at him, she slashed her hand through the air as if she could whip the word away with such a gesture. "I am not your anything." She bit out.

"You are. That means you don't get to repeat what happened the other night unless it is with me. No dating other men or *kissing* them." he hissed out low enough to where they wouldn't be over heard. "You are my woman; whether you understand this yet or not. If nothing else; the other night when I touched you should have been a clue to you."

"The other night meant nothing!" she bit out, pacing away from him.

"You didn't do anything to me that I couldn't do to myself. Anything you did that night…" she trailed off, her face flooding with color once more at the memory. "…was just you attempting to prove a point."

He stalked closer to her. His eyes flashed dangerously at her, causing her to step back. "Then you need a recap if you didn't see what I was showing you that night."

"If I never had to relive that night again; I would be very happy."

* ~ * ~ *

Lies! Make her tell the truth! Eric's wolf snarled at her words.

The scent of her lie swirled around her and mingled with the scent of her fear. From the slight tremble of her hands as he regarded her; Eric could see that Rebecca was terrified. He was pushing too hard and she was lashing out at him. Though it angered him that she would deny that what had happened between them didn't mean a thing, he forced himself to not lash out at her.

He would get nowhere with her while she was hissing at him like a cat on the defense. He would have to wait until Travis and Emma went to bed for the night, when they did; she wouldn't be able to run from him.

His first mistake had been giving her time to contemplate his actions after pleasuring her that night. He should have taken her right then. Everything else would have worked out later on. But he'd stupidly thought she would come to him on her own. She thought that she could hold herself back from him.

His lips thinned at the thought. He couldn't—wouldn't go back to before that night. He didn't understand what was drawing him to her, but he'd be damned if he listened to her fear induced words. He would give her space—for the moment. But she wouldn't be leaving this house until this was settled between them.

Rebecca stabbed both of her hands through her hair in aggravation. Without saying a word to him, she retrieved the meat from the far counter and laid the packets on the stove before bending to pull out a skillet.

"I have work to attend to. I will be in my office; in case you need anything." He stated flatly.

"I won't." she argued, not bothering to look at him.

Her stubborn response was nearly his undoing. If Emma and Travis hadn't been home, he probably would have been on her in a flat second after that. Hell; he'd probably would have dragged her up to his bedroom and kept her up there until she admitted that she felt the same hunger within her.

Taking a deep breath, he fought down his animal nature; the need to dominate. He had to force himself to walk away and head toward his office. Each step he took caused him to feel his wolf growing stronger. Rebecca had won herself a short reprieve; but it would be the only one she would ever get again.

8

A few hours later, Eric was drawn back to the kitchen at the mouthwatering aroma that floated through the house. Entering the dining room, he watched as Rebecca was serving up dinner and setting the table. His knees nearly buckled at the sight of the food she was putting out. Rebecca had made beef stroganoff with freshly made bread rolls. She'd prepared a salad as well, but he knew that he wouldn't be touching that rabbit food.

He was nearly knocked over as his children came barreling down the stairs and straight into the dining room. He watched with as Emma and Travis hovered around Rebecca at the stove; attempting to get a closer look at the food she was dishing out.

"Go sit down." She said, effectively shooing the twins from the kitchen as she finished her task.

Moving back to the dining area, Travis and Emma raised their perplexed faces to him as they seemed to notice their father leaning against the wall for the first time. He could understand their confusion. It was rare that he got to eat with his children. Pack concerns and his architecture business kept him busy. But tonight nothing would pull him away; he'd made certain of that.

When Rebecca had exited the kitchen area carrying several plates, she froze too at the sight of him. Smirking at her with a knowing look, he settled into a chair without as much as a word. Almost immediately his children followed his suit and climbed into their seats, eyeing Rebecca eagerly as she approached the table with their food.

"You're eating with us, Dad?" Travis asked snatching up his fork as soon as Rebecca placed a bowl of stroganoff in front of him.

"Yes, I am. That is if I can have some. Rebecca?" he asked with false innocence, gesturing to his empty plate. Glaring back at him she all roughly slid a full bowl at him, nearly dumping the contents in his lap had he not caught the dish.

Rebecca made several more trips back to the kitchen; bringing out the large salad bowl, drinks and a bread basket before taking her seat between Emma and Travis. Attempting to ignore the fact that Eric was sitting with them, Rebecca attempted to turn her attention solely on her food.

Taking a bite of the pasta dish in front of him, Eric nearly swore as the creamy sauce covered noodles and meat exploded on his tongue. "Rebecca?" he groaned out with pleasure, drawing her attention.

Rebecca's eyes drifted up from her bowl with a raised brow. "What is it?"

"This," he began, motioning at his food. "...is incredible. If you always cook like this I may just have to keep you." His eyes watched her for a reaction. She didn't disappoint him as her cheeks flushed before she quickly looked away.

"Thank you…" she mumbled, attempting to cover up her embarrassment.

Reaching for a dinner roll, Eric dipped it in his bowl before bringing it to his mouth. Half way through their dinner, Emma's small innocent voice cut through the silence that swelled within the room.

"Can we have ice cream after dinner, Daddy?" Emma asked, flashing him her best pleading look.

"Sure, I think I might need something sweet too." He glanced conspiringly at Rebecca across the table. "How about it, Rebecca? Do you know where I can get something creamy and sweet?" he asked with a grin. He couldn't help but smirk at the wash of color that flooded her cheeks once more as she caught his hidden meaning.

All through the remainder of dinner, Rebecca did her best to avoid talking to him, much less even looking at him. Phase one of his plan was accomplished, she was aware of his interest, and she wasn't as indifferent as she'd like him to believe. As soon as Emma and Travis were in bed for the night she would have nowhere to run, he'd begin laying phase two into motion.

After the twins had eaten as if it were the last scraps of food on the planet; they smiled with happiness as Rebecca collected their plates and returned with two small bowls of chocolate ice cream. Eric noted with a soft scoff that she had purposely not brought him one as well. After they had practically licked their bowls clean, Eric leaned back in his chair, folding his arms behind his head.

"Time for bed." Almost instantly both of the twins groaned in despair. Shooting them a firm look before they could begin to barter for more time, Eric shook his head. "Go get ready for bed."

For a brief moment the twins cast a glance toward Rebecca as she was collecting the dishes and carrying them to the sink to be washed. Seeing that she would not aid them against their father's wishes; with frowning faces, the twins slid from their chairs and headed off to do as they were told.

After collecting the last dish from the table, Rebecca returned with a damp wash cloth and began to whip the table clean. His eyes never strayed from her for a moment.

"Stop it!" she huffed out in loss of patience as she tossed a damp wash cloth in his face. Jerking the wet cloth off his face, he smiled up at her as she headed back into the kitchen.

"What did I do now?"

"Stop looking at me like that."

"Like what? Am I making you nervous?" he teased.

"No." she mumbled. Filling the sink with soapy water, all the while she was too aware that he followed behind her.

Dumping the dishes in a sink full of wash water, Rebecca stiffened as she felt his body heat at her back. He didn't move to touch her or even to speak. Ignoring him the best she could, her hands moved quickly through the water. When she found herself all too focused on her task, Eric started her by wrapping his arms around her waist and pulling her back tightly against his front.

"You should be nervous, Rebecca. If you knew the things you make me want to do to you."

"You're acting crazy, Eric." She inwardly groaned. It felt so good to be in his arms. The warm steel bands around her caused her to feel protected and loved. Which made it hurt all the more. Shoving at his arms, Rebecca forced herself to put space between them, for both their sakes.

"Why are you doing this? Why can't you just leave me alone? I work for you! Don't you have any self respect?"

His eyes flashed over her with amusement and unhidden interest. "What does self respect have to do with it? I want you and I know you want me. Why fight it?"

"So what? You just decide that I'm to be your new sex toy and I fall in line?"

Rolling his eyes, Eric scoffed. "If only."

"Look." Rubbing her tired eyes, she took a step closer to him. "I need this job, Eric. I like this job and I'm not going to risk it."

"Tough. I am willing to risk it." Quickly moving forward, Eric backed her against one of the counters.

Wrapping her fingers around the edge of the counter, Rebecca lifted her chin; refusing to shrink away from him like the rabbit he'd called her. Reaching out; Eric wrapped the length of her ponytail around his fist, using her hair like a handle to tip her head back as he pressed against her.

"Be as stubborn as you wish, but I have never backed down from a challenge and I will win."

Rebecca answered him with a doubtful glare. Before she could throw a barbed insult at his arrogant statement, his lips covered hers as if she were the last drop of water in the desert. His teeth nipped at her bottle lip demanding entre. Rebecca tried to remain motionless beneath his lips, but his kiss made her blood sing. Made her body ache in ways she'd only read about.

How she wanted to give herself to him, to love him as she desired to. But the image of her parent's bloody, mangled bodies flittered into her mind. It very may have been one of his pack members that killed her parents. Would he take her side against his own kind, people he'd played with and grew up with? No. he wouldn't.

Shoving her hands between their hypersensitive bodies, she shoved with all her might against an impenetrable wall of hard muscle. However, she succeeding in only pushing his lips off of hers. Taking a steady breathe, her hands struggled to pry his strong arms from around her waist.

"We need to stop." She whispered breathlessly, refusing to meet his eyes as he looked curiously down at her.

Eric shook his head. "There is no stopping this now. There is no going back for either of us. That chance became out of reach the moment you let me touch you."

"I won't accept." She argued in a haunting voice. Shaking her head with worried eyes, she took a step backwards, forcing a safe distance between them. "Just because we…" her hand waved between them, awkwardly indicating to what had happened between them. "…did *that*, doesn't mean that you get to suddenly own me."

"I may not own you, but you are mine and I refuse to let you run away from this cause you are scared." Eric bit out.

"I am not scared of you, Eric." It was a lie. The truth was; she was terrified of him…of her need of him. Eric had this pull about him, drawing her closer to him even as she struggled to stay away from him.

"Then prove it." Eric replied gently. Stepping closer to her, He reached out. His large hand cupped her chin and forced her eyes to meet his. "Stop fighting this. I don't understand this need I have for you, but the thought of being forced from you shreds my insides. I want to explore it. Give whatever is between us a chance."

Briefly, Rebecca's eyes searched his. She didn't know what she expected to see within his emerald eyes. It was honesty mixed with pleading. Eric…was pleading? That was a mind-boggling concept. Not once in the couple of months that she'd known Eric had he *ever* looked or acted pleadingly. Deep down, she wanted trust what he was saying, but she couldn't. Her chest ached with as a terrifying voice from a distant memory echoed through her mind.

None of my kind will let you live now. Others will come for you and you will never know mercy from my kind…

Jerking her head away, she forced herself to look at him with indifference. "I don't want to give it a chance." she whispered with a flat tone. "The other night was a mistake; one I don't want to repeat with you." Taking in a deep breath, she forced her next words out as a knot twisted her stomach tightly. "I don't want you."

For a moment, Eric had no expression or reaction to her words as he took in her words. Had he even heard her? Soon his relaxed expression shifted. His eyes darkened in reaction to her lifeless words. His lips pressed together into a tight line before he finally spoke.

"*Fine.*" his voice came out sounding more like a growl than anything and it made Rebecca shiver with fear. She flinched back as he pointed at her accusingly. "I know you feel the need—the connection between us. That won't go away. Sooner or later; you will be forced to acknowledge it and when that happens, you will come to me."

Rebecca scoffed, tossing her head back. "Get a grip! You just want sex and I'm convenient. I don't even like you, Eric, and I know you definitely don't like me. Why in the world would I *ever* come to you if I wanted a relationship?" she asked, sarcastically holding her arms out at her sides.

Eric's eyes narrowed."You think Damon can give you what I did?" he growled out.

Turning around, Rebecca grabbed her purse off the back counter. Spinning back to Eric's stubborn face, she smirked coldly up at him. "Perhaps. If not; I am sure I can find someone else."

Moving toward the front door, Rebecca was jerked to a stop when Eric's hand clamped roughly around her forearm. Jerking her fully against his front, he looked down at her, his eyes burning with anger and jealously at her words.

"Know that if someone touches you, they will be taking their life out of their hands. You are under my protection."

"I don't need your stupid protection!" she frowned; attempting to break free of Eric's restraining hand.

Eric lowered his head until their noses were touching. "I. Am. Serious." He bit out. "Don't put an obstacle between us that I will have to remove." He warned in a low voice.
Tangling his freehand in her loose hair, he held her immobile as his lips came crashing down over hers. He dominated her mouth with a near punishing force. His teeth captured her bottom lip, nipping at it before sliding his tongue over the tempting flesh. Rebecca gasped against his lips. The force of his kiss made her want to return it; all the while she knew she should fight it.

Twisting out of grip, Rebecca broke the kiss. Her lungs burned for air, and left her panting heavily. Without saying a word, she ran. Jerking the front door open, she rushed out of the house, allowing the door to slam behind her. She didn't stop her running legs until she had slid into her small car, pressing her back tightly against her seat. Her chest rose and a fell with her heavy breaths, her heart thundering in her ears.

Her trembling hand reached up to touch her pulsing lips. She could still feel him touching her, kissing her as only Eric could. Her stomach clenched and trembled all at once with need. She wouldn't go through this again, she silently promised. Eric didn't own her or own her reaction to him. She was needy and that was easily fixed. Perhaps it was time that she did.

Then prove it... Eric's rumbling words from earlier echoed in her mind.

That's just what she would do. The only way to prove that Eric had no hold; sexual or otherwise, over her was to prove it. The only way that she could prove it to Eric was to prove it to herself.

* ~ * ~*

Gulping against the lump in her throat that threatened to chock her, Rebecca stared up at the glowing red lights of the *Red Horns Bar and Grill* sign. With apprehension she looked up at the angry image on the sign of a fiery red bull's face. Within the small town of Ravenwillow the *Red Horns* was the only bar within miles, which meant this was her only option.

Rebecca had succeeded in avoiding Eric for the last few days thanks to Sarah wanting to spend for time with her grandchildren. She knew eventually she wouldn't be able to hide from him. All it would take was a touch or a kiss and she'd melt, just as she'd done that night at her apartment and a few days ago in his kitchen.

There was no way she was letting that happen again. Which was why she had to do this and she couldn't back out now. *Just go in there, get it over with and get on with your life...* she told herself, pushing away her uncertainty. She could do this. She *would* do this.

Releasing a held breath out slowly, She pulled away from the red brick wall she had planted herself against, when her mind began filling with doubts. Walking around the corner of the red brick building, she entered the side entrance to the *Red Horns* bar. With every step she took, she tried to prepare herself; mentally, for what she was about to do.

She was dressed in a dark scarlet blouse that hid her scares yet dipped low over her breasts and a short black shirt that fell just a little above her knees. Her feet were cupped tenderly within the sexy pair of black high heeled sandals that she wore. Her sinful outfit combined with her dark makeup, she was dressed to tempt.

Tonight she was going to find some hot stud, work out this need that had built up within her and forget all about Eric Daniels. Looking around, the bar was flowing with people, people ready to have fun and hopefully a mouth-watering man looking to get laid tonight.

Spying an attractive man sitting at the bar, she was just about to walk up and introduce herself when she noticed Jason; one of Eric's friends that she'd met, sitting at the bar. His eyes were focused on the flat screen TV mounted on one of the side walls as he bought his beer bottle to his lips. She wasn't getting close to him. With no doubt, he'd call Eric and then she'd have a bigger problem than she already did.

Turning to look back at the bar as patrons took drinks handed to them; she noticed that her hands slightly trembled with apprehension. A bit of liquid courage may just be what she needed. Walking up as served customers moved away from the bar, Rebecca stood across from a tall, burly man that stood on the other side of the bar. He looked more like a bouncer than a bartender. Made nearly entirely of heavy muscle and wide shoulders, the man stood nearly seven feet. He possessed dark wavy hair that he held back in a small ponytail. His expression as he served customers was far from inviting and made Rebecca want to back away. Forcing herself not to turn around and flee, she waited for him to notice her.

"What can I get you?" His tone was harsh as his dark hazel eyes bore into hers.

Jerking her eyes away from his, she nodded. Normally, she was the furthest thing from a heavy drinker, but tonight she would need the extra courage to go through with her plan. "I'll just have a scotch." She replied. With a curt the rough looking bartender moved to get her drink.

Inhaling a calming breath, she turned to look up and down the length of the bar for any appealing men, but none seemed to catch her interest. Turning around she took notice of a small group of men at a table, enjoying a pitcher of beer and laughing. For some reason none of them seemed appealing either.

She was startled when a glass was slammed down on the bar in front of her. The amber liquid sloshing over the sides of the small, ice filled glass. Murmuring a thank you, she slipped the money into his hand and pick up her drink, tipping it against her lips. The fiery liquid burned her throat as she took a small sip, causing her to cough at the sensation. She had never been much of a drinker, but now was a good time as any to learn.

Finding a table, unoccupied in a dark corner, she sat down; taking another small sip of her beverage and surveying the crowd. Several men looked her way, when they caught her looking at them, but none approached her. Hopefully she get so drunk, some guy would just take advantage of her and make it easier on her.

So caught up in her own thoughts, Rebecca didn't realize that she was no longer alone until she turned to adjust her seat. "Oh God!" She exclaimed with surprise, her free hand flatting over her heart. "You scared me." She whispered.

"So I see." Jason smiled friendly at her as he leaned back in his seat.

"I saw you sitting alone, thought you'd like the company."

"Maybe I was just waiting for you." She murmured softly as she leaned into him with an "*I want you*" smile.

Jason's friendly smile fell. "Rebecca, what are you doing?" He asked, confused.

Moving away from him, she slouched in her chair looking suddenly depressed, she took another swig of her drink. "Forget it."

Reaching over, Jason pulled her glass from her hand, bring it to his face, he sniffed the contents. "Why are you drinking scotch? I never pegged you for a heavy drinker."

"I have my reasons." Reaching over she jerked the glass out of his hand, "Give me that! It's mine." She said stubbornly, as she finished off the remaining liquor, making a face of disgust and shivering as she swallowed it down.

Turning back to look at the crowd, she suddenly felt eyes on her. Her gaze swept the room until her eye met a pair of bright blue ones. On the other end of the dance floor; lounging relaxed against the wall, was a tall, blonde haired man whom was watching her with visible interest. He was attractive in a college jock way; but she could only feel her skin crawl at his gaze. Unwilling to back down from the reason that she came here tonight; she attempted to shoot the man an interested glance.

"Rebecca." Jason called out next to her, attempting to get her attention. "Rebecca!"

"What?" She asked; irritated. If her plan was to succeed she was going to have to get rid of Jason. With his looks and presence, Jason was surly bound to scare off any potential men.

"*What* do you think you're doing?"

"Browsing,"

"Browsing?" Following her gaze, Jason noticed the tall man that leered at Rebecca like she was a treat to be devoured. This was not good. "Rebecca, why don't you just let me take you home?"

Rebecca whirled around to face him with a dark scowl on her face. "Why?" she bit out.

"Rebecca. What do you think you're doing?" He asked again, cupping the side of her face, forcing her to remain looking at him, when she turned back to her eye candy. "How do you think Eric would react if he knew what you were doing?"

Rebecca's face paled for a brief moment before she shrugged off the weight of her uncertainty. "Eric has nothing to do with this or me. I came here for a reason tonight and I'm not leaving until I do it. You can either help me or leave me alone." She stated plainly, daring him to say anything otherwise.

"You know, once you do this; you can't take it back."

"That's the idea."

Resting his forearm against the tabletop, Jason leaned closer to Rebecca. "I thought you were Eric's, did something happen?" his gaze softened and nearly pled with her to listen to him.

Teeth grinded together, her lips pressed together in a thin line, as her anger flared. "I am not Eric's anything." She bit out. "I work for him—that's it. He has no control over who I sleep with or see outside of the conditions of my contract with him."

"I don't think Eric would see it that way."

Refusing to listen to Jason's attempt to reason with her, she turned away and searched for her mystery man again; only to find he'd vanished. Rebecca immediately felt a wave of disappointment wash over her.

So much for that one, she thought bitterly. Perhaps Jason was right. Maybe she should just go home and call it a night. There was always another night.

"Excuse me." A masculine voice whispered on her from beside her.

Looking up, her eyes met the familiar blue ones that belonged to her blonde, mystery man.

"H-Hey." Her words stumbled out. *Get it together!* Straightening in her chair, she attempted to look as confident that she wished she was in that moment.

"You look like your searching for someone, anyone I know?" He teased with a wolfish grin.

"Depends," She replied coyly. Laughing at her teasing he sat down in an empty seat on her other side.

"I'm Josh."

"Rebecca."

"Rebecca." He whispered. "Nice to meet you," Smiling at her, he lifted her hand to his lips, planting a soft kiss in the center of her palm. On the other side of her she could practically see Jason rolling his eyes.

I can do this... she told herself, *Eric is nothing to me.*

Even though the very voice of this man, promise hot, sweaty nights in the bedroom. Strangely, something about the idea of going home with Josh didn't sound at all appealing. Gazing out over the small dance floor, she watched as couples clutched at each other, while dancing to the up tempo number that played.

"Are you alright? Did I say something wrong?"

"Rebecca?" Jason asked concerned. She could have mentally slapped herself. What was wrong with her?! She was going through with this even if it killed her!

Shaking her head, she smiled up at him "Not at all." Gesturing to the dance floor, she stood up. "Let's dance."

Reaching out, Jason grasped a hold of Rebecca wrist, preventing her from moving out of her chair. "Think about this, Rebecca. This will end badly." He cautioned quietly, preventing Josh from hearing them over top of the pounding music.

"I'm done thinking." She'd made up her mind and nothing would make her change it. Not Eric, not Jason, and most importantly; not even herself.

Not waiting for an answer from Jason, Rebecca grasped a hold of Josh's hand, pulling him onto the dance floor. Finding an unoccupied space on the dance floor she fitted her back against his strong frame. As the beat of the music picked up, she attempted to dance as she once had with friends before her life had been forever changed. Thrusted back against him, she grinded her ass against his groin as she teased his swelling cock.

In result; he in turn wrapped his arm around her waist, while the other stroked down the underside of her arm as she lifted her arms to circle his neck from behind. Their bodies moved as one. Thrusting and stroking against one another, leaving them panting for air—well; one of them panting, but Rebecca was determined to see this through.

Leaning his mouth close to her ear, his hot breath fanned over her neck and bare shoulder. "I never would have thought that I'd be dancing with someone as sexy as you tonight." He whispered.

Be strong, you can do this...

"Who says I *just* gonna dance with you."

The words tasted like bile in her mouth. She had lost her edge—if she'd even possessed one to begin with. It wasn't as if she'd never done this before or anything close to it. she was a virgin. The word was like a shameful badge in her mind. A reminder of how much her attack had paralyzed her in her life. No longer…

In the past; she would have instantly went for someone like Josh, but now…it somehow felt wrong. Why did her skin crawl when Jason touched her? Whenever she was near Eric, it was never like this. Just the feel of his body heat pressing to hers, his hands on her skin or his lips brushing enticingly against hers; it was explosive with Eric. What made *him* so special?!

As Josh nuzzled his face into her neck and her loose hair, Rebecca forced herself not to shrink away from him. "Really? What did you have in mind?" He breathed out, his voice weighted down with desire.

"Maybe I should take you some place and show you what other type of dancing I can do…" The words were meant to entice and from the hard evidence that stirred against her, it was working.

"Sounds like the best idea, I've heard all week." He murmured, as his fingertips grazed the edge of her breast and down the side of her body with deliberate slowness. Her head began slightly swimming with a feeling of floating, a delicious buzz as the effects of her drink hit her.

This is going to be easier than I thought…

"This is going to be the *best* night of your life." She whispered temptingly, whether it was to him or herself; she didn't know.

9

Exiting the men's room, Eric straightened his dark blue t-shirt over his tan cargo pants. Several of his workers had come to the *Red Horns* to unwind from the first day with the construction crew as they'd begun building Damon's home. His mother had taken pity on him and offered to stay with Emma and Travis while he went out for an hour or two.

With a grimace, Eric felt his thoughts turn back Rebecca. The woman was testing his wolf's patience. He'd called her several times in the last few days that she'd been able to elude him whenever he came home late nights. Frankly; he was getting at his wits end. If he didn't see her soon, he may just show up on her door step and force her to face him.

Before he could return to the table where himself and his work crew had been enjoy a large pitcher of beer, he was immediately hailed over to the bar by Mick. Mick Torus was the owner of the *Red Horns* bar and grill. He also was a rouge bull shifter, more precisely; an Ankole longhorn bull.

Mick was an enforcer that worked for Eric outside the pack. Mick's job was to police rouge shifters and maintain the peace; not only between other packs, but between ignorant humans as well. Walking up to the noisy bar, he leaned close to hear Mick as he spoke over the loud music and idle noise.

"How's it going, Eric?" Mick greeted as they gripped each other's forearms, a display of their long friendship.

"It's going. How's business and *other things?*"

"Business is good tonight. But I have some information for you that you will not like."

Frowning, Eric braced his weight on his palms that rested against the edge of the bar. "What is it?" he asked grimly.

"I looked into the favor you asked a few months back. I'm afraid you may be on to something."

The *favor* that Eric had asked of Mick was one that had to keep secret, especially from the pack elders. For several years, shifters from different packs all throughout Virginia had mysteriously gone missing. Women, men, and children simply disappeared without a cause or trace. He suspected that there were more cases throughout the U.S. but he needed to confirm his suspicions before he could take action.

Reaching into the breast pocket of his button up black shirt, Mick withdrew a thick white envelope. Laying it on the bar, he discreetly shoved it toward Eric. Taking the envelope, Eric reached inside to pull out a large pile of photos. The photos were of shifters that had been reported missing in the last ten years. On the front of each photo was the shifter's name, date they disappeared and location. Flipping through several he was dismayed to see that several of the children missing were no older than Travis and Emma. What the hell was going on?

"Do you think we may have some fanatical humans hunting shifter again?" Mick asked. His tone told Eric that he was enraged as much as he was at the unexplained disappearances.

Shoving the photos back into the envelope, he tucked it into one of his deep pants pockets. Sighing, Eric shook his head at Mick's theory. "I don't think humans did this. If this was the work of fanatics, there would be bodies and evidence. These shifters are disappearing without a trace, leaving no sign of whom or what took them."

Mick nodded solemnly with a grunt "Plus; humans would leave a scent behind. Every place I've investigated where there was a disappearance, the only scent I could find was an overly sweet scent. I've never encountered it before. Have you?"

Eric's frown deepened as his thoughts were pulled back to a nearly six months back. During his time in Darkwood Springs, he recalled the same excessive sweet scent. The scent had come from those strange enhanced soldiers that had hunted Robert Mackenzie's human mate. Could they be involved in the disappearances of so many shifters? Regardless; he would have no choice but to contact Doyle Mackenzie about it—and the elders. Shaking his head he pinched the bridge of his nose with annoyance.

"Thanks for your help, Mick. I'll keep you posted."

Nodding with a grim expression, Mick turned and walked down to the other end of the bar to several waiting customers.

Feeling the heavy weight of the knowledge he'd just received, Eric slummed down in a bar stool. He turned to look to his left as the bar stool beside him was pulled out as someone took a seat. His hard eyes flashed over the familiar face of his second beta, Jason. For a moment nether said a word to the other. Jason was busy nursing the remains of his beer as he cast a brief glance in Eric's direction.

Hesitantly; Jason finally broke the silence between them. "What did Mick say?"

Shaking his head, Eric held up a flat hand; indicating that Jason was treading on a topic that Eric couldn't or wouldn't discuss at that time. "Just something I'm looking into."

Not taking the hint, Jason pressed forward. "Is it something that we need to be concerned about?"

Flashing an irritated glare at him, Eric sighed. "It's too soon to tell. Once I have more information I will share what I know. Until then; I want you to keep your mouth shut about what you saw between Mick and I."

Jason rolled his eyes before scoffing. "You just had to go and ruin all my fun. Here I was planning on going to the elders and telling them about all your evil plans." When Eric didn't even glance his way, Jason placed his empty bottle on the bar with a sigh. "Seriously; Eric, you've been treading a thin line where the elders are concerned. I agree with what you want to do for our pack, but you need to be careful that you are not creating more enemies than allies."

Pushing his seat back, Eric rose stiffly to his legs. He was tired and his wolf was on edge. He just wanted to go home and fuck everything else for one night. "Good night." before he could walk past Jason, a scent floated from his beta that had Eric pausing. Crowding close, he scowled as he drew more of the scent into his lungs. Vanilla mixed with jasmine perfume—it was Rebecca's scent.

Catching the realization in his Alpha's eyes, Jason rubbed a tired hand against the back of his neck. "You're not going to like what I'm about to tell you." He muttered.

Eric's eyes narrowed to small slits. "You've been with my...Rebecca." He bit out accusingly.

Jason frowned before shaking his head. "No. I'm afraid it's worse than that." tilting his chin toward the dance floor and the throng of dancing bodies, Jason motioned at something.

Turning to the side, Eric followed the direction of Jason's eyes; he wasn't prepared for the sight that lay before him. Everything inside him froze at the sight that burned and taunted his eyes; causing rage began overflowing inside of him. Rebecca looked breath taking, making all the blood rush to his lower reign at just the sight of her.

With her dark makeup, her upswept hair and dress; she looked like a dream—a temptress. She danced like sin; her body flowed gracefully as her body pressed up against another man, a man that *wasn't him!* Every sensual move of her body was pure sin and it caused the flames of jealously to rise up inside him. The man began tempting fate as his body thrusted up against Rebecca's high supple ass, her arms wrapped around his neck from behind as her lips parted with a sensual smile. If that wasn't bad enough; Eric watched; as if in slow motion, as the soon-to-be-deceased man ran his fingertips along the outside of one her breast, before his caressing fingers slid back up tracing an invisible line around her succulent breasts.

Flames leapt from the depths of his eyes, as the predatory side of him emerged to the surface. Clenching his fists at his sides, his chest rose up and down in fast, angry pants. Someone had dared to touch *his woman.* He didn't care if he was acting like the possessive neanderthal. Any doubts or concerns he had about his attraction to Rebecca suddenly didn't matter anymore. She was his, case closed. She'd just have to accept it and get over her doubts about him.

Kill him. His wolf demanded with a tone that was filled with bloodlust. The thought was almost too tempting to pass up.

Placing one heavy, booted foot in front of the other; he stalked through the crowd and made his way up behind the unsuspecting dancing couple. *Couple? Hell no!* They were defiantly not a couple, the very idea of Rebecca with another man, loving another man; made a killing fury course through his veins. Rebecca and he was a couple—or at least they would be after tonight. This man was just a bug on his boot, waiting to be swashed!

He couldn't shake off the heavy pressure of rage building and tightening inside his chest as his wolf fought for freedom. It was a tempting idea to release his beast on the man, but he quickly squashed that idea—for now. Not wasting a breath; coming up behind them, he tapped firmly on the man's shoulder to get his attention. While he waited for the man to turn around to face him, Eric felt like a coiled rattlesnake; waiting to strike than a wolf in that moment.

The man let go of Rebecca for an instant to turn and see who was behind him. The second their gazes collided; Eric pulled back his fist and slammed it into the smug man's face. The impact from the punch, threw him off his feet and landing hard on his back. At the sound of Eric's fist connecting with the man's face, all dancing around them stopped instantly as all eyes turned to watch them with interest. At all the commotion, Rebecca swung around just in time to watch her dance partner get thrown off his feet. Her mouth hung open in a silent gasp as she turned her eyes to see Eric standing in front of her, panting, his eyes wild.

Walking around her, Eric leaned over her dazed dance partner; prepared to beat some sense into him. Placing herself between them, Rebecca planted her hands on Eric's muscled chest, giving him a good shove away from the bleeding man.

"What the fuck is your problem?!" She yelled at him, punching him in the chest.

Gripping her wrists he pulled her into his hard frame. "Watch your language." He whispered, scolding. His stern eyes bore into hers as she swayed slightly on her heel covered feet. Her normal soft jasmine scent was clouded with the stench of alcohol. "Are you drunk?" He accused.

"It's none of your damn business! Let go of me!" She struggled to pull her wrists out of his retraining hands.

Eric was all too aware that they were drawing every eye in the bar toward them with the commotion. He had to get Rebecca out of here where he could talk more with her without the worry of others.

Tugging on her captured wrist, he began dragging her off the small crowed dance floor. Not that Rebecca was making it a simple task for him. Behind him; she cursed, striking at his back—not that he noticed much; she possessed the strength of a butterfly.
Seeing that there was no other way around it, he sharply turned to face her just as they cleared the dance floor. His hand released her as if he'd been burnt. With fast, fluid motions; he bent down and unceremoniously tossed Rebecca over his shoulder. One of his heavy muscled arms clamped down over the back of her thighs, holding her squirming body still. His eyes glared; dangerously down at Jason, while Rebecca beat her small fists against his lower back.

"Put me down you big ape!" Rebecca shrieked while kicking her feet back and forth, her fist pounding on his back with angry strikes.

Striding past the gasping faces and shocked looks of all the on lookers, Eric marched out the back entrance and into the nearly empty back parking lot. Coming to stop beside his black hummer, he roughly lowered Rebecca back onto her feet, making her stumble unsteadily. Jerking the passenger door open, Eric held the door open for her. The harsh look on his face told Rebecca he was not in the best of moods.

"Get in." Rebecca appearance looked like she'd just been through a war zone. Her hair was tussled and her dress was full of wrinkles. To anyone else; she looked like she'd just been thoroughly pleased, were it not for her angry expression.

"Go to hell." She said in anger as she tried to walk around him, but he was too fast for her. His hand shot out and shackling her wrist in an unbreakable hold.

"Rebecca." His tone was dangerous. "Get in now. I'll take you home, we can discuss this later."

Folding her arms over her chest she didn't take a single step toward the opened door. Pursing his lips with anger, he slammed the door closed. "Fine, I was going to drive you home and not do this until tomorrow, but you obviously want to have it out *right* here, *right* now, in the middle of a dark parking lot."

"I have nothing to say to you." She stated out flatly, not looking at him.

"Well; that's a shame, because I have plenty to say. So I guess I'll do all the talking then and you will just have to listen."

"I don't have to do *anything*."

"Yes, you certainly do. You can start by explaining to me, what the hell you were doing in there." He exclaimed, pointing over his shoulder at the *Red Horns* structure.

"It's none of your business." She replied, stubbornly.

"It *is* my business! Another man just had his hands all over you, I'm well within my rights to go back in there and beat the life out of him!"

"*Well within your rights?* What rights? Big deal; you touched me and kissed me! That doesn't give you *any* rights when it comes to me."

"You're mine—"

"I am not—" She tried to interrupt, but he went on as if she hadn't said a word.

"—By now, everyone in town is aware of the fact that your under my protection and anyone stupid enough to try to touch you or anything along that line, it would give me the right to set him straight." He finished with confidence.

Rebecca stared at him with shock; her mouth slightly hung open, "Are you insane? What I choose to do with other men and who I sleep with is *none* of *your* concern or anyone else's." She shot back at him, while her hands curled into fists in frustration. "Get this through your landmine of a head! I am your employee! You are my boss!"

Beginning to pace back and forth in front of her; Eric braced his hands on his hips, his eyes burning into hers. Coming to a stop, he curled his hands into tight fists. "Then you're fired." He bit out.

Rebecca blinked up at him with confusion. *"Excuse me?"*

"You heard me; you are fired. Now that you can't use that stupid excuse anymore, perhaps you will take what I have been saying to you more seriously."

"You're insane. You can't fire me without a reason."

"You're mine. That's all the reason I need. I'm not letting you push me away because you have some ethics about dating in the workplace."

Rebecca's mouth parted, speechlessly. With a cry of outrage, she walked around him, heading for the sidewalk at the other end of the parking lot and toward her car. Her steps faltered when she heard Eric's voice again.

"You can't run from me or this anymore, Rebecca. You either get in the car with me now or I will follow you back to your apartment and we can have this discussion there. Either way; we will be having it."

She spun around on her heels so quickly that she nearly fell clear out of them. Taking a moment to right her unbalanced feet, she glared at him. Folding her arms over her chest, she squeezed her lips together in frustration. "Did it ever occur to you to take the hint that I was not interested? Why couldn't you just accept what I want and move on. Is your pride so large that you can't take rejection? Yes, I'm attracted to you and what woman with a pulse wouldn't be? But even I know when to stay away from a ticking bomb, which is why I was in there." She indicated at the back entrance of the Red Horns bar.

Eric's eyes flashed with fire. "You came here to find someone to sleep with you." He acknowledged.

"No. I came here to find someone to have sex with, because that is all that is between us; a need for sex."

"If that is the case; I am more than willing to accommodate you." He sneered, taking a threatening step toward her. "If I wanted just sex, I could get that anywhere if I wanted. But I don't just want you for sex, Rebecca. You intrigue me and that is a hard feat for many people I know. I want to know more about you."

Releasing a huff, she shook her head at him. "That's just it, Eric."She took a few steps closer to him, erasing some of the distance she'd put between them. He could help but feel pleased that she had made the first move. "I don't want to get to know you." It would appear that her unyielding stubbornness hadn't weakened.

His wolf stirred at the foul scent of her lie along with it other scents reached him; desire and fear. Rebecca may be holding him at arm's length not because of her job, but because she was truly scared of him. The realization was like a punch in the face to him. He'd admit that he had been harsh with her when he'd first met her and over the past few months out of necessity, but it was different now.
He no longer wanted her to fear him. He wanted her to trust him.

Wooing her in a traditional way was out of the question. He wasn't a gentleman. He was a wolf and he acted every bit like one. Winning her trust wouldn't be easy, but he wasn't about to give up on her. His most powerful weapons available to him were his ability to seduce her and his brutal honesty. With everything in him; he intended to use both to his full and complete advantage.

Shoving his hands into the front pockets of his jeans in an effort to look non-threatening, Eric shook his head gently. "Did you really think you could just say some words and my interest in you would vanish? You won't be able to get rid of me that easily."

Releasing a sound somewhere between a groan and a hiss of outrage, Rebecca threw her hands up. "I give up; there's no reasoning with you. But; listen carefully, because I'm only going to explain this once. If you ever try to interfere in my life again, I'll have you in handcuffs so quick your head will spin." She threatened as she turned around, stalking away from him.

Eric followed behind her with a relaxed ease, his hand remaining shoved in his pockets. "Just a little tip, angel, if I ever catch another man with his hands or any other body part even near you, I'll make what I did inside look like I just introduced myself to him. Just keep in mind; I will fight for what is mine."

Eric felt his wolf howl with victory as his words cause her to jerk to a stop. That got her attention like nothing else could. He was going to force Rebecca out of her small, orderly comfort zone even if it killed him. Before the night was out; she would be his.

10

She should have kept walking. She should have ignored him as she had always done in the past, but his words echoed in her like an annoying buzzing.

"I will fight for what is mine…"

Who did he think he was?! She didn't belong to anyone, least of all him! All her fear melted away to outrage. It was time to end this once and for all! Spinning around, she quickly stalked towards him; each slow, menacing step may as well have left a trail of roaring flames behind her.

"What's yours?" In anger she slammed the flat of her palms against his chest, barely moving him beyond a step back. "I am not *your* anything! Nor will I ever be. Take my advice and get over yourself, asshole!" She yelled, turning to walk away from him once again.

"Fuck it." Was all she heard uttered from his lips before his heavy footfalls coming up behind her.

Striding up behind Rebecca, he spun her around into his arms, His hands reaching up to clasp tightly on either side of her face. Pulling her to him, his lips came crashing down on hers. His lips felt like a hot fierily brand burning into her skin. At the touch of his lips, Rebecca felt her womb spasm and inner muscles pulsing with desire. Everything in her was reaching, aching, needing for Eric.

Still kissing her, Eric backed her against an adjacent building, effectively trapping her between a brick wall and his hard body. Rebecca broke away, gasping for air as her heart beat thundered in her ears.

"Eric…" She paused, taking in deep gulps of sweet air. "I don't think—" His hands tightened on the sides of her face, his thumbs sliding soothingly along her high cheekbones. His heated glazed eyes bore down into her soft, yielding ones.

"Don't think, just feel. Our bodies communicate far better than our words ever do." His lips covered her once again, moving with heated urgency. "For once; just once, Rebecca, don't think. Just feel what your body is so desperately trying to tell you." He breathed out against her skin.

Sliding his hands down the soft slope of her neck, over her arching breasts and down her hip to grip the firm globes of her ass. His hands molded and squeezed, causing her to gasp with pleasure at against his lips. She arched her body against his as she wrapped her arms around his neck, holding him as close as she could.

Bending his knees, Eric's hands drifted down to the back of her bare thighs. Lifting her high against his body, he wrapped her legs around his waist as he grinded his hard length into her weeping center. A thin layer of clothes was the only barrier she had between herself and Eric. She felt safe with that barrier, but at the same time she wanted him to remove that same barrier from her.

Her heels dug into the muscles of his ass as Rebecca thrusted her pulsing, center, causing chills of delight to rush up her back and through the tips of her breasts. Burying her hands into Eric's long hair, she dug her nails into his scalp while she tugged him closer to her lips. Sweeping her tongue into the warmth of his mouth; pulling a deep groan from his throat as his tongue tangled with hers in an intimate caress.

Shoving her short skirt up until it fluttered around her hips, uncovering her enough to where he could see her black silk thong, making his hard length pulse with need. The bottom of her skirt glided against their grinding pelvises, forming a curtain over their thrusting groins. Eric thrusted up against her pulsing center and began a slow grinding motion against the thin barrier of her silk black thong, causing a warm rush of liquid to flow from her undulating center and wetting the sinful looking silk further.

"Eric…I *need* you." She breathed out, lustfully breathless as his lips trailed a path away from her lips to her chin, down her swan throat.

His lips were loving, teasing, punishing, giving her everything and yet it wasn't enough. Her womb clenched, her body tightly twisted, squeezing in demand to be filled. Filled with Eric, the way only he could.

"*Please…*" She begged with an edge of need as his hands left their caressing position at the back of her thighs, roaming upward to her throbbing breasts; tugging and teasing her nipples through the soft fabric of her silk blouse and bra.

Bending down further, Eric latched onto one of her hard nipples, pulling it into the hot, cavern of his mouth. His tongue circled and fluttered against the tempting bud in between his strong suckling pulls at her breast.

"Eric, I need you, now." Her words came out between heavy pants. She was so turned on right now, if he looked at her at certain way and she'd explode.

Slowly releasing the swollen nipple, he raised his head, his breath coming out in heavy pants. "Don't say that. I'm holding on by a thread as it is. I'm not going to take you like an over eager teenager. Whenever I'm around you my control goes right out the window."

"What part of *I need you*, are you not getting? This is what you wanted, right?"

"Right here?" he questioned with a raised eyebrow.

"Right here, right now. Hurry, I can't stand it anymore." She answered hastily, panting heavily.

Eric made no move to comply with her demand, burying his face in between her neck and shoulder; he planted small, chaste kisses as he went. He didn't dare take her right here in the middle of a dark parking lot against the side of a rough building. She already mistrusted him enough as it was; no matter how much he'd want to. Rebecca began to desperately grind her wet mound against his hidden cock in search of relief, almost undoing his good intentions.

The sound of a car door slamming was like a bucket of cold water being thrown over her heated body. What was she doing? She usually had more control over herself than this. What was wrong with her? Just a moment ago this was the man that beat up a guy for just dancing with her. Granted; it was leading to more than *just* dancing, but that didn't mean he was right in what he did, did it?

For God's sake; he was a werewolf! For all she knew he was just as dangerous as the man that had attacked her all those years ago and here she was dry humping him? She must be insane—clinical-deranged-out of her mind-insane!

"Let me go." She whispered, pushing away from him. She had to get away from him before she made a big mistake.

"Why?" He mumbled as he kissed and sucked at the soft skin below her ear lobe. Rebecca was thinking too much again and when that happened; she fled. This time, he wasn't letting her run, *this* time she wasn't going to run from him.

"You weren't complaining a moment ago." He pointed out, thrusting his covered cock up against her pulsing clit; a satisfied smile curved on his face when she emitted a small, breathless moan.

Digging her nails into his shoulders, she glared at him, her teeth clenching in anger. "I'm drunk, Eric." She latched onto the excuse like a lifeline. She wasn't necessarily *drunk* in the way she implied. But whether it was Eric's kisses and his hands on her or the one drink she'd had inside, she was left feeling dizzy and highly aroused all at once.

Part of her didn't want Eric to put her down on her feet, but she was silently grateful when his expression changed from teasing to concern. Lowering her to her feet, Eric held onto her arms as she found her footing on her shaking legs. Once she was in no danger of falling, he transferred his grip to her wrist and began pulling her back toward his black hummer. Shaking her head, Rebecca weakly beat against Eric's tugging arm

"What the hell are you doing now?"

Coming to a stop beside the passenger door, Eric pulled out his keys to press a button on a small keypad. With a low beeping, the door unlocked. Shoving his keys away, he jerked the large door open before tugging her further.

Letting go of her wrist, Eric took a step back from her, his hand motioning toward the hummer. "Get in." he said roughly.
Taking unsteady step back, Rebecca groaned and rubbed at her head. How was she ever going to get away from him? "No. I'm not going anywhere with you." She stated, stubbornly shaking her head.

Dropping his arm behind her like a road block when she would have turned away, Eric stepped closer to her. His expression told her that he wasn't in the mood to listen to her. "Get the fuck in the car." He whispered firmly.

She shook her head. A faint smirk played upon her lips. "You want to talk about my language? I'm not inebriated, Eric. I can take myself home. I don't need your help." Shoving at him to make him move out of her way didn't do her any good but pissed her off when he simply watched her.

"I know that." he slowly bit out. "But I am not going to worry about you getting into an accident because you are being too stubborn. Now; get in that damn seat and buckle up before I do it for you."

For a moment, Rebecca paused. He wouldn't really do that, would he? "You can't do that." she argued with disbelief.

Without another word, Eric made good on his threat. Crowding into her space, he bent down; his strong arms scooped her up like she was no more than a child's doll. Before she could release the cry of outrage that swelled in her throat, Eric had dumped her roughly on the high passenger seat.

When she attempted to push out of the seat, she gasped when Eric laid a heavy hand over the swell of her breast, pinning her back against the seat as he jerked the seat belt over her. Making sure she was buckled in, Eric stepped back, slamming the door shut before striding around to his side.

Once he settled in the driver's seat, the close proximity between them had her mouth going dry and her heart thundering painfully in her chest. It would appear she'd pushed Eric too far this time. She just worried what price she'd be paying in the end.

* ~ * ~ *

So much for my grand plan...

Rebecca slouched in her seat with a fallen look. With a faint pout, her arms crossed over chest as she looked over at Eric. His face was set in stone, his expression dark. She knew it was her fault, not that she fully understood why. What right did he have to be so upset with her? She was nothing to him.

He knew she was human and if her past experience with his kind was any clue; they *hated* humans. Damon was the one of a few shifters that she felt safe around. She didn't feel safe around Eric. She felt hunted and constantly pursued, but at the same time she felt a pull between them, a pull that she was firm on fighting.

Bossy flea brains!

She glared at him, taking notice of how his fingers gripped the steering so tightly that his knuckles turned white. She had no doubt he could have crushed the black leather covered steel without much effort. Would he turn that same strength on her once he knew her secret?

Abruptly, Eric's breath huffed out between his lips with a near snarl.

"Stop glaring at me."

Startled, Rebecca turned to face the window so quickly she nearly knocked her forehead against the glass. She watched as they turned away from the main street and down a dark, curved road. The road was bracketed by tall pine trees as they made their way around the high incline. Brow knitting with confusion, Rebecca slowly looked away from her window to face the windshield. Where was he taking her? One thing was for certain, he had no intention of taking her to her apartment.

"Where are we going?" she asked hesitantly, before casting him a fleeting glance.

Eric sat stiff in his seat, his eyes glued on the dark road ahead and as he maneuvered the hummer around the sharp turns. His lips were pressed in their usual thin line, attesting that he wasn't in the best of moods for a chit-chat.

Much to her surprise, he replied. "I'm taking you back to my house tonight."

Rebecca didn't know what she should say first. Why was he taking her back to his home? Why was he taking some dark road that she'd never seen before? And why in all that was holy was he acting angry with her? She shook her head before slamming it back against the seat with frustration. Squeezing her eyes closed she was beginning to regret her earlier actions –or at least she regretted that he'd caught her.

"I'm not going to your house, Eric. Take me back." she ordered with a surprisingly firm tone.

He didn't reply. Opening her eyes, she looked back over at him. He looked as if she hadn't even said a word. Perhaps he didn't hear her?

"Did you hear me? Do I need to speak louder for you?" she bit out sarcastically.

The corner of his lips curled slightly. "I have perfect hearing, Rebecca."

"Then take me back." again, he didn't respond. His cold shoulder routine was really getting old. "Are you listening to me?"

"Yes. I'm just not replying to you."

"Why not?"

"Cause I am sick to death of fighting with you. As I said earlier, we are going to have a long, drawn out discussion about us and I won't let you run and hide from it anymore."

She rolled her eyes at his explanation. This again? She was really getting sick of repeating herself to him over and over. She wasn't a playing-hard-to-get girl, she was a not-interested; good-bye girl. Why couldn't he simply understand that?

Before she could toss her rehearsed retort at him, Eric glanced at her before speaking once more. "How much did you drink tonight?"

"What do you care?" she bit out turning away from him.
"I care because you aren't going to use that excuse that you are drunk on me again."

Sighing, she tossed her hands up in the air. "I had one drink. Aside from a bit of a buzz; I am fine."

"Good. Once we get at my house, I'll get you some coffee and food and then we're going to talk about your actions tonight."
Her actions? What was she? A child?

"Can't you see how ridiculous you are acting?" she scoffed.
Out of nowhere, Eric jerked sharply on the steering wheel, pulling the hummer off of the dark road and into a flat dirt patch. At the abrupt movement, Rebecca pressed herself against her seat, her eyes going wide with shock. Dropping his hands from the wheel, Eric turned to glare at her. Maybe *glare* was too mild of a term for the way he looked at her now. If it were possible his look could have fried her on the spot.

I've really stepped in it this time, Rebecca thought.

Holding up a finger at her while the rest of his hand clenched tightly, Eric bit out. "What was ridiculous was your stupid stunt tonight. There is nothing *ridiculous* about what I am feeling right now. There certainly wouldn't have been anything ridiculous about what happened in the bar if I hadn't had control over myself."

She shook her head at him. "Cut the ego-macho bull shit."

"You're getting quite a mouth on you, Rebecca." He mused with a scowl. "What happened to the woman that was too afraid to look at me? Let alone argue with me just months ago?"

Rebecca clenched her hands into fists in her lap to prevent herself from giving in to the urge to attack him. "She finally realized what a prick you are. You're just acting this way because I want nothing to do with you. Well, damn your stupid ego! I want nothing to do with you—get over it. You and I both know that you wouldn't have actually attacked Josh over me."

Pressing his lips into a hard line, Eric regarded her with a hard look. He seemed to be breaking down what she'd said to him before he would choose whether to say anything to her or not. With a shift of hard muscle, his arm lifted toward her. She flinched back out of fear of what he was.

Seeing her reaction, he paused before his hand gripped her flowing locks, pulling her close to him. Her hands flew out, pressing against his hard chest in attempt to ward him off.
Her arms trembled as despite her effort to hold him away from her, Eric pulled her face closer to his. With just a few inches separating their lips, he smirked down at her with some sort of victory.

"As you've said before, you don't know me and you certainly don't know what I am or am not capable of doing when it comes to you. Don't tempt fate with me any more than you already have." He warned. Taking in her wide eyed look, his smirk widened. "Fear?" he scoffed with amusement. "Good. I won't tolerate what happened tonight again." Without kissing her as she'd been preparing herself for; half scared and half thrilled, Rebecca found his hands falling away from her. Turning away from her, Eric pulled the hummer back onto the dark road without a further word.

Her stubbornness may have been made of iron against his words, but the look she'd just seen in his eyes left her shivering with fear. Trying to wipe the memory of Eric's hands and mouth on her would never be good enough to free her from what was between them. She was left with only one choice now. She would have to leave.

11

With a heavy sigh, Rebecca forced herself to remain sitting on the couch as Eric spoke softly to Sarah as he escorted his mother to the door. It wasn't hard to miss the look that had crossed Sarah's aged face as she watched Eric towing Rebecca inside that house like she was a disobedient child. Sarah had eyed her short dress and seducing makeup with confusion. It was only after she noticed Eric's possessive hand clutching over Rebecca's that Sarah's look of confusion quickly changed to disapproval.

That makes two of us.

When Sarah's lips had parted to question Eric's actions, but when Eric gave her a quelling look, she remained silent. After tugging her through the dining room and into the dark living room, Eric wiped at a nearby light switch. Rebecca blinked as the living room was suddenly flooded with light. Loosening his hold on her hand, he led her to the couch.

"Sit down." He grumbled while gently pushing her onto the worn cushion.

Glaring at his tone, she jerked her hand free from his grasp before taking her time to settle onto the seat. From her seat she could hear the hushed voices of Eric and Sarah in the next room. Though she couldn't discern what was being said, she suspected that they must be discussing her. When Sarah had first approached her about becoming Emma and Travis's nanny, she'd firmly told Rebecca that her son was not a man that she could get involved with. With her current appearance, with no doubt; Sarah must think she was attempting to move herself into Eric's bed.

Quite the opposite, Rebecca was desperately trying to stay away from him, not that he was making it easy. If she couldn't fight this intense attraction she had for Eric, she would have to force herself to leave and find a new home. The thought was painful. But then so would death if Eric discovered her secret.

Without even hearing a creaking floor board, Rebecca glanced up to see Eric regarding her with a calculating expression. Jumping with fright, she pressed a hand to her racing heart. Sharpening her gaze at him, she sniped. "You should wear a bell."

As before in the Hummer, he didn't respond. Instead he merely looked at her. After a moment, his nose twitched slightly. The innocent twitch suddenly turned to a full on nose curl with a look of distaste.

Sighing heavily, he approached her. "Come with me." It wasn't a request, nor where his words spoken gently. With Eric everything he said to her always seemed to be like he was ordering his dog to follow him. That reference had her frowning with anger.

"Stop ordering me around." She bit out between clenched teeth.

Again the jerk didn't respond, instead he took possession of her hand once more and tugged her to her feet. Forcibly, he tugged her across the room to the stairs before leading her upward.

"Eric, what do you think you are doing?" she practically hissed out as they reached the top of the landing. She found herself glancing toward the twin's bedroom with apprehension. She didn't want them to see her like this. She still had time to get away from him before this went any further. "Eric—" Before she could say another word to him, she abruptly found herself being tugged through the dark doorway of his bed room. Her mouth with dry and her stomach clenched. She highly doubted his intention was to take her to his room to talk.

Navigating through the dark room without difficulty, Eric pulled her with him into the connecting master bathroom. His hand angrily swiping against the wall until his hand hit the light switch. Allowing her to jerk her hand from his possession, Eric motioned to the glass enclosed shower stall. "Get cleaned up."

Had she heard him right? This night was going from bad to very, very dangerous right before her eyes. "W-Why?" for a moment he seemed to struggle with his answer before settling to wave a frustrated hand at her.

"I will not be able to talk to you like this."

"Like what?"

"Like a temptress attempting to lure a male to her." taking a breath, he released it with a moan of appreciation. "And you tempt me very much, Rebecca."

"It was never meant to tempt *you*." She bit out in anger. Instantly his eyes went hard at her words. She couldn't help her instinct to retreat from him until her back was pressed firmly against the bare wall beside the sink as he moved further into her personal space. When would she learn to just shut up?

"It should have been." Allowing his gaze to travel down the length of her, his jaw clenched tightly. "I'll find you some clothes of mine to wear for the time being, but I plan on burning those clothes so that no other will ever see you in it again." he stated with a menacing tone.

Why was he acting so…possessive? It made no sense to her. Anger and jealousy she understood coming from Eric, but this possessiveness that he was showing scared her. If she blindly followed his orders, she would be discovered. She'd been lucky to wear a blouse that covered her scars but combined with the short skirt had given her a sexy appeal. If Eric saw her scars—he would know what had caused them. In a flash her fists shot to the smooth labels of her blouse, her fingers clenched in the material as if to hold it in place against his eyes.

When he turned to leave the bathroom, she called after him in haste. "Don't bother; I'm not staying to talk to you. I'm leaving right now." she said with a stubborn lift of her chin.

Pausing just outside the bathroom, Eric turned at the waist to look back at her. To her astonishment, he was chuckling with amusement; his head shook gently at her words. When his amused expression didn't waver, she glared back at him in response; crossing her arms over her breasts.

When his laughter dwindled, he sighed, rubbing a large hand over his jaw. "How do you think you can go home? It's at least a two hour walk back to town."

"I don't care. I'll walk all night if I have to. Maybe I will get lucky and someone will see me in my streetwalker clothes and will give me a lift." She didn't know what possessed her to say the last of her words, but it gave her a small thrill to see Eric's eyes flash with anger.

"Don't put that image in my head, Rebecca." He warned. His voice hard and tight as every ounce of his previous amusement was gone.

"Why were you in that bar like this?" he asked taking a step closer to her.

Knowing that Eric's question that would lead her down a long road that she didn't want to travel, she bit her tongue to prevent from speaking. Pressing her lips together stubbornly, she moved toward the door. Moving to walk past him, she prayed that he would do what he normally did when he became frustrated with her stubbornness and just storm off.

Instead of doing as she'd hoped, his hand reached out and gripped her arm, jerking her to a halt. Turning her to face him, Eric pressed her against the doorway of the bathroom, his eyes burning over her face. Rebecca found her body trembling and her mouth going dry as he pressing into her personal space. He was so close to her that the flavor of his skin was practically on her tongue.

"*Answer me.*" He bit out slowly. "Did you go there looking for a lover? Were you on the hunt for someone to give you what only I can and will?"

"Don't flatter yourself." She hissed out, pushing at his chest in effort to put some space between them. "My personal life is none of your business."

Not acknowledging her words, he went on. "Do you really think that you can erase what happened between us by taking someone else to your bed?"

"If I'm lucky." She whispered musingly looking away from him. Shaking his head, he tucked a finger beneath her chin, forcing her eyes to meet him.

"This between us will not go away, and certainly not with another touching you. Why do you fight this?" he asked perplexed.

"Let me leave, Eric." She whispered, refusing to acknowledge his question.

His gaze softened, his hand falling away from her face. "Why do you fear this or is it me you fear?"

"Because you're a ticking time bomb." He visibly flinched at her words, but she forced herself to ignore it. "If I let my guard down with you, one day; whatever this attraction thing is, it will destroy everything. There are things about me that you don't know, Eric and I want to keep it that way. What is between us is a simple addiction and addictions can be beaten if the will is strong enough."

"I don't want to beat it." he growled out. "I want you, Rebecca." He breathed against her lips just before he covered her parted ones. At the brush of his lips, heat instantly bloomed in her stomach, spreading like licking flames to her womanhood. She fought against melting against his seducing mouth, but with a small moan, Rebecca found herself leaning against his mouth, begging for more. Her hands tightened on his bare chest, clutching him tighter to her.

Spearing his hand through her hair, pulling the silky strands free from their confines, Eric held her immobile as his lips slid from her lips to trail to her jaw. His lips parted and caressed the underside of her jaw. Nipping and sucking, he moved further down her neck as his free hand slid up her skirt from behind. Her channel clenched with delight as his hand brushed against the curve of her buttocks before his hand gripped her ass tightly.

Unwillingly her hips bucked against him with need. Desire heating her blood, she found it impossible not to touch him, not to need him. She wanted him inside her, his body covering hers, possessing hers. But could she withstand the price that she would be paying? At the thought, dazed eyes opened as she panted with need. Inwardly she cried with despair that she couldn't give up her control to him. Even for just a short time, it would lead to disaster if she didn't do something. She had to stop him.

"Eric…" she began in effort to stop him.

The unspoken words in Rebecca's mind vanished as Eric's hand beneath her skirt was ripped away. Before disappointment could settle over her, his hand returned only to move between their bodies and slid into the front of her panties. Gasping, her head fell back against the door jamb as his calloused fingers stroked over her clit and slid through the folds of her sex. All rational thought left her in that moment, leaving only him and the hunger that only he could sate.

Panting heavily, Eric lifted his face from her neck to press his forehead against hers; never did his stroking fingers slow their delicious movements. "Tonight," he began in a husky voice. "Give me tonight. I promise that nothing will harm you afterwards. I will be here with you. Let me show you how it can be between us." He pleaded with heavy pants.

Fighting against the desire coursing through her body, she comprehended his words. A pang of realization hit her like a punch to the gut. Any hope and certainty that she'd had that she could keep Eric at bay fell. Eric would never leave her alone and in that moment, she was done fighting. Either way, she would have to leave Ravenwillow. Eric was too stubborn not to leave her alone and if Damon could discover her secret, how long would it be before Eric did as well?

Like a steel door of a bank vault slamming shut, her decision was made. She would give this one night to herself. She would claim this moment with Eric for herself to remember in the years to come. She would hold him to her and give her body over to this insatiable need. But tomorrow she would leave and forever vanish from his life.

* ~ * ~ *

Eric's wolf growled with victory the moment he saw acceptance fill Rebecca's gaze. But it wasn't enough. He had to hear her say it. Swirling his thumb around her swollen clit, his growl vibrated his chest against hers as a gasp of pleasure escaped her.

Teasing her bottom lip with his teeth, he whispered against her lips. "What's your answer?"

Her nails bit into his arms as she gripped him tightly in effort to anchor herself to something as her climax began to build. Gasping for air, her eyes closed as she nodded her head quickly. When she didn't open her eyes to look at him; let alone voice her answer, Eric's stroking fingers slowed along her dewy petals, barely moving at all. Her eyes flashed open; her expression was one of need, a need that he was holding out of reach for her.

Satisfaction filled him. Good. He liked that only he was able to give her this, but he wanted her to finally acknowledge it. Because after tonight, there would be no going back to the way things were. Eric didn't full accept what Rebecca may or may not be to him, but he would be damned if he let her slip through his fingers.

"Eric..." she groaned out almost in pain.

"Say it. Tell me you want me, want this." his tone was firm, giving her no room to deny what was happening. She would tell him and when she did, there would be no way for her to pretend that nothing happened.

"I do. I want this and I want you, just don't stop." She moaned, driving against his fingers in effort to seek release.

The words had barely left her lips before Eric was jerking his hands from her. Bending, he swept her up into his arms like she was a precious possession of his. Never taking his eyes from hers, he walked to the bed, gently lowering her onto the wrinkled comforter.

Immediately, his body blanketed hers, his hips settling into the warm cradle of her thighs as they fell open on either side of him. Bracing his weight on his arms that he rested on either side of her head, he leaned closer; the sight of her parted lips was too much of a temptation to ignore. With his movement, Rebecca seemed to attempt to sink further into the mattress beneath her the closer his lips came. Slowing his decent, he smirked at her.

The action was both laughable and adorable. How had he not noticed this about her before? That was the past. From this moment, he vowed to discover all that he could about his human. He would protect her from his pack and keep her away from the eager eyes of others—including Damon. Choosing to ignore the wave of jealousy that rose up in him, he shifted his focus back to tasting her tempting lips.

Descending once more until his nose brushed hers, a tremble danced through her body as he threaded his hand in her waves of hair. He'd yet to kiss her and already she was trembling with need. Her eyes were on his, watching him with…fear?

Reaching his senses out to her, he scented her desire for him, but beneath her heady scent calling to him was something he'd not noticed before. Fear. Fear of him? His wolf whined at this realization. Unsure how to get rid of the bitter scent of fear that distracted him from everything else, he withdrew his clutching fingers from her tresses to stroke the back of his fingers down her cheek.

"What is wrong, Rebecca?" He asked softly. Closing the small space between their faces, he brushed his lips against hers. His kiss was gentle, coaxing and calming. Beneath him he felt her tense and gasp against his mouth.

His hardened cock pulsed through his pants with need. Her scent was affecting him more every second that passed. He had to have her. He would have her, but first he felt a stronger need rise up in him; the need to protect and reassure her. Easing back, he felt pride fill his chest as some of her apprehension in her eyes had faded in response to his kiss. The warm brown color now shimmered with a glazed look of desire—only desire.

Breathing heavily, Rebecca's hands rose to touch him, but at the last instant her delicate hands curled into small fists before lowering to her sides at the bed. Was she afraid to touch him? Closing her eyes, she appeared to be gathering courage to say something to him. He waited until her eyes slowly lifted to his again and she spoke.

"I've…never…I mean…" with a groan she covered her face with her hands. Eric concentrated on following and deciphering what she was trying to say to him. With realization, he felt his beast grow ten times stronger within his chest. She was…a *virgin*?

Only ours! We are her first and last forever. Claim her now!

Shaking off the possessive thoughts of his wolf, he shared down at her uncertain gaze. "You've never been with anybody? Even at your age?" Eric didn't really know how old Rebecca was in fact, but he knew enough to know that she was old enough to have had several lovers. So why hadn't she?

Shaking her head as heat flooded her face; Rebecca's next words answered his unspoken question. "I never really wanted to, until tonight or…" her worlds trailed off as her cheeks heated further.

"Until me." Eric finished, pride filling his voice.

Biting down on her bottom lip, Rebecca nodded slowly. "I want to know what I have been missing out on, Eric. Will you show me?" Eric nearly groaned aloud at her sweet, innocent plea. It was all he could do to not fall upon her, shredding the offending skirt and blouse and claim her body for his own. At the thought, his wolf rose up faster and stronger than ever before. Grappling for control, his eyes squeezed closed as his hands curled tightly into the bedspread at the sides of her face.

"Eric?" Rebecca's soft voice echoed in his ears as he fought against not only his need of her, but his wolf's as well.

Snarling with defeat once Eric's strong will overcame his inner beast, Eric felt his wolf sink back into the dark corners of his mind, relinquishing control. Once he was certain that his wolf was contained, his eyes snapped open. Not about to give her an opportunity to change her mind, his lips covered hers so abruptly that he stole the air from her lungs.

Groaning against her lips, he hands dipped beneath her skirt, following the warm skin of her thighs until her firm buttocks filled his hands. Squeezing the globes in his hands, he lifted her off the mattress to hold her loins against his throbbing shaft. The material of his stolen sweats did nothing to hide his need of her, but only served to irritate him that he couldn't feel her skin against his own.

Almost against his will, his hips bucked, thrusting his shaft against the soft apex of her thighs. With this action, Rebecca gasped against his lips, her hands rising up to clutch at the back of his neck. The moment her lips parted beneath his, he took advantage.

Sweeping his tongue forward, he explored her mouth. The taste of her exploded among all his sense, nearly taking him over the edge. Everything that he'd denied himself of her no longer mattered. He couldn't—he wouldn't wait for her a second longer.

Breaking the kiss, they both stared at each other, both of them struggling to draw in enough air for a single breath. Unable to stand not feeling her soft skin against his own, Eric swiftly ripped his shirt over his head before tossing it across the room.

"I can't decide what to do to you first." He breathed out roughly against her lips. Moving his hands from their possessive hold of her buttocks, he slid them down to cover her outer thighs, smoothing and shaping the warm, silky skin with reverent strokes.

"My mouth waters with the thought of putting my mouth here." His hand cupped her sex causing Rebecca to arch into his hand. "You want me to taste you, don't you? You want to feel my mouth on there; sucking and licking you until you can't stand it. But your sweet sex isn't the only place I plan on tasting tonight. There is so much I want and plan to do to you tonight."

Leaning back, he grinned wickedly down at her. If it were possible, her delicious scent intensified and filled the air everywhere. Closing his eyes with pleasure, he deeply inhaled. Gods, she was like a fucking drug. He wanted to be surrounded by that scent every damn day.

Still clutching at his neck, Rebecca's small nails dug into his skin at his words. "Eric…" she gasped as his hand between her thighs began to slide back and forth against the front of her panties. "Please…"

"But first," he began, pulling his hand from beneath her skirt. "I want to see you—all of you." With those whispered words, Eric slid his hands from her thighs to her hips and to her blouse. Starting from the bottom, he slipped one black button free at a time. The silky material of her blouse parted to reveal her the curve of her stomach and more creamy skin as he went.

12

Fear crept over her chest like a spear of ice at Eric's whispered words. Her wide eyes watched with tribulation as his hands began flicking each button of her blouse open from the bottom. Already the labels of her scarlet blouse had fallen open to display the plump flesh of her stomach. If he undid two more buttons he would see her scars. If Eric saw her scars he would know the truth. This couldn't be happen! She had to stop him.

Fighting against the delicious heat that pooled in her loins, her hands gripped his wrists with surprising speed, attempting to halt his movements. Eric's eyes leapt to hers with surprise.

She shook her head. "Stop…" the single word emerged with a soft gasp. "Not that."

Confused, Eric quirked an eyebrow at her as his hands stilled on the fourth button. "Why not?" Releasing his wrists, Rebecca's hands lifted to the top of her blouse, fisting the material over her heaving breasts almost protectively.

"I'm not comfortable…" her words trailed off when Eric's weight shifted away from her as he suddenly moved to lie beside her. With his large, powerful arm curling around the top of her head on the mattress, he leaned closer. His expression wasn't angry or even put out like she'd expected. Instead he looked down at her with a soft expression.

"I want you to be comfortable, Rebecca. With me and with what's about to happen between us. I've wanted this too badly to fuck it up now. But you have to trust me at some point."

Biting her lip, Rebecca looked away from him, before reluctantly nodding. "Just...not tonight?" she pleaded. It wouldn't matter anyway. There would be no other time after tonight. But she didn't' want to worry about her secretive scars or fear of discovery. She wasn't to be blinded to everything around her tonight except for Eric.

Nodding, Eric reached up to cover one of her heavy breasts in his large palm, instantly her nipples hardened, pushing at the thin material of her bra and blouse to stab at his hand. Finding the hard bud straining forward, he flicked the hard nub with his thumb as he covered her lips with a gentle touch. His lips, tongue and teeth lavished attention on her mouth as his hand slid from her breast to slide along the warm slope of her stomach before traveling upward and disappearing beneath her blouse.

At the feel of his hot hand against her stomach, Rebecca jumped, startled; she broke away from his lips. "Eric! You agreed—"

"I agreed to keep it on and I agree not to look. I never said that I wouldn't get your soft breasts into my hands though." To prove his point, Eric's hands slid up further. The closer his hand moved toward her breasts, she shivered as gooseflesh with heated awareness slid over her skin following the trail of his burning hand. Air left her lungs the moment that Eric's hand met the thin material of her bra.

Shoving the lacy cups out of his way, Rebecca found herself engulfed by his scorching hands. The moment his hand closed over her uncovered breast, her womb clenched and her hips flexed beneath him at his touch.

"Eric…" she gasped as he kneaded her soft flesh before his touch became teasing and his attention turned on her aroused nipple.

Using his thumb as forefinger, he teased the hard peak with plucking strokes. Without warning, his head lowered toward her covered chest. Before she could guess his intent, his hot mouth found her other breast through the thin material of her blouse. Finding her nipple straining against the silk fabric, he drew it into the burning cavern of his mouth, silk and all. Flames licked at her insides at the feel of his mouth on her breast as his hand and fingers caressed and teased her other. The wet silk of her blouse slid back and forth over her nipple like a teasing caress while Eric mouth began drawing hard.

Closing her eyes, she moaned at the feeling. Her hands reached up to fist tightly in the turfs of his hair, holding him to her as he lavished attention upon her heavy aching breast. Her eyes jumped open as his teeth nipped and pulled at her pulsing nipple. Who would have thought that such a simple act would feel so good? Rebecca panted as a rush of liquid heat rushed between her thighs as every muscle in her body coiled tighter and tighter. Before the flames of her desire could completely consume her, Eric's face lifted away from her breast as his hand beneath her blouse pulled away. Lifting her dazed gaze to his, she saw that his eyes glowed as he appeared nearly frenzied.

Moving quickly, his hands shot down to her skirt, franticly searching for a zipper before he gave up and simply began tugging the soft material down her thighs. "I have to taste you." He growled out. "Now." His heavy breaths emerged more harsh and rough than ever before.

Startled, Rebecca looked at him with wide eyes. Surely he didn't mean that he intended to...no it wasn't possible, people didn't do that...did they? Heart pounding faster and mouth going dry; she gulped past the nervous lump that formed in her throat.

"Eric? I don't think..." her words died on her lips as her shirt was jerked free and flung away.

Smoothing his hands over her hips, Eric's fingers hooked in her lacy thong before tossing those across the room as well. Sliding down the bed, Eric's hands cupped her trembling legs from behind her knees, spreading her for his gaze. Instantly, Rebecca rushed to cover herself, her face becoming so hot that she would had thought it was on fire. Chuckling at her attempt, his hands took possession of her wrists, pulling them up before pinning them at either side of her head as he rose over her. A spark of pleasure shot through her as his concealed shaft slid against her thigh with his movement.

"Don't do that." he whispered gently.

Her heart pounded so hard she could practically feel the heavy beats in her throat. "What?" she breathed out.

"Cover yourself. Don't do that again. I want to see, taste and touch all of you and eventually I will." He whispered firmly, his eyes sweeping over her whole body in indication.

Swallowing, Rebecca squirmed beneath him. "But...I...why would you...?"

Lord, what was wrong with her? She couldn't even say it. Though the mere thought of Eric's mouth on her sex, made her practically climax on the spot, she never actually thought he would do such a thing. That was just something people did in books...wasn't it?

Smirking at her discomfort, Eric pressed an open kiss to the underside of her chin and then down her neck, nipping with his teeth at the soft skin over her pounding pulse, he lifted his head. "Did you really think this sweet place between your hot thighs was safe from me?" Rebecca felt her womb clench at his words.

Oh God, I'm so done for…

Shaking his head, Eric's grin widened and nearly turned sinister. "I plan on thoroughly tasting you there, until you never know what it was like before I did." Pausing he let go of her wrists as he slid down the bed back to his previous spot between her spread legs. "Don't move your hands; keep them right where I left them." He ordered with a grin.

Unable to control herself, she fisted her hands in the comforter beneath her as her whole body seemed to tremble with anxiety and anticipation. As her thighs were spread wider when his shoulders pressed between them, Rebecca felt she would jump out of her skin with waiting. She was both terrified and excited. It was an exhilarating combination. When his mouth settled over her aching clit, she jumped. "Eric!"

Briefly, he lifted his mouth from her sex, his hands gripping the back of her thighs tightly. "Shh." He hushed slowly. "You cannot be too loud or else you'll wake Emma and Travis." The image he invoked nearly had Rebecca scrambling away from him. Why hadn't she thought of that? just when she was about to call the all thing off, Eric's lips settled over her clit once more, sucking and nipping at the aching flesh.

"Oh...shit." she moaned, her hips arching upward toward his mouth in reaction.

Eric chuckled against her clit as he briefly lifted his lips off her to swipe at the small, swollen bud of nerves with his tongue. "Such language. Tisk, tisk." He teased, his teasing tongue slipping lower along her sex. The sensations building at each flick and swipe of his tongue and caress of his lips were maddening her. The pressure that coiled tighter and tighter within her was too much to bear.

"Eric," she gasped out helplessly. "Stop, I can't do this. It's too much."

Not answering her, Eric flicked his tongue against the entrance of her sex before slowly drawing it back up to the top of her clit. Back and forth his tongue went, up and down always ending with his lips wrapped around the top of her clit. Just when she thought she would go crazy with what was being done to her, she felt something else touch her sex. It was his hand. His seeking fingers explored her wet petals with slow strokes.

"Damn, I knew you would feel like this. Perfect and mine."

"I'm not—" she was about to tell him that she wasn't his when one of his fingers gently penetrated her channel, cutting off her words. It was strange having his finger inside her; she didn't know how to react. His finger began to move, retreating only to return, pushing through her soft passage. His mouth began drawing and his tongue flicking against her clit as he began to move his finger faster.

Her hips bucked as the inferno inside her had grown out of control. Much to her confusion she felt her inner wall flex over and over, gripping his thrusting finger tightly. "Eric—!" she cried out as she felt the tight pressure within her explode. Struggling for air, her body was thrown into wave after wave of desire. Barely having enough time to censor her reaction, her hands shot up, clamping over her mouth as she cried out. She moaned behind her hands as pleasure shot though her over and over again like arcs of lightening as Eric's mouth continued to drive her higher.

"That's it." he cooed rising up on his knees, his hand planted on the mattress beside her left hip as his other hand was still buried between her thighs continued to move back and forth as his thumb stroked her clit in fast circular strokes. "Fuck, you're sexier than ever like this." With those husky words whispered above her a second finger joined his first, continuing their thrusting dance within her silken channel.

The small bite of pain at being stretched by his fingers was barely noticeable as the tsunami of desire continued to overtake her. When the raging waves of her orgasm began to dwindle, Rebecca felt her body fall into a nearly drugged state. Her hands limply fell from her mouth to fall at her sides. Panting, her dazed eyes met his. "So that's what I've been missing out on all this time." She remarked with a faint smile.

"Not so fast," Eric said with a smile. "It's not over yet."

Earlier she'd debated whether having sex with Eric was a wise decision. Now she knew.

I am so done for…

* ~ * ~ *

Deep inside himself, Eric's wolf was in frenzy. The taste of her had been divine and had nearly driven him to pin her down as he took her like his beast demanded. Watching as Rebecca came apart in his arms was almost enough to make him explode. Once her eyes became glazed with the aftermath of her orgasm, Eric felt his balls tighten as his shaft pulsed with painful need. There was no way that he couldn't wait a second longer.

With fumbling hands, he shoved his pants and boxers down his legs, allowing his straining hard length to spring free. Grasping the back of her bent knees, he pulled her legs up around his hips as he moved over her. Breath exploded out of his lungs as the tip of his shaft brushed against the wet petals of her sex briefly. Wrapping his hand around the base, he trailed the head of his cock up and down the length of her dewy sex. Beneath him, Rebecca gasped and writhed at the feel of his hard length.

"Eric…" she moaned softly. Though there was need in her voice, looking down he could see uncertainty in her eyes. This was her first time and he would need to remain in control for as long as he could.

Good luck with that. His wolf scoffed.

Gritting his teeth against the feel of her soft skin sliding against him, he attempted to sooth her. "I'll be gentle, Rebecca." When the uncertainty in her gaze didn't fade, he pressed his forehead against hers before brushing a gentle kiss over her parted lips. "Trust me." He whispered against her lips.

He felt her inhale deeply before she nodded. "Alright."

Sighing at her acceptance, Eric continued to kiss her as he positioned himself at her entrance. Slowly his hips pressed forward. Barely breaching her entrance, he felt his wolf howling with joy and pleasure. Fuck, she was tight, tighter than she'd been around his fingers as he'd pleasured her.

Panting heavily, he moved further into her. Rebecca's eyes were squeezed shut as her breathing was just as harsh as his own. His claws shot from his fingertips as her squeezing inner walls fluttered around his shaft. Moving another few inches deeper, he felt his spine tingle with painful need as the tip of his cock nudged her maidenhead.

His mind was swimming with pleasure of having her wet warmth wrapped around his aching cock. He couldn't remember the last time he'd felt such pure, raw pleasure with another. It was too much and his constant self control was running out quickly. He wouldn't be able to go slow this time, not even for his virgin partner.

With a groan of regret he fisted his claws in the bedspread beside her shoulders as he lowered his mouth to hers. Covering her panting lips, he lovingly took her lips, easing the tension from her at his invasion. Pulling back, barely separating their lips he met her dazed eyes.

"Forgive me, Rebecca."

Before she had a chance to question what he'd meant, his teeth grinded together as he lunged forward, fully burying himself within her. The moment he ripped through her barrier, he covered her lips as she cried out into his lips. With great pain, he forced himself to remain still, allowing her to accept the pain he'd unfortunately brought her and preparing her for the pleasure he'd soon give her.

Gasping at the feel of her hot depths, he moved one of his clenching hands from the bedspread to cover her dewy clit. Instantly he felt her passage clench and flutter around him as he awakened more need within her. Within seconds her soft cries of need began filling his ears, her body growing more relaxed.

"Eric…" she moaned softly, her soft body writhing beneath him restlessly. "Please move."

Pressing his forehead against hers, sweat beaded down his brow as he slowly pulled from her tight body only for his hips to slowly surge back against her. He had to have more of her. With a hissing breath, he lowered his mouth to her arching neck. His lips covered her flushed skin, kissing, licking and nipping. Each action caused her to flex around him like a fist.

"Next time I promise to be better." He vowed against her neck.

Ignoring the way she stiffened beneath him at his words, he began to move urgently into her. Sliding his hands down to her hips, his fingers dug into the curvy flesh there, no doubt leaving marks upon her pale skin.

If he'd known when he'd first met Rebecca that having her in his bed would be this glorious, he would have jumped her the first day; human or not. Over and over he drove into her. Each moan and cry that she tried to prevent from escaping her lips was like music to his ears. Every time he pulled from her, his hands on her hips would clench tighter before jerking her to meet his next driving thrust.

With his heart pounding in his ears and his wolf fighting to break free of his precarious hold on it, he felt his climax drawing closer and closer with every thrust inside her. Arching up against his thrusting hips, Rebecca cried out as she was thrown into a second climax. With her body tightening further around him, his balls tightened and pain shot through him as he thrusted one last time into her. Burying himself to the hilt, he made her take all of him, so that there was no doubt that *he* had taken her and that she was now *his.*

He shuttered, clenching his aching fangs as his seed shot into her. He'd never known it could be like this before and now that he had experienced this; he'd never let her go. Strength sapped from him, he debated whether he should move from the welcoming heat of her or remain buried in her until he was ready to have her again.

He scoffed silently within his mind. Like there was any question of whether he'd be having her again after this. She'd be lucky if he let her wear clothes or ever leave his bed again. Gazing down at her, he smirked to see that her eyes were closed and her chest rising and falling with heavy pants.

Pushing up on his hands he was just about to pull free of her, he gasped in near pain as his chest began to ache as nothing he'd ever felt. Stealing his breath from him, his chest—his heart felt like a fire had been lit within it. Lowering his head, he reached for his wolf. He was surprised to find that his wolf as in a mad frenzy. What was happening to draw this kind of response from him? Pressing a hand to his chest, his eyes snapped open when he felt heat radiate from his heart.

Looking down, nothing could have prepared him for the shock that shot through him at what he saw. Emerging from the center of his chest was a ghostly ribbon that swirled and danced in the air, floating like it was seeking something. Instantly, his eyes fell on Rebecca's relaxed face. It couldn't be! Jerking back, he pulled from her body before tumbling back on his bare ass. With his sudden movement the ghostly thread was pulled further from the sleeping human on his bed.

Pain like never before assailed him, it was like something was being torn from him. How was this possible? Rebecca was his…mate. His *true* mate. It wasn't possible—it couldn't be! He'd already had a mate. Though with Emma and Travis's mother; Beth, his binding thread had never emerged when he'd taken her, but he'd still claimed her. He'd long given up hope of finding his true mate and now fate had delivered her to him—as a human.

As his heart raced with the speed of a runaway train, the pain and burning heat in his chest grew. Lowering his gaze to the ribbon of white mist extending from his heart began to fade away to nothing. Within his mind he howled with pain as he'd lost the precious moment to claim her as his. Almost instantly his wolf's angered thoughts bombarded his mind.

You denied us our mate! After so long! I want her! Whether she is human or shifter, I do not care! Claim her now! Make the binding thread return!

What was he to do now? His chest ached with incompletion, with the lack of the bond that should have been cemented in that precarious moment. He had to be the first shifter to deny the call of the Binding Thread, to deny himself the one woman meant solely for him.
Rising to his unsteady legs, Eric stumbled into the bathroom, gripping the edge of the sink, he stared at his reflection. He looked pale and shaken. Eric Daniels wasn't a man to be *shaken*! He was an Alpha, a ruler over hundreds of wolf shifters. Nothing could ever raddle his control, until now.

Thinking back, he was finally seeing everything that he'd questioned over the past three months since meeting Rebecca fall into place. This explained his wolf emerging, his unexplainable jealousy at seeing Damon near her and not to mention his intense desire for her. All the signs had been there. How was it possible for him to ignore them all this time? Deep down his wolf had known, but not him. Had what Beth done to him nearly blinded him to his true mate?

The need within him to return to her and fully claim her overtook his mind like an addict's next fix. Claiming her fully wouldn't be easy. Unlike Doyle Mackenzie and his brother Robert who had both taken human mates, with wolves it simply wasn't done. Wolf shifters were traditional and their hate for humans ran deep. Eric had never thought that he would have to face this when claiming his mate. He'd always assumed she'd be a shifter or that he'd have no one at all.

When it came to claiming humans as true mates, it was a double edged sword for many shifters. Just because the person was their true mate didn't guarantee that the mating bite would turn their human mate. Doyle's mate; Aria, was living proof of that fact. Also in some isolated cases, the transformation from human to shifter proved to be too much for the fragile human body to withstand and had resulted in many shifters losing their mates forever.

Was that the fate that awaited him with Rebecca? Had he found his true mate only to lose her to a painful death? Even if he didn't give her his mating bite, he couldn't keep her a secret from his pack for long. The Act of Revealment would be issued and then it would be too late to woo her into the idea. Either way he looked at it; he may have only discovered his true mate to kill her. The only other option would be to let her go.

Glancing down at his shaft that already was growing hard once more, Eric grimaced at the sight of his spent seed mixed with Rebecca's virginal blood. Was it even possible for him to let her go now? Claws slicing against the polished wood of the sink counter, he shook his head. Looking at his reflection, he watched as his blue eyes glowed dangerously and his fangs grew. Rebecca was *his*! He may not have fully claimed her as a shifter, but he had claimed her as a man. It was enough for tonight. He would deal with the consequences later.

Grabbing a wash cloth, he quickly cleaned away the evidence that lingered on his hard length. Running the cloth under the hot water, he returned to the bedroom only to pause beside the bed. Rebecca had rolled onto her side in her sleep. Staring at the wrinkled scarlet blouse that brushed against the top curve of her round ass, he licked his lips. Damn it all if he didn't already need her again.

Claim our mate! His wolf snarled loudly.

Frowning Eric struggled to keep himself in check. He couldn't take her again, not this soon anyway. With his aching chest full of regret he moved forward. Kneeling on the bed behind her, he gently used the cloth to cleanse her between her closed thighs. In her sleep, Rebecca flinched from his gentle ministrations, her face deepening into a frown.

Bending to brush his lips against her brow, his nose nuzzling against the softness of her hair, he whispered softly to her. "Shh. I have you. Sleep for now, angel. Tomorrow everything changes for you…and for me."

Tossing the cloth over his shoulder once he'd cleaned away the evidence of their lovemaking, Eric tugged the soiled blanket out from underneath her to toss next to his closet. With care he pulled out the top sheet from beneath her. Settling on the bed behind her, he drew the thin sheet over the both of them as he pulled her closer to him. Even as close as she was to his bare skin, it didn't feel close enough and he knew it never would.

Ignoring the aching in his chest, he pressed his face into the soft waves of her hair as his eyes drew closed. Before sleep claimed him, he couldn't fight the waves of joy that echoed from his heart through his mind. Fate had given him another chance! He had a true mate now and by God he was going to keep her this time.

13

"Tell me about your family." Eric suddenly demanded early the next morning. Lying on her side with Eric's body spooning against her back, Rebecca forced herself to focus on his words and not the warm fingers he was presently trailing up and down the valley between her breasts. Brushing his caressing hand aside, she reached down to adjust the thin sheet over her breasts, effectively adding another barrier against Eric's relentless touch.

"Why?" she asked suspiciously.

It had been strange waking this morning with Eric's arms around her—if that what you could call it. The embrace she'd found herself in wasn't what she'd envisioned for a typical *morning after* cuddle. She'd awakened with one of his large hands covering one of her heavy breasts beneath her blouse while his other hand cupped her tender sex between her thighs possessively.

"Because I realized last night that I know next to nothing about you,"

Not turning to look at him, Rebecca shrugged nonchalantly. "Sarah told you about me the week I was hired."

"True. But back then I was avoiding you." He replied. She felt as though she could practically hear the smile in his voice that he must be wearing. She wasn't used to Eric being…nice. It threw her off and confused her.

"Is that what you call being a total ass face?"

Chuckling, Eric clicked his tongue at her scolding. "Such language."

Nuzzling his face in the curve of her neck, heat blossomed between her thighs as a shiver slid over her body at the contact. Behind her, Eric's grin widened at her attempt to brush him off. How could the simplest touch from him cause this much of a reaction from her?

Gulping, she forced her voice to emerge even and not to quiver like the rest of her. "You're a bad influence."

"We'll see." He responded cryptically as she felt his teeth nip at the sensitive dip of her neck. "Go on," he began, his hand trailing down her exposed arm in a gentle caress. "What is your family like? Your parents?"

Even at the heat his touch brought her, at his question Rebecca felt her chest tighten with pain at the memory of her loving parents. Her mother had been kind and gentle, always volunteering for some event in their community or filling their home with the smell of her delicious cooking. Her father was—had been reserved but a bit of a clown during the right moments. Like a flash of lightening across the sky, the memories of laughter and love were replaced by the images of her parent's deaths, their torn bodies lying in dark pools of their own blood.

Squeezing her eyes closed, her hands fisted against the edge of her pillow as she fought against the burning tears. Taking a deep inhale, with her heart shuttering in her chest, her eyes slowly opened.

"What of them?" she quietly asked, returning his question with a question.

Tightening his arm around her middle, Eric brushed his lips softly against her ear. "Is the subject of your family a hard one?" he inquired, the teasing note gone from his voice.

A part of Rebecca was thankful that he'd sensed how upset she was at the mention of her parents, but it didn't change the fact that she couldn't tell him the truth about them either. Or the truth of what she'd seen that night.

"A bit." Taking a breath, she told him what she could without calling about danger to herself. "My parents are dead."

The relaxed feel of Eric's body against her back suddenly changed as he stiffened. "I am sorry. What happened?"

Rebecca sighed wearily at his question. Obviously he wanted answers. But it had taken her years to not see that night over and over in her head. Nightmares of the monster that had attacked her and killed her parents had haunted her ever time she'd closed her eyes and still lingered in her thoughts. As much as she detested the thought of reliving it all over again, she had to tell him something.

"They were murdered and that is all I wish to say on the subject." She said curtly.

His stubble covered jaw rubbed against the side of her throat as he nodded slowly. "Very well." pausing to take a breath, Eric reached toward her face. His hand gently cupped the side of her face before turning to face him. Meeting his gaze, she was surprised to see that his blue eyes were soft with a gentle shine to them. "You know you can talk to me about anything, don't you?"

Pressing her lips together, she fought the urge to reply to him, but lost. Rolling onto her back, she forced herself to meet his gaze. "I don't talk about my parent's deaths, Eric. There are parts of me; my past and secrets that you won't ever touch."

Unaffected by her firm refusal to tell him more, Eric's wide
shoulders lifted in a careless shrug. Smirking down at her, he replied.
"Give me time and I *will*."

Rolling her eyes, Rebecca fought not to return his smile with one of
her own. She was toying with fire and she knew it. If she were smart;
she'd jump out of his arms and his bed, get dressed and leave.
Last night was meant to simply satisfy her curiosity. But instead she
now found herself lingering in his embrace.

Why? Why did it feel so good to have his arms around her, holding
her? His touch caused her body to flare with heat that bloomed in her
chest. It was a feeling she'd never known before and deep down, she
knew once she left him that she'd never know it again.

Mentally shaking herself, she moved to push space between them.
"You never speak of Emma and Travis's mother." She remarked. As
she'd predicted; Eric tensed beside her before putting a small amount
of space between them. The gentleness in his eyes faded to be
replaced by his usual cold mask.

With his jaw clenched tight, he bit out. "Why would I? She's not
worth mentioning."

Turning on her side to face him, her face rested against her palm as
her elbow braced against the mattress. "I just wonder why she's not
here. Sarah never mentions her and neither do you. I'm just curious
is all."

Eric scoffed, giving her a cynical look. "Well you know what they
say about curiosity."

When he made no move to say anything else, Rebecca rolled over onto her back, putting more space between them. Turning to glance toward the blind covered window, she could see the hint of morning light streaking across the dark sky. She needed to leave before Emma and Travis knew she was here. She wouldn't be able to look at their sweet, innocent faces and tell them goodbye. It would hurt them so much and it would kill her.

Tugging at the hem of her blouse as far as it would go, she shoved the sheet aside before sitting up and swinging her legs over the edge of the bed. Rising to her feet, Rebecca frowned when she saw that the bottom of her blouse barely fell beyond the upper swell of her buttocks. No doubt giving Eric a show as she stood. Heat flooded her face when she made the terrible mistake to glance back at Eric.

 Much to her embarrassment, his eyes were in fact on her uncovered bottom as he smirked at her knowingly. If that wasn't bad enough; she realized that when she'd shoved the sheet from her body, she'd also thrown the thin material off of Eric as well. With nothing to hide him from her gaze, Rebecca got her first real look of him. *All of him.* Her hungry eyes took in the sight of his muscled chest that was dusted with dark hair that led a hypnotizing trail down his abs, stomach and then to…

Whoa…

Air froze in her lungs as her eyes widened in wonder. If it was possible for her to blush further—she did. She'd never seen a male's body before. Well; she had, but never had she beheld any sight like this. Eric's body was the perfect mix of danger and beauty. His cock stood out, strong and proud, drawing her gaze. Mouth going dry and her womb clenching at the sight, it took everything in her not to return to the bed and touch him. Her hands itched to wrap around his hard length, to feel the texture of him and memorize every inch of him.

"If you wanted to look at me, all you had to do was ask." Eric teased his voice heavy with meaning. It was no mystery what thoughts were swirling in his mind at that moment. "Come here." He beckoned with his hand as his lips curved into a wolfish grin.

Gulping at the sudden lump in her throat, Rebecca cursed her trembling body as she fought not to cave in. Already she could feel the addicting pull of him, of what it was like to be held, kissed and touched by him. It was that same addicting need that she needed to run from…now! If she stayed even for a second she was risking everything. It was time to go.

Shaking her head at his soft command, she turned away from him. "I have to get going." With a trembling hand, she brushed one side of her tussled hair behind an ear, all the while surveying the floor for her missing skirt and underwear. Even now she could feel Eric watching her, yet he said nothing. His eyes were like a fiery brand on her skin.

Just get your stuff and go. She mentally screamed at herself.

Never hearing a single sound of movement from the bed, she let out a startled gasp as two strong arms encircled her waist, pulling her against her back against Eric's very naked form. "Stay, it's early still and I'd like you to eat with us." He whispered against the side of her throat as his lips trailed gentle kisses up to the sensitive skin of her ear.

Sparks of heat shot through her womb, making her breasts feel heavy and ache. Within seconds her body was burning with need simply from the feel of his lips. Even though her muscles echoed with tenderness, she wanted him. She needed him.

Stay strong. Stay firm. Her stupid, ill timed reason reminded her.

Gripping his wrists, Rebecca forced his enticing hands away from her waist. Though Eric was ten times stronger than her, she knew she was only able to step out of his embrace in that moment because he let her. Ignoring the warm tingling sensation at touching his skin, she released his wrists as though touching him burned her.

"No. I'm leaving, Eric."

* ~ * ~ *

Deep inside his being, Eric felt his wolf howl at her emotionless spoken words. Taking a deep breath, he slowly released it, attempting to calm his agitated beast. *"No. I'm leaving, Eric."* The simple words shouldn't have made his chest tighten with worry, but they did. Somehow he sensed that she was telling him something. Leaving? Technically today was his day off and Rebecca usually didn't work. Had she meant that she simply wished to go home or was it something else? Pondering her words, Eric was surprised to find that his wolf came to realization before he had.

She plans to run from us! Stop her! Claim her before she is lost to us!

Shock at his beast thoughts, Eric started at the stiff line of Rebecca's back as she searched for her missing skirt with a horrified expression. Did she really think she could simply give herself to him last night and then disappear?

Never!

Fists clenching tightly at his sides, he fought to keep his overwhelming anger out of his voice as he gently asked her, "What's your rush?"

After discovering her flimsy skirt under the bed, Rebecca bent to pluck it up. She held the thin material to her chest with a look of victory. Turning to look at him as thought she hadn't known he was still standing behind her, she seemed to remember his question. She shook her head with a look of regret that she quickly masked before speaking.

"I have to get home. I need to shower, change clothes and then…" her words trailed off as a shadow of doubt flashed across her eyes. He studied her in silence. What thought had crossed her mind and made her eyes fill with the dark sadness he now saw?

"Why? Shower here. I have something you can wear for now and I promise I will take you back to get your car and take you home later if you wish." He neglected to tell her that he'd be dragging her right back to his home directly afterwards. She was crazy if she thought he'd let her run and hide from him again.

To his amusement, he saw that Rebecca's heated gaze had shifted from his face as he'd spoken to take in every detail of his naked body. He felt his cock pulse with need at the touch of her eyes. A beautiful wash of embarrassment at being caught staring so blatantly at him rushed up Rebecca's neck and into her face.

He was quickly discovering that the best way to handle his human mate was to put that heat in her face as often as he could. She was less unpredictable when she was embarrassed. So if she was unnerved by his unclothed body, he would use it as the weapon it was.

Jerking her eyes from him, she quickly began shimming into her skirt. To his amusement she kept attempting to stretch the length out as the bottom edge of her skirt fell barely to the tops of her knees.

Avoiding his gaze, she kept her eyes downcast before asking, "What would delaying this help?"

"This?" what the hell was that suppose to mean? "You have no intention of returning do you?"

In an attempt to straighten her blouse, Rebecca kept her back to him. "Why would I, Eric?" Turning in a way that said she was reluctant to face him, she ran a shaking hand through her hair, hesitantly meeting his hard gaze. "You fired me, remember?"

"I accept your resignation but never your absence." He said fiercely.

"Too bad." She whispered with a hint of regret. "What outcome did you think we'd have after last night, Eric? I don't harbor any girlish fantasies about what happened last night."

Eric stood silently watching her like she was a strange mystery that he couldn't solve. She acted like last night was a onetime thing. For him it was from it. Last night had shattered his rational world to pieces. Rebecca was his...mate, his *true* mate. And she thought he'd just walk away from her?

Over my dead body.

He no longer cared about the consequences of having a human as a mate. He'd accepted her and by God she would do the same. Striding towards her he felt as surge of male pride when her eyes widened with fear as he forced her to back against the wall.

"What are you doing?" she hissed out in a low voice. Her wide eyes watched his every move like he was a hungry wolf and she the wary doe. The metaphor had him smirking.

"Proving a point."

Without touching her with his hands, his lips covered hers in a demanding kiss, without hesitation she eagerly returned it. Her hands rose to grip and knead his shoulders as she pressed her body against his. With a groan of need, he pressed her tightly against the wall at her back, branding her with his heated skin.

He knew the moment her senses returned to her as her fingers stilled on his shoulders and she jerked away from him. Pulling away from him, panting with her well kissed lips flush with color, her arms dropped from his shoulders.

"You've just proved my point, Rebecca. Last night wasn't us just acting on some pint up lust. I belong with you as much as you belong with me." Eric's words emerging rougher than normal, he sounded dangerous and fierce.

"You're wrong." Shoving at him, she slid away from him before turning to glare at him while she shook her head in denial. "You'll move on."

Sweeping up his discarded sweats from last night, he shoved his legs into them with nearly angry jerks. "When will you get that I don't want to move on? You are the one I want and that will never change." For a moment he could have sworn he'd seen fear in her eyes, but it quickly was replaced by stubbornness.

"I'm leaving, Eric. Goodbye." She said with a hard look.
At her refusal to submit to him, his wolf rose up in anger. He wouldn't allow her to escape him—escape this. He didn't' care what it took. He'd tie her to his damn bed before he allowed another mate to walk away from him. Before he could close the distance between them, Rebecca had just reached the bedroom door when it pushed open slowly.

Rubbing at her tired eyes; Emma squeezed through the door, her innocent gaze searching for him. When her eyes fell upon Rebecca whom stood frozen, Emma's face lit up like a Christmas tree.

"Becca?" Emma said with a happy smile.

Flushing, Rebecca quickly recovered and attempted to appear decent for the small child's sake. "Morning Emma, how'd you sleep?" her words echoed with the gentleness that she reserved only for his children.

"'Kay. I'm hungry. Are you staying?" Emma's innocently asked with hope shining in her tired face.

Eric smirked at how torn Rebecca looked in the face of his beautiful daughter. It would appear he had more than one weapon available to him when it came to wooing his mate. Before Rebecca could gently shatter the hopeful look in Emma's eyes, he stepped forward, dropping his arm around Rebecca's hips before addressing his daughter.

"Of course she is, Emma. I can't start my day without Rebecca's famous pancakes, can you?" After dropping the name of Emma's favorite breakfast food, Emma's smiled widened as a inner light seemed to infuse her.

"Pancakes!" Emma repeated, happily jumping up and down.

Smiling back, he motioned toward the door. "We'll be down in a minute, why don't you go watch cartoons with Travis." He said as he watched his son stumble from the twin's bedroom, barely awake as he headed toward the stairs like a robot.

With a cry of excitement, Emma bound after her brother, talking excitedly with him on the way down the stairs. As soon as Emma and Travis were out of ear shot, Rebecca turned toward him with flames of fury dancing in her eyes. The sight of her temper made his shaft hardened with the need to claim her all over again.

Damn. Had she always looked this bewitching when he pissed her off? His contemplating thoughts were cut short when one of her small fingers began stabbing into his chest above his heart.

"What do you think you are doing?" she hissed out between clenched teeth. "Why would you go setting your daughter up for her hopes to be dashed?" a flash of pain swam in her eyes.

"I did no such thing." He denied with a smug grin.

Her hands tightened into tight fists at his smugly spoken words. "Liar." She bit out with a cold glare. "You knew I wasn't staying and yet you told her anyway."

"If you think I *lied* to my innocent daughter, then by all means go tell her the truth. That you intend to leave and will never be coming back." he dared, waving his hand toward the stairs. When Rebecca bit her lip with hesitation, Eric stepped closer. Cupping the sides of her face with both of his hands he titled her head up to look at him. "Call it a battle strategy. I am simply using the weapons most effective on you."

Jerking her face from his hands, Rebecca scowled up at him with confusion. "You make it sound like we're at war."

Grasping the back of her neck as his other hand cupped her bare buttocks beneath her skirt, Eric jerked her towards him. His lips claimed hers in a rough kiss, stealing the breath from her lungs and her gasp of surprise along with it. Squeezing her against him, he smiled against her lips when her hands shot up to claw at his chest and shoulders, grappling to hold on to something as he dominated her mouth.

Pulling away nearly as quickly as he'd snatched her, he murmured, "We are. It's just a war you have no chance at winning."

<u>14</u>

A half hour later, Rebecca found herself standing in front of the stove, smears of pancake mix on her cheeks as she worked to ignore Eric. He stood at the kitchen counter directly behind her. Despite her best efforts; it was impossible to ignore the heat of his eyes against her back. She felt hypersensitive. Every hair on her arms and at the back of her neck stood on end at knowing he was watching her so intensely.

Ignore him. She told herself. *You're just going to make one last breakfast for Emma and Travis and then disappear.*

It only it would be that simple. She knew with the way that Eric was watching her that it would be nearly impossible to slip away from him.

Reaching for the bowl of pancake mix, she moved to pour another into the skillet in front of her. When strong arms suddenly wrapped around her from behind, startling her, she jumped and poured a half of a pancake over the edge of the skillet and onto the stove.

"*Eric!*" she hissed out in anger as she set the bowl aside.

Big, Bold & Bearing

Without a word, his arm tightened around her, pulling her back tighter against his body. Even through the borrowed drawstring sweats she wore, she could feel his hard length stabbing at the curve of her buttocks. Instantly, her body warmed to the feel of his solid frame. Between her clenching thighs she could feel her clit pulse with need at his near proximity.

Wasn't last night supposed to get rid of this need of him? She trembled against the need to fight what she was feeling…craving in that moment. She had to get away; away from him and whatever he was doing to her mind and body. Fighting to ignore him, she shoved at his hands, but nothing happened.

"Eric, let go of me before I toss the rest of these pancakes on you." She threatened, praying that her voice didn't shake.

With a chuckle, he rested his chin on the top of her head. "Go ahead. But know that if you do, you will be cleaning it off of me; one way or another." His voice dropped an octave at the end of his words with meaning. Instantly the image of her tongue on his neck and chest had Rebecca's breathes escaping in harsh pants as her sheath rippled in reaction. Swallowing past her sudden tight throat, she reached for the spatula to flip the misshapen pancake.

"What makes you think I would be interested in doing such a thing?"

"You forget I can tell when you lie to me, Rebecca. The thought of your mouth on me excites you as much as it does to me. Just as you were so excited last night when I was between your thighs that you shuttered like you do now." One of his hands shifted from around her stomach to slide down to her sex, cupping it through the thick material of her sweats.

"Eric!" she cried out with embarrassment as he caressed her so openly. What if the children walked in? Heart racing, she dropped the spatula to grip his wrist tightly. "Stop it."

"If it weren't for the fact that we aren't alone; I'd have you on the counter right now." a whimper escaped her lips. At the sound, she felt Eric's embrace become tender. "Are you sore from last night? Perhaps I should give you a hot bath to ...soothe you."

Knowing that he was looking for anyway to tease her, she pressed her lips together in a hard line. "Don't concern yourself." She hissed out. "I'm fine."

"I want you to stay here today and tonight as well."

Shoving her hair from her face, she turned to look over her shoulder at him. "Why should I? There can never be more than what last night was, Eric."

"Oh, my little prey, it *was* much more than that." he said with a firm nod. "And I intend to prove it to you by holding you tonight, kissing you, touching you. If you are so adamant about leaving and going to hide in your small apartment, don't be surprised to find me there with you. Because I for one know that I am not capable of letting you go."

Heart stilling in her chest, Rebecca found herself shaking her head slightly at his words. They were confusing and bewildering to her, but at the same time; they were almost...romantic? Just when she thought she had him all figured out, Eric went and showed a different side of him that surprised her.

Like a bucket of cold water dumping over them, a sharp knock at the kitchen door had Rebecca's gaze springing away. Huffing out a breath she turned away from him. How easily he had nearly gotten under her guard with just a few sweetened words. Could she be more pathetic? Shaking off his hold on her, her head turned toward the door as another insistent knock followed. Moving away from the stove and Eric, she turned to look at him with a calm resolve that she prayed wouldn't waver.

"Forget it, Eric. It won't be happening." She whispered, lifting her chin at him.

His familiar cold gaze looked down at her as if he was preparing to fight. "One would think that you'd learned not to underestimate me." As each word left his mouth, he took a several steps towards her until she found herself pressed against the fridge with Eric looming above her.

When the constant knocking finally ceased, Rebecca's gaze shot to the side as Jason and Chris came striding into the house. Uncaring that they'd just let themselves in, their expressions were dark and full of foreboding as they sought out Eric immediately. Though both saw how close she and Eric stood, neither batted an eye at it. Instead, both forced a smile at her that didn't quite reach their eyes.

"Morning, Rebecca." Jason greeted.

Returning his tight smile, Rebecca shoved some space between her and Eric until she was able to move out from her trapped position. Hesitantly glancing away from her, Chris turned his concerned gaze back to Eric.

"Alp—Eric," Chris stuttered out, glancing briefly back at Rebecca with worry, he stepped closer to Eric before continuing in a hushed tone. "We need to talk."

Not blinking an eye, Eric responded coolly. "Let it wait till tomorrow." His cold eyes returning to Rebecca's stubbornly set expression.

"With respect, *Eric,*" Jason interjected with a meaningful tone to Eric's name. "It can't wait."

Rebecca watched as Eric stood in silence, his lips pressed together so firmly that she was surprised that his whole face didn't facture from the intensity of it. It was obvious that whatever Eric's fellow werewolves had come to discuss wasn't for *human* ears.

Losing patience with the macho male staring contest that Eric was participating in, she hissed out. "Oh for goodness sake!" her outburst seemed to break the spell between the duo and Eric the second she'd uttered the words, drawing their startled gazes to her face. With a huff of exasperation, she strode closer to Eric. "It's obvious you need to discuss *business* that you don't want overheard, so I will just get Emma and Travis fed and get out of your hair." She stated with a matter-of-fact tone.

If Eric's scowl could deepen further, it did at her calmly spoken words. Turning back to the counter with enough time to simply grab the platter of pancakes, Rebecca slipped past the men and headed toward the dining room all the while attempting to ignore Eric's stern gaze. Her heart shuttered in her chest a moment later as she was roughly jerked to a stop by a heavy arm coiling around her waist. Her body pricked with familiar awareness as she felt Eric press into her from behind, his hand pressing possessively over her lower stomach. With deliberate slow movements, Eric lowered his lips to her ear.

"Don't even think for a second that this is over, Rebecca." He warned in a low voice. "I don't plan on letting you out of my sights long enough for you to escape me for long."

Tossing him a stubborn glare over her shoulder, she shrugged off his arm before heading to the kitchen table. Placing the platter of pancakes beside the pile of plates and utensils that waited, she found her reluctant gaze returning to seek Eric out once more. She shook her head when she saw he appeared to *already* be arguing with Jason and Chris about something. His clenching hand slashed through the air with the force of his heated exchange with them.

It didn't take long for Emma and Travis to be drawn from their cartoons to the table by the scent of pancakes and breakfast meats. Waiting until both were seated with their plates filled and cups of milk in front of them, Rebecca reluctantly took her seat as well.

Curiosity getting the better of her, Rebecca found herself studying the trio from across the large space to the kitchen. What was it that had them so concerned and Eric so upset? Taking a breath, she tuned out the idle chatter of the twins and focused her attention solely on the hushed voices that drifted from across the room. Despite their best efforts to keep their voices low, Rebecca was able to pick up bits of their conversation.

"Your scheme isn't a secret anymore, Eric. The elders know." Jason hissed out with a look of foreboding.

"How the hell is that possible?!" Eric's face flushed with anger, a low guttural growl surfacing from his lips. "And how the hell did you two find out?"

"You've got bigger problems than that, I'm afraid. Not only do we know, but the elders know and they're not happy about your little human either."Chris said, flashing Eric a knowing look.

Eric fisted his hands at his sides. The tips of his claws beginning to emerge from his curled fingertips. "She's got nothing to do with this!" he snarled.

"Are you ready to put your life on the line for her, Eric? Because that is what it's come to." Jason's voice asked in a soft tone. His eyes were gentle with compassion and pity.

"What are you talking about?"

Chris shifted around to Eric's other side. "There's been talk amongst the members of the pack, Eric. The elders believe that you're not fit to lead anymore. You and your pups could be in danger."

As the voices grew more hushed, Rebecca found her breakfast becoming devoid of taste, bite after bite as her inner thoughts swam. What was Eric's scheme they were referring to? The elders knew? Knew what? Just as the thought arose in her mind, so did the answer.

They knew…

Sweat broke out over her body as her fork clutching hand shook. Had she been discovered? Did Eric know too? Had Damon betrayed her? Eyes flickering back and forth in the space in front of her, she thought back over what she could have done to give herself away, nothing came to mind. But recalling Eric's behavior and his words this morning had her chest tightening with fear.

"It's just a war you have no chance at winning....My little prey."

At the memory of Eric's voice in her mind, Rebecca barely noticed when her fork fell from her limp fingers to clatter against her plate loudly. Emma and Travis sent her a confused expression but both quickly turned back to their breakfast without a word.

How could she have been so naive, so stupid? Earlier, Eric had first sought for her to tell her more about her parent's deaths. At the time she'd just dismissed it as idle curiosity, but now she saw he had been trying to glean what she knew of that night. She'd also thought that his countless offers for her to spend the day there was just some day-after attempt to spend more time with her. Could it be that he simply wanted her here when Jason and Chris arrived? Eric had warned her before that she didn't know what he was capable of when it came to her. How ruthless would he be when it came to protecting his secret?

"I look forward to your execution. None of my kind will let you live now. Others will come for you and you will never know mercy from my kind."

 The haunting words of her attacker taunted her as her fear began to climb. She had to get out of there and run. With no where left to hide and no one to trust, she was now running for her life.

Shoving her chair back, she was surprised when Travis slid from his chair as well. At her questioning look, he grabbed his empty glass.

"I want juice."

She'd almost expected him to hand the glass to her to refill for him as she usually did, but instead he rushed toward the kitchen and to the fridge before she could offer. Off to the side she could still see that Eric was arguing with Jason and Chris. It was time. She didn't care what Eric thought he was accomplishing with his head games with her, but she had to leave before ended up as the *prey* he'd named her earlier.

Taking a deep breath she looked at Emma one last time. The cute little girl had her head bowed over her syrup smeared plate as she drew a smiley face with her finger through the sticky syrup. Out of all of them; Rebecca knew she'd miss Emma the most. Tears burning her eyes, she stepped away from the table and headed for the door without a backward glance.

$$* \sim * \sim *$$

"Your scheme isn't a secret anymore, Eric. The elders know." Jason hissed out, his shoulders tense.

Eric felt everything in him freeze at the words of his beta. His interest in the missing shifters had been kept a secret for a reason. When he'd first expressed concern to the council of elders within his pack of the multiple disappearances of shifters from not only his pack but others as well, the elder's decision had been firm. He'd been forbidden from looking into the issue and told that if shifters were missing it was simply an indication that they weren't strong enough to survive amongst the pack. The reaction of the elders on the issue was the reason that he'd only trusted Mick and his long time friend, Mark with his secret interest.

"How the hell is that possible?!" Eric's face flushed with anger, a low guttural growl surfacing from his lips. "And how the hell did you two find out?"

"You've got bigger problems than that, I'm afraid. Not only do we know, but the elders know and they're not happy about your little human either." Chris said, flashing Eric a knowing look.

Eric fisted his hands at his sides. The tips of his claws beginning to emerge from his curled fingertips. It was obvious that he'd claimed her body last night. Her scent clung to his skin as his did to hers. However he'd yet to give her the mating mark that would bind her to him. It wasn't possible that the two; let alone the elders, knew that she was his mate.

His wolf rose up protectively at the subject of his unclaimed true mate. "She's got nothing to do with this!" he snarled.

"This isn't just about her, Eric. You know how the elders and other shifters within your pack feel about humans. Are you ready to put your life on the line for her or hers too? Because that is what it's come to." Jason's voice asked in a soft tone. His eyes were gentle with compassion and pity.

"What are you talking about?" he said, attempting to appear nonchalant at the mention of Rebecca.

Chris shifted around to Eric's other side. "There's been talk amongst the members of the pack, Eric. After the past few months there has been a small shift amongst the pack members. Like the elders, many of the pack members are displeased with your decision to unite with the Alpha of Darkwood Springs and your refusal to take a mate amongst your pack. Others believe that you're not fit to lead anymore and you know what could happen if others became brave enough to strike out at you. You and your pups could be in danger."

The thoughts had Eric snarling with rage. *No one* was laying a claw on his children or his mate. He was the Alpha! He'd earned the title through bloody battles and his unyielding strength. It was time for the elders and his pack to see that he didn't hide behind old traditions.

Out of the corner of his eye he saw his son, head toward them and then straight to the fridge with a look of innocence shining around him. He'd once thought that nothing would come between his loyalty to his pack. Now he knew that nothing would stop him from protecting his family; his children and Rebecca; his mate. If the elders wanted to engage in a power battle with him, he'd leave them broken and bloody in the end as well as any others that got in his way.

"Eric," Jason began, holding out a beseeching hand to him. "At least let us get you and your pups to the lodge. There we can protect them better than you could here. One of us can stay behind and watch after Rebecca in case someone tries to target her, but your home isn't built to be defended like the lodge is."

"*Rebecca stays with me.*" he whispered harshly. With his eyes glowing, his wolf echoed in his voice, making it deeper, rougher and terrifying.

Once again he sensed movement from behind him. Turning this time, he spied Rebecca. With her head down, she seemed to be quickening her strides as she entered the kitchen and headed for the door.

Did she think she could slink away from him now? Even if it weren't for the fact that she was his true mate, he wasn't about to let her out of his sight with his own pack turning against him. A frail human favored by a shifter was an easy target should anyone wish to strike out at him.

Shoving past his betas, he reached Rebecca before she was half way across the kitchen. Encircling her wrist, he was surprised when she fought against his hold, refusing for her steps to be halted. Transferring his hands to her upper arms he jerked her against his chest, preventing her from pulling from him.

"Stop this." he bit out. "Where the hell do you think you're going?"

"Let me go, Eric." she whispered with a dark tone. Her voice was lethal and sharp. She expected him to obey her, not that he had any intention of doing so.

The look she gave him had every muscle he possessed locking up. Almost instantly the smell tainted scent of fear and desperation wafted from her pours. She was afraid of him? Why? Though his beast demanded in the back of his mind that he reassure her and do what he had to make her feel safe once more, he knew now was not the time.

If Jason and Chris were correct, every second they stayed here was like walking around a firing range with a target on their backs. They had to get out of there and get to the safety of the lodge. Once they were all safe, he intended to explain *everything* to Rebecca. He would tell her *what* he was and *what* she was to him.

Hardening his features, he shook his head. "You're not going anywhere unless I say so. Keep fighting me and you will see just how ruthless I can be."

Still squirming and fighting his hold on her arms, her eyes narrowed on him. "Then don't say I didn't warn you."

Before Eric could discover what she was planning, pain exploded through his groin and throughout his whole body. Instantly his hands fell away from her to cup his aching balls that her knee had just kissed hard. When she spun away toward the door, he snarled, not bothering to conceal his wolf's reaction. Brushing the pain aside, he straightened and went after her.

Before she could grasp the doorknob, he grabbed her from behind. His arms wrapped around her chest like two steel bands, pinning her arms to her sides as he lifted her kicking feet off the floor. Backing away from the door, he snarled.

"Don't *ever* do that to me again." he hissed at her ear, rage coating his every word.

Carrying her back toward the kitchen, he ignored the confused looks from Jason and Chris. Setting her down on her feet but still holding her tightly, he was just about to rail at her when something had him shutting his mouth. The air around them suddenly felt thick and clouded. Something was wrong. Looking to his betas, he saw that they sensed it too.

With a wary look, Chris approached the widows by the sink. Instantly his body shot ramrod straight. Jerking around he shouted, "Get down!"

Before the words could fully leave his mouth, the windows of the dining room and kitchen exploded, raining glass everywhere. Jason and Chris moved to shield Travis that had frozen in fear before crumbling to the floor. Shoving Rebecca down, he pressed her against the side of the fridge, shielding her from the direction of the window. Gunfire rang through the air mingled with the terrified cries of his mate and his children. Instantly, Eric felt ice shoot through his veins.

"Emma…Where's Emma?!" his sharp gaze looked everywhere for his precious daughter but he couldn't see her. Chris was struggling to hold Travis still as the young boy fought to flee from his pinned position on the glass littered kitchen floor. Jason looked everywhere but he couldn't see anything either.

"Daddy!" a small voice screamed. Head shooting toward the voice, he saw Emma cowering beneath the dining room table. Her small body shook as tears flowed down her redden face. His gut twisted at seeing his daughter trapping right in the middle of the line of fire.

Our pup! His wolf cried in fear as he fought to get to his offspring.

Before Eric could spring forward to protect his daughter, Rebecca shot from his shielding body and ran through the line of fire.

"Rebecca!" he yelled over the loud gunshots. He managed to snag her ankle and bringing her to the floor just before she used her other foot to kick him across the face, forcing him to let her go. He watched with terror as his mate scrambled to her feet and rushed through gunfire to get to Emma.

Bullets struck the walls and the kitchen counters all around her as she rushed forward. Flitching and ducking her head as she ran, Rebecca threw herself on the floor, sliding through the mess of shattered dishes and glasses until she reached Emma. Emma instantly launched into Rebecca's arms, wrapping her small arms around Rebecca's neck as she continued to wail.

When bullets pinged off the tipped over chairs and the table; inches from two females, Eric felt his hold on his wolf slip. Shooting across the distance, with one hand he threw the table toward the shattered windows, shielding his women as he reached them. Grabbing Rebecca by her waist he jerked her up into his arms and with her; Emma as well.

"Get out now!" he shouted to his betas as they rushed toward the door, Chris holding Travis in his arms as they ran. Following behind them, Eric shot out of the front door, leaping from the porch in a single jump. In the distance he could see the camouflaged forms of several men with rifles moving to chase them.

"Get to the lodge now!" he ordered as Jason and Chris rushed to their truck, shoving Travis in the back seat.

Rushing to his hummer, he opened the driver's side door and all but tossed his daughter and mate into the passenger seat across the space. Leaping into the seat, he jerked the keys from the visor above. His Hummer roaring to life, he slammed on the gas, sending them flying over the drive way at a break neck speed. Spraying gravel behind him, he kept his gaze on his betas that followed close behind him as they sped down the road. Never when he looked back did he see anyone following them.

Glancing at Rebecca, he saw that she held onto Emma like she was a lifeline as his daughter did the same. Emma continued to bury her face against Rebecca's neck, wailing like a wounded animal. His wolf reacted strongly to the sound of his child's distress. Accepting that he couldn't comfort Emma while they were still in danger, he turned his attention to the dazed expression on Rebecca's face. Was she in shock?

"Put a seat belt around you both." He ordered, hoping his hard tone would shake her out of her shock.

Nodding, Rebecca reached out with her free hand, jerking a seatbelt around her and Emma as she pressed them back against the seat. With her movement, another scent joined the collection of fear and adrenaline in the vehicle.

Blood.

Stilling, his sharp gaze looked over his daughter's shaking form. It wasn't Emma—it was Rebecca. "Are you injured?" when she didn't respond, he snarled loudly. "Answer me, damn it!"

Flashing her eyes at him with anger at his harsh tone and language in the presence of his daughter, Rebecca responded, "I am fine. Don't worry about me."

Don't worry about her? In what universe would that even be remotely possible? He nearly lost her several times when she's charged into a rain of bullets to protect his daughter and she said not to worry? Panting he fought to keep his temper under control. He wanted to rail at her, shake her and hold her close till the image of bullets striking around her disappeared from his memory.

Someone had attacked his family in *his* home. *No* one came after his family and escaped unscathed. This wouldn't go unpunished. The peace seeking Eric was gone. The calm and yielding Eric was gone. He was out for blood now.

<u>15</u>

With his mind boiling with a deadly combination of worry and rage, Eric paced back and forth across the conference room at the lodge. At the sound of the door opening behind him, he spun around and instantly strode forward. Standing in the open doorway stood Jason with a hard look in his eyes.

"How are they?" Eric asked anxiously, his words emerging harsher than he intended.

Upon arriving at the lodge over an hour ago, he'd roared at every one of his pack members until Healer Terra had been brought to look at his children. The quiet doctor had eyed his mate with obvious disgust on sight and doing so had sent Eric's temper skyrocketing. After snapping at the wolf shifter to do her job, his mother had forced Eric to leave the infirmary, out of concern that he would upset Travis and Emma more with his outbursts.

The image of Rebecca's face as he'd been forced to leave the room had caused him to freeze. She'd looked at him with fear in her eyes as Emma still clung to her like a baby monkey. Though she had eyed him warily as he left he couldn't help but remember the small look of longing that hid deep within her gaze.

Deep down he'd worried that in all the chaos that she'd seen a hint of his beast. Was that why the scent of her fear swam around her like a cloak? Staying from his mate instead of going to her and refusing to leave her side until her fear had subsided had been agony. He'd denied his beast's instincts for too long where Rebecca was concerned. He could allow himself to lose her because of her fear. He needed to get back to her.

"Travis had a few cuts from the broken glass on the kitchen floor, but all injuries on him have already begun to heal. According to Dr. Terra; other than shock from the event, Emma is unharmed. She hasn't let go of Rebecca even for a second. Even when Dr. Terra requested that Emma let go so she could be fully examined, Emma still held onto your human like a lifeline. Dr. Tessa obvious didn't like that Rebecca was forced to stay as she looked over your daughter."

Eric found his gritting together at the actions of the young, sour faced doctor. He knew why Dr. Tessa disliked Rebecca on sight, but it didn't do anything to cool his temper. Wolf shifters were highly mistrusting of humans and with good reasons. But still; it didn't change a thing for him. Rebecca was his mate and he didn't like the thought of Rebecca being hated because of deeds of other human long dead.

With a heavy weight settling on his chest, he shook his head at the hopeless truth that loomed ahead of him. The truth was; even if he was successful in turning her, his pack would *never* accept Rebecca as his. Even if his mate had been a shifter of a different species instead of a human, wolves weren't known for accepting outsiders within their rants.

He already could predict the mirroring looks of disgust on the elder's faces when he would present Rebecca to them. Without a doubt, he knew that they would prefer to kill her than accept her. The only way he could prevent further discord within his pack and assure her safety was to…let her go.

No.

His fists clenched at his sides until his claws sliced into his palms at the thought. No one would separate him from Rebecca, not even himself. The pack would accept her in time, if not; he would exile any that refused.

Stepping further into the room, Jason ran an exhausted hand through his long ruffled hair. "Anyhow; your mother helped Rebecca take Emma and Travis to the kitchen for a treat to calm them down. While Tessa was looking at your pups, we—" Jason's words were suddenly cut off as Eric stormed away from him with a distracted expression.

"What did Dr. Tessa say about Rebecca's injuries?" when Jason didn't answer, Eric slowly turned at the waist to look at him. His beta seemed to find the long conference table interesting as he avoided Eric's gaze. "Jason?" Eric said taking a slow step closer, his muscles tightening with every step. He'd never lashed out at one of his betas before, but Jason's refusal to answer him was pushing it.

Sighing, Jason rubbed tiredly at his face before he replied, "I don't know."

Eric's eyes narrowed. "What do you mean you don't know? I left you to guard her and my pups."

"I tried to talk her, but she refused."

Almost positive that he knew what Jason was telling him, Eric still found himself asking, "Refused *what*?" his words echoing with a growl.

"She claimed that she was fine and didn't need looked over. Dr. Tessa didn't seem concerned so she allowed Rebecca to leave with your pups and your mother."

Eric's eyes flashed with light as his wolf rose up at the thought of his mate walking around injured because a member under his control thought she wasn't worthy on concern. "I *ordered* for Dr. Tessa to examine all of them. What was unclear about that?" he hissed out in a low voice.

With a snarl, Eric turned his temper on the table to his right, slamming his fist into the center of the wood. With a loud boom, his fist struck the table so hard that it split in half, as he lifted his hand the two halves fell apart with a creaking groan before hitting the floor.

"Whoa. Isn't that the third table you've had to put in this room?" a deep teasing voice said from the doorway.

Spinning around, Jason and Eric's eyes fell on the man that stood leaning against the door frame casually. Dressed in jeans and a t-shirt, Eric took in his old friend; Mark. Mark; a cougar shifter was one of the few *different* shifters that his pack tolerated. For years, Mark had helped Eric by being his level headed ambassador to other Alphas across the different shifter territories.

Taking note of Mark's appearance, Eric couldn't help but notice his friend looked…tired. His usual dark blonde hair had grown out, carelessly shoved away from his face. His tan skin along his jaw was covered in thick stubble. Dark lines of weariness circled Mark's eyes, seeing this seemed to pull Eric from his rage.

"How long have you been standing there?" He bit out gruffly.

Shrugging his shoulders, Mark straightened from his leaning position. "Long enough to see that your temper and habit of destroying furniture still needs work." Striding across the space to them, Mark nodded respectfully to Jason before reaching into his back pocket. Pulling out a thick, folded envelope, he held it out to Eric with a slight smile. "Signed as promised."

"You got your Alpha to align with us?" Jason asked with a note of awe.

Cougars, like most cat shifters normally were rouges, refusing to form packs. Mark's Alpha; Theo had managed to convince the nomad cougar shifters of Maine to band together after many of their kind was targeted by human poachers. Mark's people; like the traditional wolf shifters, kept to themselves, which was why Eric had sought an alliance with them.

Taking the thick tan envelope from Mark, Eric nodded in acknowledgement. "Any issues obtaining his agreement?"

Shoving his hands in his front pockets, Mark's shoulders slumped as though he was carrying a heavy weight. "Sort of. His alliance comes with some conditions and a favor."

"What a surprise." Eric remarked sarcastically with a scowl. "We'll talk later." With a dismissive wave of his hand, Eric turned away from him.

Ignoring Eric's rude attempt to dismiss him, Mark remained, glancing first to Jason then to Eric's stiff back. "I heard you had some excitement today? Anything I should know about?"

For a moment, Eric seemed to simmer in his own thoughts before he answered. "Some cowards came to my house with guns and attacked my home today while my children were there."

Jason nodded at Mark's surprised raised eyebrows. "It's true."
"I wouldn't want to be them once you find them." Mark murmured with a slight wince. "Any clue who it was?"

Curious about the answer himself, Eric turned his attention to Jason. "Take Chris and some trusted hunters to my property and see if you can pick up any scents as soon as possible. I will remain here to make sure my pups—"*and mate "*—are protected."

Jason's mouth opened and closed several times before he was finally able to answer. "As-as I tried to tell you a moment ago, once Dr. Tessa was done with your pups, we went ahead and looked for signs of who attacked you—"

Abruptly Mark held up a finger and interrupted Jason with a smug grin. "Am I the only one that's going to point out that Eric just said *"mate"*?"

Groaning in disgust, Eric realized he must have uttered the word aloud without realizing it.

So much for keeping it a secret. His wolf said smugly.

"Yes. I have found my true mate." He stated reluctantly. Much to his shock, Jason didn't seem shocked or even surprised by this news. His expression almost seemed as if he'd known already. Stilling, he felt like someone had punched him in the gut. His friends would never let him live this down.

"So you're finally admitting it to yourself?" Jason asked with a nearly identical smug expression as Mark's.

Shoving the envelope in his pocket, Eric moved toward the grinning duo. Yep. He was definitely never living this down. "You knew?" he asked Jason.

"Of course we knew, Eric. It was obvious from since the first time you introduced us to Rebecca. But we knew if we pointed it out it would only cause you to put more distance between the two of you. You had to come to the realization on your own."

"Told you that hard head of you would come back and bite you in the ass one of these days," Mark teased. "So, where is this mate of yours? I want to offer my condolences."

Scowling at the teasing banter, Eric waved Mark's words away. "As much as I would love to stand around the gab with you like a bunch of old women with nothing better to do, I have a more urgent thing to attend to." to Jason, Eric said. "I want answers. Who attacked us and how is it we didn't know they were there until it was too late?"

"As I have been trying to tell you, Chris and I looked into it already. There were no individual scent traces of anyone on your property."

Shocked, Eric shook his head. "That's not possible." Beginning to pace back and forth as his thoughts raced, Eric spun back toward his beta with cold eyes. "*Everything* has a scent. There is no way that there could be *nothing!* Go over the scene again. Take as many shifters as you need to do it, but I will not let these cowards think they can threaten my family without consequences."

"More trackers won't make a difference, Eric. The only thing we were able to pick up was some sort of scent that I encountered when I was in Darkwood Springs months ago when Doyle Mackenzie had gotten kidnapped."

Every muscle in Eric's body froze as his heart and lungs seized up. With suspension, he took a slow step toward his beta. "Was it an overly sweet scent? Almost like a human scent mix with decade?" Pressing his lips into a thin line before answering, Jason reluctantly nodded. "It was almost exactly that. I believe you know what we could be facing here."

"Are we really considering this?" Mark asked, perplexed. "It's not possible that they would target you, Eric. Is it?"

Rage mounting once more, Eric spun around and shoved past the both of them before he stormed down the hall to the main lobby. Heading toward his office, he took note of Chris talking with several male shifters near the door.

Uncaring what he was dealing with, Eric bellowed at him. "Chris! Get that damn bear on the phone in the next ten seconds!"

Storming to his office, Eric slammed the door open with so much force that he door swung toward the back wall and struck it with such force that it embedded the doorknob in the wall. Chest heaving, Eric was seeing red in that moment. It would appear that his new allies troubles had followed him home for some reason. He refused to allow such danger to touch his family. He had enough to deal with. With shifters disappearing and his pack turning against him, he couldn't fight an army of supernatural freaks too.

16

"What exactly are you accusing me of?" Doyle Mackenzie's irritated voice asked through the speakerphone in the center of Eric's desk.

Pacing back and forth, Eric suddenly stopped to turn toward the speaker phone. Fangs growing long and his claws slashing into the edge of his desk, he snarled. "You know what I am talking about! Your mate's messed up drama just showed up on my doorstep today!"

"I don't know what you are talking about, Eric. Are you saying that you encountered one of Malca's enhanced soldiers in your own territory?"

With a disbelieving scoff, Eric shoved away from his desk. His rage filled eyes, turning over to Mark who lounged against the far wall. With a slight nod, Mark stepped up to the opposite of Eric's desk. Folding his arms over his chest, Mark sighed.

"Doyle; its Mark here."

"Thank God, at least there is one rational person there that I can talk to." Doyle's voice dripped with sarcasm.

With a look of anger, Eric clenched a tight fist against the top of the desk beside the phone. Fearing that his temper would cause him to smash the phone to bits, Mark held up a calming hand to Eric. "Doyle the situation is…complicated down here."

"When is it ever not?" sighing heavily through the phone Doyle added, "Tell me what is going on."

"Eric's home was attacked while his children were there."

"No offense, but why would you assume it had anything to do with what we are dealing with here? How do you know that it's not members of your pack, Eric? It's widely known that you wolves are known for attacking other packs to acquire more territory."

"They attacked with *guns*, Doyle." Mark replied. "To my best knowledge, most shifters prefer a more *personal* approach when killing someone."

Before Doyle could respond, Eric bit out a snarl of frustration. His eyes glowing as his wolf attempted to leap forward, possibly in a vain effort to attack the grizzly shifter through the phone. "What I think is that when I saved your troublesome brother that your mate's problems have followed me!"

Though Doyle wasn't wrong about the possibility of it being other wolves behind the attack, Eric knew that wolves didn't possess the scent that he, Jason and Mark remembered. It had to be the freaks that were always hunting Doyle's mate.

Tension became as thick as a heavy cloud of smoke as Doyle spoke again, his normal deep voice echoing with the inner fury of his beast—of his bear. "Are you blaming *my mate*?" Instantly, Eric felt the chill of Doyle's words, but being a leader himself; he shook it off. Before he could respond to the enraged words of his ally, Eric's hearing picked up shuffling sounds on the other end of the call.

"Give me the phone." A soft feminine voice ordered.

"I've got this!" Doyle snarled, clearly still miffed about Eric's comments concerning his mate.

Was it possible that Doyle's mate; Aria, had heard their conversation? A wave of shame hit Eric at the thought and he found he was angry at himself. The last thing he wanted was to burn his new bridge with the Alpha of Darkwood Springs, but he had to know what he was facing.

Voices on the other end continued until Eric heard the sounds of a scuffle. Were they fighting for possession of the phone? As the rough shuffling sounds lessened, Eric recognized the sound of the phone being passed to another person.

"Hey this is Doyle's irritated mate, what do you want?" Aria's soft, yet stern voice asked.

"We need your help, Aria. Why would those guys be coming after Eric?" Mark asked before Eric had the chance to piss off anyone else.

"As far as we know; Malca's main players have followed her to Washington D.C. we've just arrived there and are working on another lead on her. I don't see how she would know anything about you, Eric. Which makes it unlikely that she is personally targeting you and your family. My advice to you is to look more closely at your own pack; I'm sure the answer is there somewhere."

Eric scoffed. That was *not* the answer that he needed. "Thanks for nothing, Aria."

"You called us; remember."

"My last mistake with you and your pack."

"Give me that damn phone!" Doyle bit out in the background. With a sound of a light slap, Aria sighed into the phone.

"Little tip for the day, Eric; take a Midol and go play fetch with a ball or something. Then once you've done that, maybe you want to look at what enemies you have next to you instead of working to create new ones." Without another word, the line went dead.

Reaching across the table, Mark hit a button on the phone to turn off the speaker; all the while he eyed Eric with a hard look. Catching his gaze, Eric bit out a foul curse. Pacing the length of his office behind his desk, Eric fought the need to break, tear or maim something.

"You know she'd got a point, Alpha." Jason said quietly from his spot by the door.

When Eric flashed his beta a hard glare, he was surprised to see Chris was nodding his head in agreement. Alright so maybe he could have handled that phone call a bit better. Mentally shrugging it off, he forced his mind to focus on the issue at hand.

Glancing back at Jason with a shrug, Mark turned back to Eric. "What do you want to do?"

Wincing at the only option open to him, Eric came to a slow halt. "Call a pack meeting." Eric reluctantly said. "Every wolf under my rule, call them all here. If one of them is behind what happened today, I am going to give them the opportunity to have a second try at me. When they do; I will end this threat to my family permanently."

When Jason and Chris moved to do as Eric ordered, they paused after barely taking a step when Eric spoke again. "I want the information on Rebecca that you both learned today to stay secret for the time being. Once I discover who attacked my house and the threat is eliminated, then I plan to tell her the truth."

"Eric," Chris began with disapproval ringing loud in his voice. "I couldn't be happier that you not only found your true mate, but that you finally pulled your head out of the sand when it came to Rebecca. That being said, do you think it is wise to introduce her to the pack before you claim her fully?"

"What are you getting at?" Eric raised a brow at his beta's question, his lips pressing into a hard line at the thought of not fully claiming Rebecca.

"If you introduce her to the pack before there is a bond between you, what's to stop her from running or denying your claim on her as her mate?"

"Either scenario will get Rebecca killed by the pack, Alpha." Jason agreed with a solemn look.

Rising to his feet, Mark held up a staying hand as he stepped in the middle between the two betas and their Alpha. "Hold up here. Are you guys suggesting what I think you are?" Mark asked, pointing an accusing finger at Chris and Jason. "Are you really suggesting that Eric forcibly turns his mate and then just tosses her in front of the pack? Giving her a *take it or leave it* deal?"

As if I would give her an option to say no... Eric thought with a dark scowl.

"What other option is there?" Jason asked. "It would ensure that she'd be safe from the pack. I'm sure she'd eventually understand."

A mocking laugh rang out from Mark. "Trust me, I know from experience that forcibly binding your mate to you and dealing with the consequences later *never* works out for the best." Mark replied with a heavy look of regret.

At Mark's words, Eric felt his curiosity peaked. Was there more to Mark than he knew about? Mark had never mentioned a mate or any family other than his elusive pack. Making a mental note to discuss the topic with Mark at a later date, Eric settled heavily in his chair, his thoughts returning to his own mate.

Could he really find it within himself to take away Rebecca choice as Jason and Chris suggested? Did the pros and cons truly balance in this? Sighing he began weighing the options.

Pros: Rebecca would fully be his, she would be safe from the Act of Revealment, and she would become a shifter within a week's time; making her impervious to most injuries. *Cons*: It would destroy any headway he'd made with her in the last week, she could come to hate him or even fear him, and the possibility that she would run from him regardless was still a concern. Either way he looked at it, he'd be silting his wrist when it came to Rebecca.

Go to her. His wolf urged. *You'll know what to do then.*

For the first time, Eric found solace with his beast's reasoning. He still had at least two days before all of the pack would be here. He had time to bind her him in every other way. Perhaps that would be enough to convince her to accept his mating mark. Rebecca was a reasonable person; she'd see it his way.

With his mind made up and the pull of his mate too great to ignore any further, Eric rose from his chair and passed the arguing trio. As he left, Mark, Jason, and Chris's voices fell silent. Turning down a separate hall, Eric made his way to the kitchen. With every step his wolf prowled in a nearly stalking manner as the scent of their mate grew stronger.

* ~ * ~ *

Winching with pain as Rebecca reached out to hand both Travis and Emma a small bowl of chocolate ice cream, she forced a smile as the sad eyes of the twins gazed up at her. The simple treat did little to lift the dark clouds from their minds.

"I want Mr. Stripes." Emma said with a sad expression.

Knowing that Emma needed the comfort of her stuffed tiger, Rebecca took a seat beside Emma. Looking down at her bowl of ice cream the small girl's bottom lip trembled as a single tear tracked down her face. The small drop of moisture was like a knife in Rebecca's heart.

Earlier when they'd left the infirmary, Sarah had told the children that they would be staying at the lodge for a few days while Eric tided up a few things. Their reacted hadn't been the best. The twins had instantly cried and grumbled with displeasure that not going home to their toys and seeing their friends at school for the next few days. If not for Rebecca's suggestion that they get some ice cream, the two shifter children would still be stubbornly sitting on the tiled floor of Dr. Tessa's office.

Reaching out to wipe away the fallen tear, Rebecca softened her expression as she spoke. "I'm sure your daddy will go and get Mr. Stripes for you, Emma. It's just for a few days."

With crossed arms over his small chest, Travis grumbled shoving his bowl of ice cream away. "I want to go home. I want my game boy."

Turning to look at Sarah who stood at the sink, Rebecca sighed before turning her attention back to Travis. "I'm sure you guys can go home in a day or so." Turning back to Emma as more tears continued to fall down her reddened cheeks, Rebecca looked pointingly at the untouched ice cream in front of her. "You should eat your ice cream before it melts. I think ice cream tastes so much better when it is cold, don't you Emma?"

Pressing her small lips together, the small girl nodded. Slowly, her small fingers curled around her spoon before pulling her bowl closer. With a scowling look, Travis eventually did the same. Once both children were quietly eating their treat, Rebecca stiffly rose to her feet to join Sarah by the kitchen counter. The old woman was busy working on adding spices to some type of dough in a mixing bowl. As Rebecca leaned wearily against the counter beside her, Sarah lifted her gaze to her.

Eyeing the crudely wrapped bandage around Rebecca's left forearm with a critical eye, Sarah shook her head. "You should have gotten that looked at."

Smiling faintly against the humming pain in her arm, Rebecca shrugged. "I'll be fine. It's just a few scratches." Rebecca said, attempting to downplay her actual injuries.

The truth was that when they had taken Emma and Travis to be checked out by the doctor in residence at the lodge, Rebecca had been too scared to let the glaring woman near her. Dr. Tessa was a shifter like all the rest, but even she could see the inner hate boiling in the doctor's eyes.

The extent of her injuries had been from when she'd dived under the table to rescue Emma during the attack. Shards of glass had cut into her arm that had slid along the floor on impact. Other than a few tender muscles and bruises, she would be fine in a day or so. Not that she intended to stay here this long.

Emma and Travis had Sarah to look after them—they didn't need her; which had been her excuse for lingering all morning. With Eric occupied elsewhere, now was her chance to slip away for good. Turning to Sarah, Rebecca positioned her body until her back was facing Emma and Travis.

"Sarah I need a favor."

Lifting her gaze from her mixing bowl, Sarah frowned. "What type of favor?"

"I need to get a ride back into town. There are some things I need to take care of at home."

When Sarah looked hesitant to say anything, Rebecca felt her hope deflate in her chest like a balloon. About to say something to persuade her further, Rebecca was cut short when she sensed someone else coming into the wide kitchen. Every bone in her body froze as she took in the sight of Eric standing in the doorway. His hard gaze fell on her in an assessing manner and made her nervous. She still hadn't forgotten what she'd overheard in the kitchen this morning.

They know...

Swallowing past the thick knot in her throat, a gust of breath escaped her lips when Eric's gaze dropped from hers and to his children. Instantly he strode towards them, his hands falling on the top of their heads to gently brush at their hair as he spoke softly to them. She could hear what was said, but whatever he did say seemed to put the children at ease.

Almost too quickly he turned toward her and Sarah, his eyes filled with displeasure.

Oh God. I'm too late.

Was this it? Would he expose her know in front of Emma and Travis? Did Sarah already know too? Before she could question it further, Eric stood toe to toe with her. His eyes latched on to hers like a steel clawed trap.

With a gentler expression warming his face, he turned to Sarah with a faint smile. "Could you keep an eye on Emma and Travis for a few hours?" At Sarah unconcerned nod, Rebecca felt herself become sick with fear. Too fast for her to anticipate, Eric's hand settled over her uninjured arm, tugging her toward the kitchen doorway.

"Eric, where are you taking me? Stop." She hissed out, attempting to twist from his hold. Once they were out in the long hallway that led to the main lobby, she fought harder, no longer afraid of drawing the attention of the twins. "Let go of me."

"I will let go of you when I am good and ready to do so." He stated in a surprisingly calm tone. "First thing; we have some unfinished business that needs to be dealt with."

Dealt with?

Her worst fears had been confirmed. He was going to drag her off somewhere and kill her. Just as that murderous werewolf had attempted to do all those years ago. Shoving away her fear that demanded she cry and cower, she fought harder. She struck at his back with a feeble closed fist as she kicked out at him. She may as well have been attempting to beat up a steel vault with a rolled up newspaper for all the good it did.

Still forcibly tugging her along, Eric dragged her back through the main lobby before heading toward the infirmary once more. When no others were in sight, Eric promptly stopped, spinning towards her with a hard look.

"If you don't stop hitting me, I will have to ensure you don't otherwise."

Still tugging at her captured arm, she glared at him. For the first time since the attack, her fear of what he would do to her once he knew the truth no longer held sway over her. Courage mounting, she bared her teeth at him with anger.

"If you think I'm going to make this easy for you; think again! Now let go of me before I do some real damage to you." She threatened. It actually felt good to strike back at him, almost like she'd been freed in some way.

Eric's reaction hadn't been what she'd expected. Surely at this point he would have turned and attacked her. After all; what was stopping him at this point? Instead of attacking her, his hard expression softened into a mocking grin before he carelessly shrugged his shoulders.

"Fine by me."

Her world suddenly shifted as Eric jerked her close before bending at the waist heaving her over his shoulder. With one arm around the back of her knees, he pinned her legs to his chest as he began walking again. Gasping in outrage she did everything she could think of; biting, cursing, slapping and punching at his back, though not one single effort seemed to make a difference.

 Before she knew it, she saw that he was striding through the double doors of the infirmary. Why was he bringing her here? Before she could ask, he drew her off his shoulder to sit her on an examination table with jostling movements. Quickly she gripped the edge of the table to prevent from falling forward at her abrupt landing.

From across the room, Dr. Tessa stood up from behind her desk with stiff movements. It was clear that she wasn't happy to see Rebecca back. With angry pursed lips, she attempted to give Eric a look of submission.

"Was there something you needed?"

"I am taking use of your infirmary since you cannot be trusted to do your job."

Scoffing with dismay, Dr. Tessa shoved at her long black hair, causing the glossy waves to fall down her back. "I do my job to the letter, *Eric.* I have always done whatever you've asked."

"Until today," Eric bit out shoving back from Rebecca. Giving Rebecca a hard look, he muttered "Don't even think of moving from this spot." Shoving past the glaring doctor, he began retrieving bandages and antiseptic from the tall mounted shelves against the far wall before returning to Rebecca's side.

What was he doing?

Looking past Eric as he laid out the items he'd collected, Rebecca found her eyes drawn to the glaring woman a few feet from her. If she wasn't so terrified in at moment, Rebecca may have conceded that she was pretty in an average sort of way. She wore her hair nearly down to her waist in long black waves. It wasn't until Dr. Tessa had shoved impatiently at her hair that Rebecca took notice of a thick scar on the right side of her face, where an ear should have been. From what she'd learned of shifters, they had excellent healing abilities, so why was this doctor so horribly scarred? As if feeling her scrutiny, Dr. Tessa stiffened before pulling her long hair over the right side of her face, hiding the hideous scars from view.

"Leave us." Eric bit out when he noticed that the doctor had made no move to help or speak.

With an angry huff the woman stormed from the room, the edges of her white lab coat drifting behind her with her quick strides. Once they were alone, Eric took possession of her bandaged arm and quickly unwrapped the work she'd done just hours ago.

Still surprised at why he was attempting to attend to her wounds instead of killing her, she stared at him stunned. What was he doing? Slapping at his hand, she attempted to pull her arm from him. "See the bandage, genius; that means I already took care of it. Now let me go."

"Shut up and hold still." Eric grated out as he ripped the rest of the gauze wrapping away to reveal a bloody bandage beneath. Tossing the length of gauze aside, he tenderly held her arm still as he lifted the bloody bandage away.

Eric felt his heart squeeze in his chest at the sight of her wounded arm. He supposed in retrospect it wasn't *that* bad, but inside he shook with fury that someone had harmed his mate. On the underside of her forearm was several thin cut from glass, the edges of each cut was red and irritated. The worst of her injuries was a single three inch cut diagonally across her arm. It was deep and still bled a bit.

"You should have had these seen to." he scolded, turning to rip the cap from the bottle of antiseptic. Quickly dumping nearly the whole bottle on her arm, he held her still as she cried out in pain as the wound bubbled with the contact.

"Ow! You ass!"

"There you go with your language problem." He teased. Taking a thick gauze pad, he patted the area dry then he worked on bandaging the treated wounds. "Perhaps something needs done with that mouth of yours. A good wash with soap would help your disposition too I bet."

"You're such a jerk, Eric." she grumbled out before wincing in pain at the pressure to her wound.

He inclined his head at her words as he secured the bandage on her arm with two crisscrossed strips of tape. "I may be a jerk, but I am the only jerk you will know."

Rolling her eyes, she scoffed. *Oh look; arrogant Eric is back. What a surprise.* "Why? Are you saying you're meaner than every other man?"

Lifting his amused gaze to her scowling one, he smirked. "No. But I am the only jerk that is going to be inside you." His hands settled on her thigh, as his hands squeezed and caress her muscles. His touch had her shivering within second. Bastard.

Slapping at his hands until he moved them to rest on the table beside each of side of her hips, she glowered at him. "Do you always feel the need to talk about sex? Don't be so vulgar."

"Vulgar?" A single brow rose at the word. "That wasn't me being vulgar. If I wanted to be vulgar I would tell you how I loved how you clawed at my back like a sexy kitten or how I loved being inside you. The feel of your hot body wrapped around mine..."he groaned with the memory as he leaned closer to her. "I couldn't decide whether to sink so far into your soft body and stay there or drive into you until you never remember what it felt like to be without me."

Womb clinching, Rebecca felt her breast grow heavy. Heat flooded her face as every cryptic word slipped from his lips. Gulping she looked away from him, her body trembled slightly at the feel of heat from his body as he pressed between her splayed legs.

What the hell was wrong with her? Just moments ago she was sure he was dragging her off to kill her and now he had rebandaged her arm and now was *flirting* with her. Was it possible that he didn't know her secret after all?

If that was the case then why had Chris and Jason showed up as they did and what was the scheme Eric was involved in and how did she fit it? Ugh! Too many questions crowded her brain, confusing and irritating her. Not to mention that the feel of Eric hard body pressing between her spread legs was causing her body to vibrate with need, distracting her from her thoughts.

She flinched with surprise as his hand cupped the side of her face, his face lowering closer to hers. Like a trapped animal, she held herself still. Surprise filled her when his forehead suddenly pressed against her own. Then for the briefest moment, she could have sworn she'd felt him tremble against her. It was more likely that it had been her instead or simply her imagination.

"You should have demanded that Dr. Tessa looked at your arm. What if you had been hurt worse?" When he lifted his face from hers, Rebecca gripped his wrist and tugged his hand away from her cheek.

She shrugged. "It doesn't matter."

"It does matter!" he snarled. His eyes gone wild and were glowing.

"And don't think for a moment that I have forgotten how you kicked me in the face and ran straight into a shower of bullets! I should tan your ass for that!"

"I am not a child!" she shouted at him. "I wasn't about to let Emma get hurt because…" *of me.* Was it possible that other shifters had discovered her secret and decided to attack Eric's home? Had she nearly gotten them all killed?

"No, you're right." Eric agreed in a quiet tone, his eyes still boring into hers with a look of anger. "You're not my child, but you are mine."

She would be lying if she said that his possessive words didn't make her heart swell. She wanted that. To hold onto that look that he flashed at her now, the same look that he'd given her last night as he'd taken her. With everything in her she wanted to be able to trust that Eric wouldn't turn on her if he knew her secret, but it wasn't a gamble she was willing to take.

Forcing her gaze away, she shoved at his chest. "Let me down."
With an annoyed roll of his eyes, Eric stepped back allowing her to
slide down from the tall table. Straightening her blouse, she looked
up at Eric. "Thanks for saving my life. I would be dead if not for
you." She admitted with a slight smile.

Crossing his arms over his chest, he replied. "Don't remind me how
close you nearly came to dying, Rebecca. I don't like thinking about
it. If I have anything to say about it; you won't be put in danger like
that ever again."

Her fragile smile fell. If only she could believe him. Sighing, she
looked away from him. Without a word she started for the door. It
wasn't long until the small hairs at the base of her neck stood on end
as she felt him coming up behind her. Stopping, she glanced over her
shoulder to see that he was walking beside her as if they were going
for an afternoon stroll.

"What do you think you're doing?"

"Following you. Something tells me that you shouldn't be left on
your own or I may have to hunt you down."

Hunt you down…

If that phrase didn't worry her, nothing else would. She was correct
about trusting Eric; it wasn't something she could risk. "I'm leaving,
Eric." She said with a firm look, daring him to tell her otherwise.

His eyebrows rose in mocking surprise. "Oh, are you now? Did you
really think that I would let you out of my sight, especially after
what nearly happened this morning?"

"As much as I worry about Emma and Travis, I know they will be
safe here with you and your family. But what happened has nothing
to do with me. I'm leaving." When she turned to walk down the hall
once more, her head fell back against her neck as she growled with
frustration at the echoing sound of his footsteps beside her.

"Even if I was willing to let you run from me *again*, you could be in danger after today. You will remain here until I can figure out who tried to kill us this morning."

Before she could question if Eric knew anything about who had attacked them this morning, she heard a voice call out to her from behind her. "Rebecca."

Knowing the voice wasn't Eric's; her curiosity was peaked, causing her to turn toward the voice. She froze in place as she saw Damon striding to them. Dressed in a pair of jeans and a black t-shirt with his blonde hair slicked back, Rebecca was surprised there wasn't a fan club of panting girls trailing behind this man.

At the thought, Rebecca found herself mentally slapping herself. Why was she ogling *him?* She had to remind herself that she wasn't convinced that Damon hadn't spilled her secret to Eric or the rest of Eric's pack. What other explanation was there for the events this morning? She highly doubted that as an architect; that Eric had attempts on his life.

Though Eric hadn't attempted to kill her—yet, she still felt wary as to why he was so desperate to keep her from leaving him. He had to know. He more than likely simply wanted to keep her close to find out what all she knew before he killed her, which meant that she had no ally now; least of all Damon.

Schooling her apprehension, Rebecca smiled friendly at Damon as he came to stop in front of them. Almost instantly she noticed that Eric's face had darkened at the sight of Damon. His hands fisting at his sides as a low rumble echoed so softly in his chest that she would have missed it if she hadn't been standing so close.

"What are you doing here, Damon?" she asked.

Before he could answer, Eric echoed her question as well. "Yes. *What* are you doing here, Damon? I would have thought that since your business was concluded here, you would be on your way." Eric bit out with a murderous glare.

Shrugging his shoulders, Damon chuckled. "I found something to stay for I suppose." His eyes turning to give her a lingering look before flashing Eric a knowing look.

Was she missing something here? Was Damon still attempting to make Eric jealous as he had that one night?

Waste of time, if you ask me. She thought.

Regardless of what Damon's personal game was, she had to find out what he'd told Eric and who else knew her secret. If she was lucky she could find a way out from under Eric's watchful gaze and escape to freedom. She just had to get Damon alone.

Easier said, than done. She acknowledged grimly.

* ~ * ~ *

Fire burned in his stomach as Eric watched Damon look down at Rebecca with a gentle look. *I should have killed him!* What right did he think he'd possibly have to Rebecca? As far as Eric knew; Rebecca and Damon hadn't seen each other since the night of their *date*. God; that word had never tasted so foul in his mouth before, it was even worse when he remembered that night.

Surely Rebecca wasn't fooled by Damon's playboy charm. Much to his irritation, he acknowledged that Rebecca was even able to resist his own brand of seduction. *To a degree.* Eric thought with a smug grin pulling at the corners of his lips. Despite what Rebecca may say, her body didn't lie when it came to him. She was his in every way. Without a doubt he knew that he didn't need to worry about Damon attempting to pouch his mate.

Turning to look at his soon-to-be-claimed mate with his jaw slackening, Eric felt his blossoming pride in the situation deflate rapidly as he took in her returning smile. She looked at Damon like she was…happy. Happy to see *Damon?!* Why the hell hadn't she ever looked at him like that?

Jealously filled his gut like a thick oil, sickening him and fueling his rage all the more. Damon wouldn't be getting within a foot of her after this if it was the last thing he ever did.

Grinning at Eric, Damon ran a smoothing hand over his jaw. "I'm sure you'll be happy to know that I didn't sustain any permanent damage to my handsome face from your little tap the other night."

Fighting against the need to lunge at him and remedy the situation, Eric muttered. "Ecstatic."

Shrugging his shoulders at Eric's response, he turned back to Rebecca with a softening expression. "I heard about what happened this morning." Reaching out his hands settled on Rebecca's shoulders as he stepped closer to her. "I am so glad you are alright."

Eric's eyes widened as they fell on the hands that dared to touch *his* mate. *Now I really will kill him!*

Take our mate from him! She isn't properly bound to us and he will take her! His wolf snarled as he shared Eric's rage at another touching their mate.

Before Eric could step forward to kill the back stabbing wolf in front of him, much to his relief, Rebecca shrugged his hands off of her shoulders.

"I am fine. Just a few cuts and bruises." She stated nonchalant with a shrug.

Eric bit on his tongue to prevent from pointing out that she'd nearly gotten herself killed and had injured herself badly. The last thing he needed was Damon fawning over his mate even more than he already was.

"I'm glad you both are safe; especially you Rebecca."

Not bothering to cover his scoff at Damon's sweet words, Eric stepped between the two as one of his arms curled around Rebecca's stiff shoulders. "Regardless what your *real* reason for staying here; run along. Rebecca and I are busy." He prayed that Damon was intelligent enough to understand the not-so subtle hint in his voice. Moving to steer Rebecca away from the *possible* threat, Eric flashed Damon a look that said; *this one is mine.*

"Damon, wait." Eric froze at Rebecca's pleading tone as she held a staying hand out to Damon. "I need to talk to you...privately."

Privately? PRIVATELY?! Why the hell would they need to be in private—without him there? Mere thoughts of why this would be needed had Eric nearly grinding his teeth into powder. Perhaps they wanted to pick up where their *date* had ended? There was no way in hell he was leaving Rebecca alone with this wolf.

Clearly enjoying Eric's anger at what was occurring, Damon shrugged his shoulders. "Sure. Will you walk with me?"

Returning his smile, Rebecca extracted herself from under Eric's heavy arm too quickly for his stunned mind to act. His breaths became more ragged with his control of his wolf slipping when she allowed Damon to clasp her hand tenderly within his own.

His pelt will be a nice addition to my bedroom décor.

Rebecca must have sensed his anger at Damon, because she turned to look at Eric like he was a third wheel nuisance. "I'll see you later." She stated with a distracted voice.

Had she just *dismissed* him? Oh no. He wasn't going to chase after *his mate* like some pathetic lap dog. Feeling his wolf breaking through the bonds that kept him from shifting and ripping Damon's throat out on principle alone, Eric forced himself to spin away from them and head toward the main section of the house.

He was in no way done with Rebecca, but until he informed and accustomed her to what he was, he couldn't risk scaring her. Once his rage wasn't so high he intended to drag her back to his room and have a long drawn out talk with her. The first thing he would be sure to decree to her was that she would have absolutely *no* contact with Damon ever again.

17

Moments later, after leading Damon far enough away from Eric until she was certain their conversation wouldn't be overheard, Rebecca turned around a corner to jerk her hand from Damon's tender grasp to shove at him angrily.

"How could you!" she hissed out, both her hands shoving at his powerful chest pushing him off balance until he stumbled back a step.

"Rebecca?" With a shocked look, he adjusted his footing to take a step towards her, reaching a hand out to her.

Angry tears burned in her eyes. Acknowledgement of how stupid she'd been to trust him was like a slap in the face. He'd promised to protect her secret. She'd thought him to be a friend, an ally. How gullible she was! He'd betrayed her and now he had the nerve to look hurt by her reaction to him. Screw him!

"Don't touch me!" she cried, slapping his hand away from her. "I trusted you! I confided in you!"

Holding out his hands up in surrender, he took a step closer to her, his eyes filling more and more with concern. "Rebecca, it's me, Damon."

"Oh, I know who you are, Damon." She answered bitterly. "Now I really see you for the man you are."

Eyes narrowing in question, he shook his head. Hands dropping to his sides, Damon released a heavy breath. "What is going on, Rebecca?"

"Don't act like you don't know." She snapped. "Eric knows and according to Jason and Chris so do everyone else." Curling her nose at him, her tiny finger stabbed into the middle of his chest. "I don't know if you are involved in Eric's scheme—"

"Rebecca, Eric doesn't know." Damon quickly interrupted.

Stilling, she dropped her jabbing finger from his chest. Rage lessening, she took a step back from him. "What?"

Damon shook his head as he flashed a gentle smile. "Eric doesn't know. That's why I am still here." He looked as though he meant to say more but quickly snapped his mouth closed. Casting a suspicious look around them, he stepped closer to her, pressing a flat hand against the middle of her back. "It's not safe to talk out in the open. We might be overheard. Come with me."

Too surprised at the new revelation, she mutely allowed Damon to direct her to a small room that served as a storage room. Closing the heavy door behind them, Damon pulled her amongst the maze of towering shelves until they were out of sight of the door. Placing his back against a wooden shelve, he allowed his hand to drop from her.

Taking a step back from him, Rebecca shook off her shocked expression to eye the werewolf warily. Could she trust that he was telling the truth? If what he said was true and Eric didn't know her secret, that information only left her with even more questions than answers.

Crossing her arms over her chest, she took a step back, placing a comforting foot of space between them. "What did you mean that's why you're still here?"

He sighed. "Listen to me. As far as I know; Eric doesn't know your secret and neither do anyone of his pack."

"How can you know for certain? You even said, "*as far as I know*". That means you could be wrong."

"I'm never wrong." He stated smugly. "As for why I am still here, the reason is I'm here for you." Shoving his hands into his jean pockets, he took a step towards her, his golden eyes bearing heavily into her own.

"What do you mean?" she stuttered out. "If you're trying to hit on me again; now is not the time."

Chuckling low, he shook his head. "I'm not hitting on you. I am here for you—to help you."

"Help me how?"

"You need to confide in Eric."

Air rushed from her lungs as panic swelled within her. Was he insane? She may as well as take a gun and blow her brains out herself. "Are you crazy?" she hissed out. Shaking her head, she stepped back from him like he was a dangerous animal. "You promised you would help keep me safe. How is revealing my secret to Eric helping?"

"I cannot remain here in his territory for much longer. I have been called back to my pack. I'm here on borrowed time already. But I don't want to leave unless I know for certain that you will be protected against the wrath of Eric's pack."

"I'll run and disappear. I've done it before I can do it again."

"Running and hiding will not protect you from the Right of Revealment."

Squeezing her eyes closed she shook her head. "What are you talking about?"

"The Right of Revealment. It is a law that is evoked by shifters whenever our secret is threatened to being exposed by a human. It states that if a human knows or even suspects what we are; they are to be eradicated immediately for the good of all shifters. There is only one loophole in this law that can save the human from a painful and terrifying death."

Nearly afraid of what he would say, Rebecca found the courage to ask, "What?"

"If the human is claimed as a true mate."

"Like a wife?"

"It's much more than that, but yes. True mates are rare amongst shifters. Only a small number of shifters have been lucky enough to find their true mate's. For my kind, true mates are our soul mates times thousands. Our true mates have the ability to draw out our inner beast fully and doing so; uniting the shifter and their inner spirit. True mates are our matches in every way and become our lifeline once we claim them."

"Claim?"

Waving away her question, he continued. "In all of our history, a human has only turned out to be a true mate in a couple of times, but here recently more and more shifters are finding their soul mates amongst humans. You are Eric's true mate."

For a moment she blankly stared at him. Then; a moment later a snort of laughter bubbled up from between her lips. Covering her mouth as she laughed, Rebecca shook her head at him. "You're funny."

With a stony expression, he replied. "I'm serious."

Laughter fading, Rebecca's expression filled with doubt. "No. It's not possible."

"Answer me this; do you feel drawn to Eric? Like something is tying you to him and won't let you stay away from him? Do you feel a connection to him even though you don't know why? Do you hunger for him against your own will? Do you feel possessive of him?" The dawning realization on her face was Damon's answer. "Those are all signs of true mates."

"You're mistaken. Yes, I find him attractive and feel a connection to him, but that's just because we had sex."

Nodding in understanding, he stepped into her personal space. "Let me prove it to you." His hands suddenly clasped her hips in his hands, jerking her up against his hard body. "Kiss me."

"E-Excuse me?"

"If Eric is not your true mate and you are not his; nothing should stop you from wanting another. Kiss me and you will know for certain."

When Rebecca made no move to kiss him, Damon grew impatient and reached up to grip her ponytail in his fist. Holding her still with his hand in her hair and the other wrapped around her waist, Damon's mouth crashed down over hers.

Eyes wide, Rebecca stiffened under his moving mouth. Even as she held herself stiff against him, she felt Damon's mouth move against hers, attempting to entice a reaction. She expected to feel the warm rush of sensations that always accompanied Eric's kisses. But Damon's kiss only left her feeling cold. It wasn't a moment longer until Damon lifted his mouth from hers. The hand that had held the back of her head still, now slid down to rest at the back of her neck.

With a blank look, Damon shook his head at her. "Even I know that you didn't find that kiss remotely stirring." Dropping his hands from her, he took a step back. Crossing his arms over his chest, pulling the material of his t-shirt tighter over his muscled chest, he watched her. Waiting for her to deny his words and to deny that Eric wasn't the only one she wanted.

Rebecca shook her head. "This isn't poss—"

"Don't even bother to finish that sentence. It's true, Rebecca. The longer you fight this the less time you have to save your life."

Turning away from him, her arms wrapped around her middle as she paced back and forth. Spinning back to him, her gaze was troubled as her teeth bit down into her bottom lip. "How did you know?" she asked softly.

"If you watch someone close enough and often enough, you can see things that they won't admit to even themselves. Every since you came into Eric's life, he'd been different. More on edge and almost everyone could sense his wolf rising against his control more and more. Eric simply didn't want to admit it to himself."

Her eyes narrowed with suspicion. "Why then did you ask me on a date if you knew that I was his?"

That night, Damon had said that he wanted to force Eric out of his own stubborn ways, but for what purpose? What did Damon have to gain for Eric to know the truth about her?

His crossed arms fell as he rubbed a tired hand at the tight muscles of his neck. With a groan he answered. "There is only one thing that can push a shifter's beast over the edge faster than anything and that is another male threatening to take a mate away. I knew that if Eric wouldn't see reason; his wolf would force him to."

"I still don't see why you went through all this just to throw me and Eric together. We don't even like each other."

"You may think he doesn't like you, but trust me when I say that Eric would kill anything and anyone that came between him and you." Taking a step closer a heavy weight seemed to settle upon his shoulders. "Listen to me, I am telling you this not to scare you or to push you; but to warn you. The only chance you have at surviving is to tell Eric your secret as soon as possible."

Icy terror filled her at the thought of doing what he asked. There was no way she possessed that kind of courage to lay her life on the line and pray with fingers crossed that Eric would be understanding and protect her. "I can't do that."

"You have to." he said earnestly.

"You said that you would be my protector." she pointed out, grasping for anything but telling Eric the truth.

"I *can't*." his voice strained woefully. With a defeated look, he clenched his fists at his sides. "I hoped that I could keep others from finding out your secret, but I had always hoped that you would eventually confide in Eric. But things are happening that changes all that."

Sensing the seriousness of what he was trying to tell her, she asked. "What things?"

"A power struggle is occurring within Eric's pack. Many will want him dead and anyone who stands with him. It won't matter whether others know about you or not."

"Power struggle? What about this scheme Jason and Chris mentioned?"

"Thing you have to know about wolf shifters is that we are very power hungry and territorial beings. We don't do change well and for our safety; we stick with our own. Eric has been secretly forming alliances with other packs of different castes, something that no wolf shifter has done in a long time. He's changing traditions that have stood for thousands of years and it is causing his own pack to rebel against him."

"With all that happening you still think it's a good idea to unload my secret on Eric? You're crazy."

"Rebecca, regardless how your secret comes out, Eric is the *only* person that can spare your life. I have no doubt that Eric's enemies are watching him, his children and you for a weakness. As bad as this will sound; you are a liability to Eric. Why do you think that his home was shot up this morning? You will never be completely safe until Eric claims you as his."

Eyes filling with tears at the finality of her situation, she squeezed her arms tighter around herself. Running was out of the question now. Eric's enemies would find her, whether to kill her for the secret she harbored or to strike back at Eric. Unmistakably; she was a walking target.

Seeing her watering eyes, Damon stepped forward, his arms wrapping around her and drawing her to his chest. Smoothing a flat hand over the top of her hair, he sighed. "I promise to stay until the next full moon; that's a week away. According to my information, Eric has summoned everyone to gather here in the next few days. He plans to use the opportunity to draw out his enemies. You need to tell him before someone tries again."

Tilting her head back to look at him, she blinked her hopeless tears away. Damon was right. She couldn't hide any longer. It was time for her to stop running. She had to trust Eric and trust this bond between them.

"You promise you won't leave me?" She was disgusted at how pathetic she sounded, but the truth was, Damon was her safety net, at least for the time being. She wanted to trust Eric to cling to him like she did with Damon. Though Damon was just a precarious friend, Eric was more and could be much more if their reaction to each other was anything to go by.

His hand cupping her cheek, he smiled down at her. It was a warm, caring smile and his touch against her face no longer felt flirtatious, but brotherly. "For as long as you need me, I promise."

"She doesn't need you." A dark voice said from behind them. "She's mine and you; my back stabbing friend are dead."

* ~ * ~ *

Unable to walk any further, Eric feet stumbled as he fell against the wall to his left. His claws spouted from his fingertips, leaving grooves in the wall as he fought to hold himself up. It was too much, he couldn't fight it. Beneath his skin, his beast rose.

Panting he bit back a snarl of pain as his beast rose, so did the deep ache in his chest, the ache of refusing to claim his mate. To make matters worse, he'd walked away from another mate, leaving her with another male! His wolf wouldn't accept it and now; neither could he. If he was forced to reveal what he was to Rebecca this day because of his lack of control, then so be it. He would attempt to make her understand what he was and quell her fear that would follow, then he intended to claim her until there was no chance of her ever leaving him.

With a determined look, he shoved the pain in his chest away, forcing his legs to move, he straightened to his full height. Turning back toward Rebecca's lingering scent, with his claw fisted hands at his sides, he followed her trail back to her. When he passed Doctor Tessa on her way back to the infirmary, he snarled in her direction, never breaking a stride.

Coming to a stop, Eric found he could no longer follow Rebecca's scent. Her sweet drugging scent was cut off as he came to a stop at the heavy door of the large medical storage room. Why would she need to talk to Damon in here?

Carefully pushing the door open, he stepped into the sun lit room. Immediately Rebecca and Damon's combined scents hit him in the face. It should be *his* scent mixed with hers and *his* only.

In time, He silently assured himself. *Breathe. Control.*

Past several shelves he could hear their murmuring voices, but he was too frenzied at retrieving his mate to pay attention to their words. Moving on quiet steps, he flattened his body against a shelf, peering around the edge. He needed to retrieve his mate; but he needed to know what pull Damon had over her. Observing them for a moment wouldn't cause any harm.

Gripping the edge of a wooden shelf, he felt his hands pulverize the thick wood to splinters as his eyes took in the sight before him. Just a few feet away stood Rebecca…being kissed by Damon.
His eyes took notice of how Damon held her against his body. His arm around her waist as his free hand buried amongst the strands of her ponytail, his clenching fingers holding her close as his mouth moved over her.

Killing rage seized him. It was official. He was going to let loose his wolf and kill Damon in the most bloody and painful way possible and if he was lucky, he'd have time to shift to his human form and do some damage as well before the traitor died.

Glancing away, he gritted his teeth as his wolf fought to attack. If he attacked Damon now; he risked his human mate. Sighing, he forced himself under control. He blocked out the sound of their hushed voices as they spoke. He didn't want to hear what the two were saying to each other. If Rebecca were to say that she loved Damon, there was no way his wolf would be able to remain calm.

It was Beth all over again. Why would fate be so cruel to give him his true mate and have her fall for another? He vowed silently that he would fight this time. He wouldn't another mate to leave him. Rebecca was his, if he had to win her from Damon, he would do so.

As he focused on his breathing to bring down his primal aggression, a thought occurred to him. As they had kissed, Eric had noticed that Rebecca didn't return Damon's embrace, nor had her lips moved against Damon's with willing abandon. Not like they had with his.

When he'd taken Rebecca last night, she'd clawed at him as her lips moved over him. Her body had strained against his, as though she couldn't get close enough. Even this morning she'd responded to his kiss with such passion even without him touching her. Was it possible that Rebecca didn't want Damon? The thought gave him hope.

When he could finally see past the red haze of jealousy that had clouded his mind, Eric turned back to the two. This time, Damon had his arms around her in a different way. His arms held her to his chest while his hand smoothed tenderly over the top of her head. More focused, Eric picked up more scents in the room; sadness and fear. The bitter smelling emotions rolled off Rebecca in waves, urging him to go to her. But when Damon spoke, Eric felt his feet freeze, unmoving.

"I promise to stay until the next full moon; that's a week away. According to my information, Eric has summoned everyone to gather here in the next few days. He plans to use the opportunity to draw out his enemies. You need to tell him before someone tries again."

Tell him what? Though he was furious that Rebecca had turned to Damon for comfort when she was obviously upset over something, he felt his mind whirl at what he was hearing. What was Rebecca hiding from him? He recalled their conversation earlier this morning, how she'd told him that she had parts of her that he would never touch. How bad was it that she felt more safe telling Damon than him?

"You promise you won't leave me?" Rebecca's voice sounded pleading. Like a child begging a parent not to leave them alone in a dark room. There was so much fear in her. Her fear would be his enemy and he would defeat it. He just needed to discover what she was hiding.

Gazing down at her fondly, Damon cupped the side of Rebecca's face as he said, "For as long as you need me, I promise."

Unable to stand remaining in the shadows any longer, Eric stepped from his hiding place. "She doesn't need you." He smirked when he saw Damon's and Rebecca's startling gaze turning to look at him. Focusing on Damon, Eric bit out. "She's mine and you; my back stabbing friend are dead."

Lowering his hands from Rebecca, Damon stepped away from her. Holding his hand out, Damon lowered his head in the universal shifter sign of surrender. Eric scoffed. Like that would save him in the end. The thought of wiping the floor with Damon on principle alone was tempting, but he had more important things to do first, such as discovering what Rebecca was hiding from him.

"How…" Rebecca began with a shaky voice. "How long have you been watching us?"

"Long enough to see that Damon doesn't know how to keep his lips to himself." He bit out with a narrowing look to Damon.

Turning to look down at Rebecca as her face flushed, Eric couldn't resist reaching out to her. Grabbing the front of her blouse, he jerked her to him. Ignoring her gasp, he cupped the sides of her face. He could feel her breasts rising and falling against his chest as she panted for breath. With a concentrating look, Eric smoothed the thick pad of his thumb over her lower lips, wiping away whatever lingered of Damon's lips.

When his hands fell away from her, Eric smirked at her look of confusion. "When I kiss those lips, I want to only taste you—no one else."

Aware that Damon was watching their exchange, Eric rounded on him. "This is the second time that I've caught you with your filthy mouth on my woman." as though sensing Rebecca's outraged response, Damon grinned with a boyish shrug.

Whack! With a dark scowl, Rebecca slapped the back of her hand against Eric's chest. Though she'd most likely put a good amount of strength behind her slap, it felt like a love tap to him.

"Way to make me feel like some toy to be fought over!" she hit him again, her breath escaping with frustrated pants. Shoving impatiently at a lock of hair that had escaped from her ponytail to fall in her eyes, she glared at Eric. "If you even think about attacking Damon I promise I will make you sorry."

She's so fierce, so beautiful...So mine...

Rubbing a hand over the spot where her hand had struck him, he smirked down at her. Right over his heart. She couldn't have hit a more appropriate spot. Emotions that Eric would normally scoff at the mention welled up. He had to uncover everything he could about his mate, because for the first time in years, he was seeing things with perfect clarity.

He was in love this scowling human, with Rebecca.

18

Looking around the room that Eric had just pushed her into, Rebecca took note of her surroundings. The room was nearly the size of her whole small apartment. In the center of the room against the wall was a four poster bed, king size if she had to guess. The frame was made of artistically carved wood. The heavy headboard against the wall held detailed carvings of trees with a full moon rising behind, three wolves running free. Jerking her eyes from the beautiful masterpiece, she also took note of a wide six drawer dresser to against the opposite wall. To the right of the enormous bed was three floor-to-ceiling windows covered by a heavy blue curtain.

Stepping further into the room, she noticed another door to the left of the bed. Walking over to it, she turned the polished silver knob and shoved the door open. The open doorway opened up into a deluxe bathroom. Her eyes widened as she took in the amazing sight of a gray and white covered tub that seemed to be built into the wall. Beside the tub/pool was a glass enclosed shower. Of course the bathroom also held a toilet and a large sink area; she had to admit her attention kept returning to that large bath tub or whatever it was.

At the sound of the bedroom door closing gently, she turned to step out of the bathroom to see if Eric had left her alone finally. Not surprised she watched as he leaned carelessly against her only way out of the room she was in. His arms crossed over his chest almost in a challenging fashion. Did he think she would attempt to escape from him again? Shaking her head, she thought back to moments ago.

After he discovered Damon and her in the storage room, Eric had started up on his possessive bullshit once more. It was strange that he hadn't actually attacked Damon this time though. Instead he'd shoved Damon up against a shelf, pinning him in place with just a hand to his throat. Smirking, Damon had just stood there unafraid of Eric's show of dominance, which only served to piss Eric off all the more.

With words force through clenching teeth, Eric had said. "Stay away from her. This is your last warning."

Jerking his hand away from Damon's throat, Eric had turned to face her. At that moment she'd felt her heart race as he'd strode back towards her. She had to wonder what all he'd actually over heard and she'd made a mental note to find out. Without another word to her or Damon, Eric had done what he usually did with her; shackled her wrist with his hand and preceded to drag her to where ever he wanted. Not keen on ending up thrown over his shoulder for the second time that day, she'd furiously bit her tongue as he'd dragged her past people like she was a suitcase. He'd led her through the main lobby and up a flight of wooden steps to the second level.

After being towed down a long hall, he'd jerked to a stop outside the room she was now in. was this to be her bedroom while she was here? How long would she be here? As the thought occurred, she felt doubt fill her mind. If she was in fact Eric's true mate or whatever Damon had called it, she doubted he would just let her go.

Despite Damon's advice that she tell Eric the truth, she found herself hesitant to do so. It wasn't something that she could just come out and say. What would his reaction be to having been lied to, to being fooled all this time? She doubted he would take it well. She scoffed mocking her own thoughts. He'd probably gift wrap her for his pack. Serve her up on a silver platter and all.

"Do you like it?" Eric's voice cut through the air with an almost impatient tone.

Jerking her head up to look at him, she casted a final look around. "It will do." She finally answered with a lift of her shoulders. She bit her lip to prevent from smiling as his expression tightened at her answer. Apparently her answer mattered to him. Shoving her hands in the pockets of her barrowed sweats, she walked toward the bed, taking a seat on the firm mattress, she met his eyes.

"It's nice—more than nice actually. Is this to be my room?" she asked, smoothing her hand over the soft comforter.

"In a way." He agreed with a nod. "You'll be sharing it with me."

Her hand froze against the comforter. "What?"

Shoving back from the door, Eric's face grew serious. "Why did you need to talk with Damon without me there?"

Rising from the bed, Rebecca did her best not to appear unnerved by his question. "That's between us. It's none of your business."

Like flipping a light switch, Eric's expression turned from stern to mocking. "None of my *business*?" he laughed before his words turned serious. "*Everything* to do with you is my business." Spinning away from her to pace a few steps he turned back to her. "Do…you love him?" he asked not meeting her gaze.

Rebecca felt herself go still at the question. She was used to Eric's jealous behavior. It was absurd to her the idea that she was meant to be *his*, but she'd been around shifters enough to know how *mate bonds* worked. If Eric saw Damon as a threat, it was possible that Eric would kill him. She had to put Damon out of the equation. Until she was certain that she could trust Eric fully, she had to keep her only lifeline hidden.

She shook her head. "No." she answered softly.

Instantly Eric's head jerked up towards her. "You-You don't?" the knowledge seemed to confused and gladden him. "Then why the hell did you kiss him?" he bit out, clearly remembering what he'd seen.

Sighing, Rebecca took a step towards him. "What's it matter? All you need to know is that Damon is a friend—a friend only."

"A friend that keeps your secrets, Secrets you have yet to tell me." He stated accusingly.

And just with those words, Rebecca felt the crushing weight choking her lessen. Eric hadn't heard everything. If he had; he would know *what* Damon and she had been talking about. He didn't know. She sighed with relief.

"Yes." She answered.

Turning away from Eric, she pretended to study the bed once more as her chaotic thoughts turned inward. She had to get some space from him to think. Where did she go from here with Eric? Her eyes turned toward the bathroom with a thought. Latching onto the excuse for all she could use it for, Rebecca turned back to look at Eric. He seemed to be studying her.

"I'm going to take a shower. Do you have anything I can change into?"

Raising a brow at her, he smirked. "Are you running again?" slowly stalking across the room to her, he chuckled low. "I would have thought you learned that I won't let you do that anymore."

"I'm just taking a shower, Eric."

Why did he have to smile at her like that? Already she would feel her body quaking and shivering with need to touch him, to kiss him. She was done for, absolutely done for. How in the world would she be able to share a room with him and not want to climb into that ridiculously big bed with him?

Stepping in front of the path to the bathroom door, she found all amusement had fled Eric's expression. With a pensive tone, he asked. "Why did you think you couldn't trust me with your secrets, yet you told Damon?" pausing, he took in an unsteady breath as his eyes hardened. "Did last night mean nothing to you?"

Heart stilling at his words, she resisted the urge to go to him, to wrap her arms around him and tell him everything. The truth was; last night had meant everything to her. Last night, she'd allowed herself to be held, loved and in the process; she'd allowed herself to forget about the ghosts that haunted her every waking minute. Since the attack, she couldn't remember a single time when she'd allowed herself that simply luxury.

Biting down on her lip, she paused to consider her words before answering. "It didn't mean nothing, Eric." when hope seemed to light his eyes, she quickly added. "I don't know what it meant to me. I want to trust you. I want to know that no matter what happens I can count on you to be beside me."

Reaching out to cup her face, he stepped closer, his thumbs moving in smoothing circles over her cheekbones. "Then trust me." He said, his eyes pleading.

Reaching up, her shaking hands wrapped around his wrists. "How can I? I don't even know what is going on. Why can't I go home? Why were we attacked this morning?" after taking a shaky breath, she then asked. "What is this scheme that Jason and Chris said you were involved in?"

Slowly and reluctantly, his hands slid from her face to drop to his sides. His eyes looked almost pained. His mouth opened to say something; whatever he intended to say, she'd never know. With his eyes growing cold and distant as they normally did when he was about to shut her out, he said, "I am taking care of the situation."

It surprised her when a wave of disappointment hit her at his refusal to tell her anything. Deep down, she'd hoped that he'd confide in her. If he told her something that would show her that he trusted her completely, maybe then she wouldn't feel like she was walking through a field of explosive mines when it came to telling him the truth. But he didn't even trust her to answer a single question she'd asked of him.

"Why would I trust you when you won't even trust me with your own secrets?"

With a scowling look at her, Eric jerked his eyes from hers before weaving around her to go to the covered window. "You need to trust that I know what the right decision is.

Heaving out a heavy sigh, Rebecca turned from him and disappeared into the spacious bathroom. Closing the door behind her, she leaned her weight against it.

She couldn't explain the hurt that assailed her at his refusal to talk to her, to confide in her. If this is what Eric would feel when she told him, she knew now that he would *never* choose her. She was a fool to think that she could ever trust him. There was nothing between them to ensure her that he would *choose* her. Even if she was his fated mate, the one meant for only him and him for her, if he didn't trust her, what hope did they have at a future?

What hope do I have that he will choose me?

* ~ * ~ *

When the door closed softly behind her, Eric flinched, his eyes sliding closed with regret. He was just an idiot! She'd looked at him with such urging, such need. Not a sexual or sensual need, but an emotional one. She'd wanted him to confide in her. He had wanted to tell her about him, what he was and why they had been attacked. He wanted to tell her that he feared for her safety and the need to keep her close to him was undeniable. That she was quickly becoming everything to him. He had wanted to tell her *everything*, but he hadn't.

He knew that if he unloaded the weight of the knowledge that he carried held upon Rebecca, she could collapse. He wanted them to get past the secrets they both held. He longed to be mated to her, to belong to her. Had he blown his chances with his brash words?

Lowering his large body to the edge of the bed, he dropped his head into his left hand with a silent groan. He had to fix this. He had to show her that she could trust him with her secrets, but to do that, he would need to do some digging into his own vault of them.

Remembering Damon's words from earlier only confirmed to him that he was running out of time with Rebecca. In just two days, the pack would gather. He would stand before every wolf shifter under his rule and beside him would be his mate; Rebecca. He would have to tell her before then what he was or it would mean her death.

Never before had he wished to be something other than what the creator had made him, but now he wished with his entire being that he was different, that he was just a normal human man. Would she still wish to be around him when she found out that he was a monster, a man that could change from man to beast in a blink of an eye? No. he couldn't risk telling her too soon or he would lose her.

Never before had he wished to ask that stupid bear, Doyle for advice when it came to human mates. However after his last conversation with Doyle, he doubted the bear would even take his call.

Note to self: Apologize to Doyle for snarling at his mate before I have a very big, grizzly problem to contend with.

Back to the problem at hand, he knew what needed to be done. He had to win her. Show her that he needed her in his life and that he had fallen for her. Lifting his head from his hands, a smile lit his face as an idea formed in his mind. Of course; why hadn't he thought of it before? His solution was simple. He had to get Rebecca to trust him in order to ensure that she wouldn't run in fear from him once he revealed his beast.

He needed to woo his mate.

Jumping to his feet he moved rushed from the room to find her clothes as she'd requested. With the help of his mother and after talking to pack members that lived in several of the cabins at the lodge, he had secured her enough clothing to satisfy her until he could make the trip to town and retrieve her own. His heart had warmed when everyone he'd spoke to was more than helpful and didn't ask too many questions.

Returning to the room not fifteen minutes later, he stepped into his room to the sound of the shower running. His lips curled into a smirk at knowing she was in *his* shower, naked and wet, completely exposed for him. Shoving the pile of clothes in his arms into some random drawer, he pulled off each piece of his clothing as he strode toward the closed door.

Turning the knob, he grinned confidently when he found it unlocked. Clearly she didn't want him to stay away, did she? Nudging the bathroom door open with the edge of his shoulder, he stepped into the steam filled room. His bare foot stepped down on a soft pile of discarded clothing, the same clothing that Rebecca had been in moments ago. Through the heavy cloud of steam he saw Rebecca clearly through the glass shower door. Breath slammed out of his lungs at the sight of her curvy form. His hands itched to slide over the swell of her waist and the flare of her shapely hips and grasp her perfect ass.

Unable to wait a second longer, he shoved down his boxers; the last barrier on his body, before making his way towards her. Without making a sound Eric carefully slipped behind the nearly transparent shower curtain and behind unsuspecting Rebecca.

"Want some help?" He asked teasingly, causing Rebecca to jump, emitting a small squeal of surprise.

"What the hell are you doing?! Get out!" she cried, her arms quickly crossing over her chest to cover her full breasts from him. Licking his lips he smirked at her antics. "Damn you, Eric!" She yelled. Wiping furiously at her irritated eyes, Rebecca positioned her face under the spray of hot water; in effort to rinse out the shampoo that had spilled into her vulnerable eyes when he had surprised her. "What do you want?" She bit out, still attempting to cover her soapy breasts from his eyes.

Chuckling at her reaction, he was surprised when his eyes slid down her body; he saw something that he'd never seen on her before. Across her back he spied a thin patch of white skin, lighter than her normal pale coloring. It was a scar. Four long scars stretched from the top of her right shoulder down across her spine and down to her left hip. He would guess each slashing mark was an inch in width. His teasing demeanor vanished as he thought of how she could have possibly gotten such marks and how she'd survived.

As if feeling his eyes on her scars, Rebecca glared at him over her shoulder. "I said get out!"

Ignoring her, he moved forward, his large hands cupping a shoulder and a hip to hold her still as he studied the marks closer. "What in the hell are these, Rebecca?" He asked in a hushed voice. Already he could feel her body trembling under his palms. She was afraid. Was this the secret she'd been so adamant about keeping from him. Studying the marks, Eric struggled to think where he'd seen such marks before. It seemed so familiar but so distant in memory.

"Was this the reason why you didn't want me to look at your breasts last night? Why you insisted on keeping your shirt on?" when his fingers began to trace one long raised white scar, he felt her flinch from his touch. What was the story behind them? Could this be the colossal secret she kept from him?

"…Yes." She hesitantly answered. "Now get out."

"Is this your big secret? Why didn't you tell me and what happened?"

Still holding her arms crossed over her chest, she turned to face him, positioning herself behind the reach of the shower head. Her eyes looked so haunted, so frightful. His chest ached to see so much lingering in her eyes like that. Squeezing his lifted hand into a fist, he lowered it to give her some measure of space.

"It's not something I like to talk about." She whispered, averting her eyes from him.

Stepping closer until the hot water rained down over his head and down his back, he cupped her chin, forcing her to look at him once more. "Talk to me. You can trust me. What happened?" He watched as her throat worked as if she had to swallow back a large amount of fear to answer him.

"I was attacked years ago and nearly died."

Air rushed out of his lungs at her admission. His mate—his true mate had nearly died before he'd been given the opportunity to find her? The thought angered his wolf and made his chest ache. "Who was it?"

Her gaze flinched away from his momentarily before they settled on the floor of the shower. Why was this so hard for her to tell him? What was she *really* hiding?

"I-I don't know." She shrugged her shoulders while pursing her lips, eyes still downcast. "I didn't see them—it. More than likely it was a dog or some escaped animal."

The foul scent of a lie hit him in the face like a slap. Why would she lie to him? This *was* the secret she had confided in Damon about. But if she'd just been attacked by a simple animal, why would she hide it and her scars from him? He doubted Rebecca was a vain woman that would shrink at the thought of displaying a few scars. Something wasn't adding up here and the wolf in him was curious to discover what else his mate was hiding.

Forcing himself to let it go for the time being, he slid his hands down her slick shoulders to clasp her arms gently. Smirking down at her, he pulled her arms apart, revealing her full breasts. He frowned again as he saw another set of scars leading across one of her perfect breasts. He vowed to himself to ask her more about them later. For now, he didn't plan to participate in an interrogation with his mate, but a seduction.

"I have waited so long to see these beauties that you've hidden from me. I can't wait to wrap my lips around these and suckle them." Scowling at him, she gave him an exasperated look. "Is your mind always on sex? Is that why you came in here, to get a bit of a shower quickie?"

Chuckling at her, he planted one of his hands against the glass shower wall at her back. "First off; I have not experience *anything* like I did with you last night. So; yes, I do always have sex on my mind *when—*" he paused, giving her a pointed look. "—I am around you. Secondly; with me; it will be anything but some three minute quickie."

Scoffing, she shifted against the wall, rolling her eyes. "So, what's a minute longer then?"

Raising a brow at her, he found he was liking her teasing, but it was going to get her in trouble soon. "Do I sense a challenge?" He said teasingly as his hard cock absently rubbed against her slick stomach.

"Of course not," She waved a dismissing hand at him. "I'll be out in a bit and then you can get in if you still need to." She stated matter-of-factly. Shoving him back, she turned her back towards him, her hands beginning to work the shampoo into her wet locks.

Reaching around her, Eric's warm hands reached up, cupping the slick, soft mounds of her breasts, causing Rebecca to rise up on her tip toes in surprise.

"What are you doing? I said to get out!" she gasped as his hands massaged both breasts, bringing moans from her lips a moment later.

"I don't remember you saying that. We should bath together to conserve water. I'm feeling a little *dirty* myself." He whispered against the back of her neck as one of his hand slid down her wet body to cup her slick sex. His fingers slipping between the dewy folds and into her hot core; moving in enticing strokes.

Heated chills raced up Rebecca's spine, causing her vaginal center to tremble and clutching around his fingers with pleasure. "Eric…" She moaned out.

His fingers picked up their pace, continuing to bury deep into her silken depths. The heel of his hand rolling and brushing against her pulsing clit as his other hand squeezed and molded a full breast. His straining cock pulsed and stabbed at her tempting buttocks as she pressed back against him.

Her inner muscles rippled and clenched around his thrusting fingers as her body shuttered with ecstasy. Pulling his hands from their deep caressing against her flushed skin, gripping her by her shoulder, Eric swiftly turned her around to face him. Bending; lifting her legs over his powerful arms, he lifted her, pinning her body between his hard, unyielding one and the cool, slick glass wall at her back.

"Eric!" she cried out as his hard shaft nudged against her clit causing a jolt of pleasure to sweep through her.

Breathing heavy, Eric fought against the driving need to bury himself to deep inside her that she'd never get him out. Groaning against her throat, he breathed out, "It's been more than three minutes, angel. Should I stop?"

"No." she moaned in denial. "Don't you dare."

"I want to hear you say it." Again he thrust his aching cock against her warm flesh.

Crying in reaction as sparks of need stabbed through her, Rebecca moaned. "Don't stop. Please, I need you."

Smirking, he bent to capture her mouth in a searing kiss. In one aggressive movement, he drove forward, completely burying himself inside her pulsing sheath. His hands tightening around her hips, he held her against the shower wall while his body lunged into hers with an animalistic passion. Over and over, he sunk into her. Nothing in the world could stop him from claiming her body in moment, his beast over taking his thoughts as he squeezed her tightly. Being with Rebecca; this was more than *just sex*, she claimed his heart and now he would claim her until he possessed every part of her. He couldn't think about the secrets between them, or the obstacles of their future. With wave after wave of ecstasy that had Rebecca's body clamping around his thrusting body, they gave themselves over the unending pleasure that consumed them both.

"Oh God!" Rebecca cried out with pleasure, her tight channel squeezed around his cock as he drove into her like a battering ram.

He continued to sink deeper and quicker into her without a hint of mercy in his movements. His chest echoing with a beastly rumble of need, Eric buried his face against her neck, preventing her from seeing his beast rising as his climax drew closer. He wouldn't be able to last much longer.

"Come with me, now!" He yelled out, breathlessly.

Throwing back his head with gratification, a deep groan poured out of his throat as Rebecca's tight muscles milked his release from his pulsating length. With a strangled cry, Rebecca buried her face against the warm skin of his neck as her body was thrown into another earth shattering climax, leaving both of them panting for precious air. Over and over his cock pulsed deep inside her, his orgasm marking her in the most primal way that a man could. Her wet flesh squeezed him, refusing to let him go even at the very end.

Coming down from the haze of her climax, they both became aware that the temperature of the water had turned to freezing. He didn't fight the prideful smile as Rebecca cuddled close into his chest, desperately trying to soak up the heat of his body.

Moving quick, Eric pulled his now semi-hard cock from her clenching muscles and gently lowered Rebecca onto her shaking legs. Snatching up a bar of soap, Eric worked up a quick lather and begun to wash both himself and trembling Rebecca. When he was satisfied that both of them were clean, he reached around Rebecca's huddled form; turning off the ice cold spray of water. Lifting her dripping wet form into his arms, Eric carried Rebecca into the bed room where he carefully settled her down onto the bed. He wasn't surprised when Rebecca fought against him as he began lowering her wet body onto the warm comforter.

"Eric! Stop,"

Freezing at the sound of the frantic tone in her voice, he did. "What's wrong? Are you hurt? Did I hurt you?" He asked, his voice filled with worry.

Narrowing her eyes at him, she arched a thin eyebrow at him. "What? No. Wait! Don't to put me on the bed!" She scolded as if the idea of being laid on the bed was the most unreasonable idea he'd ever had.

"Why?" He asked clearly confused.

"Because I'm wet and I'll get the covers and pillows wet too." Without another word he simple let go of her, causing her to land on the bedspread with a small bounce.

"It'll dry." Settling down next to her, he lounged on his side, facing her.

Reaching out, his fingers arranged her wet hair across the bedspread, the dark wet strands darkening the material beneath them. His eyes focused on the sight of her breast rising and falling with her heavy breaths. Already he wanted her again. When he would have reached for her to drag her beneath him, he reminded himself that this had only been her second time. She wasn't a shifter and didn't heal as quickly as they did. He grimaced at that particular thought. He would have to change her to completely bond with her. Would she welcome the claiming bite or would she fight it?

"Wow…" Rebecca breathed out with an awed tone.

Jerked away from his thoughts, he shifted closer to her, curling his naked body closer to her shivering one. "I didn't hurt you did I?" he asked, smoothing a hand through the wet strands above her forehead. "I know you're still new at this."

She giggled. "Not for long if I stick around you." Turning toward him, she sighed contently into the damp comforter. "And to answer your question; no, I'm fine. Way more than fine, actually."

Eric chuckled deeply as his chest swelled with pride. "You are very good for my ego. Be warned, I plan on keeping you around for a long time." As soon as the words left his lips, he winced.

Lifting her head, Rebecca turned over onto her stomach. Reaching out with her index finger, she began drawing teasing circles against his chest as she spoke. "Don't worry; I'm not going to run because you admit you want me around, Eric. Though; I will admit this is moving very fast for me." Her eyes met his with a meaningful look.

He shrugged. "I don't know how else to be, Rebecca. Can you accept it? I want to win you as you deserve, but I can't promise to stay away from your bed or let you set one toe out of mine."

Pressing a finger to her chin as though in thought, she flashed him a mocking look of consideration. "I don't know. It may take some *convincing*…"

With a groan at her word, he buried his hand through her wet strands, jerking her over his chest as his mouth took hers. If his mate needed *convincing,* he was just the wolf to give it to her.

19

Lifting her face to the morning sun, with a sigh of contentment, Rebecca closed her eyes. From her position on the back kitchen patio, she could hear Emma and Travis playing in the yard a few feet away. Their excited squeals were such a joyous sound. Much better improvement from how they had been yesterday. Opening her eyes, she smiled down at the scene. Scooping up another spoon full of her sliced fruit, she savored the sweetness that lingered in her mouth.

As her thoughts drifted to the previous night, she found herself smiling. Eric had seen her scars. When he'd stepped into the shower with her, she'd thought her heart would explode with fear. She'd wanted to fight his arms as they came around her, holding her close.

His finger tips had traced each one then followed his trailing fingers with his mouth. She never imagined she'd feel his hot mouth on her scars, the same scars that one of his kind had given to her. He'd seemed to buy her excuse of how those scars came to be, but she'd feared that she hadn't closed the lid on that conversation.

"It's good to see them laughing again."

Smiling faintly, Rebecca turned toward the gentle sound of Sarah's voice. Never taking her eyes from the two children playing, Sarah took a seat beside Rebecca at the small table. Following Sarah's gaze, Rebecca watched as the twin ran, chasing and tossing a large rubber ball back and forth, their laughter ringing in the air. Rebecca's heart warmed at seeing them so happy. She nodded. "It is good to see."

Laying a gentle hand on her arm, Sarah leaned closer to Rebecca. "How are you doing since the attack?"

Looking down, she set her spoon down inside her bowl, shrugging. "I'm alright." Raising her eyes, she gave Sarah a pleading look. "I just wish I knew what was going on."

Giving her arm a gentle pat, Sarah gave her a hesitant smile. Would she tell her something? Too quickly Sarah waved her hand dismissively before saying, "Eric will handle it."

With those words she felt her hands clench so hard she thought she'd break every bone. What made it worse was that she could practically hear Eric's scoffing, superior voice echoing the same words. Ugh! If he kept up with the whole *"I'm superior because I have a dick"* thing, she may not be responsible for her actions.

"My God's what is that smell?" a husky, prissy sounding voice suddenly said from the open door behind them.

Brows dipping with curiosity, Rebecca found herself turning toward the open kitchen door. Standing in the doorway was a woman that Rebecca supposed others would qualify as beautiful. She was tall and lean with long flowing blonde hair falling nearly to her hips. The woman was dressed in a spaghetti strap halter top that barely concealed the generous swelled of her breasts and a black mini skirt that would make a hooker blush.

And Eric thinks my clothes are streetwalker ware?

When the woman approached them, the heels of her flashy shoes clicking loudly against the wood, she pursued her lips rudely as her eyes seemed to be studying Rebecca.

Coming to a stop beside their table, the woman rested one hand on her hip as she flicked her long manicured nails at Rebecca. "It must be you. Your kind always did pollute the air of our world."

Rebecca felt outrage fill her. Had this woman just had the gull to insult not just her but her species too? Knowing that this woman was more than likely a shifter, Rebecca bit her tongue. Literally. Who the hell was this skank and why was she attempting to pick a fight with her?

Rebecca jumped with surprise as Sarah's voice erupted beside her with anger. "Myra! This is Rebecca, *she* is a guest here and you are *not*. You will show her the respect she is owed in *my* house." Never before had Sarah sounded so feral, so dangerous. Whoever this *Myra* was; Sarah was not her biggest fan.

Smirking down at her mockingly, Myra crossed her thin arms over her ample breasts, chuckling softly. "I don't owe her *my* respect and we both know why."

The comment had Rebecca's eyes rolling as she turned back around in her chair. Filled with disgust and irritation as the woman's "*I'm better than you*" attitude, she forced herself to focus her attention on Emma and Travis as they continued to play.

"Besides," Myra began with a musing sigh. "This won't be your house for much longer once Eric chooses me as his...partner." She said, eyeing Rebecca with a meaningful look. "This will be *my* domain." Sauntering past them, Myra came to lean against the waist high, patio railing. Her lip curled with disgust as she took in the sight of Emma and Travis playing.

Rebecca stiffened at the woman's words. Damon had said that she was Eric's true mate. What if he'd been wrong? Was Eric involved with this woman as well? The thought made her sick.

Whoever this woman was; she obviously thought she had some claim on Eric. For the first time, Rebecca felt her chest tighten with pain at the thought. In the past few weeks since her relationship with Eric had changed, she had begun fearing the loss of him. Though she also feared what her future would hold for her once she came clean with Eric, deep down; she *wanted* to be his fated mate—his soul mate. She didn't understand it; she couldn't fight how right it felt to be with him. Like needing a drug, she craved to belong to him as much as she wanted him to be hers and only hers.

Glancing back at the snide woman as she inspected her perfect nails, Rebecca felt anger and jealousy rush through her veins at the thought of this woman near Eric. God, she would have given anything in that moment for some claws of her own to tear at Myra's perfect, Barbie face.

Dropping her inspecting hand, Myra's face jerked up all of a sudden to turn toward the door. Her eyes darken like a stalking predator while her expression lit up with obvious desire. "Eric." She purred.

Meeting Sarah's eyes, Rebecca saw that she had the same look of disgust on her face that Rebecca felt. Turning around, she watched as Eric's towering frame filled the open doorway. When he stepped out into the morning light she felt her heart thunder in her ears. He was dressed in a pair of faded jeans that seemed to be made for him, a plain navy t-shirt. His ruffled dark hair and the stubble along his jaw made him look a combination of sexy and dangerous.

The only thing she could think of that would make the sight of him better would be if he didn't have a slutty bimbo pressing her fluffed up breasts against his chest. Rebecca had expected to see Eric return Myra's attention. At the least she'd thought he would be eyeing Myra like the temptress she was attempting to be. However; to her surprise, she saw that his blue eyes were locked sourly on her alone.

Not liking that she wasn't getting the reaction from Eric that she'd hoped for, Myra did her best to draw his gaze from Rebecca, but he didn't even blink. Myra looked like a cat in heat the way she was pressing and rubbing herself against Eric, but much to Rebecca's bemusement; he didn't even look at the bimbo.

"I've been waiting here for you, Eric." Myra purred, attempting to nuzzle the side of Eric's throat in a desperate attempt for attention.

Not that Eric gave it to her of course. Rebecca found herself torn between astonishment and choking laughter when Eric shoved Myra's arms away from him before nudging her aside. Myra stumbled on her high heels briefly as she watched him with a flabbergasted expression.

With his eyes locked solely on Rebecca, Eric wasted no time in coming up to the table until he stood beside her. Gulping with nervousness, she turned back around to avert her face. Out of the corner of her eye, she saw Sarah flashing Myra a smug look. Did Sarah know about Damon's suspicions that she was Eric's mate?

She flinched when a pair of heavy hands settled on her shoulders from behind. Chills raced up her body causing her to quiver with excitement. Her heart nearly leapt from her chest when a warm pair of lips began trailing from the side of her face and down the side of her throat. Normally, she would have cried out in embarrassment at Eric doing such a thing in front of others, but now; it just felt right.

"Good morning." His voice rumbled against her skin like a caress. Pressing her thighs together tightly as her clit pulsed in response, she swallowed nervously. "Morning, Eric."

At the other side of her neck she could feel his hand palm her neck with a possessive touch before sliding up into her loose hair. His fingers twisted in the soft locks, as if he needed to hold her to him in some way. The feel of his possessive hand trailing through her hair was more erotic than she would have imagined. Was he even aware of the effect that he was having on her?

"Did you sleep well?"
With a smile, she recalled how it had felt last night when she'd slept in that large bed with Eric. After spending the day with Sarah and the twins in an effort to distract them from not having their favorite toys near, she'd gone to bed alone. She had awoken in the middle of the night to a sound of footsteps in her room, before she could lift her head to inspect it; Eric had crawled into bed behind her, pulling her close.

His strong arms wrapped around her like two thick bonds, preventing her from moving even an inch away from him. With the sound of his heart beat echoing close to her ear, she'd been lulled to sleep without realizing it. Never before could she recall sleeping so well.

Turning her head to look up at him, in time to see his lips curling at the corners, she knew he was remembering their night as well. "I had a good night." she said with a nod.

Never losing the satisfied curl of his lips, he straightened up to hold out his hand to her. "Come with me." Was it a question or a demand? Regardless, she found herself thrown off guard.

Clearing the haze of her mind with a shake of her head, she asked, "Why?"

In typical Eric fashion, he clasped her wrist to pull her to her feet. "I want to show you something." When he began leading her away from the table, she scowled at him, whispering under her voice.

"This better not be a sex thing."

Sliding his hand from her wrist to weave his fingers with hers, he bent to whisper in her ear. "With you; everything is a *sex thing*."

Ignoring Myra's huff of outrage as he led her down the patio steps onto the grass, he began making his way toward the forest that circled the back of the lodge's back yard. After they walked for some time, Rebecca spoke.

"I met your girlfriend." She attempted to keep the tone of disgust from her voice, but she failed miserably.

Eric scoffed as if she'd just told him something amusing. "*Girlfriend?* What are we; in high school now?"

Rolling her eyes at him, she twisted her hand from his grasp. The moment her hand left his, Eric's long strides came to a stop. His head turned towards hers with a perplexed expression as she continued. "I'm talking about Myra; Miss Barbie-Slut back there." she explained, hiking her thumb over her shoulder toward the lodge.

Slowly, Eric's expression turned heated with pleasure as he flashed a knowing grin. His eyes dancing with amusement. "My, my, are we jealous, Rebecca?"

Hell yes! She thought silently.

Flinching, she felt heat fill her cheeks as she blushed. "No! Of course not." She replied indignantly. When his grin widened, she grew worried and hastily took a step back. Each step she retreated, he erased with one of his own. When her back it a tree, preventing her from retreating any further, Eric planted a hand on the trunk above her shoulder. "I want you to say it; otherwise I may think that I imagined it."

Pushing her shoulders back and her chin lifted, she glared up at him. "You did."

Chuckling deeply, he shook his head in denial. "I don't think so. You didn't like seeing another woman with her hands on me, did you?"

"It wasn't her hands that she kept rubbing all over you." She pointed out dryly before shifting her eyes from him.

Tucking a curled finger beneath her chin, Eric lifted her face up until their eyes met once more. "While it amuses and pleases me that you'd feel possessive of me; I feel the need to point out to you that I'm a one woman type of man. Here's a clue for you, angel; the *one* woman I want, isn't Myra."

His words pleased her, making hope bloom in her chest. With happiness radiating through her from his words, she lifted up on her toes to meet his lips as he bent forward to kiss her. Eric smiled against her mouth as he clutched the nape of her neck.

Pulling back from her, Eric murmured. "I could get used to your jealousy." Taking her hand once more, he tangled his fingers with his own. Giving her hand a reassuring squeeze, he took a step back and tugged gently on her arm. "Come on, I want to show you something before I forget and we spend the day in this very spot."

"I doubt I would complain." She murmured with a teasing look.

Following behind him, it wasn't long until the loud sound rushing water reached her ears. Where was it coming from? Looking for a direction of the sound, she asked, "Is there a river nearby?"

Turning to meet her questioning eyes over his shoulder, Eric nodded. "I use to come to his place as a boy. I know you will appreciate it."

With every step she took the sound of the pounding water grew louder to almost a roaring. Chills raced up her spine as Eric came to a stop the edge of the tree line. With his free hand outstretched toward what appeared to be a drop-off, he motioned for her to check it out. Raising an inquiring brow at him, she pulled her hand from his to do just that.

Stepping from the shelter of the trees, sunshine hit her face, causing her to wince at first. Walking close to the edge; but not too close, she peered down and gasped. Below them was a large pool at least twenty feet wide that appeared to join the river later further down. The at the far left of the inviting pool was a stone face the color of silver with a waterfall rushing over the rocks into the pool below. In that perfect moment, the sunlight hit the rushing water, casting a misty rainbow of colors up into the air. This place was paradise.

"Whoa…" she breathed out with astonishment at what she was seeing. "This is incredible!" she gasped out with excitement, turning to watch as Eric strode towards her.

Smiling at her, he nodded. "I thought you would like it." Keeping his gaze locked on hers, Eric gripped the collar of his shirt, tugging it over his head in one smooth motion.

The strong muscles in his arms flowed and rippled with movement, drawing her gaze. Apparently she wasn't the only one doing some ogling. Glazing away from the sight of his naked chest, she saw that Eric's gaze was roaming over her body like she was a porterhouse steak and he was *starving.*

She scoffed with laughter as she shook her head at him. "I thought you said this wasn't about sex."

Jerking the zipper of his jeans down, he smirked at her. "It's not—yet."

"Then why are you…?" Her question trailed off when he shoved his pants down to reveal a pair of black boxers.

Spying his erection pressing against the loose material, she felt her womanhood clench in response. Perhaps it wasn't Eric that she should worry about. If he came a step closer she very well may jump him herself. How had she kept her hands off him all this time?

Because that was before he turned me into a freaking nymphomaniac.

"Did you think I brought you out here to just look?" he laughed.

Jerking her eyes from his concealed shaft, she saw that he was looking at toward the pool and not at her. Like a child she felt so excited she felt like she would burst. She knew that she must look ridiculous with her eyes widening at his words. Quickly pulling off her shirt and shorts as well, she stood in only her purple cotton bra and matching simple underwear.

With confusion she looked left and right, searching for a path or a way to climb down to the pool below. Not seeing a way, she shook her head with disappointment. She turned toward Eric to see him striding back toward the tree line with their clothes in his hands. Carefully he laid each item of theirs over nearby branches for safekeeping.

"How do we get down there?" she asked.

Without turning around to face her, he simply said. "The typical way; we jump."

* ~ * ~ *

Eric couldn't ignore the laughable way that Rebecca's mouth parted and her body cringed at the thought of jumping over the edge. For a moment, a concern crept into his mind. Could she be afraid of heights? Taking a whiff of her scent, he didn't detect an overly amount of fear. She seemed more scared of the idea of jumping than where she was.

"Excuse me?" she gasped out with a hysteric laugh. "You can't be serious."

He shrugged his shoulders carelessly. "Do you have a problem with that? That's the way we all did it as children." He explained as he slowly made his way back to her.

"Are you insane?!" she exclaimed, her eyes wide and her face paling. "That's got to be a fifty foot drop, Eric!" she said, waving her hand toward the edge.

"It's actually a fifteen foot drop." He pointed out.

"Shut up." She bit out. "You want to go and kill yourself, be my guest. I'll stand up here and watch. I'll even write your obituary for you. It will go something like this, '*Poor Eric would have lived a long fulfilling life if he hadn't stupidly leapt to his death instead of using his brain. Too bad.*'"

Shaking his head at her with humor, he waved her words away. "I won't die from jumping at this height, so don't worry yourself. Trust me on this. I will even do it with you." He offered.

Crossing her arms over her breasts, she shook her head stubbornly. "Not going to happen. There's got to be another way." she murmured softly, as she turned away from him to look around the drop off again.

Instantly, Eric's eyes fell on the tempting curve of her waist and her luscious ass. It was a struggle not to reach out and touch her. His eyes were drawn away from her sinful curved like a magnet to the white, raised scars across her back.

Frowning, he remembered the whole reason he brought her out here in the first place. He wanted to take her somewhere secluded. Where she would feel safe and could forget that they'd nearly been killed yesterday. Hopefully, if she was relaxed enough and was not so on edge, she would finally confined in him about her most guarded secret.

He didn't want to rush her or force her; as many had advised him to. He wanted her to trust him, to cleave to him, to want *him* as much as he needed *her*. But this little road block with jumping over the edge of a small cliff may prove an issue to his plans for wooing her. Remembering the best way to handle Rebecca was to keep her off balance and take the reins himself, he did.

Moving closer to her, he waited until she turned back to face him. "I have a solution. Let's do this instead." He said in a compromising tone. When she seemed to relax, waiting for him to continue, he lunged for her. Bending to scoop one muscled arm behind her knees and the other behind her back, he quickly lifted her up in his arms. He smiled with triumph when she cried out with surprise.

"Eric!" she gasped out, squirming and fighting his arms as he held her against his chest. "What do you think you are doing?!" pausing, she followed his gaze toward the ledge.

He wouldn't…would he?

Yep he would.

"Don't even think about—" Her words ended abruptly and morphing into a scream of fear as he rushed toward the ledge and jumped.

<u>20</u>

She was going to kill him, very painfully and slowly as possible. The idiot had jumped! Worse he'd made her do it too! Her stomach was lodged up in her chest as they plummeted toward the water.

Eric held her impossibly tighter against his chest as they hit the water. When they sunk beneath the surface of the water, Eric covered her mouth with his own. Kicking his feet, he shoved them back up to the surface.

The moment her head broke the surface, Rebecca jerked her face away from his. Sputtering; she shoved at the wet curtain of hair that blinded her. "You jerk!" she shrieked. Hitting his chest with a loud slap, she demanded, "Let me go!"

Smirking, Eric inclined his head to the side as if in thought. A second later, he carelessly shrugged his wide shoulders. "Alright." With a pause, he dropped his arms around her, sending her tumbling back beneath the water.

Swimming back up, she splashed in anger at Eric's smirking face. In retaliation, Eric sent a wave of water back her. Wiping away the water from her face, she scowled at him. "Stop it."

Turning her back on him, Rebecca began swimming toward the massive waterfall, intending to ignore the big jerk. A larger wave of water hit her back a moment later, startling her. Stopping, she turned to glare at Eric, but he was nowhere to be seen. Chills of awareness, inched up her spine. Where was he?

Like a shark, Eric swam up to her unseen from beneath the surface. She gasped in surprise as two hands gripped her above her knees. Jerking her legs apart, Eric rose to the surface, pulling her against his straining cock. Wrapping her legs around his waist, he moved his hands to her buttocks, gripping them and lifting her out of the water.

Gripping her chin between his forefinger and thumb, he held her still as he reached up and claimed her mouth. With her heart pounded from the excitement, she panted into his mouth, returning his kiss. Her arms wrapped around his neck, holding him close as she took over the kiss with fevered eagerness. Breaking away, out of breath, Eric gazed up at her with heavy lidded eyes.

"It would seem I've caught you."

Her wet curtain of hair fell in twisted strands around her face as she bent towards his lips. "What do you intend to do then?" she inquired with a teasing grin, her ire at his little stunt nearly forgotten.

"Not have sex with you; that for sure." He whispered, pulling away from her.

Surprised at his words, Rebecca drew back. "What do you mean?" when had a woman ever, *ever* heard those words from a lover? "You don't want to?"

Smiling up at her like he stared up at her like she was the most precious thing in the world to him. With wonder shining in his eyes, he shook his head. "No. I plan to *make love* to you, Rebecca. Because that's what this is and will be for me from now on. I love you and I hate that I wasted so much time to realize it. If I am lucky, maybe a day will come when you understand how precious you are to me and how my life wouldn't be fucking right without you."

Rebecca's arms tightened around his neck as tears misted her eyes. Biting down on her bottom lip, she fought to keep from crying with joy. He *loved* her? This was what she wanted. What she had been waiting for. It was a sign. Eric would choose her. At this realization, she felt like her heart would explode.

I'm done for...

Seeing her watering eyes, the look of pure, unyielding love melted from Eric's face to be replaced with confusion and disappointment. "Oh hell; I fucked this up didn't I? I told you I'm not good at this type of thing. Don't cry. I'm sorry." He said, as he franticly attempted to comfort her.

Leaning away from him, she shook her head at his words. "Eric, you couldn't have said a more perfect thing."

Leaning down, she covered her lips with his. Her lips moved against his in a gentle caress as a single tear of happiness trailed down her cheek. Pulling away, when they both were gasping for air, she pressed her forehead against his.

In a teasing whisper, she asked, "Though I have to wonder how long you stood in front of a mirror practicing that speech of yours."

Pulling back, Eric scowled at her. "I should make you eat those words." He whispered in a dark threat.

"You could." she nodded with a mock look of musing. "Or you could propose a sonnet..."

"That's it!" he exclaimed with a grin. Wrapping one arm around her back, he held her to him as his other hand rose to tickle mercilessly at her stomach. Squealing with laughter she squirmed against his hard body. "Take it back or that's the last time I try to be romantic for your ungrateful self."

Gasping for air when he stopped tickling her, she reached out to cup the edge of his jaw, with a serious look, she shook her head. "I don't need romance, Eric. All I want is you."

Leaning his face into her palm, he shrugged his shoulders with a sigh. "Then you have me, Rebecca."

* ~ * ~ *

Resting her head against Eric's warm chest, Rebecca sighed with contentment as she watched the waterfall move like a curtain of liquid silk to the side of them. When Eric had said he intended to *make love* to her instead of just taking her, she now knew that he meant it. Never before had she felt so cared for, so loved. His every kiss and touch had been gentle, loving her with slow and savoring thrusts of his body. It wasn't until a little while ago he'd coaxed her to follow him beneath the waterfall into the small cave behind it. There they lay, reclining against the smooth silver rocks that rose out of the bowl shaped cave to form the high walls and ceilinged cave.

Idly, Eric rubbed his hand up and down her back as she curled against his side, the cool water gently lapping up to their collarbones. "What are you thinking?" he asked, gently squeezing her tighter against his side.

Surprised by his sudden question, Rebecca blinked, pulling her eyes from the sight of the waterfall to look up at him. Smiling, she shrugged her shoulders. "I think we're going to have to return soon."

Eric scoffed. "Not likely. I'm enjoying this too much."

Rolling her eyes, she settled her head against his shoulder once more. "Your mother can't be expected to watch Emma and Travis forever, Eric. I should be there to help." She pointed out.

Drawing his head back to look down at her, Eric raised a mocking eyebrow at her statement. "I thought I *fired* you."

She nodded. "You did. I'll bill you later." She replied with a smug look.

For several minutes Eric didn't say anything. Sighing loudly, he whispered. "You're not planning on trying to run again, are you?"

Pursing her lips at the thought, she shook her head. "No. I don't plan on running again."

From what Damon had said; running would do her no good. If they'd been attacked because others knew her secret or even if it was retaliation against Eric, it wouldn't matter. She'd be found no matter where she went. Here; amongst the strength of Eric's pack, she was safe—for now.

After Eric's earlier words she was convinced that she could trust him to protect her, to choose her when it came down to it. Her last excuse for not telling him was gone. She only wished that she felt braver in that moment.

"Why did you before?" Eric's hesitant question cut through the silence like a blade. "Was it me? Had I scared you or something? You just seemed to want to get away from me constantly." His voice was filled with doubt and concern, everything that wasn't him. She knew now was the time to come clean.

"I tried to run because it's what I'm used to doing, Eric. Ever since my parents were killed, I've lived in fear for so long. I suppose its second nature to me to run when I get too close to someone."

"There's more to the story of your parents and your scars; isn't there?" he asked, suspicion heavy in his voice.

She nodded. Pressing her lips together, she tried to will her pounding heart to slow as she fought off the memories of that night. Blinking against unshed tears, she replied in a shaking voice. "Y-Yes,"

Eric looked down at her with such heartbreak and concern. It warmed her heart to see those emotions swirling deep in his blue eyes. Lifting his other arm out of the water, he cupped her face tenderly, leaving small, cool water dripping over them both. "You can trust me, Rebecca. I would never let anything hurt you."

She gave a watery smile as she recalled his earlier words, *"I love you and I hate that I wasted so much time to realize it. If I am lucky, maybe a day will come when you understand how precious you are to me and how my life wouldn't be fucking right without you."*

It was time.

Taking a deep breath, she steeled herself for what she was about to do and what his reaction to her long played out deception would be. "The night my parents were killed…was the same night I was attacked but it wasn't…" she choked back a shutter of breath as she tried to stay calm enough to speak. Taking a deep gulp of air as tears spilled over her cheeks, she tried to finish telling him. "It wasn't—"

Pressing a finger against her lips, Eric silenced her. "Stop." He shook his head with a pain filled expression. "I don't want to see you cry."

"Eric…you don't understand." She began, only to be cut off once more.

"I understand more than you know."

Wiping impatiently at her tears, she shook her head. "I want to tell you, Eric."

"And you *will*; when you are ready. I understand more than *anyone* how a painful memory can change you and still inflict pain even years later." Pausing he inhaled deeply before continuing. "For me it was Beth or at least the memory of her that has plagued me."

"Beth?"

"Emma and Travis's mother. She was my…wife."

Needing distance from the memory of the woman that held a place in Eric's heart, Rebecca sat up, pulling out of his arms. Not noticing her when she pulled away, he tangled his hand with hers before he began telling her his most guarded secret.

"My life hasn't always been as it is, Rebecca. I had to fight; literally, for everything I have now. With everything I gained, I inherited…responsibilities and expectations. One of those was to get married young." He paused, meeting her eyes.

"You had an arranged marriage?" Rebecca didn't doubt that Eric was downplaying the parts about his shifter heritage as he told her, but she was too curious to know what had happened to Emma and Travis's mother to stop him.

Shrugging his shoulders with a hesitant look, he nodded. "I guess you could call it that. Beth and I had been best friends ever since we were children. Our families were close; I suppose it made sense at the time for us to get married."

"Did you love her?" She winced when the words fell out of her mouth. Did she really want to know the answer to that?

Please say no…

"I had hoped we would in time or at least something close to love, but no; I didn't."

"What happened to her?"

"For a time we were happy; or at least I thought we were." He finished with a cynical laugh. "We shared the typical husband and wife rituals; sharing meals, going on outing together, holding hands, and sleeping together. At the time it didn't seem to matter that we didn't *love* each other the way people should. A year after our marriage, Emma and Travis came along." He smiled faintly as he seemed to replay the memory in his mind.

"I never felt so happy in my life as when I first stood over their cradle and saw them for the first time. I had a family and I knew then that I would never want anything else." His smile on his lips faded into a hard line. A muscle along his jaw ticked as his voice turned cold and distant.
"I was so happy that I blinded myself to what was happening in front of my face. I came home one night to Emma and Travis screaming. It was a heart tearing cry to hear from your children. Rushing to their nursery, I found them in the dark inside their cradles; Beth had always left a light on in the far corner. I don't know how long they had been alone until I found them. Beth was nowhere to be seen. It wasn't until I discovered that all her belongings were missing that I saw the truth. She left me and abandoned Emma and Travis."

"Oh Eric." Rebecca gasped out, her hand covering her mouth.
Her chest filled with a physical ache at the thought of coming home to what Eric had. It was no wonder he never spoke of Emma and Travis's mother. Why would he? The person that should have been his partner, his friend, his lover; left him and their children without a word.

"Did you ever find her? Did she ever contact you?"

"No." he shook his head. "I didn't look for her and she didn't contact me. In truth; I don't know where she is or why she left. I can only assume that she no longer wished to be bound to me."

"But for her to just leave like that and without her children? I don't understand it."

"Even if she'd told me, I never would have been separated from my children." His eyes locked on hers. "Just as I could never let you go."

"Eric—"

"Listen to me," he interrupted again. "I am not telling you this to garner pity or pressure you into anything with me. There are secrets more dark and deadly than what I have just told you. In time; I will tell you everything, just as I trust you will. All I ask, Rebecca, is that you give me a chance to win your love. I will not force you to be with me if you don't wish to, but if there is a chance that you feel anything for me. Give me one chance to be the man you need in your life."

"What happened to the man that said he wasn't a romantic?" she asked dryly with a teasing smile. Inside her mind she was soaring!

So many emotions swelled up in her chest and overflowed. Just as Eric said he loved her, she knew that she was already half way in love with him. She wanted to be with him in every possible sense of the word. It was only her fear of his pack that kept her from throwing herself at him.

Flashing an irritated look, he tugged her across his body, sending a wave toward the curtain of water to his right. When she laid flat against his front, he narrowed his eyes at her. "Most women would be swooning at such words; not making fun of them."

She inclined her head mockingly. "True, but most women haven't been around you like I have." Serious now, she reached out to brush back the wet strands of his hair that fell forward. "I don't need you to say romantic things for me, Eric. All I want—all I need, is you. I…" she gulped as she gathered her courage. "I love you too, Eric."

Eric didn't seem happy at her declaration. Instead he looked bewildered. Shaking his head as his brows lowered over his eyes, he asked. "How can you be sure of this so soon? Just days ago you were fighting against giving yourself to me and then running from me."

She shook her head, pressing a hand over his heart. "I was never running from you, Eric. Like you said; we both have secrets and I will tell you all of mine. But just as you've been holding yourself back from me, I've been doing the same. I want to be with you, to stay with you. If you will have me and accept who I am."

Accept me as the human that your kind hate and would kill in an instant. She said silently to herself.

She didn't know what she was doing saying all this to him; all she knew was that she was tired. Tired of running from what she wanted. She'd been drawn to Eric from the beginning; even when she was terrified of him. After he'd opened his heart to her by telling her about Beth, about how a woman he trusted and treasured left him, she knew she wanted him to know that it was possible to be different. Between them, it would be.

Her answer was Eric tugging her higher up his chest. When her naked breasts were pressed against his collar bone, he seized her mouth in a claiming kiss. Holding her face, he poured his very essence into that kiss. Sighing against his mouth, she fisted her hands in his wet hair. Tomorrow she would tell him. Even if she had to gag him so that he couldn't stop her; she would tell him and she would pray that his love for her would only burn brighter as hers did for him. For the first time in years, she wasn't afraid of telling her secret.

She was ready.

She was ready to be free…with him.

<u>21</u>

High above the waterfall, flames of jealous rage leapt into Myra's eyes as she watched the embracing couple in the water below. Her claws flared, slashing through the bark of the tree she peered around. A growl escaped from deep within her as she watched that disgusting *human* twine her arms around the Alpha's neck pulling him closer as he deepened their kiss.

Myra hadn't wanted to believe what she'd seen earlier when Eric had turned away from her only to slink off with the human. *This* was who he wanted?! A pathetic, weak human woman! A leader like Eric needed a strong mate, he needed *her*! He was hers!

She'd had her eye on Eric ever since his mate of convenience ran off with her lover. She was destined to rule beside him and no human was going to stand in her way! Her bitter thoughts fueled her rage. She wouldn't go along with this quietly. Eric would be hers, no matter what.

Turning away from the sight of her Alpha with his hands on that filthy human, Myra called upon her inner beast. Bones snapped and reformed, skin turned to fur and her flawless face changed. In her wolf form, she turned away from the couple with a snarl. She was going to make that human wish she'd never stepped foot in Eric's territory and she knew just how to.

With her lupine lips curling, she lunged forward. Her legs rushed over the ground, scattering leaves and snapping twigs in her run. She ran and ran like the devils of the earth were on her heels. After traveling for several miles hours later, she finally reached the border of the pack's land and onto the land that now belonged to the previous Alpha. The Alpha that Eric had defeated and spared all those years ago.

Her father.

Moving through the over grown forest, she leapt over a rotten log before shoving her small form through the large brush that stood on the edge of her family home. The gray two story plantation home loomed a couple feet in front of her in the fading light like a beacon of hope. She would find what she needed here.

Shifting back into her human form, she calmly made her way up the wooden steps of the porch to the towering structure. Carefully opening the door, she entered the quiet house. Hanging on pegs to the left of the door was a spare dress of hers. With a pause, she snatched it up and pulled it over her head.

Traditionally; shifters didn't bat an eye at nudity, but when shifting without first removing your clothes resulted in destroying them. Out of habit, she had always left a spare item of clothes lying around just in case it was needed. Curling her nose at the musty scent of the short black dress, she wiped at the dust along the hips before moving past the curling wooden staircase toward the living room.

In the living room, she found her father sitting in his usual seat. The wingback chair was a faded blue, the material so worn and covered in dust that it was obvious it had seen better days as had the rest of the house. Ever since her mother had been killed by humans thinking she was just an average wolf, her father had simply existed. His hate of humans was the one thing she had in common with him.

Sensing her, Senan tossed back the rest of the amber alcohol in his glass tumbler before tossing it against the wall beside the roaring flames within the stone hearth. The glass shattered, the shards fell to join a growing pile in the floor. Her father looked out of place in just a neglected room. He was a well kept man dressed in a silk shirt, dark slacks and his fine shoes. He must have just returned from the city. His face was worn and unshaven, his eyes dark. He was like this when his anger was brewing and he was recalling the death of his mate.

Must be Tuesday. She thought bitterly.

Instead of skulking around his manor, she wanted her father to get back the fire he'd once had. The same fire that burned deep within her. It was obvious that he longed to seek revenge for her mother's death. But as an old man, he didn't have the strength to face Eric for a second time and come out alive if he wished to challenge pack law.

"Why are you here?" he said emotionlessly. His eyes never strayed from the dancing flames in front of him.

"I bring you news of the pack." She answered, stepping further into the room. She came to a stop beside the fireplace so that he was forced to look at her, pursing her lips in anger when he still didn't look at her.

Rubbing at the side of his left temple, Senan sighed. "I do not care about the *pack.*" Eyes flaring, he nearly spat the word *"pack"* from his lips in anger.

"There may finally be an opportunity for us, Father. An opportunity for you to take your revenge against the kind that took your mate from you."

Her words worked like a lure for a hungry fish. Slowly his gaze shifted to her face, interest colored his expression. "What kind of opportunity?" after a moment he asked. "Have you heard from our allies?"

"Don't worry about our allies. This is even sweeter than what those freaks have promised us. This is an opportunity for you to claim double fold revenge for your mate; against the humans and against Eric."

A dark smile curled along his thin lips. "I'm…intrigued. Tell me more."

Stepping forward, the fire light casted her shadow across the room, making her blonde hair glow with the fading light. "Eric Daniels is secretly bedding a human woman. I suspect he has for some time." Senan smirked mockingly at her. Settling his elbows on the shredded arms of his chair he tented his fingers. "Are you jealous that a human is trying to steal your prospects, my daughter?"

Expression hardening, she pressed her lips together in anger at the thought. "She is not worthy to be an Alpha's mate."

Her father gave a cynical laugh. "A human? I wouldn't worry about that happening. The elders would never allow such a thing and Eric isn't that stupid to attempt it."

"Don't be so sure. There are rumors that he's already gone against the elders and formed peace treaties with other kinds of shifters." His face darkened with the news. "*What?*" he whispered in a dark voice, laced with anger.

"There's more. According to the elder committed to our cause, he also is looking into the missing shifters. He's rule is ripe for the plucking, Father."

Standing, her father slowly approached her, narrowing his eyes in question at her. "You would want me to kill the male you have been working so hard to convince to make you his mate?"

"Of course not." She bit out. "I want him broken. Once the human is dead and the pack is back under your rule, I will spare his life by offering the protection of my line to him. With his two little brats to consider; he won't refuse me then." She said confidently.

Her father smiled conspiringly at her. "You have the blood thirst of your mother." He said proudly.

A scream of rage erupted below the floor beneath their feet, echoing through the large house. Nodding his head at her slowly, her father stepped back. "I have plans to make with our allies. Go and tell the good news to your brother." With a loving brush of his knuckles along her jaw, he turned and left the room.

Smiling to herself, Myra headed in the opposite direction toward the snarling roars of her older brother. Turning down the dark hall, she pulled open the door to the basement. The old door creaked with the movement as she crossed the threshold.

Descending down the dark stairs, the smell of the rotting foundation and moist wood filled the air making her grimace. No longer would her brother have to be locked away like an animal. Not when Eric was no longer Alpha.

Her brother, Derik was just one of many shifters that didn't allow the rules of secrecy to stop them from meeting out justice to humans for crimes done to their kind. Her brother was brave and strong. For years he hunted humans as their kind had been. But once the elders had heard of his exploits, the cowardly members of their pack had grown concerned that he would expose all shifters to the humans and endanger them all.

Nothing was more important than to keep the truth of their existence from the human world. Without hesitation, the council of elders had sentenced him to death. It was only because her father had been Alpha at the time that he'd been able to spare him. Her father had spared his life, but in return; he'd sworn that Derik would remain locked away from the world where he could never endanger their kind. At long last his freedom was near.

Reaching the bottom of the stairs, her eyes were drawn across the large empty room to the far wall. With rusty manacles around his wrists, a length of heavy chains led from each wrist to where each was bolted into the hard steel plates drilled into the cement wall. Six feet from his position were five inch steel bars forming a cage around the surrounding area. He was locked away like a savage dog.

Glaring at the sight, she walked toward the bars. Reaching out she flipped a switch on the nearby wall, with a hesitant flicker, the few lights above lit the room with a dim glow. Her brother sagged in his bonds, his head down. He wore only a pair of dirty pants. His skin was dirty and cover in sweat from his attempts to free himself. His once beautiful hair was now long and fell in shaggy strands.

"I have good news my brother."

With a growl rumbling in his chest, he slowly lifted his head. His glowing eyes met hers with feral rage overtaking them. Flashing his fangs at her, he attempted to smile at her, but locked in his feral state for years he no longer looked like his beautiful human self. His face was a mix of wolf and human, perfect and terrifying.

The elders would pay for what they did to him. Eric would pay for his actions of going against the pack law. Then the humans would finally know the strength of the shifters that no longer would hide in the dark. The humans would finally know death.

* ~ * ~ *

"What do you mean you didn't tell him?!" Damon exclaimed. Wincing, Rebecca glanced around the empty kitchen to make sure that Damon's outburst hadn't drawn any attention. "Shh!" her eyes scolding him. "Try not to tell everyone, alright?" she bit out.

"Don't you realize what you've done?" Damon hissed out as he began to pace back and forth in front of her. His eyes quickly began to glow with the presence of his rising beast.

"I tried to tell him, Damon, but Eric wouldn't let me."

Damon's agitated pacing strides came to an abrupt halt. *"Wouldn't let you?"* he eyed her with heavy suspicion. "Wouldn't let *you*?!" his voice rose once more.

Not liking his attitude, Rebecca crossed her arms over her chest, leaning back against the kitchen sink. Lifting her chin at him with a hard look, she replied. "It wasn't from lack of trying, Damon."

Eyes flashing, he shook his head at her. "How about the *lack* of a painful death, Rebecca? The Gathering is in a few hours! By that time, there will be hundreds of wolf shifters all over these grounds. You are a human alone without someone to speak for you. If you suspect that some know your secret, you need Eric's protection."

"Eric has asked me to stay in my room tonight. I'll be fine for one night."

Damon gave a humorless laugh. "If your secret is out, you will be hunted down and killed, Rebecca. You need the protection of the Alpha. You need to go to him right now and tell him." He urged, giving her a desperate look. She was surprised to see that Damon almost looked…scared.

Lips parted, she shook her head slowly, almost in a daze she answered. "Eric isn't here."

Earlier that morning, Rebecca had awakened to a note and a tray laden with breakfast food upon her nightstand. In the note; Eric had told her that he had some things to take care of before the Gathering later that night. According to Sarah; Jason and Chris had been taken with him.

No one could tell her where he'd gone or what was so important that he had to leave easily in the morning. Without Eric hovering over her as he had in the past few days, Rebecca felt her cowardice of discovery return. She should have forced Eric to listen to her yesterday at the falls. No matter how afraid she had in that moment, she should have told him!

Scrambling for a course of action, Rebecca dropped her arms, her teeth biting down harshly against her bottom lip. "Perhaps there's no proof that anyone knows."

Damon's tense muscles relaxed; not out of assurance, but with defeat. "Proof isn't needed. All is needed is a shifter stating that their existence is threatened because of a human. That's all they would need to kill you and all they will care about. Though only some shifters; that I know of, are prejudice against humans, with the wolves within Eric's pack; its worse."

"Why?" she breathed out.

"Many of my kind have been harmed by human poachers. Mates and children murdered in their animal forms and their families unable to have the closure of justice. Families have been torn apart because of it. Pain like that can become like poison within the mind and many would kill you out of revenge."

Pressing a hand to her throat, Rebecca turned away from him as the seriousness of the situation hit her. Looking out the double kitchen widow above the sink, she stiffened when Damon moved closer to her. The heat of his body brushed against her back even without him standing too close to her.

"The point of the matter is that we're out of time, Rebecca." He said gently at her back. "You need to tell Eric *now*. He is the only one that can protect you now." he stressed with a tone full of worry.

Turning around to face him, she crossed her arms over her chest, attempting to comfort herself against his words. "What do you mean?" she asked perplexed. "You told me that you would protect me. Would you just…let them kill me if it came to it?" a shuttering breath accompanied her words as they emerged. Her stomach knotted at the thought, making her feel sicker than she'd ever felt before.

Closing the space between them, Damon looked down at her with eyes filled with gentle determination. Gently, he pulled her shaking frame into his embrace. His strong arms enfolded her against his chest. In effort to calm her, his hands running in soothing circles over her back as he held her tightly.

Resting his chin on the top of her head, he sighed wearily. "I do not tell you this to scare you, Rebecca, but the fact is; I am not a member of Eric's pack. I cannot protect you if the Act of Revealment is called. I would kill anyone that tried to harm you; but that wouldn't keep you safe. The only one that has the power to spare you and prevent the pack from harming you—is Eric, your mate. You need to tell him so that he can prepare you for what will happen."

Pulling out of his comforting embrace, Rebecca shook her head dejectedly. "Eric isn't here. He left early this morning."

Damon's gentle expression turned grave in an instant. "By the time they get back it will be too late."

Desperately, Rebecca tried to search for a solution. Shaking her head at him, she waved a hand in the air between them as her hushed voice rose. "How can you say that? You don't even know—"

"I know because I've seen this happened before!" he snarled.

Eyes wide with fear, Rebecca took a step back from Damon as his eyes began to glow with the presence of his inner wolf. She'd never seen Damon this enraged. It almost was as though his worry was turning to near rage.

Ignoring the way she flinched from him, Damon gripped her shoulders. His glowing gold eyes burned into hers demanding she listen to him. "I won't let the pack hurt you." He vowed with a soft voice.

Blinking against the hopeless tears that burned her eyes, she shook her head against his comforting words. "How?"

"Wait until sunset. If Eric isn't back by then, you can't wait any longer." Reaching into his pants pocket, Damon withdrew a silver ring with two gold keys dangling from it. Forcibly taking hold of her hand, Damon pressed the keys into her palm before forcing her fingers to close around them.

Keeping his hand blanketing her closed hand, he lowered his voice. "These are the keys to my car and hotel room in town. At sunset, if you haven't seen Eric yet and told him the truth, I want you to use these. Take my car and go to my room for the night. Tomorrow; when it is safe for you to return I will come for you." Slowly, he inhaled a breath. "*If* I do not come for you and you don't hear from me—"

Sensing where this conversation was going, Rebecca recoiled from him attempting to pull her hand from his. "Whoa! What are you saying?" when he wouldn't let go of her closed hand, she glared up at him.

"If Eric doesn't declare you his before the pack and state you are under his protection; nothing can save you."

"You want me to run?"

"I don't want you to run—I *expect* you to run."

Shaking her head stubbornly, she attempted to pull her hand free once more with the intention of giving his keys back to him, but his gripping hand prevented her from doing so. "I'm not running, Damon. I promised Eric."

Letting go of her hand with a jerk, Damon looked at her with anger. "If you don't; you could die." gripping her shoulders roughly, he bit out. "*Eric* will be more upset if you let yourself get killed. Eric will find you when this is all over *if* it comes to that." taking a breath, he attempted to calm his temper. "Promise me you will do this, Rebecca." His eyes softened as he pleaded with her. Seeming to fight some internal struggle with his beast, Damon released her only to turn and stride from the kitchen, leaving her standing alone.

She didn't know how long she stood there staring sightless across the empty space of the kitchen. Her fingers tightened around Damon's keys as they pressed painfully into her palm. It seemed impossible to wrap her head around what Damon had told her.

She'd never thought that she'd be in danger for just being there. She recalled when Eric had told her to remain close to their room for the night. Had he known that she could be in danger for simply being a human amongst shifters?

Looking down, she opened her hand to stare down at the two dissimilar keys. Their slight weight in her palm felt like a thorn in her skin that she desperately wanted to pluck out and toss away. Could she really do as Damon asked her? Could she chance not running if it came to it?

She didn't want to go back to the way things had been since she'd been attacked, the constant fear and running. She trusted Eric to protect her; there was no doubt in her mind about that. But what if he arrived too late to protect her? As Damon had said, he wasn't a member of Eric's pack and therefore; he could do nothing to sway the others. Only Eric's voice carried power here.

Closing her eyes, she wished she didn't have to face the hopeless odds laid before her. She was now forced to chose between running from the man she'd come to care deeply for or risking her life.

"Eric, where are you? I need you now more than ever..." she whispered to the empty air around her.

22

Glass crunched beneath Eric's boots as he stepped into the mess of the kitchen of his home. The aftermath of the attack through his home was startling. The kitchen and dining room windows were shattered to pieces across the floor. Dark bullet holes marred the side walls like discolored pot-a-dots against the soft blue wallpaper. The dining table had been shoved away from where he'd thrown it during the fire fight; tell him that whoever had attacked them; had entered his home as they'd fled.

The thought had his wolf rising with the need to seek out vengeance. Someone had attacked his *children*, his *mate* and they'd done it with human weapons! Though the memory angered him, he couldn't help but wonder why? Typically when shifters attacked one another, it was face to face, not hiding from a distance and shooting them. It was a matter of pride for shifters to take down an enemy. You wanted your enemy to look at you when you defeated them and for others to see your strength when you did. It was even more so if someone was stupid enough to sneak up and attack an Alpha in their own homes.

None of it made sense. Shooting was something that one did when they didn't want to risk discovery. Though he doubted he or his beta's would have been killed by the bullets as shifters were difficult to kill due to their regenerating abilities, he knew that Rebecca and his pups weren't strong enough to with stand the trauma of a bullet wound.

After thinking more on it, he came to realize that it didn't matter who or why his family was attacked. It was meant as a statement. Someone wanted him out of the way. Could it have to do with the disappearances of the shifters he'd been looking into? Or the alliances he'd been making against the judgment of the elders?

Whoever had thought to take him out by such cowardly means; he would find them and make them suffer. He'd nearly lost his true mate and pups that would *never* go unpunished. At the thought of losing any of his family, his heart shuttered with fear as his wolf snarled with rage.

"Eric." the sound of Chris's voice as he stepped through the doorway of the living room.

Not turning to face him, Eric folded his arms over his chest in thought. He'd left the lodge and the warm embrace of his mate before dawn this morning against his better judgment. There was much for him to do before the Gathering tonight. He'd asked Chris and Jason to come with him to search for clues on who had attacked his family. Even if he exposed the culprit at the Gathering tonight, he couldn't just met out justice. He needed proof or he'd be creating a bigger mess than he already had to contend with.

Late last night as they'd lain together in his bed, he'd asked Rebecca to remain out of sight for the night of the Gathering, but he now worried it wouldn't be enough to prevent the elders from getting suspicious of her. It wasn't common for any of his kind to bring a human around them; much less to their sanctuary at the lodge. Many that resided at the lodge were loyal to Eric without question and they knew Rebecca was his pup's nanny. But that didn't stop the confused and discontented looks that had followed after Rebecca in the last few days.

He longed to allow his binding thread to bind them together, to mark her and make her like him. But the knowledge that he couldn't declare her his mate without exposing her to the whole pack first made him hesitate. If others discovered her first…no. he shook his head, shoving the darkening thoughts from his mind. He wouldn't let her be harmed. He would protect her by any means.

Once his work here was done, he needed to get his mate alone and tell her everything. His chest tightened when he thought of her looking at him with fear once she knew what he was. He would have to be gentle in explaining and do all he could to keep her calm, but he had to do this before others had a chance to go after her.

"What have you found?" Eric said harshly, finally responding to Chris.

"Jason has picked up that scent trail again. It's faint and nearly faded, but he believes that he can track it to its source."

Eric nodded with a grim look. "Do it." when Chris turned to leave, Eric turned towards him. Eric's arms dropped to his sides. "Not you, Chris." He stated firmly. When his second beta paused to turn and flash Eric a confused look, Eric went on. "I need you to return with me to the Gathering tonight."

Walking back to him, Chris narrowed his eyes at his Alpha assessing. "Is there something I should be concerned about?"

Sighing, Eric walked to the empty kitchen window pane. Small chunks of glass still clung around the edges like jagged teeth. Looking out over the land that surrounded his home, his eyes looked further toward the forest stretching in the distance.

"I want you to stay close to Rebecca tonight while I deal with whoever is after my family. You are to protect her from anyone that tries to come near her tonight."

"Do you expect someone to make another attempt against her?" Chris asked, tucking his thumbs behind his silver belt buckle.

"I'm not chancing it." Eric answered.

After a pausing moment, Chris approached closer to Eric until he stood a foot from him. Tilting his head to the side, he seemed to study Eric before speaking. "Are you worried about exposing her to the pack?" when Eric didn't look his way; much less respond, Chris's eyes widened with realization. "You didn't tell her did you? You haven't claimed her yet?" he asked nearly aghast with shock.

"She's wasn't ready."

"Then get her ready! Eric, why would you wait?" Chris nearly shouted.

Though it wasn't customary for a beta to speak to his Alpha in such a manner, Eric didn't allow it to faze him. Chris and Jason had been his friends long before they were his betas and he valued their opinions.

"Where is Jason now?" Eric asked, shifting the direction of their conversation for the moment.

Huffing out an irritated breath, Chris motioned toward his office through the living room. "He's waiting in your office for your orders."

Without another word, Eric strode across the glass covered floor, quickly making his way to his office. The door was wide open, allowing him to see Jason leaning against his desk with his arms crossed lazily over his chest. When Eric entered the room with Chris following close behind him, Jason straitened with an expecting look.

"You found the trail." Eric stated more than questioned.

Nodding, Jason's lips pressed together in a firm line. "Yes. Eric, I have no doubt in my mind that this is the same scent that we've both encountered before."

Frowning, Eric settled his hands on his hips. "Regardless if it is, Jason, I want you to track it but not engage. Observe."

"Is it possible that this could be related to the disappearances that you've been looking into behind the elder's backs?" Chris asked from his position by the doorway.

Rubbing a tired hand over his face, Eric looked between his two betas before answering. "I have considered it. But I need to know who is behind this and why. I cannot risk them striking back at my family and me again until I know what I am dealing with. Doyle Mackenzie and his mate do not believe it is the same people we've faced before. But I am taking no chances. Track them and report back once you've found something."

With an affirming nod, Jason straightened from his lazy position. "I won't return until I have something."

"Good." Eric said.

Turning toward Chris, Eric found that he was regarding both Jason and him with a contemplating look. Eric knew that he must be curious about what the significance of the familiar scent was. But Chris was never one to question things in the beginning. Chris was a gleaner with his personal thoughts. He preferred to gather what information he could from others by simply listening. If Malca was truly behind the disappearances of shifters, he would have to confine in Chris about what he knew.

"Come." He said to Chris as he strode past him out of the office.

"We need to return to the lodge. There is much I have to do before the Gathering in just a few hours."

The accompanying footsteps told Eric that Chris followed close behind him. Shoving the front door open with his flat hand, Eric moved with brisk steps toward his hummer. Sliding into the interior at almost the same time Chris did at the opposite side, they both looked back toward the house in time to see a large black wolf leaping from the porch before it took off toward the forest.

As if sensing Eric's inner concerns, Chris shrugged his shoulders carelessly as he jerked his seat belt across his chest. "Jason is one of the best trackers in the pack. If anyone can find out who did this and where they went; it's Jason."

Nodding, Eric pulled his door closed before shoving his keys into the ignition. "I hope so. Because if he can't we will be flying blind."

Turning the keys, the engine rumbled to life with a smooth sound. Eric's eyes flashed to the digital clock on his dashboard. He'd already been gone for too long. There were still matters that needed his attention before he could confront Rebecca.
He was running out of time.

* ~ * ~ *

Standing at the windows of her and Eric's room, Rebecca forced herself to remain still as the need to pace nervously arose in her. The day had practically flown by in the blink of an eye. After her confrontation with Damon just a few hours ago, she'd made sure she was too busy to worry about what she would do at sunset. She'd helped Sarah in the kitchen most of the day, preparing a large assortment of food.

Apparently on such occasions like tonight, food and drink was in abundant. She wondered if it was always like this when the entire pack was called together. She wasn't able to use caring for an excuse to occupy her thoughts. From what Sarah had told her; on such nights when the extended *family,* as she put it, got together, it was a private thing. The children were taken for a large slumber party of sorts. No doubt it was to keep them from seeing their parents shifting and or any violence that may ensue.

Rebecca could do all she could, she forced herself to leave when more shifters began filing into the kitchen with large trenches of meats and food. She'd searched the grounds for Eric, but she was accompanied with dark criticizing looks when anyone she asked. No one seemed to know where he was and no one was interested in providing any other information to her.

It was a strange feeling to be the outsider. Around Eric's close friends and his mother, she'd never been treated like she was an unwanted nuisance like some of the new arrivals were. She was thankful that no one had outright attacked her like Damon had warned her about. But she wasn't going to take it as a sign that it wouldn't happen.

Above the horizon of trees across the distance, she watched with a heavy heart for the next few minutes as the sky began to burn with colors of reds, orange and violet as the sun dipped low. It was sunset. She was out of time.

Gulping past the lump in her throat, she turned from the window to grab Damon's keys off the top of the five drawer dresser. Clutching the keys tightly in her fingers, she turned back to the bed where a small tote bag that Damon had found for her sat. Inside she'd packed some of the clothes that Eric had supplied her with for the last few days and some cash that Damon had forced upon her. Grasping the handles of the bag, she felt her heart grow heavy. What would Eric think when he realized she'd ran…just like Beth had?

Needed to reassure him that she wasn't running from him, Rebecca sat the bag back onto the bed and began searching the room for something to write a note. She'd leave him a note, not telling him why she'd run, but just to tell him that she was safe and where she'd be if he wanted to find her. Crossing to the nightstand, she jerked the small drawer open to find a small notepad and a pen.

Moving to sit on the bed, she braced the pad on her crossed leg as she began writing. Before she could complete the first awkward sentence she froze. The hair at the back of her neck stood straight as the sound of creaking floor boards headed toward the room. Her heart raced. Whether it was out of fear or something else, she didn't know. Setting the pad and pen aside on the mattress, she slowly rose, listening carefully as more slow creaking sounds grew nearer. Was it Eric? Damon? Or possibly Sarah?

Moving toward the closed door, she was nearly within reaching distance when the door was shoved open. The door hit the back wall carelessly, causing Rebecca to jump back. She frowned with confusion when she didn't see Eric, Damon or Sarah standing in the doorway. Instead, she saw Myra.

Dressed in another revealing outfit; this time a white dress that fell to her mid thigh. Her long blonde hair fell in waves of loose curls down her back and over the swells of her breasts. Myra barely cast a look of acknowledgement Rebecca's way when she walked into the room. Her cold eyes looked around the room with a curious and calculating look. The way she inspected the inside of the closet and dresser drawers before giving the large bathroom and bed a critical look, appeared as if she was eyeing a house that she intended to purchase.

Not wishing to draw too much attention to herself, Rebecca's gaze moved to the bed where her bag and Damon's keys laid out of her reach. There was no way she could grab them and simply run without attracting attention.

Never run from a predator, it only draws their attention and limits your chances of escape. She reminded herself.

When Myra spun around to face her, she had a smug look on her face. It gave Rebecca a sick feeling in the pit of her stomach. "Looks like you've been staying here with Eric."
Giving Rebecca a small look of disgust, Myra moved to settle herself gracefully on the bed. Crossing her perfect legs over the other, flashing more of her smooth skin, Myra regarded her with sudden amusement. Was it possible she could smell her and Eric's combined scents on the bed? The thought had Rebecca blushing with embarrassment despite everything else.

Moving to finger the bedspread with her fingers with a curl of her lips, she released her eyes from Rebecca. "How comical and original; the father and the nanny. I will have to definitely get a new bed in that case."

Unsure what Myra's game was, Rebecca hesitantly moved a step close to her. "Eric's not here if you are looking for him. I was just about to take a shower." She lied at the end, desperate to get rid of the she-wolf.

Pursing her lips, Myra turned back to look at her. "You won't need to worry about that."

"What do you want, Myra? I told you Eric isn't here."

Nodding with a grin, Myra gracefully rose to her heel covered feet. "I know he isn't. I came to see you. Girl time and all that." her smile was anything but friendly.

Rebecca felt her fear swell up in her like a sickness. Her heart nearly pounded through her chest. With a quick glance out the window she saw the sun had fully set and the sky was beginning to darken. She had to get out of her.

"Girl talk?" Rebecca asked, attempting to keep Myra thinking she was paying attention to her.

"Yes." She nearly purred. "There is something that you should have known about me, but I don't blame you for your ignorance, its expected I suppose."

"What are you talking about?" Rebecca asked, clearly confused where Myra was taking this conversation. Taking a step back, Rebecca kept the door and Myra in her vision as Myra began to pace towards her.

"Eric was never meant for one like you and I do not tolerate competition. Your time with Eric is over." Myra's words came out like an official decree from a sovereign. Did Myra think she'd just nod her head and say, *"Of course, whatever you want"?*

"Says you?" Rebecca scoffed. She didn't know what was coming over her. The old Rebecca would have meekly taken berating words and left, but here she was taunting a werewolf that already disliked her. "If you want Eric so badly, talk to him about it." she replied, attempting to plicate the woman in front of her.

"I intend to. But first; we have unfinished business between us that needs attending to." With a those words, Myra's eyes began to glow as a growl echoed from her chest.

Rebecca watched in horror as Myra's face began to become deformed, a mixture of human and wolf. With the sound of snapping bones, Myra's perfectly manicured fingers sprouted long claws. Her smirking lips parted to reveal deadly fangs. When she did nothing but stare; frozen, Myra's glowing eyes scowled at her.

Icy dread coursed through her veins the moment Rebecca saw realization light Myra's cold eyes. Her enemy had discovered her secret.

With her lips slowly curling into a dark smile, surprise and awe overtook Myra's face. "My…My..." she cooed. Stalking closer, Myra tilted her head to the side as she studied Rebecca, her long claws flicking impatiently at her sides. "Have I discovered a spy amongst us?" With a victorious laugh, her posture straightened with pride. "This will make killing you all the more…*satisfying.*" Her evil voice purred.

Edging toward the windows at her back, Rebecca kept her focus on Myra as she moved closer. She'd have only one chance at escape, she couldn't mess this up. Despite the terror that Myra obviously came here to kill her tonight, Rebecca knew she had to keep the she-wolf distracted long enough to outsmart her. Myra loved attention. She craved it. So that's what Rebecca would give her.

"How do you mean?" she asked with false confusion.

"Imagine how Eric will thank me for exposing a traitorous human amongst us."

Not waiting to say more, Myra attacked. With a loud snarl, she lunged at Rebecca, one clawed hand raised to strike. Acting on instinct, Rebecca dodged to the side as Myra flew at her. Barely missing the slashing claws aimed at her chest, she sent Myra colliding with the window. The impact cracked the thick glass, leaving behind a spider webbing pattern where Myra's head struck.

The moment Myra collided with the window; Rebecca took the opportunity of her stunned opponent to rush for the door. With a snarl of rage echoing from behind her, Rebecca willed her legs to move quicker to out run the feral beast behind her. But a human was no match for a shifter in speed.

Her fingers had barely brushed the doorway when Myra's clawed fingers seized her by the back of her neck, cutting deep into her soft skin before tossing her aside like a rag doll. Tossed off her feet, Rebecca slammed into the side of the dresser like a bowling ball against a row of pins. The dresser broke into large chunks as her frail body crashed into it.

A cry of pain escaped her lips as she attempted to crawl to her feet. Her side burned and pain exploded along her left side. Lifting her eyes, she watched as a few feet away; Myra bared her fangs at her before lifting a hand to her forehead to wipe away a smear of blood. With slow, confident steps, Myra stalked towards Rebecca's prostrated form.
Rebecca attempted in a last effort to scrabble away, but was prevented by the pain pulsing through her ribs. Crouching over her, Myra grasped Rebecca's face with her hand. Sharp claws cut at her cheekbones as she held her immobile with her crushing strength. Rebecca cried in pain as Myra lifted her into a slight reclining position from her hold on her face. Her hands rose to claw at Myra's wrist to force her crushing hand from her face, but the she-wolf was too strong.

Myra smirked at the pain she was causing, knowing that it wouldn't be long before she would be the victor. Myra scoffed, her hand tightening against Rebecca's jawbones. "Whatever made you think that you could best one like me?" Rising to her full height, Myra used her hold on Rebecca's face to force her head back against her neck, exposing her vulnerable throat. The fading sunlight streaming through the window glinted off the edges of Myra's poised sharp claws as she raised her free hand to strike.

This was it.

Not realizing she was moving, one of Rebecca's struggling hands dropped from Myra's wrist to wrap around a small, pointed shaft of wood from the wooden dresser that lay at her side. Before Myra could bring her claws down, Rebecca swung the large stake into the side of Myra's exposed upper thigh.

Blood sprayed over her hand as the shaft sliced through Myra's skin like a knife through warm butter. Howling in pain, Myra stumbled away from Rebecca to fall on her back to the floor. Moaning in pain as dark blood ran down her tan skin, Myra's eyes filled with horror as she saw the fist thick shaft protruding from her body.

Before she could turn her hateful gaze back to Rebecca the sound of pounding footsteps echoing off the walls had Myra stilling. Rebecca prayed to God that Eric or Damon had heard the attack and someone would come to her aid. But her hopes were soon dashed when three unknown males stormed into the room. All stared at Rebecca with a mix of confusion and rage as they took in the sight of Myra lying in a small pool of blood with a stake protruding from her thigh.

Shifting fully back to her human face, Myra held a hand out to the males with a fearful look. "Help me. This *human* attacked me, she knows what we are!" Myra cried like a frightened child.

Rebecca struggled to yell, cry, anything to tell them that she was under Eric's protection and that Myra had attacked *her*, but the pain coursing through her had her head spinning and left her too weak but to labor for breath.

Rushing forward two of the males, moved to help Myra like she was some delicate victim. The last one, stormed over to Rebecca. She would have thought him an attractive male if it hadn't been for the dark hatred that burned within his glowing, blue eyes. Snarling, he bent down to grip her by her neck, pulling her from the pile of broken wood. Weakly gasping for air, Rebecca cried out in pain with the movement. Reaching up, her small hands clawed against his unbreakable hold.

Growling filled the air around her as the male that held her, snarled out. "You dare to attack one of our own?!" his voice was deep and guttural.

"Kill her now!" another with a young voice demanded.

"No." her captor rumbled with anger. "Take her to the elders. They will decide her fate."

With those chilling words, the world around Rebecca grew dark as her oxygen starved body grew limp and even the pain of her wounds faded with her consciousness.

22

Pulling the hummer to a skidding stop, Eric barely put the brake on before he jumped from the driver's seat. The long drive that led to the lodge was filled with hundreds of parked cars, blocking their path. The sun had set and the Gathering had begun. Slamming his door shut, Eric barely spared Chris a glance before he took off running toward the large lit structure in the distance.

"Eric!" Chris yelled as he ran after his Alpha.

Panting, Eric's arms pumped as his legs flew across the ground. Terror and shame at how arrogant he had been nearly had his heart stopping. He was too late. He couldn't stop now. He had to make sure that Rebecca was safe and that none of the pack had discovered her. He even desperately hoped that Damon was with her. At least with the back-stabbing wolf; she was safe.

Reaching the lodge, Eric shoved past groups of shifters that eyes him warily. Panting for air, he flew across the lobby floor, not bothering to apologize when he knocked people out of his way when shifters stepped forward to talk to him. Reaching the stairs to the second level he took two at a time out of desperation to reach her. Running down the hall with his beta close on his heels, Eric reached the door of his and Rebecca's room.

Seeing the door closed, he breathed a heavy sigh as he prayed he'd simply find her sleeping in their bed. With his hand wrapped around the door knob, he froze as he took in the smell of fear and blood on the other side. Shoving the door open with enough force to wench it off its hinges, he clawed up the side wall until his hand encountered the light switch. Flooding the room with light, Eric froze as his heart ceased beating.

The window across the room was uncovered, displaying a large circular crack through the darkened window. The dresser—or what used to be the dresser now lay across the floor in broken chunks. A foot from the end of the bed was a large dark stain of crimson. It was blood. Taking a deep inhale as he stepped into the room, Eric breathed a sigh of relief to find it wasn't Rebecca's blood. Pausing he discovered it was shifter blood; more importantly; Myra's blood. His body stiffened at the thought of that manipulative she-wolf in his room with his mate. What had happened here?

On the bed Eric saw an unfamiliar bag with a keys lying no far out of reach. Approaching the bed, he turned toward the bathroom, still hoping to find his mate and an explanation on what had happened. When his mind refused to calm, his wolf rose to the surface, aiding him to search out her scent. Rebecca's scent was faint. He could detect her fear, her pain, and small traces of her blood in the air. Ignoring Myra's enraging scent, he froze when he discovered the scent of three more shifters in the room.

Others have our mate! His wolf snarled. *Find her!*

Eric allowed his restraints on his beast to loosen as he made his way to the door. If someone had attacked his mate again and had harmed her, they would meet his wrath. Fuck the consequences! Fuck the pack and the elders! Rebecca was *his* and no one touched what was his!

When Chris's towering frame filled the doorway, his face paled as he took in the sight of the room. With eyes darting from the wreckage, Chris turned to Eric, taking in his enraged state. "What happened here?"

"I don't care." Eric said slowly, "Find her!" he snarled, his face beginning to change with the threat of his mate.

Not wasting a second both males raced out the room running in different directions. Eric struggled to locate Rebecca's scent, but with so many people crowding the lobby below, he couldn't locate it. Desperate to find her, he flew down the stairs like a madman before rushing back outside. Breathing in deep gulps of air, he fought to pick up even a hint of her familiar scent.

"Eric!" a deep, frantic voice called behind him.

Turning with a snarl, he saw Damon rushing towards him with wide eyes. Not giving Damon a chance to speak any more, Eric lunged for him. Wrapping his hands around the male's throat, Eric slammed Damon into the side of the lodge so hard that the wood cracked.

Squeezing until he thought he'd kill him, Eric snarled with an animalistic voice. *"Where is she?!"*

"They…they have her!" Damon gasped out, fighting for air.

With a roar, Eric shoved Damon away from him. Falling sprawled on his stomach, Damon quickly jumped to his feet just as Chris came rushing around the side of the building with a confused look.

"Who?" Chris asked with a hard voice, revealing that he'd heard Damon's strangled response.

For a moment, fear and uncertainty warred within Damon's eyes as he looked between Eric and Chris. It was then that Eric noticed that Chris's t-shirt was torn in places, the light blue material stained with blood. Had he been attacked?

"The pack." Damon gasped out, his chest rising and falling rapidly.

"They took her. You have to come with me, Eric. I am telling you the truth."

"The pack here knows that Rebecca is under Eric's protection." Chris said, attempting to calm the two apprehensive males. "We will find her. They would never harm her when they know Eric would protect her."

"They would if they found out that she knew the truth." Damon bit out with an impatient snarl.

Eric felt his blood turn cold. She knew? Rebecca knew that he was a shifter? "What are you talking about?" he asked while taking a threatening step toward Damon.

"I told her to tell you the truth! And now her life is in danger." Damon said with an accusing look to Eric. "You should have never left her here!"

"What does she know?" Chris asked stepping forward. His voice growing fiercer as Eric's did.

"She's always known what you are, what we all are and now they have her!" Inhaling a deep breath, he stepped closer to Eric with a hard look. "Listen to me, Eric. You have to come with me. I tried to stop them, to take her from them. I tried to protect her, but now only you can." With a final look of desperation, he whispered out in a haunted voice. "They are going to kill her."

* ~ * ~ *

Coming away, Rebecca's eyes blinked with confusion. Where was she? In an instant the memory of Myra attacking her came back to her and then the men that came to her aid. Struggling to move her arms, Rebecca found she couldn't move. Behind her she could feel a hard post at her back. Moving her restrained hands, she discovered that her hands were bound together by some abrasive rope around the post at her back.

 When struggling against her bonds did nothing, she fought to discover were she was. Darkness was all around her, stealing her sight from her. The air was cool and the smelled of earth. She was outside. They hadn't killed her yet; which meant there was still time for her to escape and find Eric.

She jumped in fright at a whooshing sound to her left as her eyed closed against a blinding light thrusted near her face. When heat nearly scalded the side of her face, she instinctually jerked away. Opening her eyes against the brightly dancing flames in front of her, her sight adjusted until she could make out the form of Myra standing in front of her.

Smirking with dark intend, Myra purposely moved the torch she held close to Rebecca's face, forcing her to arch back as far as the post at her back would let her. "You're awake. Good. I'd hate to do this when you're unconscious."

"What is going on? Where is Eric? You can't hurt me, I am under his protection." Despite how firm her voice came out, Rebecca knew that it wouldn't be enough to make Myra back down. She needed to stall until Eric came for her.

Laughing, Myra took a step back from her. With the movement, the swaying flames of the torch revealed the dark shadowy figures of more shifters watching her. Looking around at the glowing eyes in the darkness, Rebecca made out at least thirty if not more. When the moon light above broke through the clouds, she was rewarded with more light. She wished then that she couldn't see their faces.

Everyone looked upon her with distain and hate. She was surprised that she wasn't already dead. Looking back to Myra, Rebecca saw the thick bandage wrapped around her upper thigh. She couldn't fight the satisfaction at knowing she'd nearly taken down a shifter with just a piece of pointed wood.

Stakes aren't just for vampires.

She jerked back when Myra approached her once more. "It doesn't matter what Eric told you, *human*. No one can know the truth and live. It's because of your kind that we live in secret. All the more fitting that we burn you like your people did to us centuries ago. No one here will lift a finger to save you now."

"Eric will." Rebecca said with absolute faith.

Myra laugh was bone chilling as she shook her head. "Eric will be the one to condemn you. You attacked one of his pack members. The penalty is death."

Fighting against the terror at Myra's words, Rebecca forced herself to glare at Myra, showing no fear. "You think killing me will endear Eric to you, Slut? Eric didn't want you before I came along, he won't want you after I'm gone."

Her words had the desired effect. Myra's lips curled over her teeth as she snarled with rage. When Myra prepared to lunged for her, she was shoved away from Rebecca as a silver wolf shot from the dark cover of trees. When they fell to the ground, Rebecca watched with amazement as mist drifted around the two tangled bodies as the large wolf's form quickly melted away to tan skin.

With swirling mist thinning around his sweat coated body, Chris rose to his feet; his eyes looked hard and held an inner rage that demanded to be let out. His muscled chest rose and fell with heavy panting breaths. Picking up the torch from where it had fallen from Myra's hand, he turned despite his lack of clothes to snarl at the on lookers.

With a slow movement, Chris took a threatening step toward the group until he blocked their path to her. In one tight fist he held the flaming torch while his other hand brandished long, sharp claws with intent. With glaring looks none of the enraged crowd approached him, but neither did they cower at him as snarls filled the air.

Rebecca gasped in fear, making her heart pound when hands grabbed hers from behind. Warm breath brushed against her face as soft words were whispered into her ear. "Shh. It's me," She'd never been so glad to hear Damon's voice before. "I'm getting you lose, hang on." He urged gently.

When others began to partially change, claws and fangs bared at Chris who stood guard, Rebecca feared they would attack, but like a flash of lighting, another wolf exploded from the trees. Coming to land on the ground beside Chris, the white and black wolf was bigger than Chris's form had been.

Snarling, the wolf bared its sharp fangs at the crowd, causing them to take several quick steps back. Still growling in challenge, white mist swirled around the massive beast as the form of the wolf grew taller until fur reseeded and skin took its place. Paws became hands and then there was no wolf standing fiercely in front of her. The sliver moonlight chased the dark shadows from the dark form in front of her, highlighting the strong muscles in the man's back and arms as he stood tensed. With a slow shift of movement the man before her, turned to look at her over his naked shoulder. With eyes glowing gold in the darkness, her heart stilled in her chest, from fear or relief, she wasn't sure.

Before her wasn't just a man. He was both beast and man, dangerous and unpredictable. Standing between her and countless enraged werewolves was the only one that could save her now.

Eric.

23

Chest heaving and rage boiling, Eric stood before most of the members of his pack. His hard gaze turned to find Myra glaring up at him defiantly as she stumbled to her legs without the usual graceful movements she was known for. Refusing to lower her eyes in submission, Myra glided around snarling Chris to stand with the rest of the pack. From behind him he could hear Damon freeing his mate from her bonds.

He wanted to rush to her. To run his hands over her and reassure himself that she was unharmed, but he couldn't. Until he was certain she was safe, he wouldn't move from his spot separating her from his pack.

When they'd followed Damon to where his pack had taken her deep in the forest of the pack's lands, he'd nearly attacked every wolf that stood before his helpless mate. They had dared to harm her and tie her up like she was a witch to be burned at the stake. This would *never* be forgiven.

Allowing his wolf freedom of its usual chains, Eric snarled at the group in front of him. In the distance he could see more gathering from the lodge. The fight for his mate had begun and he intended to win. "Who is responsible for this?" he hissed out with a voice more feral and lethal than anyone had ever heard before.

With a confident step forward, Myra smirked at him. With a sharp jerk of his wrist, Eric released his claws. Eyes glowing, he took a step forward to kill the woman that had dared to attack his mate. He would taste her blood for this.

Reaching her, his clawed hand shot out, gripping the slim column of her neck with dark intent. "I will kill you for this!" he rumbled in a low growl. Myra's heart quickened at his show of anger, but she didn't lift a hand to defend herself, which surprised him. Did she think he wouldn't do it?

"Alpha!" a hard voice called from amongst the crowd.

Not taking his threatening gaze from Myra's face as her smug grin faded, Eric heard others moving as several members of the pack stepped forward. Flicking his gaze to the side as another stepped close to him; his eyes took in the sight of the four elders coming to stand a foot from him and Myra.

"We ask that you release Myra." The female elder said with an aloof tone.

With a snarl, he tossed Myra to the ground, ignoring her cry as she fell painfully on her stomach. Ignoring the glaring gazes of the elders as several of them assisted Myra to her feet, Eric turned to look over his shoulder at Rebecca. Damon had finally untied the ropes that bound her to the tall post. With a gentle arm around her waist, Damon helped to support her weight as she clutched at her ribs with a look of pain. With the sight of her in pain, Eric's wolf nearly exploded with rage.

Turning back to the elders, he seethed. "How dare you attack this human?" his eyes glowed dangerously as he took a step forward. "I should kill you all for attacking her; she is under *my* protection; as you know!"

Taking Myra by the arm, Elder Peter directed her behind him as he stepped between her and Eric. "*That* human—" he hissed out, pointing an accusing finger past Eric at Rebecca. "—attacked Myra; beloved daughter of the late Alpha. Punishment must be honored." He said with a stiff authority that had Eric rolling his eyes.

"I do not care." He stated without an ounce of caring. "This is not how we do things." He bit out, locking his displeased gaze on each stiff expression of the elders. "We do not attack and tie up humans to murder them."

"All due respect, Alpha." the female elder interrupted with a deep scowl. "You've taken your authority too far. It has been made known that this human as been allowed not only free reign at our home sanctuary at the lodge, but in our leader's very home."

"Not to mention that you have gone against the council's recommendations not to pursue the issue of missing shifters from other packs." Elder Derik added with an accusing tone.

"I. Am. The. Alpha!" Eric snarled. "I lead this pack! You want to challenge me; do it. But understand this; I will not make the same mistake I did with sparing the last person I challenged. I will kill any that oppose my judgment from now on!"

Jonathan, Derik and the female elder took a fearful step backward, but Peter held his ground as he smirked at Eric without fear. Something was happening that Eric wasn't seeing. His wolf paced with suspicion as Myra came to step up to stand beside Elder Peter with a look of smug confidence.

"Renounce your leadership to the elder council and we will let the human die peacefully. Regardless what happens here, Eric, she will die." Myra said with a smile.

"I will kill you before I let that happen." Eric vowed, flashing his fangs in rage.

Taking a step forward, paying no heed to him when he snarled threatening at her, Myra pressed her hands against Eric's naked chest as she leaned into his tense body. Tilting her head back, Myra smiled coyly up at him. "It over, Eric. The power that you think you have over his pack is now mine to wield. Because of you; my mother was murdered by hunters—*Human hunters.* When you denied my father the right to avenge his mate, you destroyed him. When my brother decided to fight for the shifters, you would have killed him without pause."

"Your brother was attacking and murdering humans. He exposed us to them. You are lucky he will simply be chained in a basement for the rest of his life and that your father is simply exiled."

"Not any longer…" she cooed in a song like tone. "The time for hiding has come to an end." She whispered. "Chose me and allow the pack to have their human prey tonight. It is within my power to shield you and your unfortunate pups from the wrath of the rest of the pack." She whispered close to his ear. "Hiding from the humans is in the past now. We have allies now that have shown us how the world can truly be. No longer will we skulk in dark shadows, afraid of what we are. Join me."

Stilling, Eric took in her poisonous words into his mind. This was worse than he'd even thought. It wasn't just Rebecca his pack was after. They wished to war with the humans; all humans. It went against every ancient law of the shifters existence. In his bewilderment, Eric's thoughts were jerked to a stop when his wolf snarled low in his mind.

The scent…it's on her…

Jerking to look down at Myra's dark eyes, his hand cupped the back of her neck, jerking her up on her toes so that his nose could press against her throat. Inhaling deeply, he smelled it then. The scent of rotting, excessive sweetness lingered on her skin like a grimy paste. Jerking back, his hand tangled in Myra's long blonde hair, jerking sharply. When she gasped in pain, he snarled at her.

"Someone attacked my home and nearly killing my family and Rebecca. Why?"

Smirking up at him, Myra lifted her brows at him. "You've had this coming, Eric. We've found a stronger leader than you and now you will beg me to take you as mine."

When Eric released her with a jerking motion, she stepped back to look at the large mass of people that made up the pack. Her eyes locking on the elders as she raised her voice for all to hear.

"I evoke the Act of Revealment." Fear punched Eric in his gut as he heard Rebecca gasp in fear from behind him. Both Damon and Chris growled with anger at Myra's words. He knew that both would protect his mate with their lives, but he knew it wouldn't be enough to stand up against the strength of the pack.

"I am your Alpha and the right of Revealment cannot be envoked without *my* blessing." Eric growled out, his wolf furiously pacing within as a trembling hand touched his back.

He shuttered at the feel of Rebecca touching him, seeking comfort and protection. His wolf urged him to give it to her. With the Act of Revealment called, there was only one way he could see out of this. But was he strong enough to carry it out?

Walking around the elders, reveling in the protection their bodies provided her, Myra gave Eric an all too pleased look. "The Act of Revealment can be invoked without the Alpha's permission; if *his* judgment has been compromised."

"This is ridiculous!" Damon snarled. Shoving past Eric and Chris, he charged toward the crowd, turning his attention on Myra, whom; folded her arms stubbornly. "What's this? You can't have Eric so you stomp your feet like a child? Attacking this human in the Alpha's private room? Don't deny it. If you were so worried about keeping the secret of our existence you wouldn't have acted as you did. If anyone here deservers to meet some so called *justice,* it's you."

Myra's eyes flashed dangerously at Damon, "You are not a member of this pack. You have no right to speak here."

"He may not; but I do." Chris bit out, taking a step forward, he used the torch to point at Myra. The flames swished through the air with his angry movements. "This woman exposed herself to a human and doing so violated our most sacred law. The penalty is death for a shifter that attacks a human and reveals their true form!"

At the murmur of voices amongst the crowd, Myra glared with rage before turning to look at the elder council. Waiting. With a nod at her, Peter stepped forward.

"Enough." He bit out, his cold eyes sweeping over Damon and Chris like they were beneath him. Turning his attention on Eric, Peter held himself stiff as he spoke. "Alpha; as much as I hate to choose sides, Myra does have a point." The gray-haired elder turned to Myra, "What reason do you declare Revealment, Myra?"

Pointing her finger in Rebecca's direction she addressed the council. "As I have told you; that *human* attacked me. Out of fighting for my life my beast was exposed. If not for three members of the pack coming to my rescue, I knew she would have killed me. She knows our secret."

"That is ridiculous!" Eric's voice thundered.

"What, Alpha? Is she better than any of us? Are you willing to risk her telling other humans as well? How long before we're put in cages, our pups taken too? How long will we wait to take action to protect our families? We will be hunted and killed like mindless animals as our kind was in the times of old." at Myra's startling words the voices of pack members around them rose in fear and anger.

"What say you, Alpha?" Elder Derik asked.

Turning toward Rebecca, Eric was met with her terrified eyes. Lowering his voice, he attempted to gentle the aggressive tension of his body. "Tell me this is a lie and I will protect you. Tell me that you didn't hide the truth from me and that you didn't know all along."

Eric felt his heart squeeze painfully in his chest when tears streaked paths down her pale face. Unable to answer him, Rebecca pressed her lips together before turning her face away from him. He hadn't wanted to trust Damon's earlier words. He couldn't see Rebecca hiding such a thing from him; he didn't want to believe it. But was it true?

He suddenly felt anger at the knowledge that she'd lied to him, that she'd kept something like this from him. Even worse; he was angry at himself for not seeing it. Thinking of all the times he had held himself back when he should have claimed her properly because he worried that he'd frighten her if she knew the truth, made Eric's face harden.

"What is your decision, Alpha" the female elder asked with a firm voice.

Eric turned back, his eyes flashed unyielding over everyone until he turned back to look at Rebecca's averted face. There was no stopping this now. He had no choice. "I will be the bearer of the Revealment." His tone was cold. Distant. His jaw clenched tightly as his expression grew dark.

No going back now…

"Alpha, the duty falls to your hunters, not you." Derik said in a quite tone.

Eric's gaze flashed over the men of his pack that stood off to the side of the massive crowd of bodies. Hunters were the soldiers, the killers, the protectors of every shifter pack; they carried out the orders of the Alpha when others stepped out of line. His hunter's eyes watched eagerly from the shadows, the way they looked over his mate made his protective instincts go into overdrive. He would never let them near her.

Reaching behind him, Eric shackled Rebecca's wrist, pulling her to stand at his side. "I will handle this and eliminate this threat to us."

He addressed the whole pack. Hearing Rebecca's swift, fearful inhale, he chose to ignore her for the time being. Pausing, his expression turned emotionless as his voice rang out with displeasure. "From this moment forth, I hereby banish Myra; beloved daughter of the late Alpha. If she returns to my lands, my hunters have my orders to kill her on sight for risking the safety of this pack. I am assuming total and complete control over the leadership of this pack." Turning his hard gaze on Elder Peter; who met his gaze unflinching, Eric's next words had every elder's mouths gasping. "The elder's council is no more."

A hushed silence came over the grounds around him. The elders looked at him with looks of rage and horror at what he'd just done. Though as the Alpha, he held the power to lead and protect his pack, the elders had abused their power as advisors. For too long he'd allowed their threats of turning the pack against him to control his actions as leader. No more. With just a few words, he'd burned every traditional aspect of the Black Claw pack and he was grateful for it.

"If any of you have an issue with that step forward, I will tolerate no violence against the human world. Any that disobey this will be given no mercy." Many members of the pack shouted in anger, their clawed fist clenched in that air, others stormed away vowing vengeance against the humans, while the rest of the pack stared solemnly at him.

Lips curling in anger, Myra quickly shifted into her wolf form and disappeared into the woods. Staring after her retreating form, Peter glared at Eric with a look that told him that the elder would not accept his decree lightly. "You shall regret this night, *Alpha.*" He sneered with rage.

Ignoring the stunned looks around him, he tightened his hold on Rebecca's arm before turning toward the dark interior in the direction of the lodge, pulling her along with him.

24

Looking over her shoulder as they left the pack behind, Rebecca felt her stomach drop in fear. What had just happened? When Damon had freed her from the ropes that bound her, she could do nothing else but watch as Eric argued on her behalf against his pack. When he'd turned to look at her with pleading eyes, begging that she tell him that everything Myra said was a lie, she hadn't had the strength to see the look of betrayal on his face.

Instead of stepping aside and letting his pack deal with her as the others expected him to do, Eric had stood like a towering, insurmountable giant before small men. Fear had nearly caused her to run with his chilling words, *"I will handle this and eliminate this threat to us."*

What had that meant? With now knowing that she'd lied to him, would he kill her? Would his anger at her betrayal overshadow everything they'd shared in the past week?

"Eric? Where are you taking me?" he didn't even spare her a glance. Heart pounding, she tried to twist her hand free from his hold, but he refused to release her. With a strong jerk, he continued to pull her forward. "Tell me what's going on!" she demanded, her voice rising out of terror.

Coming to an abrupt stop, Eric turned to face her. His cold expression was so frightening that Rebecca had to fight not to shutter. Jerking her close, he whispered in an emotionless tone that didn't even sound like the man she'd come to love. "Keep quiet. I have to clean up the mess that you've created for yourself. It will all be over soon."

Her heart shattered as her lungs burned for air, but it was beyond her to draw in her next breath at his hard expression. Damon had told her that she was Eric's mate, that he'd protect her. But clearly his rage at her deception was too strong for him to see past.

He's going to kill me…

Well; she didn't survive her previous attack by a werewolf to die at the hands of another. Pushing aside the paralyzing fear that mounted within her, she struck out. With all her might, she fought. Kicking, and swinging her free fist at him, she fought for freedom.

"Let me go! I won't let you kill me!" she fought with everything she had.

"Stop fighting." Eric bit out as he began dragging her along once more.

Out of nowhere both of them were knocked to the ground as a heavy missal struck collided with their backs. The hard impact sent them forward, tearing her from Eric's strong hold. The sound of a loud snarl had Rebecca lifting her head to see a large, blonde wolf standing between her and Eric. Glaring unafraid at the wolf, Eric tried to reach across the grass and grab Rebecca but the wolf growled dangerously at his movements.

Lips curled back and snapping its jaws at him, the wolf prevented Eric from touching her. Not wasting the opportunity, Rebecca picked up herself and ran for the lodge as the other wolf had Eric cornered. If she was lucky, she would reach Sarah or a reach a road where someone could help her.

* ~ * ~ *

When Rebecca took off running through the darkness, Eric's wolf roared in rage. Shifting he attacked the rival wolf that kept him from his mate. Both wolves collided in a tangle of fur, claws and snapping jaws. Rolling his opponent, Eric bit down on the back of the blonde wolf's neck, holding the strong male immobile in the strong grasp of his jaws, he tossed the wolf aside. The wolf flew a foot away to hit the trunk of a tree before collapsing at the base.

The panting wolf stood on staking legs, its blonde fur stained with blood. Deciding not to attack, the blonde wolf's image melted away, until Damon stood before Eric in all his glory. With first look at him, Eric snarled in rage as he allowed the change to over take him, returning to his human form.

"I won't let you kill her, Eric. I will kill you first." Damon challenged.

Rising to his feet, Eric brushed himself off. His hard gaze locked on Damon's."This doesn't concern you, Damon."

Damon shook his head at him like he didn't recognize him. "She's your mate! And you would kill her just to please the elders? You have no idea what she's been through! You do this and you will lose her."

Stalking closer, Eric bared his teeth in anger. "You would know, wouldn't you?" with each next word, he stalked toward Damon with angry steps. "At every turn I have seen you sniffing around my mate like you have a claim to her! All this time; you knew. You should have told me! It's because she kept this from me that I have to fix this now. That's all I care about."

Damon eyed him mockingly as his temper rose. "Boo hoo, she lied to you. Think, Eric! Don't you think she would have told you if she could have! What choice did she have? Damn your pride and open your damn eyes! You've finally found your true mate—"

"I KNOW SHE'S MY MATE!" he roared. His eyes glowed, cutting through the shadows around them. A rumbling growl vibrated his heaving chest as he spoke once again. "I have to do the only thing I can to protect my pups and her."

Desperate to sway him, Damon stepped forward, giving Eric a beseeching look. "Eric, think about what you're about to do. Rebecca loves you. She refused to run and leave town when she could have all because she made a promise to you. How will she feel if you do this?"Damon tried to reason.

Using a rough hand, Eric shoved Damon away from him."I am Alpha. My word is law, and the law states that no human can know our secret can remain so and live. I do this for my pack and for Rebecca; my hunters wouldn't be so merciful."

"I can't let you do this." Damon warned. Before he could act, Eric rushed forward. Swinging his fist, he smashed Damon in the face, causing him to stumble back stunned. Pulling back his fist again, Eric drove it into his gut, causing him to gasp. Before Damon could recover, Eric fisted his hand in Damon's blond hair. Jerking his head down, he smashed his knee into his face before tossing him back into the tree behind him.

Eric watched as Damon struggled to get up, his face painted with blood. He'd broken Damon's nose and traumatized his solar plexus. Frowning down at his friend, Eric stood over him. When Damon's unfocused eyes lifted to his, Eric fisted his hand in Damon's hair once more, forcing him to hold his gaze.

"Your job of protecting my mate is done. It's my responsibility now." Using every ounce of his shifter strength, Eric drove his fist into Damon's face once more, rendering him unconscious.

Panting as battle rage heated his blood; Eric took several steps back from Damon's still form. He had to get to Rebecca and end this before a member of his pack did. Closing his eyes, he pulled his wolf to the surface, seeking out the scent of his mate. Once he located the mouth watering scent of Rebecca, his eyes snapped open, glowing in the darkness. Turning toward the direction of her scent, he frowned grimly. They were at least a mile away from the lodge, so there was nowhere for her to run, but that didn't mean that others wouldn't go after her now that they knew the truth.

With a heavy heart, Eric ran toward the scent of his mate. Damon's words reverberated through his mind like a blade in his gut. He'd once told Rebecca that he'd never let anything hurt her. Yet now he hunted her, his mate and what he was intending to do would hurt her more than anyone else ever could.

The frail trust she'd gifted him with would be shattered. Ignoring the pain in his chest at the thought he forced his legs to run through the dark forest faster. He couldn't think of his personal feelings now. *He* was Alpha and he had to do his duty and except the consequences.

Once this night was over he would lose her. But at least he could keep her safe from others.

* ~ * ~ *

Tripping in mid run, Rebecca fell heavily against the tee in front of her, her nails clawing at the bark in effort to hold herself up right. She gasped for air as her heart pounded from fear and exertion. Winching, she pressed a hand against her side as her ribs pulsed with pain, making breathing all that much more difficult. The pain was beginning to make her head swim, but she couldn't think about that right now.

She didn't know where she was going for even how much longer she could run, but she had to. The other option open to her was too terrifying to accept. Part of her told her to trust Eric to allow him to find her and talk to him. But the icy emptiness of his eyes when he'd been forcibly dragging her off somewhere had frightened her.

All at once the memory of her attack came to the forefront of her mind. Consuming and drowning her until she felt she'd go crazy. All over again, she could see the image of her attacker in her mind; only this time it was Eric. Every slash of claws, every hate filled taunting word. She had to get away until she could face him, when her terror wasn't stronger than her stubbornness.

She flinched as the air stilled around her, the night growing silent. Chills pebbled her skin as she felt as though someone was watching her. Not waiting to find out, Rebecca forced herself to run again. Her aching legs carried her a few feet before they gave out, forcing to fall to the ground with a painful jarring.
Gasping for air, she pushed herself up onto her hands. Above her the moon broke through the heavy clouds to shine light down over the trees around her. She could see that she was in an open grove; trees stood like towering pillars around her and gave her the impression of being caged.

She turned on her hip to look in all directions. All around her it all looked the same. Every direction possessed the same darkness that held no hope of a good outcome. Where should she run? Where *could* she run that others wouldn't find her? Before her mind could sort it out, the deafening sound of a branch snapping had her jerking around. The soft sounds of moment reached her ears, causing her to crab walk from the approaching footsteps.

When she could make out the dark form of a man standing in shadows, she felt her heart still in her chest. Whoever had found her didn't instantly attack her like she assumed he would, but simply stood there for a moment. Her survival instincts screamed at her to run, but her mind reasoned that even if she did; she wouldn't get far. Like an animal caught in a trap, she was out of options.

"Stay away from me!" she cried as the dark figure stepped from the shadows.

She didn't need to be able to see in the dark to know who it was a moment later. Ducking his head beneath the low hanging branch, the moonlight hit Eric's emotionless face, chasing away the shadows of the overhanging leaves above.

Taking another step forward, Eric paused to look around them with a hard look. Seeming satisfied that they were alone; he turned his attention back on her.

"Don't run from me again, Rebecca. I don't want to hurt you." The words emerged hard, almost scolding. Whether his last words were meant as a vow or a threat, she didn't know.

Scowling uncertainly at him, she crawled to her shaking legs with a wince. Making sure to keep distance between them, she braced herself to run if he made another step towards her. Eric seemed to be watching her as well. His icy gaze studied her as if she were a strange animal that he'd found.

She'd expected him to rush at her, to become the beast she knew lurked behind the face that she'd come to love. His hands clenching into tight fists at his sides, Eric continued to watch her silently, his eyes filling with a look of regret and pain.

Talking a slow breath, he took a step towards her. "Come here, Rebecca." He said softly, his hand outstretched to hers. When she simply stared at his offered hand, with no interest in taking it, he sighed. "You cannot out run me, Rebecca." He stated it like it was a fact.

Rebecca froze, her body refusing to move. What would happen if she took the few steps toward Eric and laid her hand in his? Would he hold her close and comfort her for the events of tonight or would he attack her?

I will handle this and eliminate this threat to us...

Eric's previous words echoed in her mind like a pulsing wound. Unforgettable and bringing so much pain. She wanted to run to him, but his harshly spoken words from moments ago prevented her. But his anger had her second guessing whether she could trust him.

Taking a slow step back, she shook her head at him, her lips pressing tightly together. "Leave me alone Eric." her voice soft but firm.

Eric dropped his offered hand with a hard look. Obviously he'd expected her to just fall into his arms without question and when she didn't, it angered him. *Too damn bad.* After what had happened to her; what could still happen to her, she wasn't willing to trust anyone without a good cause to.

"You know I can't do that, Rebecca. Come here. You know me. You know you can trust me." He said gently despite the way his eyes blazed with anger.

"Can I?" she asked, raising an inquiring brow at him. "I just want to be left alone. Can't you give me that at least?"

Without a pause, Eric shook his head at her. "No. I can't. Not tonight and not after what just happened. I don't have the time to explain this to you; so you will just have to trust me." He said firmly as he moved closer to her. As though they were involved in some sort of dance, without missing a beat she met his approaching step with two retreating ones.

"Trust you?" she released a shaky breath. "I do trust you. But the way you are acting...this isn't the Eric I know. I heard what you said back there Eric. Why should I not run from you right now?"

Eric flinched from her words like they were a strong blow. If she'd hurt him with her words, he didn't show it or comment on it. Instead, he pushed his shoulders back, a cool mask over took his expression as he erased the distance between them. Rebecca recoiled with a shocked gasp, but was unable to move quick enough to evade his hands as they gripped her arms.

"Let go of me!" she shouted, punching out at him.

Each time she struck him, Eric seemed to not notice. Fear and frustration mixed and caused her to strike out with her whole body. Using her leg she brought her knee to slam it into his balls as she had once before. Her hopes of hurting him long enough to escape faded when Eric anticipated her attack and used his thigh to block her strike.

Jerking her up onto her tip toes, he lowered his face to hers until their noses brushed. "The one time you did to me was the last and only time it will ever happen." He raged at her. Taking a deep breath, he made an effort to gentle his voice, but it still emerged ruthless. "Stop fighting me and hold still. I promise this will be over soon."

When Eric lowered his eyes to look at the bare column of her neck, she knew she had to act and act fast. Rearing her head back she slammed it into Eric's. Taking him by surprise, Eric shouted in pain as he released her. Stumbling onto her feet, Rebecca turned and ran. She didn't care where she ran to, so long as it was away from him.

With a loud growl, Eric pursued her. She'd not put but a three feet of distance between them before his arms came around her. Pinning her arms to her sides, Eric lifted her off her feet. Air rushed from her lungs as his arms tightened around her. The pressure of his embrace caused the pain in her side to build higher.

His arms loosened just by an inch before he shifted his arms around her. With one arm holding her immobile against his chest, Eric's free hand moved to cup the underside of her jaw before tilting her head to the side. The forced position caused her to expose the left side of her neck.

With her heart pounding with fear, tears filled her eyes as Eric used his cheek to brush her fallen hair away from the skin of her neck. His lips skimmed softly over the skin at her pulse point before they moved down to the point where her shoulder merged with her neck. His warm breath brushed over her skin, making her shiver with fear of what he would do next. Inhaling deeply, Eric's arm tightened around her middle as his grip on her jaw held her firmly.

"Forgive me..." he whispered.

Then her worst fear was realized when Eric's sharp fangs clamped down on her soft skin. Pain raced along her shoulder as he savagely bit her. The pain of her body and the overwhelming fear in her mind suddenly exploded in her mind.

Without warning, darkness began to cloud her mind. Was she dying? Was it finally over? Relief flooded her entire being like a soothing balm, drawing her closer to the darkness that pulled at her. With a soft sigh, she let the darkness take her.

It was finally over.

25

Eyes fluttering open, Pain echoed through all Rebecca's limbs as she came awake. As her vision cleared, she found the sight of the covered window of Eric's room greeting her. What had happened? Where was she? Inhaling deeply to push the pulsing pain from her mind, memories of the previous night rushed back to her. Myra attacked her and nearly had the pack kill her….except Eric came.

I will handle this and eliminate this threat to us…

The memory of his emotionless words caused her stomach to clench painfully in denial. The man that saved her hadn't been the Eric she'd come to know. He'd been just as Eric had warned her of days ago; ruthless and cold. Had everything they'd shared had meant nothing in the end, when faced with the truth; he'd chosen to attack her rather than protect her.

Her heart rate skyrocketed when she remembered how he'd looked at her as he told her it would be over soon. Eric had chased her and attacked her. Instantly she felt the spot between her neck and shoulder throb with the memory of his savage bite. She was alive? How was that possible?

"You're awake." Eyes going wide at the sound of Eric's hard voice, she turned over on her back to find he was sitting in a chair beside the bed, his chin braced atop his interlaced hands.

The abrupt movement had burning pain exploding through her side, causing a cry to escape through her clenched jaw. Instantly, Eric moved to sit on the side of the bed, pushing her shoulders down to the bed when she attempted to rise. At Eric's gentle touch, Rebecca flinched from him throwing herself against the headboard to avoid his hands.

"Don't touch me!" she bit out, her eyes watching him with wariness.

Looking down, she found she was dressed in one of Eric's sleeveless under shirts. The hem of the shirt fell loose around her hips leaving her legs bare to his eyes. Jerking her head back toward him, she ignored his concerned look before speaking. "Why am I dressed like this?" she demanded to know even as her hands shook with fresh memories of the previous night.

Eric reached for her, but with a heartrending look when she jerked away from him, he dropped his hand to the bed. "Your clothes were ruined by the time I got you back here. Dr. Terra needed them to be removed before she attended to your wounds."

"What?" she whispered with disbelief at the idea of the woman that obvious disliked her touching her.

 Pressing her hand to her aching side, she felt a thick bandage wrapped tightly around her ribs. Reaching up to her throbbing neck, she felt a wide gauze bandage taped against the area that Eric's teeth had bitten. When her hand lingered too long on the bandage, Eric reached out to remove her hand with a firm shake of his head.

"Don't touch it; it will heal in a day or so. She found bruising around your ribs as well from your attack with Myra. She said you may have a cracked rib."

Jerking her hand from his grasp, she frowned at him. "You let her touch me after everything that happened?" she asked with a look of utter betrayal. Would he let one of his pack that obviously would rather see her dead be alone with her?

Narrowing his eyes at her, he admitted softly. "I did. I remained in the room with you the whole time. I've not left your side for two days."

"T-Two days! I've been unconscious for two days?!"

He nodded grimly. "You were."

Looking from him, she released a shuttering breath. It was all too much to accept. Why would he have attacked her the way he had and then care for her afterwards? What game was he playing?

"You attacked me." She acknowledged aloud before turning her distrusting eyes to his. A shadow of regret flashed through Eric's eyes at her words. His sorrow filled gaze lowered to look at her bandaged shoulder before he forced his eyes to look at the bed.

Swallowing, he briefly shook his head before answering. "You didn't leave me a choice." He whispered with a tight voice, his lips pressing into a thin line. Did he regret what he'd done? Or could he not stomach the memory of it?

Panic swelled within her mind when she kept seeing the memory of Eric grabbing her, holding her prisoner in his crushing embrace. His eyes had held no mercy in their icy depths just before his mouth lunged toward her neck. Shaking her head, she squeezed her eyes against the racing images.

Opening her eyes, she found Eric watching her with an unreadable expression. "Why didn't you tell me?" Eric asked with a slight hint of hurt in his voice.

Rebecca opened her mouth to list her reasons but she found that it no longer mattered. Shaking her head, she shrugged uncaringly. "What would it have mattered?" she murmured with a weary look before she turned from him.

$$* \sim * \sim *$$

Eric felt his body go stiff at her coldly spoken words, as though all emotion and meaning had fled her stubborn spirit. She looked broken and lost. He scrambled to find the right thing to say to her to make her look at him with that mix of trust and love in her eyes as she had but a day ago, but he only found himself closing his mouth with a helpless groan.

Fix this! His wolf roared.

How could he? Didn't she understand he'd done what he had to in effort to save her life? He remembered that night and felt his heart strangle in his chest. When he'd held her tightly in his arms and forcibly bitten her; for the first time in his life, the taste of his mate's blood and silky skin under his mouth had sickened him.

Cradling her unconscious body close, he withdrew his fangs from her torn flesh just as tears trailed down his face to fall onto her exposed neck. The small drops mingled with his mate's smeared blood that painted her mating mark. No joy had filled him at seeing his mark on her as it should have. It sickened and shamed him to see what he'd done to her.

How could he fix this? How could he win back her trust and…love? Did he even deserve it?

He'd never wanted to mark her as he had the other night. He'd pictured in his mind something more romantic. Not that he knew anything about that sort of thing. Now because of fear of losing her, he'd destroyed what fragile trust she'd had in him. To add to it; his pack had been ripped in half because of his actions that night.

What a mess! Pushing a hand through his tussled hair, he groaned with regret. He had to fix this. He would fix this. All of it.

He found himself pondering her words as he searched for a course of action. *What would it have mattered?* The words enraged him at her lack of trust in his honor as her mate. Did she really think that he would have turned from her and left her to her fate with the justice of the pack?

Wouldn't you have? His wolf asked with a knowing tone.

Considering the possibility, Eric found that he couldn't say how he would have reacted if she'd told him the truth. One thing he did know is that he never would have left her to face the brutality of his world alone.

He didn't know what he hated more; the scared look in her beautiful chocolate brown eyes or the idea that she'd feared telling him the truth about her scars and how she knew. He had to fix that this moment. Once they got past this wall of secrets that separated them, he could focus on mending what little of a pack he had left.

Shifting his weight further onto the bed, he moved until he sat beside her feet. Getting comfortable, he took hold of both of her feet before pulling them into his lap. When he startled Rebecca with his actions, he frowned at her as he began rubbing the length of her calves to her feet with a firm massage.

"I'm not going to hurt you." He murmured when she continued to look at him as though he would bite her again.

Her lips pursed with anger and Eric found he liked seeing her fire once more. "You said that once already." She bit out, giving him a tight, cynical smile. "So, forgive me if I don't feel inclined to jump back on the *Trust Eric* train after it already crashed."

Sighing heavily, he moved his deep massaging hand from one of her legs to the other. "I had to do what I did last night to protect you." He explained.

"It didn't feel like protection to me. You may as well have let them kill me."

Eric's moving hands stilled on her foot at her words. Breath left his lungs at the thought of him just standing by as his pack killed her. After how he'd found her that night, he had no doubt how they intended to kill her. Never! He would have killed every wolf in his territory to keep her safe.

"I never would have allowed you to be harmed." He vowed. "I would have done anything to have that night turn out differently, Rebecca." His willed silently for her to believe him, but he only found her regarding him with distrust and uncertain eyes.

"Eric," she began, her small tongue darting out to flick over her bottom lip before continuing. "I know how your kind views humans. I'm weak and unworthy to even be in a place like this." she said, waving her hand around the room.

The way she spoke, it almost was like he could hear someone else saying those words to her. He felt his mind peak with interest and curiosity as he fought to find the pieces that remained of the puzzle to Rebecca's past. Damon had said she'd known about shifters. How? It was rare if shifters exposed themselves to humans and the ones that usually did didn't do so with innocent intentions.

Was that it? He froze as his blood turned cold. His eyes moved to the raised white scars across her chest. Seeing the scars as if for the first time, he realized that Rebecca had lied to him about how she'd obtained them. They weren't from some animal attacking her. They were from a *shifter* attacking her.

He forced back the rage at the thought of someone of his own kind attacking and trying to kill his mate before he'd had the chance to even meet her. Pausing, he fought against the need to know the truth and the need to let her tell him herself, but in the end he couldn't.

"Those marks on your skin, your scars; those weren't made by some random animal were they?" he asked hesitantly, never missing the way she flinched and tensed under his rubbing hands.

Drawing her legs from beneath his warm hands, she pulled her knees to her chest before wrapping her arms around them. She winced with the position, but he didn't say anything. Avoiding his gaze, she pressed her lips together. Her eyes watering when she shook her head slightly.

"No."

"It was one of my kind? A shifter?"

Releasing a shuttering breath, she nodded. "A werewolf."

He frowned at the term, but accepted it for the time being. Perplexed, he shook his head. "Why would you stay near my kind after that? From what I know you've been around shifters for years and that was before I ever met you."

"I guess I thought I was safer with your kind in front of me then sneaking up behind me."

"How did you get your scars?" when a tear slid from her right eye to trail down her face, he felt his gut clench in pain at the sight. "Please." He was actually begging. "I need to know."

Gulping past the lump in her throat she nodded. "I don't know what I can tell you other than, one night I was at my parent's house. I was on break from college. There was a knock at the door and then it happened."

"What happened?" he pressed.

"My world ended. I woke up to darkness. I found my mother and father lying in large pools of their blood. It was like a wild animal had gone crazy. Then *he* found me."

"He?" Eric asked, echoing her words with confusion.

"The monster that gave me *these*." She said, her hand rising to her scars. "He meant to kill me slowly, but he was interrupted. Before he ran off, he said that his kind would never let me live now that I knew. I was in the hospital for a week, every day I prayed that it all had been some type of nightmare."

Kill....Hunt...Protect! His wolf roared.

Eric couldn't have agreed more. If it was possible, he planned to scour the world until he found the shifter responsible for Rebecca's attack. He wanted to find the man that did it and make him suffer!

"Why would you go against your pack for me?" Rebecca's abrupt words had Eric jerking from his vengeful thoughts. She looked at him expectantly, awaiting his answer. One truth deserves another.

"Because," he breathed out. "You are my mate. My true mate." He admitted, his chest puffing out with pride at admitting it to her.

26

Watching carefully as Rebecca took in his words, he was surprised when he saw that there was no confusion or surprise in her expression. Her brows lowered before a sad look filled her eyes. Shaking her head at him, she reached up stab her hands through her hair.

"I may have been at one point, Eric, but now…" she trailed off helplessly before turning to look out the window.

His entire being rebelled against her soft, defeated tone. Deep in his heart and soul, his wolf howled in pain at her slight rejection, but his mind quickly took front seat as he quickly went over her words. Rebecca hadn't seemed surprised with this admission that she was his mate. Ignoring how she shrank from him, he moved further up the bed until they sat hip to hip.

"Why do you say that? Why do you seem unsurprised that you are my mate?" his question heavy with suspicion.

Leaning away from his crowding frame as much as her sore body would allow, Rebecca replied. "Damon told me."

"What?" he asked astonished.

"Damon told me I was your true mate the day of the attack." She repeated as she explained further. "He explained what it meant. Though I have to say; I wish I would have taken my chances and ran after all that's happened since then."

"Don't say that." he bit out, the muscle along his jaw tightening at her words. "I regret how I claimed you, Rebecca. I wanted it to be different but I feared that you wouldn't accept me. That you'd run from me if I told you the truth."

Sighing, she shook her head at him, her hand rising to cover her aching ribs once more. "I doubt the result would have been different." She admitted. "You know the truth now."

"But I didn't when I should have." He argued. The thought that she'd turned to Damon of all people for help instead of him, irked him. "*Damon* knew the truth but not me. Why would you tell him and not the man you were sleeping with?" his tone sounded jealous even to his own ears, making Eric wince with disgust. He prayed that Rebecca hadn't taken notice of that.

"I didn't *tell* Damon a damn thing." She bit out, her hand slapping at him in retaliation. Eric found he had to struggle to contain his amusement at her temper. "The night I went on a date with him, he told me that he knew. Instead of turning me over to your people for *justice*—" she said, spitting out the words like it was distasteful. "—He vowed to protect me. After the attack he urged me to tell you the truth."

"Then why didn't you?"

"How could I have?" she asked, exasperated while giving him a look that clearly screamed; *are you stupid?* "Maybe I should have told you after we had sex that first night? '*Hey Eric, last night was great, by the way; have I mentioned that I know what you are because years ago my family was attacked by a werewolf. Don't worry, I promise not to tell anyone.*' Would that have been better?" she asked sarcastically.

Sighing, he shook his head. "No. I just wish you could have come to me. I would have protected you regardless."

"You can't say that for sure." She denied, with a shake of her head. "After what happened that night it's clear that your pack wouldn't have accepted me regardless." She said with a look of deep disappointment. "It's better if I just go, Eric."

Growling low in his throat, Eric swung his legs over the bed, jumping to his feet; he paced away from her to avoid grabbing her and giving her a good shake. She thought she would run from him—again?!

"That won't be happening." He said firmly. Spinning around, he saw Rebecca carefully sliding to the edge of the bed before allowing her legs to dangle limply over the edge of the mattress. Fingers curling around the comforter beneath her, she swallowed before asking.

"What do you mean? Am I still in danger?"

He scoffed with humor at her words. "Of course you are. You're my mate. You will always be in danger. Others will come after you to get to me. It's the way of the wolf shifters to dominate other packs by killing the competition."

Scowling, she huffed out an angry breath. "Then I don't want to be your mate."

It would have hurt less if she'd stabbed him. She…didn't want him. She didn't love him. Reality was like a cold bucket of water over him. Of course she didn't. Why would she after everything? But he had too much plaguing his mind to worry about the personal feelings between them.

Burying his instincts that demanded he go to her and show her that he loved her and that she was his, Eric pulled on his emotionless demeanor that he reserved for others. "It's not like you have a choice." His words emerged flat and cold. "Not after I've bitten you."

Reaching up to cup her bandage, she raised a confused brow at him. "What does that have to do with anything?"

"The Right of Revealment comes with two outcomes." He stated, holding up two spread fingers. With each next word, he ticked off each extended finger. "Death or claiming." When she just stared at him expecting him to explain further, he did. "I chose to be the bearer of Revealment and rather than kill you, I claimed you as my mate; my true mate."

"I still don't see what you're trying to say, Eric. What does you claiming me have to do with me leaving for the best? I care for you; I do, but did you ever stop to think that maybe your home was attacked because others found out about me? I can't have your death on my conscience."

Expression softening, he strode back across the room to her. Cupping her face, even though she tensed, Eric bent to brush a tender kiss over her lips. She *did* care. She may not think she loved him anymore, but he was stubborn and ruthless enough to keep at her until she admitted it again to him.

Pulling back, he sighed before falling to his knees in front of her. When she lightly brushed her fingers though his tussled hair, he had to stiffen a groan of desire. Her touch was a drug and he was content on being addicted to her until the end of time.

"There is more to the claiming bite or as we call it; the claiming mark." He admitted. Raising his eyes to see she was paying attention, he revealed the ugly truth that he was certain Damon hadn't shared with her. "In a few days to a week of a shifter claiming a human for his true mate, during the next full moon, the bitten mate will change."

Stiffening, Rebecca's hand fell from his hair with dead weight. Her fear filled the room around him like a foul stench. "What do you mean, *change*?" her voice was firm, but the tremble of fear still echoed out, hidden deep.

Rising to his feet, he braced both arms on either side around her, caging her in as he towered over her. "Shifters live for nearly three times longer than the normal human lifespan. The claiming mark allows shifters to make their human mates like them, so they will be forever tied to each other."

"As romantic as that sounds, I can still feel that you aren't telling me something." she observed with a frown. "There's more than just a longer life involved, isn't there?"

Looking away briefly, Eric nodded. "The bite allows us to change our human true mates into shifters. At the next full moon, you will take your second form for the first time." He explained, proudly.

"What?!" she cried out, shoving away from him. Stumbling to her feet, she cried out when her ribs protested. When Eric moved towards her to help her when she staggered away from the bed, she slapped at his hand, angrily. "Let me get this straight; you've *infected* me?!" she questioned in outrage.

Eric's eyebrows lowering with confusion at her outburst. He nodded, dumbly. "Not the way I would put it, but yes."

Face falling to one of panic, Rebecca turned away from him, pacing as fast as her weaken body would let her. Hand going to stomach, she moaned while shaking her head. "I think I'm going to be sick."

Fearing she was telling the truth, Eric lunged toward her to help her to the bathroom, only to have his assisting hands slapped away from her again. "Don't touch me!" she bit out, her eyes blazing at him in anger.

"What can I do?" he asked, feeling out of his limit with Rebecca for the first time.

She seemed displeased with the news that she'd be turning in less than a week. He didn't know what Doyle had encountered with his mate; Aria, but he knew from rumors that Robert Mackenzie's mate had been ecstatic at the news. The small Latina had even had the event filmed so she could study it later on. Rebecca on the other hand appeared to be in the midst of a panic attack. Should he hold her? Kiss her and tell her it would be alright? Or should he call Dr. Terra?

"Take it back!" she demanded. Coming to a stop in front of him, she stabbed her puny finger in his chest, punctuating her words. "Right now!"

Aghast at her at her words, he shook his head slowly. "What? I can't and even if I could I wouldn't." he answered with absolute confidence. "It's a gift, Rebecca." His hands settled on her shoulders before sliding down to tangle with her hands. "It's a gift I can only give to you. It means you will become nearly as strong as me and beyond living longer, your senses, your ability to heal and resistance to injuries will increase."

Jerking her hands from his, Rebecca shook her head at him. "*Gift?* Gifts can be returned!"

"Not this one." He bit out firmly. His gaze turned hard at her refusal to accept what she was being offered.

At least she'd not scared of you anymore... his wolf mused teasingly.

Shut. Up. Eric fired back.

"This is part of being my true mate, Rebecca. I will be with you through all this. I know you are scared, but you can trust me."

Jerking away from him, she yelled. "Damn it! I never wanted this, Eric! I want no part of being your mate!" she seemed surprised at her own words, but she made no move take them back.

His world shattered around him at her words. Anger filling his being at her thoughtless words, he strode past her, only stopping long enough to whisper his parting words. "You are my mate. I accepted you when you were just a human and I will do so when you change. Perhaps you should think about that." he gritted out between clenched teeth.

Moving past her, he jerked the door to their bedroom open. Striding out, he slammed the door behind him as he left. Growling in anger and in confusion at her odd rejection, he rushed down the stairs to the lobby, leaving his mate alone for the first time in days.

27

Moving quickly through the forest, Jason dived over fallen logs and under heavy brush for what seem like hours until he came to an abrupt stop. His claws bit into the dirt beneath his feet as he stilled. Pointing his nose to the mid-day sun above, he searched for the scent that he'd been trailing for the past two and a half days. Through the night it had grown stronger and fouler the closer he got.

Within his wolf form, he sighed wearily. Though he knew that his mission to find who attacked his Alpha and his family was important, he couldn't shake that he should have been with Eric at the Gathering two nights ago. Deep down he worried what the elders had told the rest of the pack and if Rebecca; Eric's human mate was safe still.

For a while now, he knew that the retrained violence and discontent within Eric's pack was reaching a boiling point. It had nothing to do with his friend's rule over the past few decades either. Eric was a fair leader and a harsh one when it came to humans. However many wolf shifters were unhappy with Eric's need for peace.

 Many shifters in the Black Claw pack wished for war, not just with other wolf packs for power but against the humans as well. It was only a matter of time before Eric would be forced to cull members from his pack for the safety of the humans, but Jason feared even that wouldn't stop the rage that was brewing in others hearts.

The leaves above him rustled eerily though the sudden silence of the forest, drawing his attention as a strange sound drifted on the wind. Ears perking in the direction, he turned and moved with cautious steps. In the light of day, Jason's black pelt stuck out like a sore thumb, meaning he had to be vigilant for danger. He could easily be killed by a hunter if he wasn't careful.

Moving closer the strange sound grew louder; finally able to hear it more clearly, Jason shook his lupine head in confusion. It was a distant moaning on the wind, a ghostly choir of several eerie moans of despair. What was it?

Reaching the edge of the tree line, Jason moved onto his belly to peak through the outreaching branches of a large honeysuckle bush. In the mist of the unfamiliar forest stood a tall building; more of a warehouse or large barn. The haunting melody was coming from there. Remaining still, Jason lifted his snout to the air once more. The souring sweet scent was here. Who ever had attacked them at Eric's home was here.

Sliding back onto his four powerful limbs, he glanced around his surroundings once more. It was then that he noticed that he was no longer in Eric's territory. He didn't know where he was, but it had to be miles from Ravenwillow.

Turning back to stare at the rotting and dark stained, wooden structure, Jason remembered Eric's earlier orders; "*Observe but do not engage.*"Shaking his head, Jason found himself darting from the tree line toward the imposing building ahead. He would follow his Alpha's orders, but he had to find out who had attacked them and why.

Coming to a stop by the door, he found a discarded pair of jeans. His nose curled at the stench of muck and rain water that clung to the fabric, but forced himself to pull them on before entering the dark interior. If he had to fight in this form, he could but he wasn't about to do so in his human form with his favorite parts exposed.

Stepping inside, he felt air leave his lungs at what he encountered. Rusty cages were positioned along the length of the building lining the walls. Muck and fecal matter covered the ground, seeping into the base of the cages. Each cage contained a large padlock, preventing the cage from being open by just anyone. Looking up he saw more cages were positioned up on the second level. The choir of moans and cries grew louder as he stopped before a cage.

Inside, he found a person! Not just a person; a shifter. The woman lay on her side, what once was a shirt and pants clung to her skin, torn and frayed. The woman looked at him with sightless eyes, as if he wasn't there. Turning to the other side of the building he found a burly man. Chains encircled him as he lay in a heap at the bottom of his cage, his beaten face and body trapped in a partial shift of a jaguar. Moving stealthily along the rows of cages, Jason found men, women and even children, all shifters, caged and appearing nearly catatonic or drugged.

It all came together in that moment. The disappearance of shifters that Eric had been secretly looking into, it was them! They had been attacked not because of Eric's choice to unite with other packs or even his choice to claim Rebecca. They had been attacked because of this! He had to get back and tell Eric what he'd found. Before he could turn to rush out the building he heard a loud roar of anger.

"You swore you could hold up your end of the deal!" a deep rumbling voice shouted in rage.

Stilling, Jason moved toward a side door halfway along the length of the cages. Moving inside, he found himself in a large room that must serve as a loading area. Stacks of large empty crates were positioned by the door, giving him something to hide behind as he took in the rest of the room. Along the far side was a large metal door, no doubt it was used to allow trucks in for loading purposes. In the middle of the room, Jason could see four figures.

As realization hit him at who was in front on him, Jason remained perfectly still. The loud rage filled voice was none other than Senan, the previous Alpha that Eric had defeated all those years ago. Senan had been an Alpha that few respected, but all feared.

Like a malicious dictator, he'd ruled the Black Claw pack with an iron fist and with no sense of mercy. Senan and his son were just a few among many that were responsible for the gruesome murders of countless humans. When Eric had defeated him for the right to rule, most expected and hoped that Eric would kill him, but instead he'd banished the old Alpha.

Beside him, Jason saw the willow frame of Elder Peter. He scowled at Senan's angry tone and replied. "How was I to know that Eric would dissolve the elder council? None other would stand up to challenge him as you assured me they would! I am not at fault here. Blame your whore of a daughter." Peter spewed out with an offended tone as he pointed a bony finger at Myra that leaned uncaringly against another empty crate.

Crossing her arms over the bodice of her short, blue cocktail dress, she snarled at Elder Peter. "You should have allowed me to kill that human woman before Eric got there and then we wouldn't have this problem!"

"And how do you think that would have come back on *me*?!" Peter asked bitterly.

A dark chuckle erupted from behind the arguing three as a towering man stepped forward. He stood at least six feet tall, enough to tower over the others with his massive frame. His hair was the color golden wheat, falling around his shoulders in long waves. When he stepped closer toward the others, Jason found it odd that they quickly stepped back, as though they feared him.

Looking closer at him, Jason found the man's eyes glowed with a bright blue. The sight made his heart still in his chest. A shifter's eyes always glowed golden when their beast was close, but it was nothing like this. This man radiated power like a radioactive missile. Breathing deep, Jason found he was shocked to discover that he was the source of the foul, sweet scent that he'd been trailing. Worse than that; he was a shifter, but what kind was unclear.

"You failed me." The man said in a voice do deep that it nearly sounded demonic. "The deal was that Eric Daniels was to stop looking for these shifters. I even tried to make it easy for you by sending my men to attack his home. But perhaps I should relay this information to my boss of your worthlessness to our cause."

Senan squared his shoulders before stepping forward. "You promised us that your leader would guarantee us a way to destroy the humans. You cannot back out now. Eric will give up on these shifters eventually. Besides; we can always try again to kill him."

"It won't be that easy now." Peter sneered. "According to my spies, Eric has formed alliances with not only the Grizzly shifter Alpha of Darkwood Springs but also the elusive cougar shifters."

"The cougars will never come to the aid of a wolf. They do not matter." Senan said with a bored expression, waving of his hand dismissingly.

Not appearing to care. The towering male released a lion-like roar of fury. Striding forward, he grabbed Peter by the front of his shirt to lift him off his feet. Peter squealed with shock at the quick movement as he found himself dangling in the air.

"You allowed him to form an alliance with *Doyle Mackenzie*?!" the man roared.

"What does one stupid bear shifter from Canada matter?" Myra
asked with almost bored tone. Sighing heavily, she shook her head
as if she found the thought of them fearing Doyle to be absurd. "He's
all strength and no brain. Just like all bear shifters, trust me."

Tossing the quaking elder aside, causing him to land with a hard
thud, the towering male rounded on Myra with a look of hate. With
eyes still a glow, the man rumbled. "Doyle and his mate are the only
ones that have the means to bring down our plans! If Eric discovers
what is really happening with these shifters our plan would be for
naught!"

Jason slowly moved back from the crates with a shocked look. Mark
was right! This wasn't just shifters just turning up missing. If this
involved Doyle's mate; Aria, it could only mean one thing. Malca
was involved. He had to warn Eric. When he turned to move from
the room, Jason found his way blocked by two tall shifters standing
in the doorway. Like the man across the room, their eyes glowed
with an eerie blue color.

Before he could fight his way out, one of the men lunged for him,
shifting as he did so; Jason found a large lion inches from his face.
Wasting no time, Jason shifted to his wolf form and darted out of the
lion's reach. With a loud crash, the lion collided with the empty
crates, smashing them to bits.

At the commotion the others turned in time to see the remaining man
shift into large black bear. Jumping from the smashed pile of wood,
the lion snarled and stalked toward Jason. Jason's eyes flicked back
and forth between the two shifters that moved closer and closer to
him with their eyes glowing bright blue.

Snarling, he fought to reach their minds as all shifters could while in
their animal form. *"Listen to me! I do not want to fight you. You do
not know who you are working for. Come with me and we can
protect you."* To his utter bewilderment, the snarling shifters never
so much as blinked at his words. It was almost like he'd never
spoken at all.

What was wrong with them? They were nearly mindless with only the need to attack him. Suddenly a popping sound echoed through the air a moment before pain exploded in Jason's side. Slowly the shifters began backing away from him, quickly changing back into their human forms. Looking from him, Jason looked to his side to see that he'd been shot.

Weakness filled his being as his blood dripped to the ground beneath him. Within seconds, his powerful legs shook with the effort to hold him up. Before Jason could prevent it, his legs crumbled beneath him, causing Jason to fall onto his side. Dizziness swarmed his vision, making his world spin. Footsteps approached him as Jason looked up to see Myra holding a long barrel gun. She'd shot him. A simple bullet wouldn't have this effect on him. Something else had hit him. A sedative?

Attempting to shift back to his human form to combat the drug, Jason felt his heart still in his chest when his wolf was quiet. Again and again he tried to call upon his wolf to shift, but something was preventing him from doing so. He was trapped in his wolf form.

"I would know that wolf anywhere." Elder Peter said aghast. "It's Jason De'Van; he's Eric's beta."

"We can't let him live to tell Eric what he's seen." Senan said casting a worried look to the towering male beside him.

The immense male grunted in response. "But we cannot kill him."

Whirling around, Myra scoffed in anger. "Why not? He could ruin everything!"

Briefly looking at her unconcerned, the male shrugged his shoulders before answering. "If he is found dead, Eric will send more to track us here. We have to move all the subjects to another location. As for the spy…" he said musingly as his glowing eyes shifted over Jason's still form. "Leave him to me. I will make sure he disappears forever."

Struggling to fight the drugs that coursed through him, Jason looked up to memorize the blonde male's face. He had never met him before and but he spoke of Doyle Mackenzie with such hatred and that could work in their favor of discovering who he was. But why they were kidnapping shifters and what they were really doing with them?

Unable to fight any longer, Jason allowed his body to relax as the drugs in his system took over and darkness descended.

28

Gripping the edge of the doorway, Rebecca leaned her forehead against the back of her gripping hand before releasing a tired groan. It had been nearly an hour since Eric had stormed angrily from their room. Needing something to distract her from the startling information that Eric had given her, she'd decided to get cleaned up. Still unsteady on her feet, with her limbs feeling like wet noodles, she'd forced herself to get into the shower.

After a simple five minutes she found that taking a shower was the worst idea she'd ever had. Several times she'd gripped the towel bar inside the shower to prevent from falling on her face. With her head swimming and just a towel wrapped around her, she stumbled to the door, only to have the remaining strength to grip the edge of the door.

Once she was certain she wouldn't fall on her face, she pushed herself to exit the bathroom. Walking to the closet, she opened it to pull out a white tank top and a simple pair of jeans. Leaning her back heavily against the now closed, closet door, her eyes drifted around the quiet room. Where the dresser had once stood was now an empty spot, the evidence of her battle with Myra that night had been cleaned away.

Staring intently at that empty spot where she'd lain when Myra had crouched over her, ready to end her, Rebecca couldn't believe how close she'd come to dying. If it hadn't been for Eric; she would be dead.

Shaking her head, she fought to hold onto her anger with him. He had taken her choice from her. It was bad enough having to accept that you belonged to a temperamental and stubborn werewolf in some mystical way; it was worse to know that you would be changed against your will. Was it even possible for her to fight this?

Would you rather be dead? Her inner thoughts chided her.

With a strangled sound of frustration, she allowed her head to fall back against the door. Even after what Eric had done to her, she knew that she loved him. The stubborn bastard had wormed his way into her heart despite her many efforts to prevent him. He'd saved her life several times and how had she rewarded him; by yelling at him for risking everything for her.

 She wasn't ready to admit that she was wrong in her anger at having her choice taken away, but she knew that she had to make things right with him. Feeling her lightheadedness from being in bed for the last couple of day began to fade, she moved to the closed bedroom door.

Opening the door, she frowned when she found Chris lounging in a chair outside the door. With one arm slung over the back of his chair and his left ankle resting on his right knee, his eyes looked straight ahead; lost in his own thoughts he looked relaxed, as though he'd been there a while. Narrowing her eyes at him, she closed the door behind her with a loud bang.

Instantly, Chris's head snapped to her at the abrupt sound. Had she actually snuck up on a werewolf? A smug smile curled along the corners of her lips at the thought. Dropping both of his feet to the floor, Chris pressed his hands against his knees as he rose to his full towering height. For a minute he seemed to give her a look over, his eyes searching for something.

When his gaze strayed to the bare skin of her shoulder, Rebecca stiffened. She'd forgotten to replace the bandage over Eric's bite mark. She'd kept the ace bandage around her rips mostly dry, but she'd removed the gauze from her shoulder. The wound was red and pulsing, displaying a perfect mold of Eric's fangs.

"Why are you out here?" she asked, nervously. Her hand reaching up to adjust her damp hair until it covered Eric's mark. Snapping out of his thoughts at her question, Chris shook his head before answering.

"Eric asked that I make sure that no one tries to bother you."

Wincing, she crossed her arms over her chest, glaring at him. "I don't need a bodyguard."

Shrugging, uncaring, he scratched at the back of his neck before replying. "Not my problem. You don't like it you can take it up with him. I just do what he tells me to."

"As his *assistant*?" she inquired with a raised brow. When she'd first met Chris, Eric had introduced him and Jason to her as his *assistants,* but after everything, she knew that it had been a lie.

"I'm his beta, his enforcer and so is Jason."

Sighing, she dropped her arms, shaking her head. "Do you know where Eric is?"

Chris nodded, his lips pursing in thought before he answered gruffly. "He's in his office."

"I need to see him." she whispered, her eyes shifting from his, preventing him from seeing her need to find Eric.

With a slow nod, he moved out of her way, waving a hand toward the stairs. "Let's go. I'll take you to him."

Moving past him down the stairs, she felt her mind fill with doubt. Would the other shifters look at her strangely now? Did she need to be worried? Her chaotic thoughts had her steps faltering until she stopped half way down the stairs. When Chris came up behind her, his hand pressed against the side wall as he leaned down toward her.

"Is something wrong?" His voice was actually filled with concern and it gave her something to hold onto in the mist of her uncertainty.

Clamping her lips together, she closed her eyes. She refused to tell him that she was scared to be around anyone after that night. She wasn't a victim, hiding in fear from the unknown.

Pushing her shoulders back, she opened her eyes before shaking her head at his concerned question. "I'm fine." she responded curtly. Taking a calming breath, she forced her legs to move once more, never stopping or looking back.

* ~ * ~ *

Sitting at his desk, Eric stared down at the blue prints of another commissioned house he'd been asked to design. He was supposed to be making the final changes to the floor plans but he found he couldn't focus. Most of the pack had left the lodge or made themselves scarce. He didn't doubt that many of the pack members that still remained under his leadership were cautious of his decree at the Gathering. Many feared that he'd seek revenge against others because of Myra's actions toward Rebecca and he was too angry with the memory to tell them otherwise.

Shoving the blue prints aside, he growled with frustration. He needed to clear his mind. Rising to his feet, he left his office to go to the kitchen for a cup of coffee. Returning a moment later to his office, he'd nearly closed the door behind him, before he paused. Standing at the window against the far wall of his office, he saw the familiar lithe figure of the woman that had haunted his thoughts for the past eight years.

"Beth…" he breathed out with a ghostly voice.

Glancing over her shoulder at him, Beth's finely shaped lips curled into a friendly smile. "Hello Eric." turning around to face him, she rubbed idly at her elbow as she felt his shocked expression.

Taking the few steps toward his desk, he carefully set his mug down on the desk. The sunlight streaming through the open blinds made her tan skin glow. She had to be an apparition. Why would she be here?

"Beth?" he repeated, his eyes narrowed while he studied her with a distrusting eye.

 The years hadn't changed Beth overly much, her jet black hair that once fell to her small hips was now cut in a short bob that framed her face. Dressed in a simple t-shirt and jeans, she still wore the facade of *girl next door* well. He'd once found her pretty; not beautiful that made drove every though from his mind like Rebecca did, but now; he felt nothing but emptiness.

His expression hardening, he took a step back as he crossed his arms over his wide chest. "Well, this is a surprise. But I must say not a welcomed one." He stated, bitterly. Unlike Rebecca, Beth didn't flinch at his harsh words.

She didn't expect him to be gentle with her feelings. Good. After all these years; the last thing he had to offer the mother of his children after she'd abandoned them all without a word was *kind* words.

Meeting his glaring gaze, Beth's expression remained cool. "I don't expect you to welcome me, Eric. Especially after what I did and left you do deal with the consequences."

He scoffed. "That's an odd way to phrase what you did, Beth. You left me. You left your pups and you did so without a backward glance."

Beth rapidly blinked as her eyes watered at the mention of Emma and Travis. Clearing her throat softly, she asked. "How are they; Emma and Travis?"

Brushing her question aside, he leaned his hip against his desk. "Why are you here? You no longer have a place here, you know that."

"I've come to plead with you to rejoin the pack." Her melodic voice matched the pleading note in her eyes.

"You think you can just walk out on your family without a word and then just show up?" When she looked away from him with a sigh, he growled in anger as the memories of the past were brought to the surface. "Just answer a question for me that I have asked myself since that night you ran off. Why?"

Seeming to steel herself against his angry gaze, she pressed her lips together before nodding slowly. "The night I left, I met my true mate."

Eric frowned. He knew more than anyone the pull of a true mate; undeniable and phenomenal.

"I won't apologize for finding my true mate and falling in love, Eric." Beth added, her soft voice growing firm. "Be honest, Eric." she began, taking a hesitant step toward him. "You knew I wasn't your true mate from the beginning. I was just your friend and it easier to pick me as your mate with our families being so close." Rubbing a tired hand over his face, Eric released a pent up breath.

"You're right. I knew you were not my true mate. But I am not angry that you broke your vow to me; not anymore at least. I am angry that you left your children with a backward glance."

Narrowing her eye at him with disbelief, Beth shook her head at him. "You think that was easy for me? You think it was easy for me to stay away from them all these years? I wanted to take them with me but after I found my mate in Victor, I couldn't. I knew as Alpha you wouldn't and couldn't let me go without losing face. My choice was to leave secretly or have Victor challenge you as he wanted to. To protect you, the children, me and my mate, I accepted what was happening and I made the hardest choice of my life." Her voice hitched with emotion. "I left."

Releasing a sound, half growl and half sigh, he rubbed a frustrated hand over his face before meeting her sad eyes once more. "Why are you here now?" he asked gruffly.

"I came to plead with you."

"For what?" he scoffed at the idea that a simple apology would make the past eight years of pain and not knowing go away. "If you want forgiveness for embarrassing me, you wasted your time."

Ignoring his mocking tone, Beth stepped closer to him until she stood but a foot from him. Looking up at him, her eyes pleaded with him to understand. "Victor and I wish to rejoin the pack."

Eyes widening at what she was asking his breath burned in his chest. The pack would never accept her back into the pack. As Alpha it would be his job to deal out punishment for her betrayal from all those years ago. "Beth." he breathed out, shaking his head in denial. "You know our laws. You betrayed your pack and your mate. I may not have marked you, but others knew you were mine. If Victor and you try to return I cannot guarantee your safety. If justice is demanded for your crime, I would be forced to challenge your mate. This isn't just about you anymore; I have to think of our pups and my true mate."

Instead of disappointment at his words, she smiled warmly up at him. It was the same smile she'd given him as children. "I heard you found her. I am glad."

Heart growing heavy, he shoved away from her to spin around and face her. "Save your words of congratulation." He bit out, rubbing furiously at the back of his neck in anxiety. "You don't know what you are asking."

Closing the distance that separating them, Beth nodded solemnly. "I do, which is why I came alone tonight. I want to be a part of Emma and Travis's lives more than anything, Eric. I will do what must be done to make right how I wronged you. I want to see my mother and live my life within the pack." Slowly dropping her gaze, she sank to her knees before him. "I will face any punishment you as Alpha see befitting." Tilting her head to the side, smoothing her hair away she exposed her neck, her gentle eyes rose to his, waiting for his decision.

Bending at the waist, Eric gripped her upper arms, lifting her to her feet. Startled, she watched him for a sign of what he planned to do. If in his shoes, any other Alpha; hell, even any other man, would have lashed out at her without mercy. But despite the pain of the past, Beth was his friend. He remembered how she'd sat with him at the falls the day Senan had slain his father. She'd only been thirteen at the time and still she'd known exactly what to do to take his sorrows away. How could he return her years of friendship back to her with spiteful vengeance?

Groaning, he pulled her into his embrace, hugging her. She stood stiffly in his arms with her hands held up in defense before a shutter moved through her body. With a soft sob, Beth wrapped her arms around his waist, returning her childhood friend's embrace.

Pressing his cheek against the top of her head, Eric sighed. "Don't expect others to be as merciful as I, nor as forgiving."

Pulling back, she raised her surprise filled eyes to his; her lip trembled, "I'm really sorry—"

"Don't." he cut her off, shaking his head at her. "Wallowing in the past won't help. I'll see what I can about minimizing your exposure."

Overfilled with joy at his words, a smile crossed her face before Beth threw tightened her arms around his neck, causing Eric's hands to grip her shoulders to steady them both.

"Listen to me Beth..."

29

Walking beside Chris, Rebecca attempted to ignore the looks that the other shifters gave her as she descended the stairs. All speaking had ceased and all gazes followed her every step. Some looked at her with a stunned and wary expression. Then there were the ones that glared at her with outright hatred. Several went as far stride towards her, intent to confront her.

With a growl, Chris had put himself in front of her with a warning look to the others brave enough to approach her. When they would reluctantly clear a path for them to pass, every once in a while she would hear someone hiss out beneath their breath, *"Changeling."* The way the word was spat out toward her direction made Rebecca think that it wasn't meant as a friendly term.

Raising her gaze to Chris's tense expression as he watched the other shifter around them, Rebecca quietly asked, "What's a *changeling?*"

Pressing his flat hand against her back, he directed her through the small groups of shifters that littered the large lobby. Still keeping a sharp eye on those around them, he flashed a raised eyebrow at her words. "What?"

"I heard one of them call me a *changeling.* Somehow I doubt it was meant as a compliment." She stated with a shrug.

Sighing, he explained. "*Changeling* is our term for a human that is bitten and later turned into a shifter. Like you said; it's not meant as a compliment. To others you are an enemy that's been allowed to remain among us. Many are not going to be as welcoming as others."

"You all must really hate humans." She mused with a wary look.

Chris simply shrugged his shoulders. "Some more than others." he conceded.

"Do you? Hate humans, that is?"

A brief look of anger and regret flashed behind Chris's eyes, before he jerked his face from her to look over her head toward Eric's closed office door. Gulping softly, he nodded his head before lowering his eyes back down to hers. "I do. But I stand with Eric's policy on humans."

"Which is?" she prompted, her hands tangling together with worry.

"Remain separate from the human world, keep to our own, protect our own and most importantly; we do not allow others to reveal our existence. I once had two sisters, a mother and a father." For a moment he remained silent. His chest rose and fell in even breaths before he softly admitted. "Now I am alone."

Rebecca felt her heart still in her chest at his look of pain. Not wanting to intrude on a painful memory, she looked away from him. "I am sorry." Shoving at her damp hair as it fell past her ear to brush against her face; she hesitantly looked back to him.

Chris was watching her with a hard look. Did he hate her too because of what other humans had done to him? "That night," the look of recognition in his eyes told her that he knew what she was referring to. "You stood in front of me and against your pack."

Chris gave her a look of confusion. "Of course I did. I never would have let them harm you."

"But I am human; or at least I was or currently am, temporary. Why didn't you agree with them when they wanted to kill me?"

"You are Eric's mate." he said as though those four words explained everything. "As his beta, that makes Eric my closest friend, my brother and you my sister. I may not have been able to protect my own sister's from their deaths, but I will never stand by and let harm come to you. It is our way. Besides," he said, lifting his shoulders in a casual shrug. "You are different from the other humans. You knew our secret and you could have done so many things differently; but you didn't. That tells me a lot about you, Rebecca. I am proud that you will our Alpha female."

Eyes misting at his kind words, Rebecca rapidly blinked her eyes, smiling warmly up at him. "Thank you."

Suddenly looking uncomfortable, Chris nodded before gesturing to Eric's office. "There's his office. I'll go to the kitchen and see if there is any food leftover from lunch since you slept late. Meet me there once you and your mate make up." Without another word, he spun on his heels and strode away from her.

Taking a calming breath she approached the door. She was about to knock when the sound of Eric's hard voice along with a soft female one pierced though closed door. Who was in there with him? Lowering her clenched fist, putting her ear to the door Rebecca remained perfectly still, listening.

"Listen to me, Beth. Because of our past and my feelings for you I will protect you. But you must not tell anyone I saw you here tonight. I will do whatever I can for you to be safe here again. I care for you more than you know. I will do whatever I must so that you can be a mother to your pups again."

With Eric's gently spoken words, she felt her world crash around her like a shattered window. Beth. This was the woman that Eric had once treasured and Travis and Emma's mother. She was back?

"I'm scared, Eric." The sound of the woman's gentle voice as she pled with Eric made Rebecca sick. Eric was her mate. He'd claimed *her*. She had to be misunderstanding this.

"Don't be. I will take care of everything. You just focus on watching your back. I could never live with myself if something happened to you."

His tender vow was like a stab to Rebecca heart. With her heart stopping dead in her chest, she braced herself to turn away from the door. Accidently, her hand slipped on the door knob, turning it and allowing the door to slide open with a loud groan.

Freezing like a deer in headlights, she looked at the sight revealed to her. In Eric's office stood a short slender woman wrapped tightly in Eric's arms. The woman's hands pressed fearfully against Eric's hard chest as her eyes widened at the sight of Rebecca.

Caught, the woman looked from Rebecca to Eric with a look of uncertainty. "Eric...?"

Eric released a deep sigh, his body relaxing once he saw Rebecca. "It's okay, Beth. She can be trusted." Letting his arms drop from around the woman, he took a step away from her. Turning to Rebecca he spoke softly. "Rebecca, this is Beth; Emma and Travis's mother..." The rest of his words drowned to silence as Rebecca's heart pounded in her ears, blocking out everything else he was telling her.

Releasing a shuttering breath as her breaking heart ravaged her chest; Rebecca felt tears filling her eyes. There was no need for him to explain any further. She could guess what was happening. The mother of his children was back. The woman he'd chosen all those years ago was back in his arms, a woman of his own kind. How could she possibly have a place in his heart compared to *that*?

"Who are you? Do you work for Eric?" Beth's gentle voice cut through the smothering cloud of heartache, forcing Rebecca to meet her gaze. Before Rebecca could respond, Eric spoke, "Rebecca is Emma and Travis's nanny."

Rebecca felt her breath explode from her chest with pain. Not his lover, not even his friend; she was just his children's nanny. Was he ashamed to admit to her that he'd claimed her? That a *changeling* was his true mate? How stupid she must be to think she was more to him.

Grasping tightly at her emotions that rushed to the surface, Rebecca held her voice in check. She wouldn't show how much he'd hurt her with just a few simple words. If he was ashamed of her, she wouldn't bother him with her *human* presence. "I'll leave you guys. I just—"

Unable to come up with an excuse other than the real reason she was seeking Eric, she turned and rushed down a nearby hall. Tears clouded her vision as she ran. She didn't care where she was running. She didn't even care about the shifters that meant her harm. She just needed to get away, to run.

Lifting her head as tears burned a path down her face, she found herself running toward a door that seemed to lead outside. Before she could reach the door, she collided with a tall, muscled body as someone came striding around the corner.

A pair of strong hands reached out, grasping her shoulders when she would have fallen. "Rebecca?"

Looking up in surprise, she felt sobs rack her chest as she saw Damon looking down at her with confusion. The tight rein on her emotions suddenly broke, allowing all her pain to over flow. Lunging forward, she buried her face in his chest, desperately seeking to disappear inside his chest.

Cupping the sides of her tear stained face, Damon pulled her back to study her stricken face. Concern filled his voice. "Rebecca; what is it? Where's Eric?"

No sooner than he'd spoke, the sound of Eric's voice rapidly approached. "Rebecca?" he called.

Looking fearfully over her shoulder in the direction of his voice, she turned to raise her tear filled eyes to Damon's. Beseeching, she spoke quickly. "Don't let him find me. I can't face him right now."

Not understanding, but still willing to help her, he nodded solemnly. Pulling her against his side, Damon wrapped an arm around her shoulders as he led her down the hall he'd come from and toward a stair case. Moving hurried up the steps, Damon directed her down several twists and turns until he reached a door. Without a backward glance, he opened the door and ushered her inside before closing it behind them.

Barely glancing around, Rebecca could only assume she was in Damon's room. She opened her mouth to thank him, but nothing came out. In her mind's eye, all she could see was Eric holding Beth close to him, his reassuring words echoing forever in her ears. Unable to breathe, Rebecca gasped, her hand going to her chest. It felt like someone was squeezing her chest, her lungs, and her heart.

This was what heartbreak must feel like.

As though he sensed what was happening to her, Damon moved closer to her, his big arms wrapping around her shoulders and back, pulling her against him. Gasping as ugly sobs racked her chest, Rebecca shoved against him. She didn't want to be touched. She wanted to be left alone to allow this pain to consume her.

Ignoring her feeble strikes, Damon held her as she cried. When her legs gave out, Damon sank down to the floor with her, his hands moving in soothing circles against her back.

His voice murmuring softly against her ear as her hands fisted in his shirt. "I have you, Rebecca. I'm here."

"You were wrong." She wailed while she sobbed like a wounded animal, full of unrelenting pain and agony. She was never his true mate as Damon had told her. She had been just some stand in until Eric's *real* mate returned.

She had no place here.

She never did.

* ~ * ~ *

Rushing down the halls, Eric searched franticly for Rebecca's scent. When she'd looked at Beth with a look of utter pain, he hadn't understood what was wrong at the time. Needing to be alone with her, he'd explained to Beth that Rebecca was a trusted friend. He hadn't divulged that she was in fact his mate.

He would have shouted it to the world if he was able to, but even after he'd let go of his anger toward Beth, he wasn't certain he could trust her. Beth's parents were just a few among many that despised humans. He refused to risk that they would come after Rebecca until she transitioned in a misguided effort to avenge their daughter's reputation.

After assisting Beth sneak out of the lodge without the notice of others, with the promise that he would contact her when he was able to address her petition before the pack, he ran after his mate. The scent of her pain in the air as he followed her trail made his chest clench. He didn't know why she'd sought him out after their harsh exchange in the bedroom, but he had to find her and make sure she was alright.

He followed her trail down the stretching hall toward the infirmary. Coming to an abrupt halt, his beast rose when her scent suddenly merged with another. Damon. Growling low in his throat he followed their combined scents up toward the stairs to the opposite end of the second level. His strides quickened as he moved toward the room that Damon had claimed for his stay at the lodge.

Coming to a stop, chest rising and falling with rapid movements as he fought down his beast's need to find their mate and kill Damon, he glared at the dark oak door. Why would she be in Damon's room? Anger filling him with the possibilities he shoved the door so hard that the locking mechanism snapped, sending the door hitting the opposite wall. Growling with eyes a glow, Eric felt his anger fade slightly when he found no one in the room. Damon's and her scent floated in the air, but no one remained in the room. Where were they?

Taking a retreating step out of the room, he focused all his senses on Rebecca, on the addictive scent of his mate. With the faintest of brushes against his skin, he found it. With her perfect scent was Damon's. He had gone with her! Why? This habit that Damon was developing with following his mate around was going to cause him to get killed. With a stormy expression, he turned toward the main staircase; he headed back down, the scent growing stronger with each step he took.

30

Tilting her head back, Rebecca closed her eyes against the feel of the warm rays of the afternoon sun and the soft caresses of the slight breeze that ruffled her hair. Sighing, she opened her eyes to look up at the towering trees around her. There was something about being outside calmed her mind, but it did nothing to take away the ache in her heart.

"Are you alright now?"

Turning she saw that Damon stood a distance away. Smiling faintly, she nodded at his question. When she'd collapsed in his arms, crying and wounded, she couldn't have been more grateful that Damon had been there for her. But deep down she knew she couldn't hide behind Damon when it came to Eric. She had to face him.

When Damon had gently brushed her tears away from her face, he begged her to tell him what happened. She hadn't. When she refused to tell him, Damon had looked helplessly at her, needing to help her in any way possible. He asked her what he could do to help her. But all she wanted was to be away from everyone for a moment to get her thoughts together and with a gentle nod of his head, Damon had given her that. They now stood a stone toss distance from the lodge. No one would bother her here.

*Except Eric...*she thought sourly.

She knew that soon or later she would have to talk to him. She found herself surprised that she actually *wanted* to talk to him. Even as painful as it was to replay in her mind; she wanted to know what had she truly seen back in his office.

With a slight sound of rustling clothes, Damon was at her back, watching and waiting. After a short silence between them, Damon finally spoke. "I can stay if you want me to." he offered.

Shaking her head, Rebecca turned around to face him, her arms folding around herself. "No. I can face Eric on my own."

"What did he do this time?" he asked, repeating his question from earlier once more.

"It's not important. I'll deal with it." she replied firmly before glancing away from him.

Shrugging his shoulders helplessly, Damon stabbed a hand through his blonde hair with a heavy sigh. Dropping his hand, he reached into the front pocket of his jeans with a grim look. "If you won't tell me and you won't let me stay to watch your back; take this at least."

Glancing back at him, Rebecca saw that he held the keys he'd given her the night of the Gathering. Narrowing her eyes, she gave him a questioning look. "What are you doing?"

"Eric tossed these at me the night he brought you back to the lodge; the night of the Gathering. I'm giving them to you if you should need them. With everything that's happened since the Gathering, Eric's power over the members of this pack is strong but tilts on a razor's edge of collapsing. Until you transition, you are vulnerable. I don't want you to be trapped if you need to get to safety." When she still looked at the keys like they were a spider that he was asking her to pet, he added. "Take them for my peace of mind at least. Please."

Nodding, she accepted the keys into her open palm before shoving them into her pocket. When Damon nodded, pleased with her acceptance, he turned to leave her. Watching his retreating form, Rebecca felt her curiosity peak at Damon's behavior. She'd never really paid attention to how protective he was of her. She knew it wasn't because he *wanted* her in that way, but if not that; then why?

Calling out to him, she took a step after him. "Damon!"

When his steps halted, he turned to the side to look back at her with a perplexed look. "What is it?"

Coming to a stop in front of him, she hesitated to ask what was on her mind, but she felt she needed to know. "Why do you care so much about me?"

Appearing confused at her question, Damon reared back from her, his eyes narrowing slightly. "You're my friend, I suppose." He answer was slow coming, as though he was hesitant to lie to her. He was hiding something.

Rolling her eyes, she scoffed at his answer. "Do me a favor, Damon. Don't lie from me. I am sick to death of people around here keeping things from me and then just expecting me to accept the truth when it finally comes out. Tell me. Why did you offer your protection to me when we first met? Why have you orchestrated everything to help me and protect me since then? Why is it that you are always there to shield me?"

A flash of pain flooded his eyes, before Damon looked away from her. Rubbing a large hand over his mouth, he sighed heavily. "Eric has been a friend for years to me off and on. We have our differences and our fights. Coming from two different wolf packs will do that I suppose. Anyhow; the moment I knew that you were hiding our secret and knowing you were meant to be Eric's, I had to do what I could to keep you safe until he could. Eric deserves happiness, even if he's too stubborn to reach for it himself."

Rebecca shook her head at him. "I don't understand how you could know that I was Eric's true mate."

Damon chuckled. "It wasn't that hard to spot. Since meeting you; Eric lost all interest in other women. Plus the night we met, his wolf was so close to the surface that you could practically see it."

"So that's the reason for everything you've done?" she asked skeptically.

Like a light turning on, the look of sorrow was back in his eyes. What was it that pained him so much? Folding his arms over his chest, Damon regrettably shook his head at her. "No. It's not the only reason." He paused for a moment before continuing on as if his words pained him. "I lost my true mate years ago and you remind me of her." smiling though the pain darkening his eyes, he seemed to recall a member of her. "She was fierce like you and beautiful and she was my world."

Pain seized Rebecca's chest. Reaching up to cover the aching deep inside her at his obvious pain, her gaze softened sympathetically. "What was her name?"

He smiled softly. "Talia. She was a human like you."

"What happened to her?" deep down she feared she already knew the answer but she waited to hear it from his lips.

Drawing in a shaky breath, Damon turned from her, presenting her with his back. When she thought he'd simply storm off after she drudged up such painful memories, she was surprised when Damon began telling her. "Like Eric's pack, my own pack is very traditional when it comes to humans. My pack lives deep in the woods, far from civilization. I was twenty at the time and despite the laws of my pack, I journeyed into the city. When I saw her; my world stopped. She was a student at the local college.

To make a long story short; I snuck away from my pack's lands to meet with her. I kept my secret from her to protect her. But it wasn't just a couple of months later that my pack members became suspicious of my frequent absences. Someone discovered what I had been doing, they discovered Talia."

A lone tear slid down his face. "A Gathering was called and I was brought before the pack. For disobedience; I was beaten, nearly every bone in my body was broken. Then; I saw her and in that moment; I truly knew fear."

Covering her mouth with fear, Rebecca whispered as she lowered her hand. "What did they do to her?"

"The same thing that would have happened to you if Eric hadn't stepped in like he did the other night. Talia was so scared and she looked so betrayed. She probably thought I didn't want to fight for her. I tried to, but my Alpha was so furious at my actions to risk the lives of my pack members for a single human that he denied my right to bear the Act of Revealment.

My best friend at the time stepped forward and dragged Talia deep into the woods to kill her. He came back with the smell of her blood on him." Turning back to look at Rebecca he sighed. "Now you know why I've remained close to you. I know what it is like to have your true mate and then have her ripped from you, to see the fear in her eyes at seeing the brutality of our world. I wanted to spare you and Eric that if I could."

"But I thought that once you meet your true mate; that's it. I've seen you look at other women before. You don't look like a man morning his dead mate."

"What you've seen is just me wishing for her. I've not touched a woman since that day nearly a decade ago. What you've seen is for show. It's not something I want others to know about."

"Why? Her death wasn't your fault, Damon."

His expression turned bitter. "I can see no other reason but me for her death. The only ones that know about Talia are you and my pack members. I carry a shame that wish I would forget sometimes and I'd like to keep it that way." Pausing, he explained. "When a shifter loses his true mate after they've bonded, the will to live for the surviving shifter is no longer there. But when Talia was killed, I wanted to die so badly, if nothing else to just join her in the next life, but my wolf wouldn't let me and still won't to this day. Others think I should have died that day, but I didn't."

"Don't worry; you won't be for long." The sound of Eric's voice cut through the air around them like a whip.

* ~ * ~ *

Turning around, Rebecca found Eric striding toward them with tense, angry strides, his fists clenched tightly at his sides. His burning gaze settled squarely on Damon who still stood close to her. "If you want me to stay, I will." Damon whispered low enough that only she heard.

Not looking at him, she shook her head, keeping her eyes on Eric as he quickly made his way toward them. "No. Please go."

With a grim nod, Damon tore off his shirt and pants; quickly shifting to his wolf form. Grabbing his discarded clothing with his teeth, he looped off in the opposite direction before disappearing from sight.

With a heavy sigh, Rebecca met Eric just as he closed the distance between them. His dark gaze glared over her shoulder toward the direction Damon had run. With a low growl in the back of his throat he took a step back to turn his hard gaze on her.

"I warned you not to put an obstacle between us, Rebecca." His lips pressed into a thin line in anger.

Crossing her arms over her chest, she pursued her lips, her expression turning just a stubborn and irate as his. "Leave Damon out of this, Eric. If anyone is putting obstacles between us; it's you."

"Me?" he asked confused. "What the hell are you talking about?"

"I saw you, I saw you with Beth." Pain filled her chest at the memory.
Eric's anger quickly disappeared at her accusing tone. Moving closer to her, he gripped her arms, his eyes boring down into hers. "It's not what it looked like, Rebecca."

"So she's not back?" She hated that she sounded so cynical, but what else was she suppose to think? Beth was real competition when it came to Eric. What if Eric wanted his pure blooded she-wolf bride back? The though brought tears to her eyes.

With a hesitant look, Eric reluctantly nodded his head. "Yes. She is back. But not in the way you are thinking."

"Then why didn't you tell her that I was your mate? You told her I worked for you, Eric! Which by the way; is not only a lie, but hurtful. I thought this mating-thing meant more to you than that."

"It does!" he exclaimed. "You are my mate. That's all you need to know." He stated with a shake of his head.

Crossing her arms over her chest, she sighed wearily. "You won't even answer the question? Are you ashamed of me? Because you mated a *changeling*?"

"Where did you hear that?" he asked, his expression going stark cold.

She shrugged her shoulders dismissively. "Does it matter? It must be an easy choice for you if your pure blood bride is back."

"*She* is not mine, Rebecca. You are. She wants to be a part of Emma and Travis's lives. She wanted my help to rejoin the pack."

Shaking her head, Rebecca swiped away an escaping tear that slid down her face. She was already losing him and he didn't even care. "I heard you, Eric. I heard what you said to her."

"What do you want me to say?" uncaringly he shoved his hands in his jean pockets. "What of it?" he bit out. "Beth is my past. I will always care about her, but changes nothing between me and you."

It would have hurt less if he'd slapped her.

"Eric I am not some toy for you to play with and toss aside later on. If I am your mate, why wouldn't you tell someone that? What is the point of me accepting this bond between us and accepting the changes in my life while you treat me like I'm some...some..." Her words trailed off in frustration as she furiously paced back and forth in front of him.

"Outsider?" he supplied coldly.

Jerking away from him as if he actually had slapped her, Rebecca's face washed with the pain from his verbal blow. "Eric?" his name fell from her lips out of shock. "Why would you say that?"

"You're human; or at least you were, Rebecca. Until you change you arc an outsider in these matters. You couldn't possibly understand what I'm going through or Beth for that matter. Because I chose you, my pack is now ripped in two. As Alpha of this pack I have to do what I have to. It's time you accept that."

Rebecca felt as if he had ripped open her chest and torn out her heart. What that all she was to him? A human? An outsider? Someone beneath him? Within her mind, she felt something shift. A cold tidal wave wash over her, helping to compose what was left of her pride.

Reaching deep inside her, she could almost touch the second being that reached towards her pain, seeking to comfort her. She could feel her newly found wolf, pacing beneath her skin. She wasn't human anymore; Eric had seen to that. Not yet a werewolf either; then what was she?

"Your right, I don't understand. But what I do understand is that I am unbelievably stupid." Walking around him, she headed back toward the lodge with long angry strides.

Within her closed fist, she could feel Damon's keys biting into her palm. For the first time since he'd forced them on her, she was thankful. Emerging from the tree line, they faced the side of the towering lodge structure. Pausing at the tree line, she attempted to ignore the quizzical stares that she was receiving as other shifters looked her way. Just like Eric, they would never accept her here.

"What do you mean?" his voice still restrained and cold.

"I love you, Eric. I am sorry that you had to choose between saving me and your pack—"

Eric's wolf leapt to his glowing eyes in denial. "You're being childish. That's not what I meant." He attempted to say over top of her words, but she ignored him.

"—But I refuse to stay somewhere if you only want to acknowledge me before strangers when it's convenient for you. You are still keeping things from me." Spinning around to face him, she looked at him with her heartbreaking every second. "You want me to trust you and to accept that you've changed what I am, but you won't do the same. You refuse to treat me like your equal and share things with me."

When she saw that he had no intention to say nothing further, Rebecca willed the tears in her eyes not to fall. Turning back toward the lodge, she made her way toward Damon's car. She had to get away from him. He didn't really want her, not when he had his perfect she-wolf back at his side. She wouldn't remain in the shadows because his pack wouldn't accept her and because he truly wouldn't either.

Before she got a foot toward the car, she was jerked to a stop when Eric's steel hand settled over her arm. His tone was as cold and unyielding as iron. "Your first change will happen in just a few days. Do you really want to risk hurting someone because you can't control your emotions?" his words were meant to scare her into staying, because he couldn't let her go. But those few words had an opposite effect.

Shoving his hand off her arm, she twisted around to face him, when she looked at him, she saw the ruthless man that she'd seen when she'd first met him. The man that saved her life and made tender love to her down at the falls wasn't there anymore. Was this the true man that she'd bound herself to?

"Don't worry, Eric." she softly said with an emotionless voice. "I've had my experiences with dangerous animals; I'll make sure no one is hurt."

Before she could take another step, the door of the lodge flew open with the sound of innocent laughter. Eyes locking on the both of them, Emma and Travis ran to her side, each holding a large painted picture in their small color smeared hands.

"Becca look what we made!" Emma exclaimed, proudly holding up her paining of an amateur of her house with crudely drawn replicas of the four of them

"I did this one." Travis held out his that showed an image of a chocolate brown wolf with obscenely long eyelashes. "This is you." He added proudly.

Her heart warmed at the smiles on their faces. She wanted more than anything to stay; at least for them. But she had to remind herself that their *real* mother was there now. What need would they have for her?

Bending down, she wrapped her arms around both of them. She memorized the feel of their small arms around her as they returned her hug. Know this could be the last time she held them. Not wanting to risk the tears that were threatening to fall, Rebecca abruptly stood and calmly turned away without a word.

She rushed across the thick grassy yard to Damon's small car. Jerking the door open, she climbed in without putting on her safety belt, immediately starting the engine. Driving down the long winding dirt driveway, her misty eyes flashed to the review mirror. Watching as Emma and Travis raced toward her with confused and hurt expressions.

What was left of her breaking heart shattered with Emma fell to her knees crying out for her to not leave with tears falling down her small face. Confused, Travis fell beside his twin, his small arms wrapping around her as he watched Rebecca drive off. Behind them, stood Eric with a determined look focused on her. Forcing herself to look away from him, she finally allowed her tears to fall and the pain of losing the family she'd nearly called her own consume her.

* ~ * ~ *

At the sound of wailing, Sarah appeared in the open doorway to see Robert bending to pluck up his wailing daughter. With a look of concern she turned to look at Travis who stood bravely by his father's side, but sadness lingered in his young eyes.

Fearing she already knew what had happened, she took a step toward him, her arms out stretched to take Emma from him. With a grateful look, Eric relinquished his daughter to his mother. When Emma's sobs had settled a bit, she finally asked. "What happened?"

Appearing to carry a heavy weight on his shoulders, Eric replied in a low tone, "Rebecca left."

Shocked, Sarah shook her head. "What? No, that's not possible, you two are bound. She is your *true mate*. What happened?"

Flashing a knowing look at his son and daughter, he remained silent. Whatever he needed to say wasn't meant for their ears. Rubbing a gentle hand down Emma back, Sarah nodded. "Travis come with me and lets see if we can't cheer up your sister." With a small glaring look in his father's direction, Travis followed after his grandmother without a word of complaint.

When his pups and his mother disappeared toward the kitchen, Eric made his way to the conference room. He had to leave and go after her. There was so much he wanted to say to Rebecca, but he didn't know where to begin. She was right. He didn't fully trust her. The way his pack—the way *he* had come to regard humans; as if they were weak and inferior had caused him to treat his mate like she was less. She was never less! She was more than his next breath to him.

He couldn't get the image out of his head of her looking up at him, begging him to explain why she'd found him with his arms around another woman; and not just any woman; his ex-wife. Inwardly; his wolf howled at the memory of the tears that had swam in her eyes as she'd looked at him, shattered. The sight was pure agony. He never wanted her to cry, especially not because he'd caused it with his thoughtless actions. How was he going to fix this now?

You really screwed up this time... his wolf bit out. For the first time in his life, Eric found himself agreeing.

Walking through the open doorway of the conference room, he found Chris sitting at the *new* long, conference table. A pile of papers scattered out in front of him in a chaotic mess. See Eric as he entered, Chris leaned back in his chair with a questioning look.

"Eric?"

"Rebecca has left the grounds. I have to go after her."

"What?!" Exploding out of his chair, Chris made his way to his Alpha with a look of concern. "Was it Myra or someone else from the pack? If anyone has done anything to her I vow to rip them to shreds!" Chris promised venomously, his devotion to his new Alpha female evident.

"You would have to attack your Alpha then." Eric imparted with a weary look. When Chris scowled at him in confusion, he took a step back, not replying. "I have hurt her and I must make it right. I need you to get in touch with Jason and get him back here. I need the both of you to watch over the pack until I return."

"With all due respect Alpha; is now really the best time to be having a tiff with your mate? The full moon is in just two days."

"I will handle it." Eric reminded harshly before he took a calming breath and added softly, "I have to fix this."

"Damn right you will." An angry voice bit out from behind Eric.

Turning at the sound of the voice, both men watched as Damon came charging into the room. To both their surprise, Damon charged straight for Eric.

Before he could guess his intention, Damon gripped the front of Eric's shirt and tossed him onto the long table with a snarl. Hitting the table on his back, the force of his body caused the table to break, sending Eric to the floor a top a pile of broken pieces.

When Chris would have attacked to defend his Alpha a scalding look from Eric had him holding his ground. With a shrug of his shoulders, Chris mumbled grudgingly, "I just moved that table in here…"

Moving toward Eric, Damon snarled as he pointed an accusing finger down at him. "You have no idea how hard she cried over you. I don't know what you did or said to her, but you had better fix this, Eric!"

Leaping from the floor, sending chunks of wood flying with his abrupt movements, Eric grabbed Damon by his throat before delivering a blow to his stomach. When Damon's knees crumbled beneath him at Eric's quick attack, his arms wrapped around his middle as he choked for air.

Growling, Eric allowed his wolf free reign to attack Damon, but he held back, barely. "Who gave her keys to your car, Damon? You had no right to interfere! Now I have to hunt down my injured mate and talk her into returning before she transitions."

Wheezing, Damon stumbled to his legs with a hard look. "If you don't fix this and you hurt her again, Alpha or not; I will make you sorry."

"Don't threaten me. I have had enough of you thinking you're her protector. She is mine!"

"Then let go of your stubbornness and your pride and be her mate! Rebecca is my friend and if I have to help her stay away from you, I will interfere again."

Tossing his hands up in the air with a look of disbelief, Eric shook his head. "I don't have time for this. I'm going after her." Turning to Chris, he said. "Find Jason and get him here." Moving to shove past Damon, the sound of Chris calling after him caused him to stop.

"I can't." Chris said with an unsure tone.

Turning at the waist, Eric looked back at Chris with quirked an eyebrow. "What do you mean?"

"That's just it. I can't. I don't know where Jason is."

Moving back toward his beta, Eric looked confused. "He's missing?"

Nodding, Chris replied. "He never checked in after the Gathering. I can't find him anywhere and he's not answering his phone. I believe something happened to him. It's not like Jason to just disappear."

"Find him." Eric commanded before turning to leave once more.

"We don't have the man power to; at least not anymore. Many of our trackers and hunters have left the pack and Elder Peter has disappeared. If we are going to find Jason, we need you, Alpha."

Right then and there, Eric was prepared to damn his responsibilities as Alpha and go after his mate, but he knew deep down that he couldn't. Jason had been by his side when others refused to. He'd fought alongside him and even traveled to Darkwood Springs to assist Doyle's mate when asked. He couldn't abandon him now.

Where ever Rebecca was going she would be safe for the night and tomorrow. He could go after her and beg for her forgiveness after he'd found out what had happened to his friend. There was still some time before the full moon, but it was time that he didn't have.

With a groan of loathing, he turned toward Damon that watched the interaction between him and his beta with concern. He couldn't believe he was about to do this.

"I need a favor." He practically spit the foul tasting words out of his mouth.

Crossing his arms over his chest, Damon smirked at him. "The great and powerful Eric Daniels is asking me a favor? I wish I had a camera to capture this moment." He said, looking up musingly.

"I am serious. I had Jason tracking the men that attacked my family and me at my home. If he has disappeared I need to know what he found. I ask that you watch Rebecca. If I do not come for her after tomorrow, I need you to bring her back here. Human transformations are unpredictable. The change could come over her before the moon even rises. I need someone to be there for her if I cannot. Can I trust you with this?" he asked with a hard glare.

His wolf snarled at the thought of allowing this rival near his mate, especially since the binding thread had not bound their souls together. But if his beta was in trouble, he couldn't desert him to his fate without at least trying.

Damon's face softened with seriousness as he nodded firmly. "You can always trust me when it comes to Rebecca, Eric. I want only for her to be safe and happy."

Tilting his head in agreement, he turned back to Chris who looked at him with a shocked look. Ignoring his look, he moved straight into Alpha mode. "Gather half of any trackers and hunters we have left. Half will be coming with me to follow Jason's trail. The other half will remain here under your command until I return. I will not leave our pack unprotected if this is a trap."

Striding from the room, Eric moved toward the kitchen to tell his mother of the situation. He had no doubt she would protect her grandchildren with her life. Once this mess was cleaned up and Jason was safely back within the pack's borders, he would devote everything in him to earning Rebecca's forgiveness. He refused to lose his mate after finally finding her.

31

"Get that stuff away from me." Rebecca groaned in agony, from her fetal position on Damon's couch. It had been two days since she'd fled from the pack's lands back to the city of Ravenwillow. For some reason this morning, pain had begun to rack her body worse than anything she'd ever felt before.

Taking a seat on the couch beside her, Damon reached out to help her up into a sitting position, thrusting the steaming mug of some sort of tea at her. God, it smelled awful. She'd been raised to always be grateful when someone went to the trouble of making one something. But there was no way that rule applied to *this*.

Grasping her hands, Damon forced her to take hold of the steaming mug. The foul liquid was a mud brown with a leaf and root or two swirling amongst the other contents. Gulping past the bile that rose in her throat at the smell, she attempted to pass him the mug back.

"There is no way in hell I am drinking that!" she exclaimed as she dry heaved at the smell.

Flashing a firm look, Damon's hands held hers around the mug as he pushed it toward her mouth. "You will and you will now. This will help with the pain, just be the big girl I know you are and drink it."

Unable to pull away, the rim of the mug was pressed to her lips, forcing the warm contents down, leaving her no choice but to swallow it. Instantly her stomach attempted to rebel but she was able to force it to calm.

When Damon pulled the mug from her lips, she made several gagging sounds as she tried to rid the taste from her mouth. "What in God's name was that crap, you dirt bag?!" she exclaimed.

Setting the mug aside on the coffee table, he grinned at her grossed out expression. "It's an herb concoction that we usually give children before their first transformation. In the past in rare cases we've had to use it on the few human mates that shifters turn. The main ingredient is wolfs bane."

"You're making that up." She groaned as another wave of pain it her. Narrowing her eyes at him, she stilled. "Isn't wolf's bane poisonous?"

"To some; yes, but for shifters it can slow down a first time transformation. You are already a shifter, Rebecca. That's why you feel this pain. Your bones are growing stronger and so is the rest of you. Once you transform tonight, it will go away. The tonic will dull most of the pain, but not all."

When she curled back onto her side, he crossed one leg over the other, resting his ankle on his opposite knee as his arm stretched along the back of the navy colored couch. "Eric called earlier. He wanted to know how you are doing."

Pressing her lips together, she shook her head. "I can't talk to him right now."

Sighing, Damon scratched absently at his chin. "You won't have a choice tonight."

The heavy weight of sadness filled Rebecca's chest at the thought of
Eric. Even after everything that happened the day she left, fleeing to
the seclusion of Damon's hotel room, she missed Eric. She longed
for his touch, his embrace, his kiss, and even the sound of his voice
like a drug. But the pain at knowing he considered her inferior, an
outsider; prevented her from going back to him. If he couldn't see
her as an equal, as his mate; what hope did they have?

Doubts and fears of what the night would bring her began to creep
into her mind, making her stomach knot painfully. She knew the
reason Eric hadn't come charging after her was because Damon had
told her that there was trouble at the lodge that had pulled Eric away
from Ravenwillow. What would happen to her if he didn't return
when the moon rose tonight? How would she get through this
without Eric?

"Damon, you once told me that if I ever needed anything you'd help
me." She stated, her voice shaking.

Damon nodded. "Yes and I stand by that promise. Do you want me
to go get Eric on the phone for you so you two love birds can make
up?" He teased with a playful smile.

"No." she answered, shaking her head. Closing her eyes against the
next wave of pain that exploded down her back, she breathed out, "I
want you to kill me."

She knew she'd shocked Damon with her request, but her fear of
transforming, of losing what she was, terrified her. There was a
slight pause before Damon finally answered. "Come again?"
Damon's features froze at Rebecca's haunting words.

"In less than a few hours, I'm going to be forced to become something else. I have no control over it. I can feel something pressing at my mind like a cool touch of a hand and I know what it is. I can't do this if Eric won't truly accept me. I can't live my life like this. What if I can't control it? I couldn't stand it if I turned into that monster that killed my family and nearly killed me. Don't let it come to that, Damon. I beg you. I want you to kill me."

Gripping her upper arms Damon jerked her back into sitting position before he shook her gently, "Are you insane?" When tears filled her eyes, forcing her to look away from him, he growled slightly before he released her.

"First of all; shifters—even newly turned shifters can change whenever they want. The full moon has no sway over that. It's more like a special occasion that we use and the lunar energy from the moon helps to draw out our beasts the first time. The shifter that attacked you did so of his own choice, not because the beast within him forced him to. Just because you become a shifter doesn't mean you have no control over your beast. It is part of you, it *is* you." He stated harshly, his fingers stabbing at his heart.

"Secondly; your mate will be there to guide you. Whatever argument you too had, won't even matter after you transform. Eric is bull headed, you knew that going in. It's your job to give him a kick into reality when he gets out of line." He said with a light teasing note.

"So, you're saying you won't kill me." she stated emotionlessly

Releasing a fake sigh of regret, Damon released his hold on her to lift a hand up to his face as though to examine it. "Well, you see I just got my nails done." Damon teased, before lowering his hand. "What's the real problem, Rebecca?"

"What if I can't control it? I can't go to Eric for help, he doesn't want me anymore and I don't know what to do."

A silent pause swept between them as Damon fought against his need to comfort her. According to pack law—he wasn't allow to interfere between Eric and Rebecca; at least, not any more than he already had. More importantly; Rebecca's first change was a sacred thing. It was meant to be shared between mates, not friends. He wouldn't be allowed to be there with her when the time came. But what could he do? Without direction she could hurt herself or even die.

Groaning, he knew he didn't have a choice. Deep down, he knew that Eric would move heaven and hell to be there for Rebecca tonight. But even if he wasn't; this was something Rebecca would have to face on her own, with or without her mate. Turning to look out the window, he saw that the afternoon sun hung low in the sky. Dusk would be upon them in just a few hours. He had to get her back to the lodge where she could transform safely.

Patting her knee, he rose to his feet. "Get ready to go, Rebecca. Dress in something that's easy to remove."

Giving his retreating back a quizzical look, she asked. "Why?" Turning back to look at her over his shoulder, he replied, "It's time."

* ~ * ~ *

An hour later, Damon had quickly gotten some food forced into her and ushered her to the car. It was a long drive from the heavy populated section of Ravenwillow, and the sun had already begun to set. With each second, she could feel the pain of her muscles and bones fade to an icy burning. Fear sought to choke her, but she fought to remain calm. She had Damon with her; he would never let anything happen to her. It would be fine.

Rebecca found herself taking in an unfamiliar sight as Damon carefully pulled off the back road he'd taken into a heavily wooded area. He'd told her that he would bring her back to the lodge, but this looked nothing like the familiar forest that surrounded the property.

"Where are we?"

"This is the wood toward the back of the lodge's property."

"Why didn't you take me straight to the lodge?" she asked, concerned. She didn't like how Damon wouldn't meet her gaze. What wasn't he telling her?

"I don't want to risk some resentful member of Eric's pack thinking they can take a run at you. This part of the wood will offer you the seclusion you need."

"This was your idea?" she asked, hesitant to get out of the car as she fearfully took in the sight of the darkening forest in front of them.

"It was Eric's idea."

"Will you be with me? When it happens?" she asked, turning back to look at him. This time, he met her gaze with a sad look.

"No. I cannot. This is one of the most sacred of our laws, Rebecca. This is something you must face on your own. It's too personal for me to be a part of. Your wolf will know what to do. I have no doubt that Eric will be close by, ready to be at your side when the moon rises."

Shaking slightly at the finality that his words held, Rebecca undid her seat belt. Opening her door, she shifted to get out of the car, but froze. Reaching out, Damon's hand settled on her back in comfort.

"What is it?"

"What am I suppose to do?"

"Start walking into the forest until you find a place within the forest that feels right to you and your wolf. You will feel it deep inside when you get there. After that; when the moon is at its highest, you will feel your wolf rising. Don't fear this. Accept it and let her come forth."

Releasing a shuttering breath, she nodded. "Anything else?"

"Be certain you're naked."

"What?!" she exclaimed, unsure if he was teasing or not.

"Just a little piece of advice for you to remember," he said with a grin. "Now; this is the part of the evening where I kick you out of my car and leave you in the middle of the woods." With a shooing motion, he motioned for her to get out.

With a look of uncertainty, she climbed out of the car, slamming the door closed. Not a moment later, Damon's engine roared to life, his headlights turning on as he slowly put the car in reverse and back onto the road. With a final wave, he disappeared down the road, leaving Rebecca standing at the edge of the tree line with a heavy stone sinking in the pit of her belly.

Turning to look in the distance, she saw the last of the day's light was quickly fading. Steeling herself, she turned back around, looking straight ahead. Inhaling a steady breath, she took the first step.

32

Running fast through the woods, Eric allowed his long strides to carry himself closer and closer to the scent of his mate. He'd run for the last day to get back to Ravenwillow and now he was quickly running out of time. He along with one of his trackers and two hunters had tracked Jason's scent far beyond his boarders in Virginia to the deep forgotten forests of Massachusetts.

They'd found the charred remains of a building where Jason's scent ended, and found nothing. No matter how further they traveled in their wolf forms, Jason's scent had vanished and no other scent could be found. The whole situation concerned him deeply. As there was no established pack of shifter in the surrounding area, Eric was forced to be cautious on any shifters they scented around them.

Leaving his hunters and tracker behind, he had left orders that they continue to comb for signs of anything that could lead to Jason's whereabouts. He was desperate to discover what had happened to his friend and beta, but he'd already failed Rebecca several times over as her mate, he refused to let her face this night alone.

In his wolf form his long legs allowed him to cover more distance. He'd passed into his territory an hour ago was nearly at the lodge's property. He'd bade Damon to take her to the boarder of the property, to make sure she would be away from lingering members of his pack until he could reach her.

Her scent grew stronger with each powerful lunge of his legs. He knew he'd found her before his eyes had even spotted her. In the middle of a grove, the moonlight flowed down over the open area beside a flowing stream. In the mist of the silence and beauty of the night, he saw her. Never had she looked more beautiful to him.

Standing in the open with her back to him, he watched her shiver slightly as Rebecca allowed the flowing green, gypsy shirt she wore to fall to her ankles. When she unbuttoned her white blouse and pealed the material over her shoulders, the moonlight hit her naked skin, caressing it to his eyes. The soft material of her blouse slid down her arms before joining the discarded skirt.

Standing bare foot in only a pale pink, cotton bra and panties, her shaking intensified. Pausing, he wondered if the trembling of her body was due to the cool night breeze around them or from apprehension.

The thought of her going through this with no one to lean on, pained him. No longer would she feel hurt or fear around him. He'd made so many mistakes with his mate. He'd underestimated her at every turn. His only excuse was that he thought he was doing the right thing, shielding her from the harsh reality that he had to face. But he had to face the facts when it came to his mate.

Rebecca was strong in mind, strong in heart and most importantly; she was strong in spirit. Rebecca wasn't a woman to run away screaming for her life. She'd survived a fucking werewolf attack, for goodness sake!

She was made for him in every way. She deserved his respect and deserved the opportunity to come into her own strengths as a shifter. Most of all; her place was to stand by his side.

Note to self: grovel, grovel, and beg for her forgiveness...

Shifting to his human form, he stepped from the shadows of the trees and into the open space. Moving down the slight incline, he watched her shoulders stiffen as she heard him approach. Turning to look over her shoulders, he watched as need and happiness flared in her eyes at seeing him. The sight eased the tightness in his chest.

"Eric…"

Before she could say anything more, his hand cupped the side of her tilted face before lowering his mouth to hers. His free hand lowered to wrap around her waist, gently pulling her against his front as one of her arms reached up to circle around his neck while the other gripped his restraining hand.

Every word that he wanted to say to her, every emotion that he wanted to convey to her, he poured through his kiss. Finding the will to break the kiss, he sighed at the wondrous feel of completion at holding her once again. He never wanted to be without this and he would make sure he never was.

Lowering his cupping hand, he undid the closure of her bra at her back. Immediately, she stiffened with confusion. "Eric…?"

"Shh…" he whispered gently against her ear as she turned around to grab her loosened bra before it could fall. "I can smell your wolf. She's nearly ready to emerge. We can talk after this night. Tonight is about you, nothing else."

Sliding his hands down her arms, he pushed the limp bra straps down, forcing her to allow it to fall to the ground. Smoothing a caressing hand over the tempting swell of her full breasts, he allowed his hand to drop to her waist before drawing her panties down until they pooled at her ankles.

Carefully unwinding the ace bandage that still remained wrapped around her ribs, he toss it aside as well. Standing just as bare as he was, Eric turned her to face him, his eyes focused on no other part of her other than her eyes.

Her body began trembling more as her eyes widened with fear. "Eric…I don't think I can do this…" she whimpered softly. Uncertain and terrified.

This was his fault. He'd allowed her to think he wouldn't be there for her with his thoughtless words. He couldn't allow her to go through this thinking that.

Cupping both sides of her face, he bore his eyes into hers. "Listen to me, Rebecca, because it isn't often that I apologize for anything."

Her eyebrow rose at him with a '*gee, you think?*' look. "There's a bit of surprising news…" she jibed at him, fighting to keep the tremble from her voice.

Ignoring her comment, he pressed on. "I was wrong. Since I brought you here, I have been so fearful and prideful that I sought to keep things from you, things that I never should have."

"What could you possibly be afraid of?" she asked, disbelievingly.

"Of losing you and your love that you have weakened me with. When Beth left me all those years ago, I gave up the thought of feeling anything for someone else. If I could go back, I would do it all differently. I would trust you, when I didn't. I would tell you everything, when I withheld things. Please forgive me. Let me stand by your side and you by mine." He pled, his eyes searching hers. Rebecca's hands settled on his chest over his pounding heart as he waited for her answer.

Licking her lips absently, she raised her eyes to meet his. "What about Beth? She's back and she would make a perfect mate for you other than a changed human like me."

Leaning close, he pressed his forehead against hers, holding her gaze the whole time. "I already have a perfect mate and she is in my arms right now. Beth is my past and I would never choose her over you. You were right, I was wrong to introduce you as my help to her. But I was worried for your safety. Beth's parents live within my pack and I feared they'd retaliate against you. I wanted to wait until you had safely transitioned before I introduced you to my pack."

Softening against him, Rebecca sighed, pulling away from him. She appeared like she was about to say something more to him, but stopped as her body tensed. Wincing, she gripped his arms so tightly that her nails bit into his skin. At the bite of pain, he looked down to see her small rounded nails had begun to grow into deadly tipped claws. Jerking his awing gaze up to her face, he found her eyes glowing brightly in the darkness.

It was time.

Shoving away from him, Rebecca stumbled to the ground as her legs gave out beneath her. Falling to her hands and knees, she panted as her bones began to painfully reshape from her human form to her wolf. She was fighting it.

Worried that she'd harm herself with her stubbornness to allow the change to happen, Eric shifted back into his wolf form. Moving toward her lowered head, he bumped her chin with his muzzle.

"Rebecca, you have to let this happen." He said through the mind link that all shifters shared.

Her eyes widened impossibly further as she heard his words in her mind. "H-How?"

"Your wolf wants to be freed, let her take over. She will know what to do." He urged gently.

"I…" she winched in pain as her hands began contorting and reshaping, slowly and painfully. "I don't think I can. What if I lose myself? What if I can't find my way back?"

"That's why I am here. I will never let you be lost. Accept her and let go."

He knew the instant that she'd done as he asked. Instead of the slow random shifting that had occurred when she'd fought against the call of her beast, now her imaged blurred with white mist around her as her wolf came forth. Before his eyes, Eric found himself seeing the birth of his true mate in all ways. Lying with her legs tucked under her, Rebecca lifted her muzzle toward his hovering one. Eyes going wide with wonder, she leapt onto her feet with a chuff of shock.

"I did it…?" she asked hesitantly, lifting a brown paw to look at it suspiciously. He felt his lips curl in a slight smile as she turned her head to inspect her long silky tail behind her.

"You did." Moving toward her, he nudged her toward a different direction. Stepping in front of her, he tilted his head forward.

"Follow me. There is much I want to show you about being a wolf."

"Cool it, Mr. Daniels." She said with air of superiority. *"I got this covered."* She stated confidently, clearly taking to her new form quicker than he'd anticipated.

"Oh really?" he asked mockingly, moving to circle her smaller frame. *"I'd like to see that."*

"You asked for it." slapping his side with her tail, Rebecca raced forward, his eyes following her until she disappeared from sight. With a smile of pride, he followed after her.

Under the light of the full moon they ran together. He'd pursued her like the prey she was to him. Just when he thought he'd caught her, Rebecca would dodge out of his reach, sending him into a tree or over grown bush. When the moon sat low it he sky, they found themselves at the base of the falls, near the edge of the deep pool.

Exhausted, Rebecca's wolf receded, leaving her lying naked along the bank beside him. Following suit, he allowed his ecstatic wolf to retreat as well before pulling her against his pounding heart. Relaxing against the soft grass beneath her, Rebecca shoved a hand through her hair, sending the waves of soft brown hair fanning across the ground.

"You lied to me." She mumbled sleepily.

Looking down at her in confusion, he shook his head. "I don't understand. What did I lie about?"

Jabbing her thumb over her shoulder at the water fall and the deep pool, she raised an accusing brow at him. "You said the only way down here was to jump. Apparently there was another way."

Smirking, he stretched out on his back with a sigh. "I suppose I did."

Moving onto her stomach, she braced an arm over his chest as she leaned closer to him. "That will be stopping, Eric." she commanded with a firm voice. "You can't lie to me anymore and that includes keeping things from me."

"How will our life be interesting if you know everything?" he teased with a blank look.

Skimming her lips over his, she rose up to smirk down at him. "I have ways to keep plenty of interesting things in our lives. Which from what I remember, is going to be a long time."

Covering her hand that rested over his chest, he leaned up to place a slow, deliberate kiss on her lips. "It will never be long enough, my love."

Rebecca smiled warmly down at him, before lowering her head to press against his chest. For a moment they simply laid there, holding each other. Eric wanted to remember everything about this moment for when he was grey and much wrinkly version of his current self. He would never be happier than he was in this moment.

He felt Rebecca shift away from him with a gasp. "Eric, why the hell is your chest glowing?"

Snapping his eyes open, he looked down to see the binding thread emerging from his chest. With his heart full of joy at a second chance to fully claim her, he sought out her gaze. She started as if hypnotized at the rippling thread appearing like mist before her eyes.

"What is it?"

"It is the binding thread; it only emerges for a true mate. The first time mine sought you, I denied it. This time, it is your choice. Do you accept me, Rebecca? As your true mate?"

Her lips parted to answer, but her hand flew to her chest as she sat fully up. "My chest," she gasped. "It feels like it's on fire." Letting her hand fall, Eric watched in wonder as bright light emerged from the center of Rebecca's chest, her own binding thread.

Both of them stared at each other in wonder as the two threads coiled around each other until the threads became as one. With an explosion of heat, the threads disappeared, leaving both of them gasping at each other at what they had just seen. Rebecca was the first to recover, crawling over him; she straddled his hips to lean over his chest. Cupping the edges of his strong jaw, she lifted his face slightly as her lips claimed his. Her kiss held heat, passion and need. Need for her mate, her true mate.

"You have some explaining to do, Eric." she moaned out against his mouth as his hands reached up to grip her hips. Rolling them until their positions were reversed, Eric grinned down at her after breaking away from her siren lips.

"Later."

With a nod, she agreed. "Later." She whispered as his lips crashed down over hers.

Eric sighed with contentment against her mouth. Nothing would take her from him now. She was his! More importantly, she had claimed him as well. Not because she was his mate, but because she loved him.

The world fell away in that moment. The night stilled around them. The fate's giving them that moment of perfection. Troubles of tomorrow would continue to come. War was brewing, death and destruction would come to both sides. But for some reason the nagging fear of the future held no power for Eric's mind as it once had. He didn't know what future they would be facing in the morning, but he did know that as long as Rebecca was by his side, nothing would stop him or tear him from her. His Rebecca.

His true mate.

His heart.

His salvation.

Author's Note

From the bottom of my heart, I want to thank each and every one of you that purchased this book. I hope you enjoyed this book as much as I did writing it.

When I first began my journey of writing, *"Hunger of the Heart"* actually came before the *Grizzly Affairs* series was even thought of. After only getting to the fifth chapter, I put the beginning of this novel away for two years and nearly forgot about it.

With the help of my overactive muse and the release of the romance and suspense filled stories of the Grizzly Affairs series, I was finally able to share Eric and Rebecca's story.

If you enjoyed this book, look out for the next installment of the Wolves of Ravenwillow series, "Hungry like the Wolf" (Coming soon)

Show your appreciation for this and any of my books by taking a moment to write a review at Amazon, Smashwords or at any other locations of purchase.

Reviews help authors more than many realize. They not only help me to stay sane, but also help me to see what you are thinking about each book. Remember it's only because of readers like you that I am able to follow my dream and create these awesome stories. You are all my superheroes.

As readers your thoughts matter. Share them with me anytime.

Don't forget to head over to my site to sign up for my newsletter for information on new upcoming books and future giveaway drawings.

Facebook: https://www.facebook.com/magentaphoenixbooks

Twitter: https://www.twitter.com/Magenta_Phoenix

Pinterest: https://www.pinterest.com/magentaphoenix/

Google+: https://plus.google.com/115176721315670176631

Email: magenta.phoenix.books@gmail.com

Website: http://magentaphoenix.wix.com/magentaphoenix

Want more books by Magenta Phoenix?

Check out these titles!

Bearing It All (*Grizzly Affairs: Book 1*)

Big, Bold & Bearing *(Grizzly Affairs: Book 2)*

Dream Of Me (*Dream seekers: Book 1*)

Hunger of the Heart *(Wolves of Ravenwillow: Book 1)*

Light of the World (*Rebel Hearts: Book 1*)
(Coming Soon)